IMMORTALMAN

IMMORTALMAN

Scott Parson

Whiskey Shallows
Press

This is a work of fiction. Names, characters, places, and incidents are either the product of the author's imagination or are used fictitiously. Any resemblance to actual persons, living or dead, events, or locales is entirely coincidental.

Immortalman was serialized on Amazon's Kindle Vella December 2021

Whiskey Shallows Press
eBook Edition 2022
Paperback Edition 2022

ISBN 978-0-9996378-2-1

Cover and interior design: Slade Withers
Front cover image: Scott Parson
Back cover image: fruitcocktail @ fotosearch.com Stock Photography
Find out more about the author at www.scottparson.com

to Mom and Dad
for all the laughs along the way

and to Lisa, Vergil, and Maggie
the funniest people I know

"For an angel went down at a certain season into the pool, and troubled the water . . ." – *John 5:4*

IMMORTALMAN

Part One

Chapter One

Hudson River Valley – 1830s

ON A SANDY WEDGE OF LAND by the river, soldiers and rivermen gathered in front of a large fire to drink and play at dice under the stars.

Squared off over an upturned biscuit box, sat Solomon Durnley, younger than most of the other men standing around, but seasoned by adversity. Across from Solomon sat Captain Curtwood, an officer of the local militia. Curtwood glistened with sweat and poured out profanities against his run of bad luck.

The more Curtwood lost, the harder he squeezed his lucky piece. A peculiar shard of worked metal of no familiar ore to Solomon's eye. The bauble gleamed like obsidian with a lustrous translucence, hammered into its shape, rather than knapped like flint. More teardrop than oval, slightly bowled, with an eye-hole drilled into the larger end.

Curtwood scooped up the dice and dropped them into the cup. He gave it a mighty shake and slammed it down onto the biscuit box. He lifted the cup.

Ones. Another loss.

"Mine again," crowed Solomon.

Curtwood bellowed foul oaths, slapping the odd metal token down on the wooden box. The rivermen roared with delight. Curtwood, cleaned out and breathing hard, stared as Solomon took up his winnings.

The dice rattled in the cup as Solomon offered it up to fresh blood. But the gamblers shied from this display of unnatural young luck.

Curtwood snagged Solomon's wrist, a twig in the grip of the big soldier's paw.

"I smell a river rat," snarled Curtwood, sniffing the air like a grizzly bear scenting blood on the breeze.

He lowered Solomon's arm and twisted his wrist, dumping the dice out of the cup onto the biscuit box.

Solomon had reached behind him for his bowie, when Curtwood slammed his pistol butt down onto the first die and crushed it to bits, poking through the dust with the pistol barrel.

The men stood watching, tense.

He smashed the second die, then poked through the shards.

He smashed the third die and swept away the pieces.

"Guess we need new dice." Curtwood smiled at Solomon.

"You've got nothing left to play for," said Solomon.

"No?" Curtwood twisted Solomon's hand up in front of his face.

Rivermen and soldiers clasped their sheath knives and side arms, waiting. Curtwood laid the pistol on the table, unaware or unconcerned how he'd ratcheted up the men, ready for a bloodletting.

"Griffin!" growled Curtwood, giving the soldier nearest him a back-handed swat to the thigh. This soldier, a lieutenant by the epaulet he wore, held out a small, leather pouch.

The lieutenant's features caught Solomon's eye. Nothing so different from the rest of the pocked, freckled, or alcohol-blushed faces common among soldiers and rivermen. It was his silver-blue eyes and the unnaturally bright, almost luminous glow of the lieutenant's face in the gleam of firelight. So fixed on the game and its stakes, Solomon had not noticed him before.

The lieutenant opened the pouch and dropped the dice into the cup. Curtwood plucked the cup from Solomon's hand and set it down on the biscuit box.

"A triple. For all of it," said Curtwood.

"What's your stake?" asked Solomon, although allowing him off the sandbar alive was probably stake enough.

Behind Solomon the rivermen muttered, their sense of gaming offended by the challenge.

Solomon could see Curtwood do the quick mental mathematics of his own survival, counting heads, multiplying by the number of fists, then adding up cutlery and small arms. His eye twitched just the merest mite. He released Solomon's wrist and held his lucky piece up in the light for everyone to see.

The muttering stopped. A man playing for his own skin was beyond the game they'd gathered to join. But this curious object seemed to satisfy the onlookers.

Solomon laid his own stake back on the table. All of his winnings. Cash money he needed if he hoped to prove himself a man of means to Lavinia Kantlingher's daddy, Luther.

But the pistol lying on the biscuit box, the bloody eyes of Captain Curtwood, and the soft sandy stretch of shore with no good cover for at least thirty yards put survival at a premium. Solomon cursed his own good luck.

Curtwood snatched up the cup and gave it another hard shake, the bones rattling. He stopped, his eyes never leaving Solomon. He slammed the cup, mouth down, onto the biscuit box and then tilted it ever so slowly.

As the cup tilted, Solomon and the men could see that the first die was a four.

The cup tilted further revealing a second four. Solomon had given up breathing, afraid his breath on the cup would crimp the Captain's fortune.

The men leaned in.

The cup moved ever so much more slowly.

A six. Curtwood lost.

Solomon slapped his hand down on the pistol barrel, a vain hope to gain a few more seconds before the much bigger man lifted and fired at him.

Curtwood reared up, the enraged grizzly again, but he wasn't reaching for the pistol. Or for the money. Or for Solomon. Curtwood grabbed at his chest, his face twisted up in pain. Blood smears appeared under his hands, staining his uniform. He seemed to fold into himself, like cotton wadding rammed down the mouth of a cannon barrel as he disappeared in a sucking blast of sandy wind, yanked from their midst.

Solomon stared. Curtwood hadn't fallen backward, nor had he stumbled off into the trees. The Captain had simply—vanished.

But the soldiers weren't looking where the Captain had been. They'd seen the bloody blooms on the Captain's uniform. They were ready to believe the wiry young riverman with a pile of filthy lucre in front of him had played some villainous chicanery on their Captain.

As one furious man-mob, they dived at Solomon.

Braced and ready, Solomon couldn't out-punch the bruisers descending on him, but they would remember he was on his feet when they pummeled him to Kingdom Come.

A powerful hand yanked him by the collar as the first haymaker whistled past his chin.

Rivermen and soldiers exploded against each other, fist to jaw, tooth to ear, knee to neck, a melee of cursing, cracking, crunching, and caterwauling.

Suddenly released, Solomon tumbled clear of a collapsing riverman.

On hands and knees, Solomon grabbed for the money still on the biscuit box, snagging Curtwood's lucky piece as well. He snatched up his knapsack and bedroll, crawling baby-swift through the boiling riot of men.

Once clear, Solomon stood and fairly flew despite the sand sucking at his shoes.

He kept to the treeline, using the shadows to hide as he ran until he realized no one chased him. He slowed to look back at the figures in the firelight, still hammering, elbowing, slugging, kneeing, and flinging each other around on the beach.

Solomon cursed his luck again. It was clear from the blood on Curtwood's uniform he'd suffered a wound of some kind. The soldiers would blame him.

Solomon again considered the look on the Captain's face. It was the loss of something far greater than a fickle lucky charm, however pretty.

Chapter Two

SOLOMON REACHED THE CROSSING over Esopus Creek. The ferry was still on the other side. If he rang the bell, he might alert any soldiers hunting for him. It could be hours before the ferry returned.

The Esopus was called a creek, but was river-wide at this point, finishing its run into the Hudson. There were only two ways across—ride the ferry or row a boat.

Solomon threw his knapsack and bedroll into one of the skiffs tied up alongside the landing. He settled himself on the thwart, fit the oars in the locks and rowed for the far bank.

The Captain's strange disappearance and the enraged soldiers meant Solomon would have to make himself scarce for a time.

Solomon hoped a direct appeal to Luther Kantlingher's avarice with the money he'd won tonight would open the way for Solomon to pay true court to Lavinia—after it was safe to return to the valley.

When Solomon first approached Luther for his permission to call on Lavinia, Luther listed his objections to any such courtship.

First, Solomon was an orphan with no family to vouch for him. Second, he held no steady occupation, knocking around, taking all manner of mean employment up and down the river. Third, he was of low character, smoking, drinking, dicing, playing at cards, and betting on horse races.

Solomon pointed out the potential hypocrisy since Luther himself smoked, drank, diced, played at cards, and bet on horse races. Therefore, in Solomon's humble opinion, those attributes should not count in the list of his deficiencies.

This is what got Solomon pitched headlong off the porch by Luther himself, rather than simply being invited to depart by the house man.

But tonight, he should have more than enough to prove himself a man of substance to Luther.

More ticklish was explaining to Lavinia the need to disappear for a time so soon after his visit to her bedchamber last night.

He tumbled words around in his head to defend his absence, words that would encourage her to wait for him, solitary and chaste. Especially chaste. And if not solitary, at least chaste. Solomon sighed. It was a lot to ask of the English language.

With a half-dozen strong strokes, he drove the boat onto the sandy edge and tied the painter around the wooden bollard on the landing. He shouldered his knapsack and bedroll, heading off along the coach road that paralleled the Esopus, toward Kantlingher House.

A stage stop and hotel, Kantlingher House was set back from the road, joined to the coach road by a rutted and tree-shaded drive. The house sat square to the drive, a broad, deep porch fronted the main building, with two smaller additions attached to either end of the center building.

Solomon could see that the house was dark except for one window on the second floor at the far end of the house. The light cast from that window fell on a fine horse and buggy standing hitched up and pointed toward the road.

The stage wasn't due until morning, and anyone staying at the hotel would have their rigs and horses stabled in back.

A ladder, carried by a dark figure, wobbled out of the darkness and into the light. The dark figure struggled to set the ladder against the siding, smack dab in Mrs. Kantlingher's flower beds just under the lighted window.

Lavinia's room.

Solomon threw aside his knapsack and bedroll, and ran full out toward the dark figure. "Edwin Greene, you miserable merchant," he shouted.

Edwin, visible at last in the light from the upper window, gave a cry of alarm. He let go the ladder and scampered around behind the buggy. Solomon doubled back to cut him off on the other side as he came around. Edwin slid to a stop, catching himself as he fell, rolled over, got his legs pumping again and ran back around the rear of the buggy. Solomon caught the front wheel, stopping himself and heading back the other way, ducking under the horse's neck to catch Edwin as he rounded the back end of the buggy. Edwin barely evaded Solomon's outstretched arm, churning through Mrs. Kantlingher's flower bed, spraying leaves and petals.

"Lavinia!" Edwin yodeled, as he tore around the front of the house, vaulted the porch railing, and lunged for the front door.

The dark paneled door swung open and Edwin scrambled inside, slamming the door shut behind himself just as Solomon reached it.

"Edwin Greene, you come out here and take your licks like a man!" Solomon pounded on the door. It swung open. A pair of smooth-bore pistols poked out of the dark.

Solomon stumbled backward, landing butt first on the porch.

Luther Kantlingher, barefoot, dressed in a nightshirt and cap, stepped out, both pistols aimed rock-steady at Solomon's manhood.

"Thank God you're awake, man. A thief's come to rob you of your most cherished possession—my intended. My Lavinia."

"You git!" said Luther, "or there's going to be one mighty big hole where all your future generations used to be."

Luther's aim was true and point-blank as he advanced. Solomon scuffled to his feet, backing down the steps and into the yard, keeping his hands cupped over his crotch.

"You're going to let him waltz Lavinia right out from under your nose, stand before a justice of the peace in the middle of the night, denying her a white wedding in the parlor of her daddy's house? Something every girl since Eve has hankered after?"

"Edwin shows good sense, times being hard. He's got a keen head for a dollar and it'll put an end to worthless boys like you ever setting foot in my house again!"

"That ain't at all sporting, Mr. Kantlingher. Where's my chance to speak now or forever hold my peace when he asks why this woman shouldn't be joined to that low-life, scum-sucking, addle-pated, half-wit sourpuss of a store clerk?"

Solomon danced sideways and shouted toward the house, "Edwin Greene, you miserable merchant! I'm calling you out to fight me, man to shopkeeper."

From inside the house, Edwin chirruped back, "I'll thank you to leave me and my rightful bride-to-be alone."

Solomon whirled back around on Luther. "You'd leave your daughter go off with a man ain't got the spine enough to fight for her? At least sic the dogs on him. Make him break a sweat for her."

Solomon shouted up at the lit window overhead, "Lavinia! You said you'd wait for me to make something of myself!"

Luther thumbed back the hammers on the pistols, the double snap harsh and loud on this beautiful night of crickets and cicadas. "You're just another no-account. Always will be."

"Death holds no fear for me, Mr. Kantlingher," said Solomon, "but

I'm too good a potential son-in-law to put the temptation in your way."

Solomon turned and ran for the trees, his skin itching where the likely ball would pass between his shoulder blades.

Chapter Three

IN THE DIM LAMP GLOW behind the house, Solomon climbed the trellis up to the roof and across to Lavinia's window. The window he'd climbed through only last night to offer himself body and soul to Lavinia.

Pushing aside the curtains, Solomon saw Lavinia, her older sister Abigail, and her mother, Esther, packing and making preparations for Lavinia's elopement.

He eased over the sill onto the floor, the women unaware of his presence.

"I don't see why you encourage such fellows, Lavinia," said Esther.

"They have their uses," said Abigail. "What better way to liven up those dreadfully dull dinners, dances, and band box socials." Then, with a glance back at Lavinia, added, "Or so I'm told."

"Now don't you start with me. My Edwin may not have a playful personality, but he more than makes up for it as a practical, hard-headed man of business." Abigail spotted Solomon's reflection in the bureau mirror. "Oh!" She whirled to face him.

"Lavinia, please!" Solomon stepped toward her, his palms out.

"Solomon Durnley! How could you even think it the least bit proper to climb in at a lady's personal and private chamber window uninvited? I'm—I'm—I'mI'mI'm—" stammered Lavinia.

"Shocked?" suggested Abigail. "Completely mortified at the familiarity you would never give the least encouragement? Something like that?"

"Yes, thank you. Shocked! And completely mortified!" said Lavinia.

"Lavinia, you said you'd wait for me to make something of myself."

Lavinia gawped like a trout, "I—I—thought you'd be long gone by now, seeking your fortune."

"How can you think I'd leave when my every thought is taken up with the only woman in this whole wide creation that means the world to me?"

"You've done precious little to prove it," said Abigail, pushing between them to drop another valise on the pile by the door.

"I did." Solomon took a pair of lockets from his vest pocket, holding them up to Lavinia. She took one from Solomon. Abigail reached for the other, but he swept it from her grasp.

Lavinia popped open the locket. Inside were two tiny portraits. One of Lavinia and the other of himself.

"Ori, the sexton, painted them for me. Fella can't play at cards for nothing. Them lockets—"

"—are a gambling debt," said Abigail. She turned to Lavinia. "There's nothing he has but by cards or dice."

"I can hunt and fish—" he started, his manhood offended.

"—and gamble and talk the shine right off the moon," said Abigail. "But it won't build a barn or put beans in the pot." Abigail pushed between them again, taking another valise to put by the door. "Don't just stand there," she said to Lavinia. "You and Edwin have to get over the Esopus before the German ties off the ferry for the night."

"Lavinia, there must be some task, some charge I could accomplish to prove my worthiness."

"It's a little late for that," said Abigail. "She's getting married tonight. Tonight."

"Well, it's not fair. Leaving me so little time."

"Mister Durnley. Solomon. The only boon I crave of you this night—"

"Yes!"

"—is to be a blessing to my children should you ever in this life cross paths with them."

"You and Edwin intend on having children?"

"What did you think?"

The idea of Edwin Greene under the same sheets as Lavinia was nasty.

"You might want to wait on that. Edwin, puny as he is, might break his neck with a hard sneeze. You'd be a widow before you know it."

"I'll be *old* before I know it."

"What about a dog? Dogs make fine companions. Loyal."

Lavinia chuffed and grabbed up her handbag.

Solomon realized it was time to mention the unmentionable.

"How can you forget what we shared last night?"

"Last night?" asked Lavinia. She seemed confused.

Pushing past Abigail, Solomon made himself as warm and buttery as he could. "It's not the kind of thing anyone soon forgets."

"I don't remember sharing anything at all with you."

"Don't remember? Or won't remember."

"Mister Durnley, nothing passed between us last night. Or any other night for that matter."

"You don't remember me climbing through your window."

"No."

"You don't recall how I ended up on the roof at daybreak."

"No."

"What do you think happened, Mister Durnley?" asked Abigail.

Lavinia whirled on Abigail. "Nothing happened. He was drunk and Daddy had to sic the dogs on him. That much I do remember."

"Was that you, Mister Durnley?" asked Esther.

"It's not all completely clear to me," he said to Esther, "but, yes, I climbed through Lavinia's window last night, and, yes, Luther sic'd the dogs on me." Solomon turned back to Lavinia. "It's kind of hazy in between, but surely we exchanged something of a deep and lasting nature in those precious hours."

"Naked as I recall," said Esther.

"I was a chrysalis, Missus Kantlingher, caught in the very act of transforming into a butterfly, leaving my old nature behind."

"More like a snake, shedding its skin," said Abigail.

"Is there nothing I could say to change your mind?"

"There's more to life than charming words," said Lavinia.

Charming words were all he had. They'd always been enough.

"A man who can't remember where he was or who he was with one night to the next isn't fit for any good woman," said Abigail.

"Maybe you'd like your daddy to sic the dogs on me again," said Solomon, weary of her venom.

"Of course I wouldn't."

"That's a relief."

"I'd be satisfied with the sound of a lead ball passing through the meaty part of your buttocks, and a last warbling, blood-curdling cry as you ran for the woods."

"Abigail!" said Esther.

"Just—thinking out loud," said Abigail.

"Sooner or later, Mister Durnley, your eye will light on another, and I'll be forgotten."

"Just like the Almighty brought Adam a helper suitable for him," said Solomon, "so the Almighty's done for me, whether any here realize it." He gripped Lavinia's hands in his, reaching for some snatch of poetry that might in one sentence undo his reprehensible reputation, dislodge Edwin, and restore himself in her affections.

"If it took a hundred lifetimes, you'd never be forgotten." He braced himself. "With the Almighty standing witness, I would be steadfast." Solomon brought her knuckles to his lips, kissing them hard, then said, "I want to live forever. I will proOOooOoo—" his voice trailed off in a quaver. His eyes went wide as his knees wobbled and his skin prickled, like swimming in warm lard.

Inside his vest pocket a blinking, streaky golden glow leaked out from under the lapels of his jacket. Lavinia could feel in her fingertips the tingle surging through Solomon. Breathless, convinced the jolt came from Lavinia, Solomon sighed, confident he'd rekindled her passion.

But Lavinia stepped back, wiping her hand, twisting on her fingers, startled by the electricity that passed between them.

Luther burst through the hallway door, into the room, both pistols leveled.

Behind him, Edwin followed, holding onto Luther's night shirt, keeping the old man between him and Solomon.

"Dimsley! It'll ease my sense of guilt having to shoot you," said Luther, "seeing as I've caught you in the very act of trespassing my daughter's bedchamber."

"Durnley. Solomon Durnley," said Solomon, backing up, circling to keep the women between himself and Luther.

"Step into the hallway, woman!" Luther bobbed to get a clear shot at Solomon.

"Don't leave, Missus Kantlingher. You'll be washing innocent blood out of the bedlinen for weeks."

"Oh, no, dear. I have help."

Luther moved Esther to one side with his forearm keeping the pistol aimed in Solomon's general direction.

"I'll remember you fondly," said Lavinia, as she helped steer Esther and Abigail out of the bedroom.

"Momma, does Daddy have to shoot him?" asked Abigail. "We'll have to repaint the room."

"Mister Durnley is awfully stubborn. May not be any other way, hon," said Esther.

Luther fired the left-hand pistol, filling the room with sparks and smoke, knocking Solomon backward through the open window, carrying the curtains, frame, and glass crashing after him onto the roof.

Abigail and Lavinia both shrieked. Abigail rushed to the window in time to see Solomon roll off the roof and hit the ground with a thud and a grunt.

Solomon laid still.

Then squiggled.

Then raised himself up, surprised to be ambulatory after being shot point-blank. He pulled open his vest, looking for blood. He'd just sighed with relief at Luther's poor aim when he saw the freshly scorched, powder-burned hole right at heart level. He clasped his hands to his chest feeling for anything wet and sticky. Nothing.

Above, Luther stepped onto the roof and edged out to see where Solomon fell.

Solomon scrambled to his feet and ran a few steps, looking back at the window.

Abigail clambered out behind Luther.

"How in hell did I miss you?"

"I'll take that as an apology," said Solomon, but not for long. Luther pointed the other pistol and fired, catching Solomon in the thigh, stinging him, but not slowing him down.

"Great Gawd A'mighty!" shouted Luther, shaking his pistols at the heavens.

Abigail clutched her bosom and whispered, "Thank God."

Lavinia looked at Abigail.

"I'm grateful he didn't die in the yard and bring the law down on us," she said.

Solomon didn't stop running until he reached the coach road. Winded, he finally looked back to see if Luther followed. He doubled over, hands on his thighs, breathing hard. A scratching inside his shirt made him pull out his shirttails to find the intruder. His fingers found something solid. But not alive.

He held it up in the moonlight. A spent pistol ball, flattened. Still warm.

There was something in his shoe. Slipping it off, he dumped out a second slug. Flattened. He felt where the second shot had hit him. Another hole in his breeches and his long-johns opened all the way to the skin.

A peculiar courage washed over him. He turned back toward the house.

Edwin and Lavinia came barreling around the bend, the buggy piled high with luggage. Solomon had to jump sideways to avoid the vehicle bearing down on him, Edwin sighting in on Solomon between the ears of the galloping horse.

"Lavinia," he reached out as they drove past. "Lavinia! I'm a man fit by the Almighty for you." He ran after them but they were already too far ahead.

Not sure what to do, he ran for the ferry landing. Maybe intercept them. Force Edwin to fistfight him. Take Lavinia back by physical force. He was ripping ripe with a sense of destiny.

The ferry had already separated from the landing when Solomon reached it. The ferry drifted out onto the Esopus, poled by the German along the guy ropes stretched from bank to bank.

Solomon backed up and then ran in a burst for the dock edge, prepared to leap for the gunwale of the ferry, already ridiculously far out on the water.

He ran and as he planted his foot to launch himself over the impossible distance, an arm caught him across the chest and hauled him to a stop.

"Too far, Solly. You'll be swimming all night."

Solomon took no note of his rescuer, shoved away the arm, reconsidered the distance, then scrambled down into the nearest skiff and rowed after the ferry.

The fellow didn't say anything else, but watched Solomon haul on the oars trying to overtake the ferry.

Pulling even with the ferry, Solomon stood up to grab hold of the ferry's weather board.

"Lavinia! I'm a by-God man of purpose!" said Solomon. He pulled the slugs from his pocket. "See? I've been shot twice without effect. I'm divinely preserved. It's a sign."

"A sign your momma loaded the pistols," said Edwin, refusing to be impressed by Solomon's survival or his determination to catch them, spurred on by true love.

But Lavinia didn't look back at him.

"Lavinia! Providence must've stopped the lion's mouth once more!"

With a shudder and a chuff, Lavinia whirled to face Solomon.

"Solomon Durnley, you can quote Scripture with the Pharisees. Be grateful Daddy elected not to kill you on my wedding eve."

Edwin, who feared a confrontation with Solomon here so far out of pistol shot from Luther's handguns, passed a handful of coins to the German.

Solomon, by now, was standing, his arms thrown wide to show off the proof of his preservation. From up front the German lifted his long pole and with a jab, swatted Solomon out of the skiff, into the river.

Coming up, spewing water, sputtering and splashing, Solomon swam after the swiftly departing ferry.

"Lavinia! Lavinia!" he called out, coughing water and swimming for all he was worth.

But the ferry made the opposite bank, knocking against the pilings loud enough to be heard over the water. The gate opened and the buggy rolled off, Edwin slapping the reins like mad.

As the buggy disappeared up the road, Solomon stopped swimming, just treading water, out of ideas.

The prow of the skiff knocked against the back of his head.

He turned and climbed in, collapsing in the bottom of the boat, exhausted, the boat drifting along with the current.

Chapter Four

SOLOMON, SPENT AND SPRAWLED in the bow of the skiff, wiped the water from his face. He palmed his eyeballs, squeezing out the mortifying disgrace of a townsman like Edwin Greene besting him right there in front of his true love.

Although, to be fair to himself, it was the German, not Edwin, who'd dunked him in the river and set him to floundering and spewing like a gaffed carp. The German was twice his size and, as he thought about it longer, no more than a hired assassin. Couldn't Lavinia see Solomon was the better man? Willing, if not exactly able, to fight his own battles?

He roused himself, gave a dog-shake of his head, flinging water and blinking the wet from his eyelashes, ready to take the oars once more and give chase.

Solomon stopped, his hands on the gunwales. A glistening halo outlined the figure of someone sitting on the stern thwart of the skiff. The figure leaned forward, forearms crossed on knees. The shoulder epaulet jogged Solomon's memory.

That lieutenant back on the beach. The one Captain Curtwood called Griffin.

Solomon scrubbled to get his feet and hands under himself, ready to pitch himself back into the river. But Griffin lifted the oar out of its oarlock and pinned Solomon to the bottom boards.

"I didn't cheat him. I got no idea what happened to him," said Solomon, eyes locked on Griffin and the oar.

"I guess nothing makes much sense tonight, does it?" Griffin lifted the oar. "I'll bet you've got a few questions. Your kindly old country parson won't be of any help."

Solomon relaxed but kept his eye on Griffin.

"Can't think of any."

"Really?"

Solomon was about to shake his head 'no,' when it hit him. B'gad, there was that one bit of peculiarity twingeing at the back of his mind.

"Yessir. And it's been gnawing at me from the git-go."

"I thought there might be," said Griffin.

"What'n hell makes Lavinia Kantlingher think an old pus-pocket like Edwin Greene is better than me?"

Griffin seemed a tad puzzled, then said "Maybe we should let your kindly old country parson handle that one."

"How on God's green earth could she ever consider giving that warm, sweet self of hers to a gap-toothed, pasty-faced pile of pudge?"

Griffin continued to blink. "Nothing else about tonight strike you as odd?"

Solomon thought another long minute.

"You mean being shot at point-blank and coming away without so much as a scratch?"

"Yes. Like that."

Solomon fished in his pocket. "The Captain's lucky piece." Solomon turned the token to catch the light, causing it to give off an odd luminescence. "It got all warm and buzzy, just before Luther shot at me." Solomon concentrated trying to remember what happened. "When I took Lavinia's hand, I said, 'I want to live forever' and that set me to tingling with some kind of holy fire."

Solomon reared up onto his knees, the boat rocking. "It grants wishes, don't it."

"It doesn't grant wishes," said Griffin.

"How many wishes do I get?" Solomon held the token out before him.

"That's not what it does."

Solomon squeezed his eyes shut. "I wish—I wish—for Lavinia Kantlingher to appear, right now, in this very boat, entirely in love with me, and only me, and Edwin Greene somewhere up to his neck in horse manure." Solomon opened one eye to check.

"It doesn't grant wishes, Solly."

"If it ain't wishes, what is it? I wished I could live forever, and then Luther shot me. Look at my shirt. That ball should've passed right through my heart, leaving a hole as big as a goose egg."

"When you chose to say those particular words—"

"Lucky I did. My blood was up. I was grabbing for any little bit of sweet-talk that'd catch Lavinia's fancy."

"Well, Solly, m'lad, you sweet-talked yourself onto a whole new plane of existence. You have silver-tongued your way into an unusual state of being for your kind."

"I always had a way with words."

"It's not what you said, Solly. It was everything going on inside that noggin of yours when you said it. The alignment of neurons, the inter-linking synapses of your brain, setting off a unique electro-chemical re-action that passes for a thought in your species, sending out a precise amount of voltage along an interconnecting network of ganglia in just the right amplitude to the muscle membranes that make up the human articulatory system which turns into speech, and, whammo, you're im-mortal!" Griffin finished up on one breath, inhaling deeply to recover.

The look on Solomon's face made it clear wishes would be easier for him to understand.

"You have no idea what I'm talking about, do you? That thing there is tuned to the mental activity of its bearer." Griffin sighed. "What are the odds that the neurological impulse that becomes the phrase you chose to utter in your primitive, unimaginative, puny little language is the same exact neurological impulse for the angelic phrase 'activate?' "

"One in a million?" offered Solomon, being more at home with cal-culating odds than comprehending biology.

"Try one in never It's not even a common phrase."

Solomon sank back down into the bottom of the skiff.

"It ain't wishes?"

"Okay. Let's say it's wishes. But! But, it's just the one. You wished for immortality and you got it, Solly. Well, more like indestructibility and that's almost the same thing."

"Indestructible? As in not destructible?"

"Solly, the intelligence of your species has always amazed me."

"Really?"

"That you all live as long as you do without any."

"Can't be destroyed, no matter what?"

"If you like. Or if you don't like. Whichever way, that's about the size of it."

"Then what in hell're we sitting here jawing about?" Solomon grabbed up the loose oar, dropped it back into the oarlock and set him-self to stroking for all he was worth, causing Griffin to grab the gunwales to steady himself as Solomon heaved and stroked.

"I gotta get to Lavinia and show her I'm a man of means. Luther can't say I ain't worthy now. This thingamajig's better than money." Sol-omon was heaving, stroking, chuffing with the effort, his head turned to keep the river in view over his shoulder. He wasn't making any progress.

He turned to look toward the stern. Griffin was out of the boat, standing on the water, leaned over, holding the transom. The boat wasn't moving.

Solomon stroked faster, spraying water everywhere.

"Let go! I gotta catch up to her before Edwin has her down to her smalls." Solomon stroked faster and faster. "Let go the boat!"

"Solly, wait. You don't understand."

"No, *you* don't understand. There never was a gal more ready for her wedding night than my Lavinia. I got to get to her before she says 'I do,' and then does."

"Solly, there's way, way more you need to know."

Solomon stopped rowing, worn out rather than curious, which actually made him curious.

"If I'm immortal, why'm I so tired out?"

"I'm trying to tell you. The human anatomy was never designed to bear this kind of immortality. Your nerves didn't stop working. You still get tired like everyone else. You still get hungry. You still feel pain. Maybe not as much."

Solomon pulled the token out and held it where he could look at it in the moonlight.

"What is it, then?"

"A piece of scale armor off an angel's breastplate."

"What's angels need with armor?"

"It came in handy when we were all locked in a great cosmological war over who should be in charge of the universe."

"Who won?"

"Who do you think won? That," Griffin pointed to the artifact, "could be considered fallout. The debris of battle. Just finding it lying about, your kind wouldn't know what it was. But, once it's activated, a short-timer like you can live forever. I've traveled the earth for thousands of years, looking for these. Finding them when they turn up. Recovering them before they fall into the wrong hands."

"What's that got to do with me?"

"I've come to take it back, Solly." Griffin held out his hand.

"Over my dead body." He jerked the shard out of reach.

"That's one way."

Solomon pulled his bowie and Griffin laughed. "What good is a knife going to do you?"

"This doo-hickey is the only thing of any real value I ever possessed in my life. I'm not giving it up without a fight."

"Solly, it wouldn't be much of a fight."

"Jacob wrestled himself an angel, didn't he? Good Book says so."

"Got himself a bum leg for his troubles."

"Aha! You just said yourself I'm indestructible."

"Solly, this is a dangerous thing for anyone to have. I figured you for more sense than Captain Curtwood."

"Why didn't you get it from him?"

"You know what the second most irresistible force is in all the cosmos?"

"A card sharp with five aces and a hidey pistol under the table?"

"Free will, Solly. Free will. You can't take a step in any direction without tripping over somebody's free will. And if you want my opinion, insofar as I'm allowed to have one, free will is the number one most lousy principle in the cosmos. But like it or not, I can't violate it. I mean, I can, but not without some serious personal consequences. The only thing you can do when you come up against free will is try talking sense into it. Captain Curtwood didn't have any. I figure you to be the kind of man who appreciates the odds."

Griffin held out his hand.

"Why'd that captain of yours risk it on a throw of the dice?"

"He didn't think he could lose."

"He was counting on loaded dice of his own?"

"He was counting on me."

"I don't see why I can't use it to prove I've got me some prospects now."

"Solly, it's a danger."

"I'd risk anything to win back Lavinia."

"Think for a minute. You can say you're immortal, but you can't prove it. Luther will think your insane. Maybe you can prove you're indestructible. But, if you do, they'll think you're a monster. Once that becomes known, you'll be hunted for the secret. The very worst of all creation would come looking to get hold of this."

"I can take care of myself."

"I mean the very worst of *all* creation. Not just your fellowman. There would be no stopping them. Is that what you plan to offer Lavinia in addition to your charming self?"

"So you just want me to hand it over."

"Yes. You go back to being mortal, with the biggest whopper of a story to tell the grandkids, which, fortunately, no one will believe. But at least you'll have survived to tell it."

"Then, thank'ee kindly for that word of warning, but if this is my only chance to win Lavinia, I've got to take it." Solomon leaned into the oars again his tongue stuck out in sympathetic effort.

"I've misjudged you. I really have. Sure, on the outside you appear to be a wastrel. A rake-hell. A conniver. A drinker of hard liquor. Given to gambling, chasing lewd women—"

"If this all's a way to butter me up and get this bauble, you got a mighty daft way a going about it."

"I was going to say that deep down, really, really deep down, I thought there might be a spark of intelligence and good sense."

"That'd make me just hand it over, pretty as you please?"

"I was hoping, yes."

"Whatever the reason, it's mine now. There's a divine purpose back of this and I mean to make the most of it. You're right. Abigail was right. Maybe even Luther's right. Everything I have, I got by cards or dice or other knavery. This is my chance to be something worthwhile."

"You can't let anyone know about this. They'll lock you up for a lunatic. You'll grow old—very old—in a mad house somewhere."

"I gotta try and make something of myself for Lavinia."

"Solly, she'll be married to Edwin by the time you reach her. Look. I'm not without influence. I can get you a dozen other Lavinias or Elizabeths or Gretchens. Just give it to me. You have my word."

"I don't care if she's married a hunnert years to that mangy manpoop. I have to win her away from Edwin. Don't you see? Saying she'd choose Edwin over me was her way of putting the spurs to me. I bet, right now, she's patiently waiting for me to come to her. It's all part of her plan."

"She nearly ran you over with the buggy."

"I wasn't ready to be the right kind of fella for her. I see that bright and clear now. However long it takes, I'll get back to her."

"Honestly, Solly, if it weren't for your looks and your sweet talk, do you think Lavinia would've given you the time of day?"

Solomon wasn't about to answer that.

"Well. I can see you're determined to hold onto it."

"I am."

Griffin seemed to appraise Solomon. "I tell you what I can do. I'll let you keep it for the tiniest little while. Long enough to make your fortune. Then you give it to me."

"How long?"

"Three days."

"That wouldn't be much of a fortune."

"You'd be surprised."

"Gotta be longer than that. A year."

"A week."

"A year."

"Okay, a month. But that's it."

"One whole year. Or I join a circus side show, travel all over creation, letting folks shoot me, a nickle a shot, until the whole world knows about this doo-hickey."

"All right! All right, Solly. One year."

"How long'd that captain have it?"

"You do remember what happened to him, right?" asked Griffin. "That's the deal. You can keep it for one year. Make your fortune, win Lavinia away from Edwin the old-fashioned way—with money. Then you give it to me."

"And maybe I don't."

"And maybe natural disasters follow you around like little lost puppies. I said, I'm not without influence."

"What's stopping you now? Are you some kind of guardian angel? Now I got this thing you have to watch over me?"

"Don't flatter yourself. I'm more the avenging angel type." Griffin straightened up, crossing his arms. "I've been at this uncounted millennia," said Griffin, studying Solomon. Then he said, "I guess one more pass around the sun won't kill me."

"Time don't mean all that much to you, does it?"

"No."

"Then let's make it a couple years."

"Solly—"

"Maybe till me and Lavinia get settled. Somewhere out west. After the kids are grown. Maybe after we've got a passel of grandkids."

"Solly, don't presume on my good nature."

"What's twenty or thirty years to a fella like you?"

"You give it up now, even a year from now, you'll barely feel it when you go back to being mortal. But the longer you wait, the more time will take its toll all at once. Everyone who ever got hold of one of these, who figures it out, who makes a deal, they say, oh, sure, tomorrow, or next week, or next month, I'll give it up and live my life like normal. But that day never comes and pretty soon it's too late. When you finally decide to give it up, Time takes it all back in an instant. Immediate death. They've stretched the strand of their life long past the breaking point. Nothing but that little disk keeping them from going dust-to-dust all over the shoes of some innocent bystander."

Griffin looked off toward the stars. "You'll see. When you start outliving everyone around you, people get suspicious, start asking questions, and pretty soon they're blaming you for what time and age are doing to them, and not to you. Next thing you know, you're on the run, hiding, pretending you never were the person you used to be."

Solomon watched Griffin, who seemed to take no more interest in him, only watching the bank slide by.

"The Captain called you Griffin. That your name?"

"Yes."

"What's that? Irish?"

"Mythic."

"Is that someplace up around Albany?"

Griffin didn't answer.

Solomon studied Griffin, who now seemed intent on the scenery. What would an angel know about a flesh and blood woman like Lavinia? Solomon knew women. Lavinia appreciated him for his whole natural self. Not just his looks and charming ways. Solomon could make book on that.

Chapter Five

SOLOMON FIRST SPOTTED LAVINIA and her sister Abigail while walking along the road toward the Second Evangelical Lutheran Free Church, not far from Kantlingher House. The day was heavily overcast, with the smell of rain on the breeze, and in the distance the dark curtains of a downpour.

He'd just left the *Clement C.*, docked a little before sunup to off-load goods from Albany. Now he was headed for Miss Monroe's place where he often rented a room whenever he dropped anchor in Saugerties.

After working until midday, he'd slipped off, making for town to find recreation before returning to the *Clement C.* to take on cargo bound for Manhattan.

As he approached the two women, Abigail shot him a fierce look to warn him against approaching them. She was older, taller, darker complected and with much darker hair. Except for the pronounced pinch of disdain she aimed at Solomon, her face was quite attractive. He'd have given them both a wide berth, if Lavinia hadn't smiled. Solomon could see the shorter girl took his presumptuous gawking as her due.

Even as he moved past them, he kept his head swiveled to watch Lavinia as she walked by him.

The two young women were a study in contrasts for Solomon, who knew something of such things.

Abigail's gait seemed to dampen the flow of her skirts. For all the ruffles and ribbons, there was no movement to suggest that hips and legs were at work under that cloud of fabric.

In contrast, Lavinia's skirt swayed and swooped deliciously. She was a fascinating figure in motion.

Lavinia was not quite as tall as her sister, but certainly taller than most women Solomon knew. Her figure and her complexion told of a healthy, outdoor vigor, rather than the cloistered look so many women affected. The ringlets of hair framing her face were honey amber and flowed from beneath the hat she wore tied off under her chin. Solomon could imagine its fragrance, even over the dockside aroma of his own pea coat.

Abigail didn't look back, but ensnared Lavinia's arm and kept them walking, lengthening her stride.

Heaving to, he hauled up and watched them move on down the road. Solomon had sufficient experience with young women of better quality to know not to approach them without a direct invitation.

That is, until he caught the barest tilt of Lavinia's head and the sweet cream flash of her jawline as she turned back ever so slightly. Not enough for her to see whether he was still looking, but enough to suggest the barest wisp of interest in whether he might be.

That tilt of her head exerted over Solomon the power of a summoning whistle by the bo'sun. He about-shipped, pivoting on his heel and followed after them.

Abigail walked faster, her shoulders squeezed upward, while Lavinia seemed to slow her pace.

Following behind, Solomon kept his distance while he considered how best to approach the young women without coming off as boorish and low in hailing them without a proper introduction.

Abigail, her arm still linked with Lavinia, didn't bother with decorum and fairly ran from Solomon, with Lavinia in tow. She planted her foot on a loose stone, slipped, and went tumbling into the gully along the roadway.

Struggling, Abigail sat up and grabbed her ankle, moaning and rocking as she massaged her damaged member.

Solomon ran up, took Lavinia by the hands, and looked deep into her eyes.

"Is she all right?" he asked.

Abigail stopped rocking and shot them both a dark look.

"I'm sure *she'll* be fine after a little major surgery," said Abigail. "I, on the other hand, am just peachy."

Lavinia broke the lock of Solomon's gaze and took his wrist, steadying herself as she side-stepped down the embankment to kneel next to Abigail.

"Are you hurt?"

"Of course I'm hurt! Did you see what that—that—that hooligan made me do?"

"That's terrible," said Lavinia, then turned to Solomon. "Are you a hooligan?"

"No," said Solomon, a bit wounded.

"Thank goodness." She turned to Abigail. "I have it on good authority he's not a hooligan."

Lavinia then stood astride Abigail to help pull her upright. But when Abigail put her full weight on the turned ankle she cried out. Lavinia lost control and Abigail sat down hard, causing her to cry out again.

"Go on to the church and get help."

"All right," said Lavinia, then turned to Solomon. "Would you please stay here with my sister while I bring help?"

"No! You'd leave me in the hands of this—this—"

"We've already decided he's not a hooligan."

"—assassin!" she finished.

Lavinia turned back to Solomon. "Would you do us the kindness and go up this road about a mile until you come to a church."

"Where they were having that big old oyster supper?" Solomon had smelled the mixture of aromas and had considered stopping in, but was reluctant to put himself within reach of the Almighty's long arm.

"Which we'll have to miss because of your clumsiness," said Abigail.

"Yes, that church. Fetch the sexton or his wife, and have them bring a buggy." She dug in her purse and held out a coin to him.

"No!" Abigail shouted.

"Now what?" asked Lavinia.

"He'll run off with your money and leave us here to die."

"I wouldn't blame him now if he did!"

"It'd be an honor," said Solomon, waving away her money. He tipped his cap and started to back away, when the cascade of rainfall finally reached them, the heavy drops pelting down.

"Don't stand there gawping," said Abigail. "Run. We'll be soaked." She opened up her umbrella as the rain came down harder.

Lavinia pulled her shawl about her and opened her own umbrella.

"Wait," she called after Solomon. "Come back."

"Let him go. We'll be drenched."

"The gully's starting to fill. You'll float away before he gets back with help. He'll carry you." She waved Solomon back to them.

"He will not," she said, even though the water in the gully was streaming along her legs and slowly rising.

"He will, and there's no more to it."

Solomon was inclined to let Abigail float away. It'd be a relief to let her float on down to the Esopus and into the Hudson, not stopping till she reached the Atlantic, her umbrella a convenient sail to speed her on her way. Then he'd be left alone with this winsome creature.

"You can carry her, can't you?" asked Lavinia.

"I've been toting potatoes all morning. I can certainly heft the likes of her over my shoulder. If she don't mind the view."

"She's not a sack of potatoes. She can ride. On your back."

"She will not," said Abigail.

"Yes, she will, and that's all there is to it."

Working together, with Lavinia steadying and Solomon levering, they got Abigail upright. Then, with an *allez-oop*, mounted her on Solomon's back.

Abigail, blushing a deep rose, now astride the living, working spine of a flesh-and-blood man, held herself back, bracing herself away with one hand on his shoulder while holding up the umbrella with the other.

In his own effort to keep from being over-balanced and tumbling backward with her, Solomon leaned forward and with a sudden jolt, hefted her up higher on his back, flattening her against him. He fought the fabric of her skirts to slide his forearms under her knees and locked his hands to keep her securely fastened in place.

He walked quickly and with an ungainly wobble as the rain picked up. Abigail slipped an arm around his neck. Solomon regretted his half-day's growth of chin whiskers that must certainly scrape and tickle along her forearm, underscoring his low character.

"I'm so glad you came along," said Lavinia.

"So am I." His breathing was as shallow as he could make it to avoid any sign of exertion. Talking didn't help the illusion.

"We're not at our best right now."

"Beauty strikes without warning," said Solomon. "I often stroll this way, enjoying the flowers by the road. I feel sorry for them. They don't stand a chance when real beauty turns up."

"Oh, puh-*lease!*" said Abigail. Solomon hitched her up again, landing her hard on his spine. He'd have preferred having Lavinia's thighs clasped hard against his ribs, the way Abigail had herself locked around his waist, the heat where she rode against the small of his back—intoxicating.

"It's going to take me a week of scrubbing to get this smell out of my clothes from whatever rat trap boat you came off," said Abigail. Nevertheless, she kept her knees in tight against his sides, her heels pressing hard against the tops of his thighs.

"Is she heavy?" asked Lavinia, with a quick smile at Abigail.

Solomon would blush if his face weren't already crimson from the effort.

"I could carry her all the way to New York for you, if you like." As long as New York wasn't more than fifty paces from where he now staggered.

"You're going to drop me."

"You're quite gallant to go so far out of your way."

"Good Book says love bears all things, believes all things, hopes all things, endures all things," said Solomon.

"Good Book also says that donkeys can talk when the Lord lets them." That got her another hitch and another hard landing on Solomon's spine, knocking another grunt out of her.

"Won't you miss your ship?"

"They won't sail without me."

"Why wouldn't they? River sailors being a dime a dozen these days." Nevertheless, Abigail rested her cheek against the back of his head, closing her eyes, her curls dropping down alongside Solomon's face.

The sweet fragrance of Abigail's hair surprised him, as did her warmth against the back of his head. Her hard looks and sharp tongue made him expect only cold flesh and a sour corpse smell. These sensations distracted him, and his pace slowed.

Abigail opened her eyes and she caught Lavinia watching and smiling. She jerked her head erect.

"Stop jostling me, you clod. I'm nearly faint with the pain!"

It wasn't as warm and sweet as before.

"It must be exciting to be a sailor," said Lavinia.

"Soooooometimes," said Solomon, breathing through his nose to hide the strain. "I could captain my own boat if I took a mind to it. But—"

"But, what?" asked Lavinia, when he didn't finish right away.

"I would never want to be so long gone from a sweetheart—if I had one like you."

"I'm going to be sick. On an empty stomach!" said Abigail.

Lavinia pointed out Kantlingher House when it came into view.

"Thank God," said Abigail.

Solomon agreed, and then with a superhuman effort powered by his desire to please and impress Lavinia, he broke into a gallop and whinnied, bobbling and jouncing Abigail along.

"Oohhhhh, deeeeeeear Gawwwwwwwwd," exhaled Abigail, her breath bursting in time with the galloping stride of a sweaty Solomon playing the man-stallion between her legs.

Solomon reached the porch of the house, nearly spent, but staggered up the steps with Abigail still astride his back. At the top step, he could feel himself tipping backward. Abigail, perhaps sensing their danger, leaned hard against his hot back, arms wrapped around his heaving chest, his breath rasping hot on her wrists.

He released Abigail who let herself slide ever so slowly down off his back. She kept a firm grip on Solomon as she tested her weight on her damaged ankle.

Once safely on the porch out of the rain herself, Lavinia laughed and clapped, which made Solomon smile through the pain.

Luther Kantlingher, very much a patriarch to Solomon's eye, had stepped out onto the porch, his thumbs in his waistcoat pockets.

"Well now, Abigail. Who's your beau?" he asked, wearing a broad smile.

Abigail looked back at Solomon who'd already moved closer to Lavinia.

"How should I know? Ask Lavinia. She's the one who found him on the road."

"You owe him thanks, Abigail," said Lavinia.

"Lead him around to the stable and let Custis give him some oats and a good brushing." Abigail stumped past Luther, into the house.

Solomon doffed his cap. "Is there anything else I can do for you? Anything at all?"

"Why, no. But thank you."

"Well. Good day, miss."

"Wait. Even horses have names."

"Solomon. Solomon Durnley."

"Lavinia Kantlingher," she said, then gestured to Luther. "This is my father, Luther Kantlingher."

Solomon offered his hand. "Luther."

But Luther was no longer smiling, and didn't bother to unhook his thumbs from his waistcoat.

"Mister Kantlingher will do for you," said Luther. "Lavinia, get in the house and out of those wet things." He kept his eyes on Solomon.

Lavinia sailed by Luther, and into the house, leaving behind only Luther's scowl for Solomon to look on.

Solomon stepped off the porch and into the driving rain, but he hesitated to turn away. He was rewarded with the sight of Lavinia's face appearing in an upstairs window. She gestured for him to keep watching, pointing toward the end of the house, and disappeared from the window. He continued to walk backward trying to appear fixed on Luther even as he kept watch for Lavinia.

She appeared at the next window over and again pointed toward the end of the house. Solomon turned and walked away from Luther, hands in his pockets, whistling, throwing back an occasional glance, until Luther went back inside.

Solomon dashed to the far end of the house where Lavinia had pointed. She appeared at the last window, this time pointing around back of the house.

He continued around the house, almost sashaying to keep his eyes on the windows for her next appearance, as he sped along. Lavinia again showed herself, this time at a window on the other side of the house, at the end, just over the long, wide single floor attachment that served as the kitchen for the hotel. She stood for a long moment, then stretched up and closed the curtains. He realized it was the window by which he could reach her.

He was still standing there when Luther stepped out through the back door.

"Which way's the road back to town?" asked Solomon.

"That way." Luther pointed the stem of his pipe square at Solomon, then swept it toward the front of the house, dismissing him. Solomon tipped his cap and made for the main road, dancing to avoid the water puddling in the drive.

From the next window over, Abigail watched him go, her forehead pressed against the glass.

Chapter Six

SOLOMON STEERED THE BOAT UP against the pilings of the small dock at the end of the street leading off to Miss Monroe's rooming house.

He stretched the kinks out of his sore muscles.

"You could've taken yourself a turn on the oars. Pull your own weight for a while."

"I don't weigh anything."

Grabbing the knapsack and bedroll, Solomon stepped out of the boat.

"Where are you going?"

Solomon headed for the street. "My rooming house."

"You need to get out of the valley."

"I been shot, dunked in the river, and rowed a boat this whole long way by myself. I'm wore out and hungry."

Griffin stepped out of the boat, following Solomon. "So you've given up on the idea of interfering with Lavinia's marital bliss."

Solomon stopped. Griffin's choice of words filled Solomon's head with the revolting image of Edwin in long johns, back flap open, chasing Lavinia in her night dress.

"I have not. Maybe I can't stop the wedding. But—she'll find a way to save herself from him. You can be sure she's got a plan worked out, after what we shared last night."

"What was that exactly?"

"I don't remember it all. There's still a few hazy spots. But you can bet it'll come back to me."

They walked on. Griffin's steps made no sound. Solomon realized there was a lot to learn about Griffin.

"You been at this a while, haven't you," said Solomon. "Chasing down these little doo-hickeys."

"Quite a while. Why?"

"There anyone still left out there? Like me, I mean?"

"How could there be, Solly? You're one of a kind."

Walking on a bit longer, they reached the rooming house. Miss Monroe catered to regular travelers as well as the rivermen who worked the Hudson between Albany and Manhattan.

This stretch along the river wasn't much of a place for making fast fortunes. Solomon figured to sleep until breakfast, eat, then settle his bill and head out for greener pastures. He still had his winnings, wet from his ducking in the Esopus. It ought to be enough for passage somewhere more hospitable.

Reaching the rooming house, Solomon saw light in the parlor windows.

Miss Monroe was much older, unmarried, and slightly sweet on Solomon. But she was too tight-fisted to leave lamps burning so late into the night on his account.

He paused on the porch, scraped his shoes on the iron dog, his concession to her fury for boarders tracking mud across the floors. He opened the door.

Solomon found himself facing a room full of soldiers in torn and sand-crusted uniforms. All looking at him.

Miss Monroe pushed out from between them. "There you are!" she said.

The front door closed behind him.

Two more soldiers stepped shoulder to shoulder, blocking his retreat.

Griffin's face appeared from behind the soldiers. "Get him!" he shouted.

Solomon bolted for the window and dived headlong, hitting the glass with a bang, and knocking himself to the floor, the glass unbroken.

Solomon's head rang with the impact but didn't stun him.

The soldiers were on him instantly. He thrashed and squirmed as the blows rained down on his head and shoulders, setting his skull to vibrating.

Solomon wriggled and kicked, crawling out through the legs of his attackers. He saw Miss Monroe lift the sash of the window opposite. He dived for the narrow opening.

"Sorry," she said as he flew by, launching himself into the night beyond.

He rolled into the hedge, snapping branches and coming up with a mouth full of leaves and twigs. Spitting, he got to his feet as the front door banged open and the soldiers poured out, some leaping the railing, others taking the front steps two and three at a time, hot on Solomon's heels.

Not likely to outrun a body of men whose livelihood was traveling by foot over long distances, Solomon shinnied up the nearest tree, only to discover he'd chosen a tree too short and with no reach to anything higher.

Hands gripped Solomon's ankles and hauled him out of the tree, slamming him to the ground with a bone-jarring thud. He lay there amid a forest of blue-piped trouser legs and muddy shoes.

A pair of soldiers lifted him onto his feet, shoving him up against the tree. Another soldier step forward, gripped Solomon's shirtfront, and cocked back his fist.

"Wait, wait, wait!" said Solomon, his hands up. The soldier hesitated. "There's something very important you should know."

Solomon's fist shot up, catching the soldier hard under the chin.

"Dang!" Solomon shook his hand as the soldier smiled, showing off a mouth nearly empty of teeth. Then he hammered Solomon, rocking him back against the tree trunk, bouncing him forward onto his face.

Griffin, on hands and knees, peeked through the legs of the soldiers.

"Uh, Solly? We're trying to keep your condition a secret, remember?"

"*You* set these johnnies on me."

"They recognized me. I had to say something."

Spitting gravel, Solomon raised himself up. "You said I was indestructible! What good's this thing if they can knock me down?"

"It makes you indestructible. It won't make you any better in a fist fight."

Soldiers grabbed Solomon by the collar and hauled him to his feet.

Griffin winced and ducked as the next soldier landed a smacking blow to Solomon's jaw, laying him out again. "Also, you can still feel a little pain."

Solomon struggled to lift his head. "How much do you think's a little?"

Griffin looked down at Solomon. "Okay, maybe more than a little."

"Maybe a whole lot more than a little."

"But not as much, right?"

Solomon flipped over onto his stomach, getting his hands and knees under himself, his head ducked. Then he launched himself, running full out, ramming the nearest soldier in the guts. With no effect. The butted soldier bashed Solomon with an upper cut, knocking him onto his back again, his head bouncing off the ground.

"At least I ain't out cold yet. That's an improvement."

"They'll figure it out if you keep this up. You have to get out of here."

Solomon jerked sideways out from under a stomp to the belly. He sprang to his feet as the soldiers encircled him.

"Okay, okay," said Solomon, "I give. I give." He had his hands up again, holding them off, turning, looking at each of the men closing in on him. Solomon advanced toward the shortest soldier, keeping his hands up, then kicked the short soldier square in the stones, doubling him up. Solomon leap-frogged over his back and out of the encirclement.

At a dead run, Solomon disappeared into the dark, angling away from the street. Vaulting fences and dodging livestock, he put as many obstacles as he could between himself and the pursuing soldiers.

The soldiers closed in on him, calling to each other as they bore down on him in the dark.

At the river's edge Solomon plunged headlong into the dark waters and swam out toward the middle.

When he finally broke the surface he saw that he'd drifted down river from where the soldiers prowled the banks looking for him to emerge. Angling with the current he swam toward the opposite bank, the waters pushing him toward the Hudson.

Reaching the tangled growth along the bank, Solomon pulled himself out of the water. He gasped as he struggled up from the entangling roots and limbs.

Blue-piped trouser legs stood over him. Solomon rolled sideways, up onto his hands and knees and looked up. It was Griffin.

"You were trying to get the Captain's lucky piece back, weren't you? Going back on our deal."

"I'm the one who gave Miss Monroe the idea to open the window. So you could escape."

"She could've come up with that herself."

"No. She's a sweet old lady, but things were happening much too fast for her."

"So, wait a minute. All that talk of free will. That's just a bunch of malarky?"

"Okay. In theory, it's a fine idea. But out here in the everyday cosmos, you're always walking a fine line. Sue me. I said my job is to keep it out of the wrong hands. Secrecy makes that a whole lot easier. For both of us."

Solomon turned and headed back upriver.

"The soldiers are still out looking for you up there."

"I lost my knapsack thanks to you."

"You mean this?" Griffin held out the knapsack and bedroll. "I picked it up while you were keeping the soldiers busy."

Solomon turned around and came back. He stood a moment glaring at Griffin.

"You led them right to me, didn't you, so they would be waiting for me."

"I was with you the whole time."

"You're a danged angel."

"Ah. But I'm not omnipresent."

Solomon swiped for the knapsack, flung it over his shoulder, and started downriver.

They walked in silence, Griffin making no noise, only the sound of Solomon's shoes on the roadbed.

"What's the first?" asked Solomon.

"First what?"

"You said the second most irresistible force in that cosmos of yours is free will," said Solomon. "So. What's the first?"

"True love. That's about as rare as lips on a chicken."

Chapter Seven

THE ROAD LEADING BACK to the river was dark. The moon was long gone behind the clouds. Solomon was so keen on the road under his feet to avoid the water-filled ruts, or sliding off into the muddy underbrush along the roadside, that he failed to appreciate the peculiar light on the roadway.

When he did look up to get his bearings, he realized that the milky gray light was coming off Griffin. It wasn't so much an emanation as an envelope, sufficient to see by on a moonless night. It reminded him of the phosphorescence he'd seen in the wakes of the river schooners. Especially on dark nights above the point where the Harlem River met the Hudson on his north-bound voyages.

Solomon stretched out his stride to get closer to Griffin and out of the disconcerting darkness.

Griffin walked along whistling, paying no attention to Solomon or the ruts and rocky places under their feet.

"Rain's coming," Griffin called back to Solomon. A few more steps and the first heavy drops of the rainstorm started falling. "Lightning's going to be bad. You may want to get under something."

"Angels can see the future?"

"Don't need to." Griffin pointed off to their left. The sky was bursting with the artillery of a great lightning storm, the cracks of the thunder finally breaking over them.

The rain caught up with the peals of thunder and fell hard, thick, and drenching.

Griffin's evanescent glow didn't diminish.

With another syncopated crack, the sky lit up and a streak of lighting lanced to the ground, passing straight through Solomon, scorching the dirt on which he stood.

Solomon shook hard, the hot buzz of electricity still vibrating his body. He shivered and exhaled every last bit of air from his lungs.

"I told you to get under something!" said Griffin. "Look out!"

Another lightning strike snappity-snapped and cut through Solomon, making his bones flash white through his skin, scorching his shirt collar, and popping the buttons off his vest.

Solomon was more of a rusty automaton than man of smoking flesh as he staggered toward the fence along the road in a series of creakity jerks. His knees gave out as he reached the fence, and he caught himself on the top rail. He raised up a leg, stretched it along the rail, then let it drag the rest of him over, rolling, to land back-flat on the other side. The rain pelted him, his clothes smoking and steaming from the heat and water.

Griffin ran back, grabbed Solomon by the wrist and pulled him to his feet. He pointed across an open meadow to a light barely visible through the trees beyond.

"Let's head for that farm. Bound to be a barn there so we can get out of this storm!" Griffin shouted over the cacophony of beating rain and rumbling thunder.

Griffin took a few steps toward the bright yellow point off in the distance. Thunder cracked as lightning flashed, and the smell of newly scorched wool filled the air. Griffin looked back at Solomon, struck again, standing stock still.

"Come on!"

"I ain't moving. Lightning don't strike in the same place twice."

Another lance of lightning struck Solomon, with a power that caused even Griffin to flinch.

"Physical laws seem to have made an exception in your case, Solly. You can't stay out here in the open!" Griffin grabbed Solomon by the collar and hauled him across the meadow toward the light.

"This being indestructible ain't worth warm piss, you know that!" Solomon's body continued to buzz, his blood stream and nervous system nothing so much as a swarm of angry yellow jackets flying up one arm and down the other, with a loop through his entrails, down to his toes and around again.

"Come on." Griffin aimed for the buildings silhouetted in the stabbing arcs of light. They clambered over another rail fence, keeping out of sight of the farmhouse, with its one window showing a dim glow. As Griffin and Solomon dashed across the meadow, the lightning followed them, tearing up the ground, burning the vegetation under their heels.

Solomon ducked under a scrawny tree just this side of the fence the same instant another electrical bolt struck, splitting the tree right down to the ground, the odor of burnt bark and boiled tree sap cutting through the heavy rain.

Reaching the barn, Griffin pulled the broad door open just enough to let them squeeze inside, then working together they dragged it closed again, the lightning flashes illuminating the barn's interior through the gaps in the siding.

The livestock snorted and snuffled in the dark around them.

"You'd think the whole blamed storm was called up on account of me," said Solomon, but Griffin and his handy glow had vanished.

By the flashes of light between cracks in the barn siding Solomon could pick out the red-gold glow of eyeballs peering through the slats of the stalls. That halo of Griffin's was right handy, and sure would be useful about now.

The glow reappeared in the hayloft above him. Griffin's head poked over the side.

"Solly," hissed Griffin. "Up here."

Solomon hauled himself up the ladder and collapsed in the hay. With a groan, he rolled onto his back and stared up at the rafters overhead. Bats, clinging to the ridge beam above, stared down at him, their eyes glittering.

The storm outside seemed to be passing.

"You coulda took a couple of them bolts, maybe saved me a scorching." Solomon held out his charred shirt front.

"I told you. I'm not some kind of guardian angel."

"A little bit a lightning can't hurt you none."

"I'm not omnipotent, Solly. I don't want to get struck by lightning any more than you do."

Solomon picked at the blackened spots of fabric.

"It's a danged uncommon thing, the lightning catching me out that way. You'd think I'd done it some personal injury and it tracked me the whole long way just for spite."

"Who can understand nature, Solly." Griffin didn't seem ready to offer any more insight.

"At first light, I'm heading back to the river. Maybe catch a flatboat or schooner for New York. There's bound to be more quick money to be made down river than up."

"Solly, I see only two ways this could go. Banditry or hard work. You've never had much of a stomach for either one. Face it, a man makes a living with his back and he makes a fortune with his head. There's nothing inside that noggin of yours worth any real money."

"There's gold in the Carolinas. Georgia, maybe. Swirl me up a pan full of nuggets and be back before spring. Fur trapping's good money, too. A couple months in the mountains. Having this thing with me, I won't waste time worrying about Indians or grizzly bears or whatever might come along."

"Facing tomahawks and bear claws will be easy as pie, no doubt. But that thing hanging from your neck won't protect you from the misery of long hours doing manual labor, Solly."

"I ain't afraid of a little hard work."

"Anyone who's ever had to pay you a day's wage might beg to differ."

"I give fair work for fair wages."

"And never an inch more."

"I been working up and down the river going on four years now, making bricks, cutting ice, sorting mail, loading barges, shoveling horse barns," said Solomon, ticking off his work history, finger by finger. "You can't tell me that ain't hard work."

"From one job to the next. Just long enough to pay for a jug, pay your way into a card game, or pay your way out of jail."

"I believe hard work's a good thing. But I also believe what my daddy, God rest his soul, said about too much of a good thing."

"You didn't know your daddy."

"It's the sort a thing a man's pap'd tell him if he got the chance."

"And these last few months? Cleaning out bilge on a river sloop, calling yourself a riverman? Come on, Solly."

Solomon shook himself free of that memory.

"I could captain my own boat if I took a mind to it."

"You will be better off going back to a normal life, working the river, or whatever it is you plan to do next, and leave Lavinia and Edwin to their future."

"It was you said I should make my fortune and come back for her."

"I had to say something. You were talking crazy."

"Crazy to go after the one true love of my life?"

"Really? She's planning to get married while you're playing at dice with your pay."

"I was winning. If I hadn't crossed that Captain, I'd be—"

"—still there. Rolling dice. Never knowing she was gone. What about all the other true loves of your life? Not exactly the freshest flowers of maidenhood. Am I right? Am I right?"

Solomon didn't answer. He'd been partial to willing, wayward women before, but not a single one since he'd clapped eyes on Lavinia.

And, surely, never again after the night he shared with her. Pretty sure he shared with her.

"You are decidedly partial to the professional practitioners of the womanly arts."

Solomon stared up at the bats overhead. He must have consorted with others who didn't make a specialty of fellas with a pocket full of money.

"Face it, Solly, the women who manage to hold onto your attention are the ones within arm's reach of a tankard of beer, a cup of dice, or a deck of cards."

"Lavinia changed all that for me."

"Isn't it possible Lavinia dallied with you as some kind of peculiar adventure? Make her daddy mad? Feel wanton without the risk?"

"You watch yourself. You'll be answering to me, angel or no angel. My Lavinia is no kind of wanton."

"No, she's not. She cut you loose once the adventure ran its course."

"Who knows what goes on in the minds of women."

"You gave it your all. Time to move on, Solly."

Solomon was tumbling it all over and over in his mind. Lavinia choosing to run off rather than have herself a white wedding, her accepting the locket, him surviving Luther's pistol shots. There had to be something she said or did that would make it all clear to him, something he was missing.

"I told you. I don't care if it's one year or a hunnert years—"

"In one year or a hundred years, Lavinia will be up to her apron strings in Edwin's progeny."

That was it. That's what Solomon missed. He sat up, pointing at Griffin.

"I asked her straight out if she and Edwin were having children. She said, and I quote, 'What do you think?' What does she think I would think? Of course, I know what I would think. No!"

Griffin shook his head good and hard. "That's amazing how your kind moves so easily from one delusion to the next."

"Ain't no delusion. It was there in front of me all this time. I wasn't giving her enough credit."

"If she is an upright woman, like you say she is, don't you think she'll keep her vows of eternal matrimony?"

Solomon hadn't quite worked out in his head how she would reconcile all of this in her scheme. But he trusted in the wiliness of women and that spark of true affection he knew to be burning deep in that delicious bosom of hers.

"Any woman can see when it comes to the upstanding department, you don't hold a candle to a fellow like Edwin."

Solomon rolled over, hugging himself against the damp cold air. Then he rolled back.

"Maybe there is something useful you can tell me," said Solomon.

"Light starting to dawn finally, is it?"

"Where's that glow coming from?"

"What glow?"

"That glow coming off you?"

Griffin looked down at himself and stretched out his hands. "Oh. Yeah."

"How is it you shine like that?"

"It's not me. For you to see me, be able to hear me, I have to step out of my—" Griffin stopped, clearly struggling for a word that would fit Solomon's grasp of cosmology. "—dimension?" Solomon looked slightly stupefied. "It's like standing in a doorway between where I am and where you are. Not quite in, not quite out. What you're seeing is the light from the other side."

"Oh," said Solomon, nodding with comprehension. "Well. Put yourself out so I can get some sleep."

"Solly, I thought we were going to have a deep, meaningful discussion about your relationships."

"I'm through talking with any fella who hasn't got any useful experience with women."

Solomon hunched up and hugged himself tighter against the cold, making his back as inhospitable as possible to any further talk. The light in the hayloft faded, leaving only the dark.

Chapter Eight

A SLATE GRAY DAWN FILLED THE BARN. The wet morning air, the itch of straw, and the stink of livestock joined the hazy light to rouse Solomon from the deep grip of sleep he had been enjoying. He pulled at the straw, pillowing more of it under his head, fighting off the new day.

A brand new store-bought pitchfork with long, shiny, well-sharpened tines hovered over Solomon's buttocks.

At the other end, gripping the pitchfork's shaft, stood Louisa Jugenheimer, a full-figured farm wife in a faded blue dress, dirty collar, and half-apron, with a tight-fitting, white cap tied off under her chin. She stood with legs apart, arms bared to the elbows, the pitchfork raised and ready.

With a grace and power gained by years of working the plunger on a butter churn, she stabbed the pitchfork into Solomon's butt-cheeks.

Solomon's eyes popped open in surprise at the painful wake-up call. He inhaled, ready to give out with a yowl of indignation. Instead, he got a mouthful of straw dust and started coughing. He scuttled from under the pitchfork, flipping over to locate the source of the attack.

"It's mein eggs you stole, ja!" She held the gleaming tines at Solomon's throat.

Solomon kept his nose pointed toward Louisa while his eyes darted about for any sign of Griffin. Nothing.

Much more awake, he remembered that he was in no real danger from this corn-fed Valkyrie and her barn-yard lance, but Griffin's insistence on the need for secrecy kept him cowed.

"I didn't eat any eggs. I came up here last night to get out of the rainstorm. I've been asleep the whole time."

Griffin reared up out of the hay.

"Where've you been?" Solomon demanded.

"Right here," said Griffin, stretching and yawning.

"Did you eat this woman's eggs?" Looking up at her, Solomon pointed at Griffin. "He might've eaten your eggs."

"Solly," said Griffin, low, urgent.

"This is a serious woman. Can't you see she's got a pitchfork?"

"Solly."

"Standing there like Missus Lucifer on the front porch of Hell."

"Solly!" Griffin shouted.

"What!" Solomon shouted back.

"She can't see or hear me."

Solomon's eyes slid from Griffin to Mrs. Jugenheimer then back to Griffin.

"Those soldiers could see you just fine when you sic'd 'em on me last night."

"I'm not visible when I sleep."

"You're awake now." Solomon fixed his eyes on Mrs. Jugenheimer, trying not to move his lips.

"Well. Ummm. I thought it might be less threatening for her to find only one of us in her barn. Keep her from over-reacting."

"You know, this little fact would've been handier before she showed up."

"You may not appreciate this little fact about me now, but I guarantee it will come in handy later."

"So where's that leave me?"

"Looking like an idiot, talking to a clump of hay in front of an armed and angry civilian."

"You a kook?" demanded Mrs. Jugenheimer.

"No, I can't cook," said Solomon.

"Kook! Kook! Sick in d'head?" she tapped her temple, the pitchfork still rock steady in her other hand.

"If I say I am, can we forget about the eggs?"

"You ate 'em, you pay me up," she said, with a jab of her pitchfork.

"Pay her for the eggs, Solly."

"Okay, okay. I pay." Solomon got to his knees. "How much?"

"Two dollars an egg. Ten eggs. Twenty dollars."

"Twenty dollars! What kind of chicken lays a two-dollar egg? That's barnyard robbery!"

Mrs. Jugenheimer jabbed the pitchfork at him again.

"Finefinefinefine!" Solomon checked his vest pocket. Then he checked his other vest pocket. Then he checked his coat pockets. Then he checked his pants pockets.

"It's gone." Solomon, fished in every pocket, a hand-dance going faster and faster. Then he stopped. "My money's gone."

"Gone?" asked Griffin.

"It's gone! It's all gone!" Solomon tore through the loft, throwing hay everywhere. "All my money's gone!"

"You must've lost it in the fight back at the boarding house."

"What about my eggs?" She pointed the pitchfork at him again.

"I don't have any money."

"D'en," she said, lowering her pitchfork, "You work."

Solomon slumped, sitting on his heels, spent.

Mrs. Jugenheimer reached out and took hold of the locket around Solomon's neck.

"No, nononono. Not for sale." Solomon tugged it from her hand. He popped it open and held up the pictures of himself and Lavinia. "That's me. And the other one is the future Missus Durnley."

"Who paint? You paint?" A smile actually seemed to creep onto her face, crinkling ever so slightly the corners of her eyes and mouth.

"Uh, yes," said Solomon, seeing a tiny breach in her wall of hostility that he might exploit. Then with a wink at Griffin, Solomon got to his feet and turned on the charm. "I paint all kinds of things. I'm quite the *artiste*. People. Landscapes. Every day objects artfully arranged." She began to nod her head. "You know, I bet I could paint you a picture worth every single one of those eggs. More, even." With a hypnotist's charm, he dangled the locket before her eyes.

"A surprise for the Mister," Solomon crooned. "Something to brighten up the old farmstead." She was nodding along with him now. "I don't have my paint box or my easel with me, but I could slip into the village and gather a few things, then come right back here to paint you a jim-dandy picture."

"Ja," she said, looking up. "It's my barn you'll paint." Her smile was gone. If it ever existed.

He studied the pitchfork, the determined Mrs. Jugenheimer, and the distance to the ladder.

"You know," Solomon said to Griffin. "I could just walk out of here."

"Of course you could. And she'd send for the sheriff, tell them about the egg thief, and how she bent her shiny new pitchfork on his stubborn hide. Then we'd have the entire county out looking for Sasquatch."

Solomon looked at Griffin, then looked at the scowling farm wife standing in front of him.

"Or, I could paint the barn," said Solomon, his smile for Mrs. Jugenheimer more of a grimace.

She turned and climbed down the ladder. At the bottom she looked up. "First breakfast, then the barn." She marched out.

"Hey, saw what you did there, Solly. That was truly an instructive bit of chicanery," said Griffin. "It kind of tingles to be in the presence of such a con *artiste*." Griffin followed her down the ladder. "I hope she has sausage," he said, catching the eye of the hogs, snouts up and snuffling. "Nothing personal," he added as he jumped from the last rung landing in front of the hogs in the pen under the loft. "I've never actually had sausage."

Solomon followed him down.

In the morning light outside, Solomon turned back to calculate the square footage confronting him. He wished Griffin had chosen to hide in the outhouse.

The kitchen was warmed by the fire in the hearth where Mrs. Jugenheimer cooked breakfast.

At the far end of the table, Solomon sat, a napkin tucked into his collar, a fork and knife under his hands, and his eyes on Mrs. Jugenheimer. She twisted off a piece of bread, dropping it on the plate filled with sausages and gravy.

She dropped the plate on the rough wooden surface, and banged a mug of hot coffee down beside it.

Solomon began to fork up the food.

"Mitout grace, you eat my food?"

He stopped, mouth open, eyes upward. He ducked his head.

"Lord, thank you for this food I am preparing to consume." He raised his head and lifted his fork. She was scowling down on him. He bowed his head again. "And bless this dear woman for her kindness to this lonely wayfarer. Amen." She gave a bob of her head and turned back to her work. Solomon went back to forking food furiously.

In spite of the disdain that seemed to ooze from her pores, she hummed some old Teutonic hymn, her hips swaying as she shuttled between the hearth and the pantry. If he were more of a churchman, he'd have hummed along to put her at his ease.

Sausage was disappearing off Solomon's plate as Griffin snagged links and chewed furiously. It was unsettling to think someone from the very throne room of the Almighty had such lousy table manners.

Griffin sucked the grease off his fingers. "Have you noticed? She hasn't set a place for the man of the house." He leaned close to Solomon. "This could be a sweet deal for an otherwise itinerant ne'er-do-well without any hope of a future, fortune-wise."

"Who?" Solomon whispered, watching Mrs. Jugenheimer.

"You. Here's your chance."

"To do what?"

"Settle down here. It's a splendid possibility."

"Splendid?" barked Solomon causing Mrs. Jugenheimer to stop and look around. Solomon held up the sausage. "Splendid." She chuffed and turned back to her cooking.

"What's here to be had?"

"A big old farm, a not-half-bad looking farm wife. Sausage and biscuits for life. I certainly would enjoy eating these the rest of *my* natural life. If I had a natural life."

"You have any idea how much work there is to farming? No, you don't, having things done for you. Little cherubs shuttling back and forth, fetching and carrying. Here on earth, there's no end of work. No making port. No tying up and paying off. I'd be living like the Flying Dutchman, sailing on forever."

"That's not the only consideration." Griffin nudged Solomon to take another, longer look at Mrs. Jugenheimer.

"She's nearly twice my age." But not unappealing, he had to admit.

She took more sausage off the platter on the sideboard and dropped them on Solomon's plate, making no mention of his appetite, then turned back to the hearth.

"She's certainly more available than Lavinia, from the look of things. She didn't put out a plate for Mister Farmer."

"Maybe he's already up. Out milking goats. Stuffing a scarecrow for all I know."

"So. Ask her."

"She'll either get the wrong idea and I'll be stuck painting barns and plucking chickens the rest of my own natural life. Or she'll get the wrong idea and use that shotgun on me." Solomon pointed his fork at the fowling piece leaning against the door jamb.

Still, the idea was not entirely unattractive to Solomon. Watching Mrs. Jugenheimer out of the corner of his eye, he could appreciate that she was vigorous and healthy. And strong-willed, which had always been appealing in the women to whom Solomon gravitated.

Griffin nudged Solomon again, nodding toward her.

"Don't seem safe, taking to wife any woman who'd hold a pitchfork on me first thing in the morning, then feed me breakfast."

"One way to keep married life thrilling and fresh, if you ask me."

"What would you know about such things?"

"Just what I see."

Solomon kept his head down, loading his fork with the help of his bread, keeping himself fixed on Lavinia.

"At least ask her about Mister Farmer." Again with the nudge.

"If you'll stop jabbing me." Solomon washed the food down with a swallow of coffee and cleared his throat.

"So. The Mister out milking cows?"

Mrs. Jugenheimer stopped stirring and slid a side-long glance at Solomon.

"Mister Jugenheimer is det, Gott rest his soul."

Griffin, beaming with smugnacity, nudged Solomon harder, causing him to grunt.

"I appreciate your sympathy," said Mrs. Jugenheimer, and went back to stirring, humming louder, her hips swaying with a mesmerizing lustiness as she worked.

Chapter Nine

AFTER BREAKFAST, SOLOMON STEPPED into the work shed, finding it a disorganized scattering of hand-tools, rope, pieces of metal, wood-scraps, and chicken droppings.

"Yep," said Griffin. "Looks like the place could use a man's touch."

"Why's everything got to be work with you?"

"You know what they say. Idle hands are the devil's workshop."

"I can't picture you all saying that up where you come from."

"We don't. We say, why do for yourself when you can get a mortal to do it. I'm just repeating what I'd heard around here. Thought it might buck you up."

"Well, it don't."

"Sorry."

Solomon found a bucket, a sack of store-bought pigment, linseed oil, and some lime. He measured out quantities into a bucket all a-slop with dried red paint, and stirred it with a scrap of wood, scraping the bottom as he blended the ingredients.

Solomon toted the bucket around to the side of the barn facing the house. Mrs. Jugenheimer scuttled about the door yard, setting up a kettle for laundry. Solomon caught glimpses of her between his dipping and brushing on paint. She made quite the display of industry, drawing water and carrying firewood.

To distract himself from watching her healthy figure and admirable vigor, Solomon turned his thoughts to ways he might acquire large sums of hard money.

"There's bounty money scouting for the army," said Solomon out loud.

"You have to know the country, read animal sign, and shoot," said Griffin.

Solomon slapped more paint on the barn.

"Fur trapping in the northwest territories."

"Requires peeling the skin off small, dead animals."

"I could trade for 'em. I've got a gift when it comes to dickering."

"You have to start with something worth trading."

Solomon slapped more paint on the barn side.

"Face it, Solly, when you get right down to it, you're pretty helpless. You've always depended on the industry of others."

"You know, you might help. Point me toward some big old nugget just under the ground. Maybe scrape a little dirt and turn up a diamond as big as my fist. Or lead me to buried pirate treasure. I'd have my fortune and you'd have your doo-hickey. Make everybody happy."

"Except Edwin," said Griffin.

"Who cares if Edwin's happy?"

"Edwin? Edwin's saintly old mother?"

"I'll bet Missus Greene's as tired of him as I am, if you asked her."

"You're missing the treasure right here."

Solomon dipped his brush and snuck another look at Mrs. Jugenheimer paddling clothes in the kettle.

"Marry a landed farm-widow. Make a go of it here. Give me that thing. You surely won't need it with that barnyard Brunhilde watching over you."

Solomon slapped at the barn side with the brush, paint spattering.

"Don't you have anything better to do than pester me?"

Griffin didn't answer, intent on blowing a note on the blade of grass between his thumbs.

As far as Solomon could tell, being an angel seemed a sedentary sort of life. Not much of consequence going on in it. Sitting around watching is about all Griffin seemed good for.

Solomon kept brushing the thin concoction of red color onto the boards, which, to his mind, didn't need painting.

"Way I see it," said Solomon, dipping and daubing paint, studying the results, "being a human being beats whatever it is you are. I read the Bible. And I don't recall anywhere anyone in heaven doing any real work. The kinda work that needs doing down here."

Solomon dipped and daubed, stroked, and studied.

"Yep. People gotta know a whole lot more'n a fella in heaven to get along. If you ask me."

Dipping and daubing, stroking, and studying.

"Like painting. You ever paint in heaven? Or wherever it is you live?"

"Never needs it."

"Then when you get right down to it, who's the more helpless? The one who needs things done for him? Or the one who does for himself? I can rig a sail. Can you?"

"If you can, I'm sure I could."

"Prove it."

"Next time we're at sea."

"I can cut ice from a frozen river, neat and square, six by two in under five minutes. Can you?"

"Not much call for ice where I'm from. But if you can, I could."

"Prove it."

"Next time hell freezes over. Which happens a lot more often than you might imagine."

"What is it you can do, really? You're handy with lightning bolts, I'll grant you that."

"That wasn't me, Solly."

"They sure seemed to find me out and you standing right there next to me."

"I'm made of different stuff, Solly."

"Calling me helpless," said Solomon, more into the bucket as he dipped his brush, "It's not me that's helpless. Human beings have it all over your kind. I can paint a barn. Can you?"

Griffin looked up at the barn and along its broad side. Solomon held out the brush.

"Solly. I may have been created out of nothing in the black of night, but I wasn't created out of nothing in the black of last night." Griffin pointed to a bare patch between the streaks. "You missed a spot, Mister I-Can-Paint-A-Barn-How-About-You."

Scowling hard, Solomon whipped the paint-filled brush up and down, slapping and spraying, slapping and spraying, paint droplets going everywhere.

Solomon's angry effort continued as the sun climbed higher. He took off his vest and shirt, draping them over a rain barrel out of the flying paint.

Hard-muscled in spite of his aversion to physical labor, Solomon was not a bad looking young man in face or physique, lightly browned by his short time in the sun-cooked river life.

As Solomon moved around the barn, Mrs. Jugenheimer seemed to find tasks that let her keep an eye on the bare-chested young man.

Chapter Ten

COMING ON DUSK, THE FIREFLIES STARTED to blink and roam the grasses around the farmyard.

Solomon dropped the brush into the empty bucket, the last few boards finally painted. The grass was dappled with red paint along the length of the barn's wall. Solomon had splashed himself from head to foot with paint as he grew increasingly careless trying to do more work with less effort. He was a red-splotched mess.

His arms ached, his back stiff and sore. He was dog tired, bone tired, dead tired, and every other kind of tired in between. From the looks of the place managed under Mrs. Jugenheimer's stern and never-ceasing scowl, it was a good bet there was no jug handy to ease the aches.

He backed up to check his work, colliding back-to-front with Mrs. Jugenheimer, who was planted right behind him, checking the work as well.

"Not half bad. But," she said, "not half good, either."

She looked him up and down with a scowl. "Come. You need a good scrubbing." She headed for the house. "You eat. You sleep in the barn. More for you to do tomorrow." She was already up the two steps to the porch and into the house, not waiting for his answer.

"I'm done with all this." Solomon grabbed up his shirt and vest.

"Solly, that's as close to a proposal of marriage you're ever likely to get from a woman."

"I'll have me the bath. I'll have me the grub. But I won't be worked to death by some farm fatale." Solomon headed for the house, scratching at the swatches of dried paint covering his skin.

Inside the house, a quilt had been draped over a length of rope tied off between two nails driven into the ceiling planks. The quilt divided the kitchen area from the front part of the house. Up against the hanging quilt was a washtub filled with steamy water. On a stool next to the washtub was a crude bar of cut soap and a towel.

Solomon kicked off his shoes, peeled down his stockings, unbuckled and unbuttoned his britches, shoving them down around his ankles, tugging and hopping trying to get loose of the wadded-up fabric.

The quilt was swept aside, and Mrs. Jugenheimer stood in the gap, arm raised, holding back the quilt, wearing nothing, not a single stitch of clothing. She was majestic, nude, bosomy, her hair unpinned and flowing down her back. Quite becoming in a sudden, startling, too-quick-to-let-morality-get-the-better-of-you kind of way.

Solomon stood there, thumbs still twisted in his britches, staring, his balance starting to give way.

"Don't dawdle. Der's two of us to bathe before the water gets cold." Mrs. Jugenheimer dropped the quilt and stepped into the bath water. She bent over, dunking the washcloth in the water around her calves.

"You do my back und I do yours. She turned her back to him, lifted a surprising great quantity of auburn hair and displaying an amazing backside. She turned her head and smiled at him. A real smile.

"I love the Germans," said Griffin. "They're just so danged efficient."

The britches leg came loose, which Solomon wasn't expecting, and he sat down hard, still watching Mrs. Jugenheimer.

Her eyes and mouth opened up in shock, and for a brief second Solomon thought she was worried that he'd damaged himself.

"Louisa!" shouted a brand new, male-ish voice from behind Solomon, which caused Mrs. Jugenheimer to whip the towel from the stool and cover what little it could cover.

"Again you paint der barn?"

Solomon popped to his feet and spun around to see a middling tall man, dressed in a white shirt, black suit, and flat straw hat. His jaw sported a trim white beard pointed up, angry.

"Early to home, you are," said Mrs. Jugenheimer.

"Jesper threw a shoe. I had to walk him back the whole long way." Pointy-beard man peeled off his coat and hat.

"You must be Mister Jugenheimer." Solomon tried to keep a smile in his voice as he struggled back into his britches.

"Ja, ja."

Solomon looked back at Mrs. Jugenheimer, who had her arms crossed, holding the towel up, looking more like an offended ship's cook than a maiden of compromised modesty.

"You said he was dead, God rest his soul." Solomon kept the smile in his eyes and the sweet reason in his voice.

Mr. Jugenheimer placed his hat and coat on the pegs by the door with methodical deliberation.

"I said he was dead *tired*, Gott rest his soul." Mrs. Jugenheimer scowled at Solomon, as if to share in her husband's ire at this ruffian breaking in on a decent woman at her toilette. "Und look how my prayers were answered. Fresh as a daisy and all back home." She smiled at Mr. Jugenheimer, clapping her hands together then making a hasty grab for the towel as its slipped from her bosom.

"Tired? Dead tired? I didn't hear 'tired' " Solomon looked at Griffin who was sitting in a chair and watching the three of them. "Did you hear 'tired?' "

"Who can tell with that accent of hers."

"You wicked, wicked woman. Luring another poor young man, to make him look on your nakedness. A fella dat never do us no harm. Prob'ly comes from a goot home." Mr. Jugenheimer rolled up his sleeves. For a simple farmer, he had really big forearms. "Well, Louisa, I told you what I do."

Mrs. Jugenheimer ducked her head ever so slightly, resigned. "Ja, ja, you must do what you must."

With a shake of his head and a tsk-tsking smack of his tongue and teeth, he took up the long-barreled shotgun and aimed at Solomon.

"Whoa!" Solomon held out his hands to ward off the impending hail of buck shot. "What're you shooting me for? I just painted your entire barn!"

"Always the same, ja? Paint the barn. Shhcrub the back. Dibble the Frau. Just like the last one." Mr. Jugenheimer raised the gun to his shoulder.

"It's a weakness," said Mrs. Jugenheimer, sheepish and small.

"Why not shoot her?"

"Because the weakness for young men she can't control?" Mr. Jugenheimer lowered the weapon.

"Well—when you put it like that—yes."

"You look like such a smart boy. Who'd feed my chickens, churn my butter, cook my dinner?" He raised the weapon and sighted once more. "Nein, it's better this way. Sorry."

"How about you don't shoot either of us."

"How would she know I'm serious this time?"

"I think we can both agree, you're serious." Solomon looked back at Mrs. Jugenheimer. "We're agreed, right? That he's serious?"

"Mein Gunter is a man of his word. When he says he'll do a thing, he'll do it, you betcha."

"Time to run," Griffin stood at the raised window sash and gestured out the opening to the dark door yard.

Solomon looked at Griffin and then at Mr. Jugenheimer.

"Go ahead," said Solomon, his jaw set.

"I knew you was a smart lad."

"But you're going to be a mite surprised after you pull that trigger." Solomon folded his arms across his breast.

Griffin cleared his throat. "You realize the likely reaction if you survive a gunshot blast in front of two God-fearing, if completely backslidden, Christian witnesses?"

Solomon blinked, playing out the likely scenarios in his head.

"Again?"

"Again." Griffin gestured with a sweeping hand to the open window.

Solomon's head flopped, his chin to his chest.

"T'ank you for painting mein barn," Mr. Jugenheimer squinted to aim.

Solomon turned and dived out the window, the blast of birdshot flying through the spot where Solomon had been, peppering the wall opposite.

Flopping on the dirt of the door yard, Solomon bounded to his feet, remembering he'd left his clothes on the floor by the wash tub. He turned back toward the house.

Griffin held up Solomon's clothes and shoes. "Here."

"I'd like to go back to leaving by the front door, if you don't mind."

Another shotgun blast lit up the window and pellets flew by Solomon as he turned and ran for the dark field beyond.

A third shot rang out, but Solomon was over the rail fence and into the grass, disappearing across the field into the moonless night.

Solomon reached the far side of the field, vaulting the fence, landing on the soft ground alongside the road. He clutched the top rail, breathing hard.

Griffin appeared, dropping Solomon's knapsack and bedroll at his feet.

"The least you could've done was warn me her husband was still alive."

"How am I supposed to know?"

"Or warn me he's coming down the road or something."

"You see how dark it is out here? I'm not omniscient."

"I can't fathom they'd let an angel of the Almighty roam around so entirely helpless."

Griffin shrugged.

"Let me ask you something."

"Sure."

"Are you omni at anything? Anything useful?"

Solomon didn't wait for an answer, hoisted his gear and started walking.

"That's just the buckshot talking." Griffin jogged to catch up.

Chapter Eleven

Hudson River Valley – 1830s

SOLOMON SPENT A COLD, RESTLESS NIGHT balled up under his blanket, huddled against the chill as he slept between the exposed roots of a large cottonwood tree.

He woke as the fingers of mist reached across the meadow beyond, grayed up by the light of day just coming over the horizon.

Like it or not, he'd have to clean himself up. The only water available was the frigid creek nearby. But he couldn't go on painted up like a red Indian. Stripped down and taking a quick deep breath, Solomon flopped into the clear running water.

"Da-a-a-amn!" Solomon leaped up flinging himself about, like a carp fighting at the end of a fisherman's line.

He scrubbed at the dried paint, rubbing it into a faded rosy tint, working as quickly as he could bear.

When he'd done all the bathing he could stand, he danced up out of the creek, onto the matted grass and weeds growing along the bank.

He toweled himself off with his shirt and then hop-stepped into a clean pair of duck trousers, the only other britches he owned. He sat to tug on his stockings and shoes.

Done dressing, Solomon cinched up his blanket and slung it over one shoulder then shrugged into the straps of his knapsack. He set out walking, not bothering to take bearings, but aimed toward the sun, now a sliver on the horizon.

Griffin came along side Solomon.

"People always say cleanliness is next to godliness, but there's no bathing in the Hereafter. Did you know that? I'll bet you didn't. Little known fact." Griffin skipped a bit to get in stride with Solomon. "No soap in your eyes, no water to heat."

Solomon stayed fixed on the horizon and the growing dish of sunlight sparkling now through the trees.

"Did you know that already? About no bathing in the Hereafter? Maybe you did. You said you read the Good Book a lot, am I right?"

Solomon still said nothing.

"But—I'll bet you don't know *why* there's no bathing in the Hereafter. Right? Right?"

Solomon shifted the load on his shoulders and kept walking.

"Aw, come on, Solly. You don't think you can get to me with the old silent treatment do you? I can outlast you. I can go centuries without talking."

Solomon gave him nothing.

"Aren't you the least bit curious what they do about sex if there's no marriage in heaven?"

Griffin gave Solomon a sidelong glance.

Nothing from Solomon.

"Solly! You can't blame me for Mr. Jugenheimer showing up like that."

Solomon stopped, turned and studied Griffin.

"I got me a question."

"Well, you know there's lots of things I can't talk about—"

"Are there horses in heaven?"

"Yes. Why?"

"Least you could've done was brought one with you."

Solomon turned and kept walking. Griffin hurried to catch up with him again.

"What? You think I can just go borrow one from the four horsemen of the Apocalypse? It's not like they rent them out when they're not using them." Griffin twisted his face up in thought. "Although, I wonder what they'd charge? Probably a lot. I mean it's not like they ride your typical hay burners."

"So if you can't provide me a horse, how about you figure out what I can do for some ready money."

"You're a sea-faring man, why not take up whaling. A good ship making a decent haul pays off handsomely. Or so I've heard."

"It's hard, it's dangerous, and takes as long as two years to do it. I don't have the time."

"Wait. You still think there's time for you to get it right with Lavinia? Okay, since we're on the subject of horses, it seems to me you're trying to close the barn door after the horse has been put out to pasture. Or, however that saying goes."

"Being married doesn't mean she's out to pasture."

"I meant the horse."

"And I'll thank you not to call my Lavinia a horse."

"You're deliberately missing the point."

"I'm not missing a single thing. Lavinia's got everyone fooled. Now it's up to me."

"To do what?"

"Rescue her from Edwin."

"She did not look like she wanted to be rescued."

"You weren't there."

"In point of fact, I was. The whole time"

"Then you'd've seen she was playacting. To get free of her daddy's thumb."

"I know a lot more than you think. I know Lavinia isn't the kind to fake a marriage, a honeymoon, a consummation—to put it delicately—and a childbirth or two—"

"You're gonna turn my stomach."

"—just to make you into a man of purpose. No one's that saintly. Or conniving."

"Lavinia is."

"Saintly? Or conniving?"

"It's plain you don't know her at all."

"Solly, can you even remember the first time you kissed Lavinia?"

Solomon stopped walking. "Of course I can."

"You never did. She never let you."

Solomon laughed and waggled his finger in Griffin's face. "That spring picnic at the church! We all snuck upstairs at the church and played Postman Knocks. I kissed her then."

"No, you did not."

"I should know who I kissed."

"Would you like me to remind you who it was you *did* kiss?"

After that first meeting on the road between Kantlingher House and the Second Evangelical Lutheran Free Church, Solomon became a regular fixture at every social to-do held at the church, if it meant getting close to Lavinia.

He wasn't the only smitten swain with the same idea. There were others, but the most obvious, and most odious to Solomon, was Edwin Greene.

The way Lavinia kept playing up to Edwin convinced Solomon she was angling to make him jealous.

A late April day, at a hymn sing and picnic sponsored by the church, the young people gave their chaperones the slip and took refuge up in the church's Society Room, out of the warm spring air, and away from the music. They were looking for something more thrilling and intimate than blind man's buff, leap-frog, or three-legged races.

Evading the watchdogs, they gathered in the half-light of the Society Room to play Postman Knocks. Solomon, having little experience among genteel folks, didn't know the game. He hung back as he joined the other young men on one side of the room while the young ladies gathered on the other. Two chairs were placed facing each other in the center of the room.

Huddled up for secrecy, each side chose a player, blindfolding both and leading them to the two chairs. The onlookers giggled and hissed at each other for silence.

It was shaping up to be a tame afternoon. Arm wrestling or mumbly-peg would've shown him off to better advantage among the boys here.

Stepping forward, Lavinia took for herself the role of referee. "Remember, no touching, no peeking." The two players nodded.

"Well, let's get to it," said Lavinia, and the spectators called out, "Postman knocks!"

Amid catcalls from both sides of the room, the blindfolded couple leaned into each other until their lips met, to the glee of everyone.

"Don't just sit there!" cried Lavinia, catching herself before she blurted out the name. "Who delivered the letter?"

The girl called out "James!" and from the general groaning, Solomon figured she guessed wrong. Their blindfolds were whipped off them and the onlookers laughed at the blushing couple. "Don't hold up the mail, Vernon," Lavinia scolded. "Your letter goes to someone else."

Energized by the scolding, Vernon charged across the room. The young ladies scattered, leaving a pale, thin girl alone in his path. But she waved him off.

"The letter goes to James now. I'll see he gets it." She marched to the other side of the room, taking James by the shoulders and, stooping slightly to meet him face to face, kissed him long and hard.

When they finally broke, someone called out, "That was a mighty long letter!" which set the onlookers cackling.

Solomon considered himself a quick study when it came to games of chance. This seemed no different.

The rules were simple enough as far as he could tell. They blindfold a couple, sit them down in front of each other, and they have to kiss. If the girl guesses who it was kissed her, the boy had to kiss her again. If she refused the second kiss, the boy had to choose another girl for his kiss. If that girl refused, then he was out, but the second girl had to kiss someone else of her own choosing.

If, however, the blindfolded girl guessed wrong, then the boy chose another for the second kiss. The same penalty applied if the second girl refused his kiss.

Relationships could be made or broken on the etiquette of such a game.

Solomon was beginning to see some merit after all, and the way he gamed it out there was an excellent chance he would kiss Lavinia, maybe twice, right here in front of everyone. Including Edwin Greene.

He watched and cheered along with the others as players were chosen, blindfolded, and kissed. He cheered their success or catcalled their failure, keeping an eye out for the moment the young ladies might choose Lavinia.

Then, as it seemed the girls had their designs on hauling Lavinia into their secret circle, Solomon edged forward, making great noises of reluctance, finessing the boys to choose him next for the blindfold.

While they tied on the blindfold, Solomon ran through the likely outcomes. If they chose Lavinia next, she'd surely guess it was him, and he'd get a second kiss. If she guessed wrong, even if she was pretending not to know him, his choice would be to kiss her again. It wasn't exactly in the rules, but it was his choice. If they chose one of the other girls, it was a pretty good bet they wouldn't remember his name, not being a townsman, and his choice for the next kiss would again be Lavinia. Even if the other girl did guess, she wouldn't want a second kiss from a stranger, which again would leave him free to choose Lavinia. Solomon wished there was money riding on this.

Now blindfolded, he let them guide him to the chair and seated himself. Almost before the spectators called out "Postman knocks," Solomon leaned far forward, almost immediately colliding with the lips of the young lady opposite.

The sweet fragrance of the face so near to his provoked so strong a memory and the soft touch of the lips on his so electrified him that he shivered. He couldn't believe his luck, that he might truly be kissing Lavinia. All he needed now was for her to call out his name and he would kiss her again, for real, his eyes open to take in the rose bloom of her face against his.

"Jehosaphat!" shouted Abigail.

Solomon whipped off his blindfold to find Abigail sitting opposite him. She was leaning back, drawing herself as far away as the chair back allowed. The onlookers howled.

He'd completely forgotten she might be among the young ladies. It hadn't occurred to him she would play.

"No fair! A clear foul! It has to be someone in the room!" the onlookers sang out.

Solomon hesitated, still thinking of that soft sweet mouth, delicate fragrance and the slight breathlessness he still felt. He would have guessed that kissing Abigail would be no different from kissing a crab's barnacled backside, cold and scratchy. That is, if he'd bothered to think about her kisses at all.

"Choose! Choose!" they chanted as he broke from his spell, looking around for Lavinia. Spotting her, he made straight for her, not looking back at Abigail.

Edwin, despite being the pudge that he was, still stepped in front of Solomon, barring his way.

"Don't hold up the mail!" the others shouted. "Road agents!" all laughing at the entertainment to see jealousy rear its ugly green head. Solomon tensed to shove Edwin aside when Lavinia pushed between them.

"I'll deliver the letter myself," she said.

Edwin, giving Solomon a smirk, turned to accept delivery from Lavinia.

But Lavinia sailed by Edwin and grabbed Abigail, giving her a sisterly kiss on the lips to everyone's delight, especially any of the swains who loathed to see Solomon or Edwin collect a kiss from Lavinia.

"You kissed Abigail. Not Lavinia."

Solomon reassembled this shattered recollection, then said, "She stole a kiss meant for Lavinia."

"Lavinia chose to kiss Abigail, who, I might add, is a far better sport than you."

Abigail allowed them to choose her to wear the blindfold next, accepting with a good grace and trusting the ordeal to be over quickly. She had gone along with Lavinia and the other young people to the Society Room more to watch out for Lavinia than join the frivolity. If she'd expressed any misgivings they would have consigned her to the chaperones.

Abigail knew instantly who was on the other side of that kiss, and just as instantly regretted being there. She knew if she guessed it was

Solomon he'd have to kiss her again and likely make a great show of displeasure to impress Lavinia. She couldn't bear that.

Nor could she bear seeing him rush to kiss Lavinia and leave her sitting there, rejected, if she deliberately guessed wrong.

She would not dignify the game any further by naming anyone else in the room, giving rise to romantic speculations. So she pulled Jehosaphat's name from the Bible and let them to chew on that.

Solomon glared at Griffin. "You said you weren't omniscient."

"I don't need to be."

"Well." Solomon thought a long moment. "There were other times."

"Like when?"

Solomon looked back toward the horizon, not yet setting out. He shrugged his shoulders trying to settle the knapsack.

"Don't you have better things to do than spy on us?"

Griffin considered this, then said, "Not at the moment."

With a snort, Solomon headed down the road.

Chapter Twelve

SOLOMON WALKED ALL DAY, having only eaten a few cattail roots and some apples he'd picked from a tree along the road.

Solomon reckoned he was not too far from Glasco, south of Saugerties, where he might work his passage on a brick barge back to New York. At least he'd have a better chance there of making his fortune.

The sun had set and the chill was returning. Solomon stopped to unroll his blanket and wrap it around himself for extra warmth as he walked.

The noise of a rumbustious crowd reached his ears. Through the stand of trees along the road, he spotted a large stable and outbuildings all lit up.

He came up on Griffin who held out a handful of plants.

"Can you eat any of these," asked Griffin as Solomon trotted by him. Griffin looked at the dirt-caked vegetation. "Right. Why would anyone want to." Griffin dropped the bundle and followed after Solomon.

Reaching the front of the largest building, Solomon slowed. The place was crowded with men all shouting, smoking, and swigging. Solomon's kind of place.

Two men pushed through the crowd bunched around the door. Between them they lugged a third man, his face wrecked and bloody.

They dumped their burden in a watering trough, splashing two other men slumped beside it, one holding his swollen eye, and the other nursing his broken nose.

Solomon squeezed his way into the lighted interior.

Inside, a ring of spectators perched on stall railings, ladders, feed sacks, and barrels, all watching a giant of a man in the center of the impromptu ring.

This was, to Solomon's eye, the biggest pugilist he'd ever seen. A prize fighter's prize fighter. Stripped to the waist, wearing knee britches, stockings, and soft leather boots, he was speckled with blood, none of it his own, Solomon was certain.

"Ten dollars American to any man who can go one round with Big Arne Blaine," shouted a thin, natty gent in tight coat and britches. "The best bare knuckle boxer out of Brooklyn's fourth ward!" He waved his bowler hat at the crowd. "Twenty-five dollars if you can go three rounds."

"What do you get if you knock him out?" shouted Solomon.

"I'll give you a unicorn to ride home on!"

"Then go ahead and saddle it up for me." The men around him hooted and howled with laughter.

"Tell you what, Shorty," said the natty gent, "I'll give you two dollars just to take one punch from Big Arne. Wha'd'ya say?"

That set the crowd roaring.

Griffin appeared at Solomon's elbow.

"Solly, this is not a good idea."

"I need me some ready money."

"This is extremely dangerous."

"Not for me."

"I mean dangerous if they find out there's more to you than meets the eye."

"I'll act hurt. Long as I keep my feet, I collect the prize money."

"So what's it gonna be, Rumplestiltskin?" the natty gent called out.

"Solly!"

Solomon stepped to the center, stripping off his shirt, then rotated his shoulders, loosening up. The crowd seemed tickled at the little squirt's presumption.

Big Arne blasted out laughing.

With elbows out, Solomon twisted from side to side.

Big Arne strode up to Solomon, who found himself staring at the pugilist's rock-ribbed, hard-muscled thorax.

Lowering his head to Solomon's ear, the pugilist rasped, "I'll take it easy on you. Give you a shiner to impress your girl. You fancy it on your right eye or your left eye?"

Solomon stepped back and took his stance, flexing at the knees, his fists curled up and ready. Big Arne socked him with a quick left that landed solid, snapping Solomon's head back. Solomon gave a shake to throw off the sting, recovering quickly, and resumed his stance.

The pugilist flexed his hand, eyeing Solomon.

"Hey, Big Arne! You hurt yourself?" one of the onlookers shouted.

Big Arne circled back to the natty gent.

"Something ain't right," the pugilist whispered to the natty gent.

The natty gent peeled off two dollars and waved them toward Solomon.

"Fair's fair. I said two dollars if you took the punch, and by gum you did."

The crowd was laughing and pointing now. But not at Solomon. At Big Arne.

Solomon held up his hand and shouted to the crowd, "Fifty dollars says I can go one round and I walk out of this ring without a mark on me. Fifty dollars!"

"Solly, you don't have a dime to your name," said Griffin.

"I will in a minute."

"Gambling's a sin," said Griffin. "Cheating's worse. By my count, you're breaking the seventh and eighth commandments. Not to mention a piece of the tenth."

The crowd shouted and cursed a mixture of delight and bloodthirstiness.

"All right, Samson," the natty gent said to Solomon. "One round." The natty gent turned to Big Arne and hissed, "Take his head off."

The natty gent went to the center of the enclosure and dragged his toe in the dirt marking the scratch.

Both Solomon and Big Arne stepped up and toed the mark, took up their stances, fists at the ready.

With lightning quickness Big Arne landed another solid blow, a right.

Solomon shook his head, dazed, but not incapacitated.

Again, Big Arne stepped back shaking his hand, shifting his shoulders.

"Sump'n's not right, I'm telling you," he said to the natty gent.

"Get back in there!"

Big Arne took a much more fearsome stance, hunched, ready to uncoil on Solomon.

"I don't wanna hurt you, squirt," Big Arne hissed at Solomon.

Solomon popped Big Arne twice, to no effect, drawing more laughs and jeers from the crowd.

"I'm warning you," said Big Arne. "I'll give you one more chance. Fall down and take the two dollars."

Solomon popped the pugilist with another two lefts and followed up with a right.

Big Arne reared back and let fly with a haymaker that was known to stun cattle. Solomon reeled sideways, his arms windmilling, fighting to keep his balance. The crowd rattled the walls with its cheers.

Big Arne retreated to his corner.

"It's his face. It feels funny. Like it ain't skin or bone."

"Then hit him in the guts, make him puke. Finish him off." Again, the natty gent shoved Big Arne back toward Solomon.

Again, Big Arne swung, delivering a left-right combination to Solomon's teeth, driving him back through a knot of onlookers and against the rails. Solomon shook his head again to clear it and bounced back to the center of the field.

"The body," shouted the natty gent, "I said the body!"

"He's too short," Big Arne shouted back.

Bounding inside Big Arne's reach, Solomon went for the belly, which might as well have been a rock wall.

Big Arne planted a hand on Solomon's forehead, keeping him just out of reach as Solomon stretched his swing to connect with something worth hitting.

Then the pugilist gave Solomon a trademark Big Arne Blaine upper cut that was known to lift better men off the floor and out of their shoes.

Solomon flew backward into the arms of men crowding the edge of the field. It rattled him. He felt around his mouth and nose for any blood that would lose him the bet. Clean. No one seemed to think it strange he was still unbloodied.

Big Arne was getting tired. He didn't carry his arms as high and wasn't protecting his face. Solomon kept hitting.

Breathing heavily, Big Arne backed up to his corner.

"Ain't natural," said Big Arne. "Sump'n—ain't natural."

"You finish him off, or you're finished."

Big Arne gathered himself and stalked back to the center of the ring. He let fly at Solomon with whirl-winding fists, swinging, landing, missing, drooping, getting more and more tired. All the while Solomon kept coming back, bouncing and bobbing and dancing until he saw an opening. With a swing that started low down between his knees, Solomon swung upward, catching Big Arne a resounding crack under the chin that sent him staggering through the crowd, back into the wall of the stable. His head slammed against the boards with a mighty thud that shuddered the walls and creaked the joists.

With a shake to clear the sweat and the blood from his vision, Big Arne fixed his ice cold eyes of fury on Solomon—until those ice cold eyes rolled up in his head and the pugilist fell forward, flat on his face.

The crowd burst into cheers and huzzahs and tossed caps, a thrill to see an unfair fight, lots of money changing hands, impossible odds, and sheer, cussed good fun. Men were grabbing at Solomon's hand to shake it. He danced, his arms in the air, scanning for Griffin's face into which he planned to gloat mercilessly.

Griffin's face appeared among the well-wishers. He studied Solomon's unmarked face.

"Oh, you're going to feel those," said Griffin.

"Nah," said Solomon, pressing spots on his face. "Stung for a little bit, but I don't feel anything now."

"You will. I told you. When Time takes it all back, in that instant, you'll feel everything."

One of the men, portly and florid, wearing a slouch hat and great coat, grabbed Solomon by the hand, shaking it hard.

"I'm mighty glad I got to see Solomon Durnley beat Big Arne Blaine in the gol-darnedest piece of pugilism I've had the pleasure to witness," said the portly man, shouting to be heard.

"I tried to go easy on him," said Solomon, "but the fella didn't know when he was beat."

"Folks sure got their money's worth," said the portly man, then folded back the lapel of his coat revealing his sheriff's badge.

The crowd evaporated, leaving a haze of hay dust clouding the air.

Solomon turned to flee, but the sheriff had him by the arm. With his other hand, the sheriff flapped open a flyer.

"Short, wiry, dark hair, ruddy skinned and answers to the name of Solomon Durnley. Wanted in connection with the disappearance of Captain Benedict Curtwood, Ulster County Militia. Possibly murder. A known gambler and cheat. And I guess we can add prize fighter."

Solomon stomped on the sheriff's instep, yanked his arm free. He grabbed the brim of the sheriff's hat, snugging it down over his eyes.

The sheriff swung wild, but Solomon was already out of reach, running.

Bounding over grain sacks and hay bales, Solomon dashed for the door. Sliding to a stop just outside, he threw a quick glance around before aiming for the dark stand of trees between the horse corrals and the roadway.

The portly sheriff was no match for the speedy Solomon.

Solomon ran on, and after what felt like a mile, slowed to a walk, breathing hard.

Up ahead, in a pool of his own light, Griffin stood holding out Solomon's shirt, knapsack, and bedroll.

"I don't need a butler. I need someone who can throw a punch on my side when I need it."

"Never was much for fisticuffs."

"How am I supposed to make my fortune if I got the law hunting for me now?"

Solomon yanked his shirt on, shoving his arms through the sleeves, angry and wanting something to suffer.

"That's a problem, I suppose," said Griffin.

"I didn't do anything to that Captain. But I can't be sitting in jail while I try to explain."

"A nice long sea voyage might be just the ticket."

Solomon settled his knapsack and bedroll on his shoulders once more.

"Damned odd that sheriff having a handbill on me the same time I show up at an illegal prize fight."

"Yeah, damned odd."

They walked deeper into the dark.

"Why couldn't you have been a horse?" asked Solomon.

Chapter Thirteen

SOLOMON TRAVELED ALONE for nearly three days. Hunger and chill gnawed at him, providing him with an abundance of aggravation and fatigue, but no serious impairment. Certainly an effect of that damnable object.

"Yes, I said damnable," said Solomon to no one in particular. Griffin had absented himself, objecting to all the walking, the scant food, and poor accommodations associated with Solomon's fortune hunting so far.

Solomon finally reached Bridgeport, on the northern side of the Long Island Sound and east of Cold Spring Harbor. But those ships were bound for the South Seas. Not only did it mean years of cruising in the South Pacific, it also meant a dangerous transit around the Horn and the unruly waters at the southern tip of South America. Every seaman knew the stories of sailors thrown off a wrecked vessel and stranded on some small, unreachable divot of land, waiting years to be rescued.

Scuttlebutt among the dockside loungers was that a few of the ships across the Sound at Cold Spring Harbor were aiming to fish the much closer whale grounds off Newfoundland. That was more to Solomon's liking.

Finding a friendly fishing smack that worked along the Long Island coast, Solomon crossed the sound. The boat's fisherman landed Solomon close in so he could wade onto the sandy beach and from there continue on to Cold Spring Harbor.

Passing through the village, he found Griffin studying notices pinned to the clapboard planks of a store front. One handbill, with block text and a simple drawing of a whale, announced that ships of the Cold Spring Whaling company were looking for whalemen, both experienced and green hands, to ship immediately.

With no other likely prospects, Solomon pulled it down and continued toward the docks.

Following his nose, inhaling the fetid stench of the whale ships, Solomon found the wharves of Cold Spring Harbor in the wet, early morning dew with its congestion of vessels tied up along the piers, the air filled with the sound of timber on timber, the rattle of tackle, the creak of line, the hammering of shipfitters, the gentle snap of those few limp sails hanging to dry, and the sloshing water against hulls. All the sounds and smells that reminded Solomon of the hard work of seamanship.

"I thought the sea was more—I don't know—romantic smelling?" said Griffin.

The piers were abustle with the offloading of newly arrived ships, and the provisioning of ships preparing to depart.

Tradesmen jostled among sailors who pulled hand trucks, maneuvered wagons of cargo, loaded hardware, studied manifests, or greeted sweethearts and wives.

Solomon stopped under the peak of a ship that looked to be two hundred tons. With its tubby hull, sails rigged fore-and aft at the mizzen, and smelling to high heaven, he knew it to be a whaleship.

The vessel carried four long, slender whale boats on davits at the rail and the try-works shed forward for rendering blubber. All about her was quiet, not pestered with the same bustling traffic, suggesting it was most likely undermanned and open to hiring new hands.

Solomon tapped the shoulder of a lean, shaggy-haired sailor pulling on the lead of a goat that refused to set hoof on the ship's gangway.

"What ship is that?"

"The *Mary Hoppe*," said the sailor.

"Where y'bound?"

"Grand Banks to fish for whale if there be any. Walrus if thur ain't."

Solomon turned to Griffin. "It's a year if it's a day," he said. But Griffin seemed more engrossed in the plucky goat twisting at the end of her tether.

"At least it's on this side of the world."

"I don't want to be in the middle of the ocean when I have to give this back."

Griffin turned from studying the goat to studying Solomon.

"You actually plan to keep your end of the bargain?"

"I do. What did you think?"

"A novelty, that's all. Not something I've come to expect from mudfoot short-timers like you."

"Excuse me?"

"Sorry, slip of the tongue. Meant to say 'mortals.' What if you don't have your fortune by then?"

"I hadn't thought that far ahead."

"Then—however long it takes."

Now it was Solomon's turn to study Griffin.

"Mighty generous of you all of a sudden."

"I've taken a liking to you, Solly." Griffin turned back to watch the struggling goat. "You've got spunk. If there's one thing in short supply where I come from it's spunk. Besides, a whaling voyage puts you out of reach of the law. Less chance they discover your special qualities if they can't lock you up."

"Where the profit in it for you?"

"I said I took a liking to you, didn't I?" Griffin clapped Solomon on the shoulder. "So, what say ye, me hearty? A little time on the ocean blue, nostrils filled with the good salt air. New mates. Nothing but water as far as the eye can see?"

Solomon wondered if being insufferable was a trait common among angels that went unreported in the Good Book, or if it was a trait unique to Griffin alone.

"You shipping hands?" Solomon asked of the sailor.

"Talk to Howell, the first mate." The sailor jabbed a thumb toward the head of the gangway.

At the top of the gangway stood a muscled man of medium height, sunburnt coloring and wispy hair, marking in a ledger.

Solomon called out, "Ahoy, the ship."

"Ahoy, yourself," he said without looking up.

Solomon strode up the gangway and stepped onto the deck.

"What's your business?" the mate asked, still not looking up.

"I wish to ship for whale," said Solomon.

He finally looked up at Solomon. "We're bound for the Grand Banks. Off Newfoundland. No warm breezes, coconuts, nor island girls to bid you welcome, if that's your inclination."

"A shorter voyage suits me."

"Oh, it does? That'll be a comfort to the captain. You ever fished for whale a'fore?"

"No."

"You ever sailed anything more'n a paper boat around your mamma's wash tub?"

"My last ship was the *Ardith* of sixty tons. A river sloop. I was rated able."

"A river sloop?" Howell laughed. "What sort of sailing have you done out of sight of land, lad, where you can't wade ashore if your ship sinks?"

"I'm seaman enough for you."

"I don't need another one-buttock sailor. I need a man who can throw the harpoon. I've got green farm boys wanting adventure, drunken old men hiding from termagant wives, and a one-eyed Negro that can smell whales before any white man born can see them, but can't hit one standing on its back. A harpooneer with a steady hand and a sure eye is what I need."

Howell lifted a lance off the workbench where the smith had been sharpening the iron. He held it out to Solomon.

Taking the heavy lance, Solomon hefted it to find the balance point.

Griffin appeared at Solomon's elbow.

"Throw it," said Griffin.

"I've never thrown anything this heavy," said Solomon under his breath.

"I thought as much." Howell reached for the lance. "Go back to the river. Leave whaling to men what's got the mind and muscle for it."

Solomon flinched, holding tight to the lance.

"You may have better luck than you think," Griffin sing-songed.

Solomon raised the lance and threw the iron across the deck, over the rack with the spare whale boat, driving it deep into the middle of the mizzen mast behind it.

"Thirty feet if it's an inch and dead center of the pole," said Howell. He turned back to Solomon. "You mean to hit that?"

"I did."

"Not bad for a scrawny fella. You'll sign on as boatsteerer for a short lay of the shares."

"What's that in Yankee dollars?"

"One-seventieth of whatever the oil fetches when we return. Take it or leave it. You won't do better if the captain made you second mate. I'll put your name in the book and get the articles for you to sign."

Howell ducked down the companionway.

Griffin popped back into view, his eyes wide and full of innocence.

Solomon pointed at the lance still quivering where it stuck in the mizzen. "Don't that count as interfering with free will?"

"Extraordinary feats of skill or strength don't actually fall under the heading of free will. And, if I may ask, when did you get particular?"

Solomon fit himself in with his shipmates as they made the *Mary Hoppe* ready to sail, joining the work with a will, and gamboling with the men at the end of watch.

Once at sea, Solomon showed no fear in the rigging, moving with ease on the footropes even on the highest spars, in rough seas or calm, scrambling about in the shrouds as if it were no more than a walk down a church aisle.

When it was time to relax and make music, Solomon played the squeeze box with a fine hand, enough to keep the tune lively, as they took turns jigging and horn-piping to Mad Moll, or Follow the Peacock, or Kiss in the Kitchen. He had a tolerable voice, and carried a tune with the best of them, singing along with their songs of whiskey, women, and whales. However, he talked little of himself or his home, or engaged in the usual speculation about what he intended to do with his share from the voyage.

Griffin seemed to have nothing better to do than skylark about the ship, chittering away as Solomon worked. Maybe it was Griffin's way of fending off boredom. Not much for an angel to do aboard ship. But even that was too thin a reason. How was it even possible for an angel to be bored, having the will and the way to gad about the earth without benefit of conveyance? That seemed both daft and unnatural to Solomon.

Sometimes Griffin would break out with some peculiar or outrageous observation or disparagement, provoking Solomon into a tirade of a reply. Which lasted until he caught sight of his shipmates all stopped, watching him.

In all that, Griffin never offered anything useful about the muddy crossroads of mortality and immortality where Solomon found himself. Despite the aggravation, Griffin was easier company, since he understood Solomon better than could his shipmates.

Like the night he stood leaning on the rail, watching the bow wave rush by, as men of his own watch stood nearby, smoking and talking low.

Griffin stood on the other side of Solomon, staring out.

"On a dark and lonely night like tonight, floating on top of all this mystery, I can see where you sailors get your crackpot notions about the secrets of the oceans. King Neptune. Davy Jones' Locker. Krakens. Mermaids."

Such things, to Solomon's own way of thinking, were nothing but the feverish imagination of a sailor too long at sea. With the exception of mermaids.

"You think mermaids'd come this far north?" Solomon gazed into the waters over side. "Or do they keep to warmer waters, lacking proper jackets for their nakedness?"

The sailors at the rail got quiet, listening in on Solomon.

"No such thing as mermaids," said Griffin.

"Not this far north?"

"Not this far anywhere. Mermaids don't exist."

"Of course there's mermaids. I sailed with two different fellas who swear they've seen them up close."

"Solly, there are no mermaids."

"There could be cold water mermaids. Like there's Eskimos in the arctic and Hottentots on the equator?"

"Solly. No mermaids."

"How would you know? You said you're not omniscient."

"I'm not, but I know there's no such thing as mermaids."

"We net a mermaid, that'd fix my fortune for sure. To hell with this whaling business."

"There are a great many strange and wonderful things all over creation. Some of them not yet seen by mortal man, but mermaids or unicorns or fire breathing dragons are not among them."

"Ah, ha! There is so unicorns. Says so in the Bible. 'Save me from the lion's mouth: for thou hast heard me from the horns of the unicorns.' If there's unicorns, there could be mermaids. Fire breathing dragons for that matter. Thinking you're so smart." Solomon turned to look at the sea once more, imagining what a mermaid might fetch by the pound.

When Solomon turned from the rail, the eavesdroppers scattered.

Once they reached the whale grounds they reefed sails and let the ship drift while the lookouts scanned the distances searching for the aerial mist of a spouting whale, or the scavenger birds that circled, indicating a whale below the surface.

In the bow, Hieronymus, the one-eyed Negro of the fabled nasal passages, sat astride the bowsprit. With his one good eye rolled to the heavens, he aimed his legendary nostrils this way and that to catch a scent.

But the whales weren't there.

"Soon," said Hiram Dunn, the captain, a man grown up on the sea pursuing whales. "Soon."

So here they would remain, wallowing in the swells, waiting.

As much as Solomon disliked the tedious labor of keeping ship, he discovered being idle was worse.

When they first left port, and the Block Island North Light finally disappeared below the horizon behind them, the distance between himself and Lavinia was magnified, both in miles and in circumstance.

Solomon found a thin comfort in the most unlikely place—hard work. It dulled and dissipated his imagination, holding back the frustrating fantasies of Lavinia in someone else's arms.

When called upon to holy-stone the deck, he scrubbed hardest, erasing Edwin from the face of the earth with each stroke of the pumice stone.

When called upon to scrub out the try-pots with ash, he reached into the deep bowl of the pot, imagining his hands in Edwin's chest cavity scraping it clean down to the white of his rib bones.

When called to mend sails, he pierced Edwin's pasty hide with the needle over and over, sewing him up, alive, in a shroud suitable for a sea burial.

It was at night, smoking alone by the rail and watching the moon when the sky was clear, that Solomon imagined how Edwin and Lavinia might be sharing the lustrous lunar light between them at that very moment. He no longer saw Edwin as a physically repugnant, unworthy rival. Instead, Solomon saw him as Lavinia might see him—a handsome devil, with flowing locks, a perfect mouth, and gleaming teeth. This Edwin was taller, more muscular, and right now leagues closer to Lavinia than Solomon.

Had it been Lavinia's plan to land Edwin and not Solomon? Had Solomon become a pawn in Lavinia's chess game to force Edwin's hand to marry her?

He thought back on a day picking apples, how clearly she'd shaken off Edwin to share a basket with him. Solomon simply assumed she was showing good sense to be rid of that gadfly. But now, in the serpent's coils of jealousy, Solomon brooded on the motives behind her flirtations. Was he, in the end, the bait to land Edwin all along?

About the fifth day on the fishing grounds the ship suffered a string of mishaps that spooked the hands.

First, a dead eye broke loose and cold-cocked the third mate, who regained consciousness, but not his senses. Bereft of speech and gasping for air, he flopped around the deck, acting like a landed mackerel. The other hands netted him and tied him in his hammock, occasionally throwing water in his face so he would remember to breathe.

Next, the dogs on the anchor windlass gave way and the anchor chain spun off the drum, dropping the anchor to the ocean bottom. The chain paid out so fast it nearly took the legs off the leadsman standing between the shrouds forward. It would have done if not for his presence of mind to leap onto the ratlines, his knees drawn up to his chest. The heavy black anchor chain snaked across the deck, through the hawse-pipe, snapping up at the rail one final time nearly catching him in the buttocks before the last link disappeared into the froth of water.

Not long after that, the rudder pins sheared off from the stern post, and the ship wallowed and bobbed without steerage until the ship's carpenter and two hands working over the side could refit the pins and secure the rudder once more.

It was clear to all hands. The ship had taken on a Jonah, a sea-going jinx.

Solomon was convinced it had to be Griffin, bored and making mischief. But as long as Griffin remained unseen, Solomon had no safe way to lay blame on him.

It did seem odd to Solomon, how his shipmates took to smiling at him, avoiding his company.

Again, Solomon was left to find companionship with Griffin.

Solomon sat cross-legged, mending sail, as Griffin faced into the breeze blowing across the deck.

"I've decided."

"Decided what?" asked Solomon.

"I will never get the smell of this stinking ship out of my nose hairs."

Solomon inhaled. "What smell?" He cherished the moments when Griffin experienced discomfort and discombobulation.

"What say we climb to the foremast top and get a little fresh air?" asked Griffin, "Because it stinks to high heaven down here."

"It's what Hell smells like on a good day."

Ears around Solomon perked up and work stopped.

"Actually, Hell doesn't have all that much of an odor."

"It's a pit of sulfur and roasting humans and all the trash of Man's filthy sojourn on earth," said Solomon. "Of course Hell stinks."

"Have you ever been?"

"No. Have you?"

"I talked to someone who'd been."

"Someone who's been to Hell? For a visit?" asked Solomon. "What's his name?"

"Just somebody. I didn't ask his name."

"You come across a stranger, and give a shout like, 'Greetings, mate! Where y'hail from? I hail from Hell, how about you? I hail from heaven. How's the weather there? Cloudy. How about you? Hot and steamy, but it don't smell half-bad. You should stop in for a visit sometime.' " Solomon bit into his pipe and continued his stitching. "Don't tell me Hell don't smell."

At the end of watch, Solomon took the ladder down to his berth below. He found his shipmates waiting for him.

A spokesman stepped forward, nervous. "We've found the Jonah."

Of course. They'd tumbled to Griffin's presence, and he wasn't here to accept the blame.

"What've you to say for yourself?"

"Me?" Solomon saw a very long swim in his future. "It's not me."

"No one else it could be."

They spoke fast, giving Solomon no chance to answer.

"Who else is so unnatural brave, scampering in the rigging without any fear of falling into the sea," said one.

"Who else never says a word about where he's from or who his people be," said another.

"Who else would summon up mermaids? Hellish creatures with female enticements to lure sailors to their doom," said a third.

"Solomon Durnley, if that be your name, you were caught redhanded debating with Hell's denizens about the nature of its smell."

"So we ask again, what've you to say for yourself?"

Solomon knew the fate of any Jonah. Put him off the ship without delay if the men expected to survive. And Griffin nowhere to be seen.

From above deck came the lookout's cry, "Breaches! She breaches!"

Immediately the second mate was below decks driving them topside.

Topside, the lookout in the crosstrees cried out again, "Breaches!" as the shape of a whale far in the distance lifted nearly out of the water, splashing back down. "White water!" the lookout sang.

Forward, the men squeezed up out of the fo'c'sle, the tedium-ending whale was their single thought.

"Where away?" Howell called up.

"Four points on the starboard quarter," the lookout shouted back.

Despite confronting Solomon, this break from the dreary days of idleness and busy work to keep the devil at bay, sent everyone crowding the rail. All looked toward the spot pointed out by the lookout.

"Stand by the boats," shouted Howell, which set the men hustling and leaping to make all ready.

Captain Dunn appeared, barefoot, shirt untucked. "Lower away," shouted Dunn.

"Mind the tackle," Howell shouted, as the men pivoted the whale boats on the davits.

Dunn smoothed back his hair, tucked in his shirt. "Don't stand mucking about! It's whale you've come for! Don't he oblige ye!"

The line squealed as it passed through the pulleys until the boat touched the ocean's surface.

"To the boats with you. Lively there," called Howell.

Crews scrambled into the bobbing whale boats, each man into his own place, Solomon taking his place in the bow of the lead boat.

"Shove off, the beastie won't wait all day for you!" the captain cried out from the rail.

"Put your backs to it," snapped Howell, a tight grip on the tiller bar.

Three boats gave chase, rowing hard, sweat freezing to frost on the men.

"She sounds," called out Howell, who could see forward, keeping the whale in sight. "Don't turn to gawp! Keep to your oars!"

The boat slipped through the water, finally reaching the spot where the animal had first been sighted. They rowed on, keeping to the course, confident that the beast would rise up for air without deviating from its path.

And rise it did, not ten yards ahead of Solomon's boat, foam and breaking water marking the spot of the whale's return.

"Quickly, lad!" urged Howell. Solomon stood up, taking the lance in hand and bracing himself with his knee in the notch of the forward cleat.

If he could lance this whale, it might prove to his shipmates he was not the Jonah.

The animal was enormous, powerful, and utterly unaware of their presence. Solomon tried to judge the spot behind the flipper where he needed to drive the iron.

Solomon felt a chill breath on his neck.

Griffin was tight behind him.

"You ever see anything that big?"

"Not now," said Solomon, a gravel hiss.

The two men nearest Solomon glanced at each other and then at the tub of whale line, ready to be spun out when the whale was pierced.

All eyes were on the two men nearest Solomon.

"Now," said Griffin.

"Now!" cried Howell.

At Griffin's gentle gesture, Solomon let fly the harpoon and sent it firm into the whale's flesh, but not a deep thrust, only hooking the hide and alerting the whale to its mortal danger.

With a ferocious venting blow and a mighty slap of its fluke the whale sped off. The whale line whirred through the chock, spinning out of the main tub.

"Tie off, tie off," shouted Howell.

Solomon turned back to take his spot at the tiller, and give his place to Howell who would direct the effort bringing the creature to haul.

But the line paying out snagged Solomon's ankle, snatching him out of the boat and into the water, dragging him askim across the waves, slicing, skipping, rooster-tailing through the water.

"Griiiiiiiii-ffiiiiiiiin!"

Howell looked down at the rope still racing out of the tub.

"Don't just sit there, make it fast!" he shouted.

Before the sailor could tie it around the loggerhead, the line parted and disappeared after Solomon, leaving the sailor holding the other end, a limp cord of hemp.

The boat rocked quietly.

Griffin stood looking into the bucket, hands on hips "Don't that beat all."

"That's damn odd," said Howell. "Who paid down this line? Come on. Fess up! Who paid down this line?"

The men kept their eyes averted from the first mate and from the rapidly disappearing Solomon.

"Griiiiiiiii-ffiiiiiiiin!"

Now on the deck of the *Mary Hoppe*, Griffin leaned on the rail watching as the whale dragged Solomon toward the ship.

Griffin experimented with a bowl of tobacco, lighting it and testing the taste of the smoke in his cheeks. He looked up as Solomon came skipping along behind the whale as it passed to starboard of the ship.

The men along the rail watched as the whale and Solomon passed.

"Griiiiiiiiii-ffiiiiiiiin!"

With another great slap of its fluke, the whale sounded. Solomon popped out of sight as the whale pulled him under the water.

Below, Solomon, with his arms splayed out for a sea anchor in hopes of slowing his descent, watched the surface of the water fade above him, the light dimming as the whale dived for the depths. The twilight blue of the deep engulfed him.

Back on the *Mary Hoppe*, Griffin blew a long stream of smoke, carried away by the wind.

"So long, Solly."

Part Two

Chapter Fourteen

The Fiji Islands – 1850s

THE BRIG *SAMANTHA*, OUT OF PROVIDENCE, backed sails to keep position about a cable's length beyond the break in the coral reef enclosing a mile-wide lagoon of glimmering blue water. The lagoon embraced the eastern approach to the island, a buffer against the open ocean. The island beyond the lagoon, overgrown with a lush and luminous green vegetation made up of exotic trees, vines, and spectacularly large flowers, was the object of intense and squint-eyed curiosity by the *Samantha*'s master, crew, and passengers. Eyes shaded against the radiant reflection of sunlight off the water, the entire ship's company studied the bit of land before them.

The island was belted in greenery. At its southern end a stubby, clenched fist of a volcanic cone thrust upward, the southern face of which dropped straight into ocean surf that churned and thrashed the rocky base beneath it. The volcano's northern face sloped gently downward, disappearing into the verdant cover of tropical forest over the island's northern point.

The gas and smoke vented by the volcano made for a languid veil riding high above the strong breeze blowing along the surface of the water. The darkness and the density of the smoke hinted at a molten vitality not far from violence just beneath the surface.

From the treeline, a watcher, careful to remain unobserved, kept an eye on the *Samantha* riding gently on the waves that swept under its keel, rushed across the coral, to break over the sand.

On the *Samantha*, the ship's captain called out orders to make ready and lower a boat, which set the hands scurrying about the deck.

A landing party gathered at the ship's accommodation ladder and clambered down into the boat as it bobbed and knocked against the *Samantha*. Once the sailors had arranged themselves, four women, in bonnets and heavy dark skirts, were handed down and helped into the boat. After the ladies were seated and secured, the crew pulled for the island. They made their way through the break in the coral reef, into the lagoon, and across the expanse of tranquil water. With strong finishing strokes they drove the boat up onto the beach.

Two sailors hopped out and drew the boat out of the water as the surf helped shove it higher onto the shore. They handed the ladies out and dragged the boat up above the reach of the retreating surf that might drag it back out to sea. A third sailor stood with his musket at the ready.

A tall and fearsome woman, apparently in charge, hiked her skirts and marched up toward the high-water mark. Behind her a trio of lesser ladies struggled to keep up, staggering in the soft sand.

The commanding female scanned the treeline, while the other women seemed unsteady on their feet, as if unused to solid, unmoving ground, suggesting a lengthy time afloat. The sailors made no secret of their mirth at the ladies' discomfort.

Another of the sailors, perhaps the mate in charge of the boat, came up even with the tall woman.

"Captain Creech expects us to be back aboard before the tide turns," said the mate, "and the men unable to row against it."

"How much time do we have to explore this island?" asked the tall woman, clearly exasperated.

"You have the better part of the morning, Miss Samples."

"That is hardly enough time."

"See along that line there just where the water reaches? The tide comes in hard and high. You'll spend the night ashore if you don't return when I signal, and I will not answer for it."

Miss Samples scanned the island fully north to south, then turned to the ladies following. "We will split up and explore the island for any hint that Man the Corruption has been here prior to our arrival."

"Could be a trick," said one of the other sailors. "Islanders leave no sign, hoping to lure in mariners desperate for wood and water and whatever edibles might be found."

"Then they fling themselves upon us, cut our throats, and roast us for their heathen feasts," said another.

"Are you trying to scare us with cannibals?" asked Miss Samples.

The other bonneted heads snapped round to fix Miss Samples and the mate with a look of severe concern.

"It's a peculiar pastime still practiced by many in this part of the world," said the mate, "your meddling missionaries notwithstanding."

"I am tired of your captain's efforts to frighten us from our goal." Miss Samples stopped at the sight of her followers clutching each other, transfixed by something behind her. One of the ladies fainted dead away.

Miss Samples turned to see what had so shocked the ladies.

Striding out of the treeline was a man of perhaps twenty-five or thirty, vigorous, his long strides kicking up sand as he came toward them. Fair-skinned and clean-shaven, his face was unmarked by sea or sun, and his hair tied back with twine made of coconut fiber. His head covering was a halo of long palm leaves encircling his brow, giving shade to his face. He was dressed in a bushy skirt of pili grass and a tapa cloth waistcoat, very much of a European style, hanging open, its bamboo buttons more ornamental than functional. A crudely made, short-handled knife was thrust between the loops of hemp rope that served as a belt to the skirt, and over his shoulder he carried a satchel made of thick-bladed grass plaited together. On his feet he had banana leaves trimmed and twisted into the likeness of shoes. Trailing along behind him was a coal black pig on a leash.

The sailor with the musket aimed to fire a warning shot and pulled the trigger. The flint fell on the empty pan with a sharp snap. It was all over the sailor's face that he'd forgotten to load the musket and charge the pan. The strange-looking islander made straight for the sailor and his empty weapon. The sailor fumbled and juggled to get to the powder flask, biting out the stopper, pouring powder down the barrel and into the pan, just getting the hammer cocked in time to take aim again.

The island oddity held up his hands, clearly a gesture to calm the sailor. He tip-toed up close and put his nostril to the bore of the musket barrel, sniffing deeply.

"Your powder's too damp. Won't catch," he said, then closed his mouth on the barrel and blew a mighty tuba-toot. A cloud of powder burst out the touch hole in the sailor's face and set him to coughing.

"Oooh, looks like somebody didn't load the ball. You'll never hit anything that way," he said, and then turned to give Miss Samples a studious appraisal. Circling her, he examined her from every angle. The other women circled behind Miss Samples to keep her between themselves and the man.

When he'd finished his circuit, he put his hands on his hips. "I'll take her. I expect she's a layer, because she don't look like much for frying."

"I beg your pardon!" demanded Miss Samples.

The man leaned back, slid a look at the sailors. "That seem odd to you? A talking chicken?"

"Excuse me?" The glare she gave the man should have cooked him.

The man swooped right up close to Miss Samples, his nose to her neck, sniffing hard and quick before she could flinch away.

The man stepped back and made deep, courtly bows, his left leg extended, sweeping wide with an imaginary hat. "My humblest apologies. I took you for a very bad dream."

"Who are you?"

"Solomon. Of Durnley, I believe. It's not a question I've been asked very often in the last—the last—what year is it?"

"Eighteen hundred and fifty-three. April."

"Nearly twenty years," he said, staring away into the distance for a long moment. He snapped back, smiling brightly, "Shall we go? We'll have to take your carriage. My horse threw a shoe and ran off with the footman. Terrible scandal. It was in all the papers. No one talks about it. Come along, Hamilton." Solomon tugged on the pig's lead, striding down the beach to the boat, offering deep bows to the ladies and the sailors as he went. He lifted the pig into the boat.

"I will allow no such thing," said Miss Samples, catching up to him.

"I suppose we could walk. It's a lovely day for it." Solomon shaded his eyes, checking the weather.

The volcano gave out with a rumbling belch.

"They promised to fix that thing." Solomon shifted his gaze to the volcano's summit. "The neighbors will insist on coming over to throw in another virgin, for all the good it seems to do."

The ladies clustered close to Miss Samples.

"Of course, then they'll insist we stay for dinner. Delightful people, but terrible table manners, don't you know." Solomon climbed into the boat and seated himself on the midship thwart.

"Cannibals?" asked the women.

"Why, yes they are."

Again, the volcano grumbled long and low.

"Going to be a bad one. May take more than one virgin this time."

"We have armed men and a ship with two cannons."

"Please. They're not blood-thirsty savages." Solomon turned to the sailors. "They'll buy the lot of them off you for a few gallons of the island liquor," he said, gesturing at the ladies. "Don't settle right away. They love to dicker."

The mention of local hooch seemed to appeal to the sailors.

A shot boomed from the *Samantha* and echoed across the lagoon.

From beyond the northern end of the island, three large, ornately carved outrigger canoes rounded the point. The speed, precise strokes of the rowers, and the sun glistening off sweaty backs was impressive even from this distance.

"I hope you brought enough for everyone," said Solomon, counting noses among the ladies.

With skirts flying, the ladies sprinted for the boat, spraying sand as they ran, tugging Miss Samples along with them.

The sailors stood by as the ladies pushed the boat back into the surf and hopped aboard, taking to the oars.

"On the other hand," Solomon called out to the sailors, "They may just cut you all up for pork chops and keep the liquor for themselves."

The sailors chased after the ladies, high-stepping through the surf to catch the boat before the ladies pulled out of reach. They tumbled in over the gunwales, the ladies pulling fiercely with the oars.

The boat sliced a wake making toward the *Samantha*, racing to get through the breakwater before the outriggers cut them off, trapping them inside the lagoon.

Ferocious, tattooed men could be seen in each canoe, paddling with high, arching, and powerful strokes.

The boat passed through the breakwater of the inlet and into the open ocean with only the cable length's distance left to go.

The outriggers gained on the boat, with pursuers on the starboard side angling toward the huffing and heaving oarswomen.

A cannon boomed again from the *Samantha*, sending a shot plunging between the boat and the starboard side pursuer, the shower of water soaking both vessels.

The ladies cracked on harder and the boat pulled away from the outriggers.

As the boat came within a few yards of the ship, the men of the outriggers quit paddling, and let their vessels slide in close, then veered off, away from the ship's side.

When the boat bumped against the *Samantha* the men clambered up the ladder and through the gangway, leaving the ladies to follow, dragging their soaked skirts up after them.

The watch on deck had already unreefed sails and were straining at the ropes, adjusting canvas to catch the wind, steering the ship to make for the open water.

Solomon was last up the ladder, taking his time, the pig under his arm. Once on deck, Solomon looked around the ship, getting his fill of civilization's sights, sounds and smells after so long a time away. He breathed a deep, deep sigh, then turned to the men in the outriggers and waved.

The steersman of the closest outrigger raised his paddle in reply. The warriors rode silently, rocking on the waves as the ship left them in its wake.

"Who's this fella." Creech, the ship's captain, came down from the afterdeck for a closer look at the newcomer.

"A madman. Most likely a deserter hiding out on that island," said Miss Samples, flinging the water from her sleeves.

"How'd you come to be on that island?" asked Creech.

"I came by whale."

"By whale ship? Which you deserted," insisted Miss Samples.

Solomon got in close to her ear.

"Bi-ee-yuh. Ooo-way-ul-uh," he said again, drawing out the syllables to simplify the words for this idiot.

She jerked her head away, his breath lacking a certain freshness.

"Remarkably well-fed for someone who's spent nearly twenty years on a deserted island." Miss Samples turned to Creech. "He's a deserter and a liar to boot."

"I was fishing for whale in the North Atlantic. A whale yanked me out of my boat. That critter must've dragged me halfway round the world, by way of the polar ice cap. Then he swum down through the Bering Sea. Can't say for certain, me being unfamiliar with those waters. Then, he made for the South Sea islands, where I washed up on that very beach. Somewhere in the Feejees most likely. Without charts, chronometer, or sextant, I had no way to tell. By the stars, I reckon it's where I washed up."

"What did I tell you, Creech," said Miss Samples, "I insist you put this man in irons. He was going to feed us to those cannibals."

"I'll put no man in irons on your say-so, Miss Samples."

"You believe his—his—fish story? That he was pulled overboard? By a whale?"

"Been known to happen."

"The man is a lunatic and needs to be locked up."

Creech looked Solomon over. "What's your name? What's your ship?"

"Solomon Durnley. Off the *Mary Hoppe* out of Cold Spring Harbor."

"Cold Spring Harbor? Don't know any ships of that port out here."

"It weren't bound for these waters. It was bound for the Grand Banks off Newfoundland." Solomon rubbed his hands on his grass skirt.

"Would you happen to have some tea and a crumpet? I'm famished. Being marooned on an island for nearly twenty years leaves a man with a powerful hunger for civilized fare."

"Seems awfully far-fetched, you ask me," came a familiar voice from among the sailors still huffing and puffing from the race with the outriggers.

Solomon stood stock still, then shook himself, as if rousing from a long, bad dream. He smiled before turning to see who'd spoken. His eye settled on Griffin, standing there, big as life by the rail.

"You look like you got some color," said Griffin.

Solomon threw wide his arms and gave Griffin a welcoming smirk as he moved toward him. "I can't tell you how good it is to see you," said Solomon, and when he got close enough, walloped Griffin right square in the snoot. "Because it ain't!"

Griffin blinked hard and shook his head, more annoyed than injured, then touched his nose to check for jointedness.

"You'd hit an angel who's not allowed to defend himself?"

"I heard you were more the avenging angel type." Solomon, his fists up, danced around in front of Griffin. "I've been practicing on coconuts so's I'd be ready when you showed your face again. Come on, come on. What've you got to say for yourself?"

"You're asking for it, you know."

"I am asking for it. I'm ready for you and your whole angel army."

"Oh, you don't want that, I assure you. You should be glad I don't take it personally."

"Take it personal all you want, you no good, low down dirty bastard!"

"It's not our fault we don't have fathers. Or mothers. I'm reminding myself it's just the years of eating bugs and berries on a deserted island talking,"

"It's the whole danged business talking. Leaving me roped to a whale's fundament, dragged clean under the ice cap, down the devil only knows how deep, eating nothing but krill for who knows how many leagues, having sharks gnaw on my legs, until I wash up on that god-forsaken island!"

"It's not really god-forsaken. Just sort of out of the way. Way out of the way. All right, way, way, way, way, way out of the way."

Solomon swung at Griffin again, but Griffin dodged, leaving Solomon to punch empty air.

"You're really asking for it," said Griffin.

"Come on, come on, what're you going to do about it?"

"What am I going to do about it? What am I going to do about it?" Griffin braced himself, standing ready, his voice rising. "I'll show you. I'll show you what I'm going to do about it," he said, hauling back his fist in a powerful wind up, and then with a swoop, gestured toward Captain Creech.

"Clap that man in irons!" shouted Creech.

"They can't see or hear me," said Griffin. "Sorry. Meant to tell you first thing. But I was just so excited to see you again!"

Three extra-large sailors snatched up Solomon.

"No hard feelings?" Griffin called out after him as the sailors carried Solomon, kicking and squirming, below deck.

With his legs locked in chains, Solomon sat on a pile of ballast stones in ankle-deep water down in the ship's bilge. The stench from the flotsam, jetsam, and then some, of the *Samantha*'s every voyage hung heavy in the humid space.

The single lantern gave out with a sickly light, filtered through its mica shades. From just beyond the cast of the lantern's light came the noise of skittering cockroaches and squeaking rodents.

A familiar glow filled the space, augmenting the lantern's feeble light.

Griffin sat on the highest mound of ballast stones, above the water level. Solomon, no longer dressed in the grass garments of the island, wore a shirt, trousers, and shoes taken from the ship's slops.

"I'll bet living among cannibals for so many years wasn't all clarified butter and seasoned salt, was it," said Griffin.

"Next time you're solid? I'm going to find me something heavy and knock that halo of yours down around your ears."

"It's not really a halo. Just a trick of the light. We don't wear actual halos. Except maybe on formal occasions."

Solomon was still for a moment, then slapped the water in which he sat. "You just watched that whale yank me right out of the boat and drag me away to hell and gone."

"You're still mad about that? Solly, that was almost twenty years ago."

"It's amazing how the passing of time don't mean anything when you've got so much of it ahead of you."

"What do I know about whaling? Could've been how you land one of them big monsters for all I knew."

"My predicament didn't strike you as odd?"

"It's not like you were in any kind of danger as long as you held onto that—" Griffin lowered his voice and tightened his lips, "—that object."

"There's more than physical dangers, you know. That doo-hickey ain't proof against them."

"I thought it was all part of your plan for making your fortune. I can't read your mind, Solly."

"Least you could've done was come after me."

"Hey? Remember free will? I'm not your guardian angel."

"I'm beginning to think there's more than two kinds of angels. There's three. Guardian angels, avenging angels, and good-for-nothing angels."

"Solly, you cut me to the quick."

"You lured me aboard that whaler like you were some common crimp, playing me the fool for money. When I didn't come back, you never thought to come find me?"

The rats squeaked and skittered at the edges of Griffin's radiance.

"How was I supposed to know where you washed up? The way that whale took off, he could've dragged you anywhere. I told you, I'm not omniscient."

"That's right. You did." Solomon picked up a large stone, tumbling it in his hands. "So. What're you doing here, now?"

"Now? As in right now, now, or now earlier topside?"

"On this exact ship, at this exact time, on this exact patch of ocean!" Solomon slammed the rock into the water. "Yes, right now!"

"I'm here now, aren't I? Boy, there's no pleasing you, Solly, you know that? After all we've been through together."

"Together?" Solomon was about to say the next profane thing that came to his mind, but stopped, seeing there'd be no use of it. He turned away from Griffin and rested his chin on his arms, watching the beady red eyes of the rats scuttling back and forth along the bulkhead.

"Solly, you think I had any idea you'd turn up? It's a full-time job scouring the earth looking for those things."

"You saying it's all one big coincidence?"

Griffin thought a long moment.

"Okay."

"Not buying it."

"You'd be surprised how much of life is accidental. It's frustrating and exhilarating all at the same time, don't you think? You're a gambler. You should appreciate that."

Solomon pulled on the tangled loops of lanyard and thin gold chain around his neck, lifting the locket and the worn leather pouch from inside the over-sized shirt he'd been given.

"So. You ready to hand that over and go back to being a normal mudfoot, like I suggested in the first place?"

"No."

"You're not still thinking about joining the circus, are you?"

"I'm going back for Lavinia." Solomon popped open the locket. The paintings intact, if slightly water-damaged around the edges.

"What's the point now?"

"You don't know the first thing about love, do you? I told you, no matter how long it took, even if it took a hunnert years, I was going back for Lavinia once I made my fortune."

"You made your fortune. Out here. In the middle of nowhere?"

"Yep."

"O-kay." Griffin leaned to address the rats congregated about. "Mad as a hatter." Then he turned back to Solomon. "I would've bet money it was an act. If I actually carried money."

"There's something else."

"Do tell."

"I learned there's only two kinds of love in the world. The kind that holds fast and the kind that leaves go."

Chapter Fifteen

The Fiji Islands – 1850s

"THERE WAS NOTHING ON THAT ISLAND. Aren't you the least bit interested how I survived, plunked down smack dab in the middle of nowhere without any help from you all those years?" asked Solomon.

"You do understand that for those of us traveling by way of eternity, all that time of yours is a walk to the corner for cigarettes."

Solomon glared at Griffin.

"Okay. How?"

"Don't strain yourself getting all excited."

"Solly, I'm about to slip into a coma with anticipation. How?"

"I had to find food and water, build a shelter, cover my nakedness. Not to mention keep an eye on the horizon for passing ships and building signal fires to catch their attention."

"There wasn't a single sign you were even on that island when we showed up. What happened?"

"Glad you asked. Took you long enough."

The Fiji Islands – 1830s

The rope ensnaring Solomon with the runaway whale finally parted near the breakwater of the uncharted island. The tide deposited him high on the beach then ebbed, leaving him to dry out in the tropical sun.

He was salt encrusted, and his clothing in tatters, entwined with seaweed and small jellyfish.

Lying on the sand, Solomon drifted upward to wakefulness as the sound of the breakers against the coral and the call of sea birds increased and sharpened. The light of day slipped under his eyelids now fluttering against the scratchy seal of encrustation.

A deluge of clouded images, indistinct impressions, and discon-nected ideas flashed through his recovering mind, until a giant whale's angry eye raced by him and he was once again flying from the whaleboat, yanked out to sea.

He startled and roused to a half-sitting position. He rolled over onto his hands and knees, resting there, gathering strength and equilib-rium. He raised up, rediscovering his center of gravity, then staggered to his feet. Weaving, but upright.

Still all a-wobble, he wiped his face and shaded his eyes to look around himself.

He saw shadows. Against a blazing yellow sun. Women, it looked like. Women in full skirts and broad brimmed hats and carrying shep-herd's crooks. A band of shepherdesses? Solomon squinted and stretched his face to regain his eyesight.

One shepherdess approached him, a hand out. Was he supposed to kiss it? Solomon looked down at himself. He wasn't dressed to receive.

The out-stretched hand slammed him hard in the chest, knocking him back to the sand.

His eyesight cleared and he saw a dozen or so grass-skirted, tattooed warriors armed with spears. The one standing over him was wizened and wrinkled, a dark, hickory husk of a face. The old man looked to be some sort of witch doctor, streaked and scarred for his profession. The kind of harum-scarum conjured by crusty old shellback sailors to tease the lubberly green hands when ship's work was done.

The witch doctor wore a lacework of bones and feathers, and carried a staff topped with a human skull, its jaw tied loosely with gut. The witch doctor shook the staff in Solomon's face, then pointed away.

Solomon raised up to look where the witch doctor was pointing. It was the water from which he must have come.

The witch doctor made shoveling gestures toward the water, then waited for Solomon to respond. Solomon didn't move. The witch doc-tor jabbed toward the water with his staff, the jawbone of the skull clackity-clacking.

Solomon again struggled to his feet, but before he could get fully upright, the witch doctor shoved him toward the water's edge.

Now Solomon understood.

"Get your paws off me," croaked Solomon, staggering about in the soft sand. He slapped at the witch doctor's hands as he tried to corral Solomon back into the sea.

He knew he was no longer in the Atlantic half of the world. From the appearance of the islanders, he guessed he was in the Pacific some-where. Solomon could recall sailors telling how Pacific Islanders were usually very hospitable to stranded sailors. Except for those still prac-ticing cannibalism. But these islanders didn't seem inclined to practice on him. They wanted him off their island. So, having no means of trans-portation with which he might oblige them their request he shook his head.

The witch doctor stepped back and looked at the circle of warriors. The stockiest of the islanders, the headman perhaps, given his ornate breast plate and headdress, pointed at Solomon and barked a single word of command. The biggest of the warriors pushed forward, took aim with his spear and gave it a mighty fling at Solomon. It landed against Solo-mon with an equally mighty *doink* and then fell to the sand.

The warriors looked from the headman to the witch doctor.

Clearly fed up with this breakdown in communication, the witch doctor reached into a pouch tied at his waist and took a handful of a powdery something and threw it over Solomon.

Then with a gesture of impatience, the witch doctor backed away from Solomon and invited the warriors to let the troublesome outsider have it. This time all the warriors stood ready to oblige, hefting their spears.

At a word from the headman, the warriors launched their spears, and with a *doink-de-doink-doink* the spears bounced off Solomon onto the sand. Solomon shivered, his skin crawling at the sensation of the spear points striking his flesh.

The warriors looked to the witch doctor, who sniffed the powdery residue between his fingers. He seemed to ponder what he smelled, then broke for the sea, running toward the canoes. The warriors didn't need further explanation but dashed after the witch doctor.

They scrambled over each other to get their canoes launched. As a gesture of apology or perhaps island hospitality, they pitched the witch doctor out of the first canoe, while the headman shouted back at Solo-mon. By the headman's tone and gestures, Solomon took it as an invi-tation to dispose of the offending witch doctor in whatever manner seemed right to Solomon.

The witch doctor, unwilling to remain behind and find out what manner of disposal seemed right to Solomon, swam for all he was worth in pursuit of the swiftly departing canoes, managing to catch hold of an outrigger, and haul himself canoe-ward as they passed through the mouth of the breakwater.

Standing rooted there on the beach, Solomon felt very much alone.

Lost at sea. That would be the sum total of his obituary reported in the shipping news once the *Mary Hoppe* returned to port. Three words alongside his name on the ship's muster.

How much time had passed? A few hours? A few days? A few thousand years?

He grabbed his shirt front. Relieved, he could feel he still had the locket and the peculiar artifact both still hanging around his neck.

"Griffin!" The noise of the surf pounding the breakwater, and the call of the gulls wheeling overhead swept away Solomon's voice.

"You want this thing?" Solomon yanked the metal bauble from his neck and held it out. "You have to come get it." Solomon strode out onto a little bit of a basalt jetty. "You listening to me?"

He held it out again.

"How about I drop it to the bottom and let it lie there to rust clean away? How about that!"

A gull dived for the bright object, causing Solomon to flinch out of the flight path.

"You got God's ignorant creatures doing your dirty work? That it?"

Nothing.

He stepped down onto the sand.

He was a very small speck of a man, on a very small spit of sand, atop an unimaginably vast and empty ocean.

"All of you so cock sure you took my measure and found me wanting. All of you."

Griffin allowed him a year, didn't he? All right then. A year it is. He'd show them.

He marched to the treeline, and disappeared into the island verdure.

Solomon walked the island in little more than a day, surveying his new domain, leaving only the volcano unexplored. There seemed to be precious little at hand with which to make a life. No fresh water, nothing he recognized as edible, and no building materials readily available for constructing a raft or a permanent shelter.

It didn't take long for Solomon to realize the extremes of hunger, thirst, or exposure were not life-threatening. That was some comfort. On the other hand, hunger, thirst, and exposure still had a powerful bite and would be a constant goad to the hard work of survival.

Recalling how musket flints could be knapped to razor sharpness, he used a hand-sized stone to work a chunk of the basalt into a serviceable dagger-like blade keen enough to draw blood.

With the new knife he fashioned a fire plow. Securing the log between the soles of his feet and using a pointed stick of the same hardwood, he worked the point in the trough with fierce, swift strokes. After much effort the tinder finally caught. He kept working the point in the trough until he judged the smoke thick and lively enough, then blew the smoldering tinder into flame. He carried the tiny lick of flame to his fire pit and lit the kindling.

By that same firelight Solomon fashioned a three-pronged fishing spear of bamboo and hibiscus vines.

When he'd finished the fishing spear, he created a segmented bucket out of hollow bamboo stalks tied together with more hibiscus vines.

Wore out from so much hard work on his first full day of consciousness, he stretched out against a palm trunk, the lick of the heat from the dwindling fire warm on his face. He dozed, waking in the deep of the night when the fire had burnt down to embers. He fed the glowing coals with more twigs to keep the flame going inside the pit.

With his flint knife, he cut a hash mark in the palm trunk, just over his head, then rolled over and went back to sleep.

With the simple tools he'd fashioned, Solomon set about making a living off the beautifully vegetated, brilliantly colored, and incredibly inhospitable island.

In sheer defiance of good sense, he'd taste-tested everything he could get his hands on. He had no fear of any flower, leaf, pod, root, berry, bark, or stem. But he only swallowed those things that didn't make his mouth tingle, give off a bitter taste, or excrete an acrid odor that made his nostrils itch. He found much he could eat and ease the knot in his belly, but it wasn't all that satisfying.

As he further surveyed the edibility of the island wildlife, he added insects, mollusks, starfish, snakes, and green sea turtles to the few tiny birds and leathery iguanas he managed to trap. He caught sight of small, black feral pigs, but didn't yet have a weapon sufficient to bring one down.

He built a simple lean-to of woven palm leaves lashed to a bamboo frame braced against the trunk of the palm tree that grew horizontally toward the beach. He added a corduroyed floor of larger bamboo trunks laid side by side.

Solomon's days had become very simple and repetitive.

He visited the lagoon in the early morning hours to spear the small, frisky fish that fed in the shallows. He kept to water that was no more than knee deep, to avoid being taken unawares by sharks hunting close to shore.

Solomon gathered and husked coconuts, keeping the milk in bamboo canisters covered with waxy ti leaves tied off with vine. He kept his bamboo bucket filled with fresh rainwater, the edibles he'd gathered in a simple rock-and-bamboo larder, the firewood he'd collected in a crib that also served as a windbreak.

When his clothing finally disintegrated off his body, he constructed a skirt of pili grass and more of the hibiscus vines. Using the strips of bark fiber from paper mulberry trees, dampened and pounded, Solomon managed to make a workable fabric from which he fashioned a tolerable loincloth and waistcoat.

Once he'd secured food and water for the day, Solomon patrolled the beach, both morning and evening, watching for passing vessels in the daylight, and for lantern or firelight after dark. He'd light a signal fire when he spotted a patch of white sail or a yellowish glow on the horizon, and he'd add a dance that was a mix of hornpipe, jig, reel, mazurka, and a passable imitation of a trotting horse, to attract the attention of the more frequent island outriggers that raced by, just beyond the breakwater.

He'd been on the island quite a number of days before he investigated the volcano that dominated the island. On that first day's exploration he followed a worn footpath leading to the summit. Given the stories he'd heard about Pacific Islanders, he was uneasy about what he might find at the top. He reckoned the island was their church, and the mouth of the volcano the focal point of their religious practices.

It was a short climb, no more than half-an-hour. On reaching the top, Solomon was relieved to find a simple, unadorned platform that allowed him to stand securely at the crater's edge and look down on the magma in the vent not all that far below. He'd always imagined a giant, bubbling bowl of glowing hot, yellow-white lava. Instead, he saw a tranquil, burbling pool of the boiling rock, mostly crusted over, with the magma shining through creases between the crusted places. The heat was something sharp, almost cutting. Without the protection of the token, the heat would have driven him back from the platform's edge after only a few moments. But the beauty of the near-living quality of the molten rock, surging and rolling and popping down below, like spooned molasses, enticed him to watch as long as he could before the discomfort from the heat drove him off the platform.

There was something in the pulsing heat and luminescence of the magma that reflected his feelings for Lavinia and, he hoped, her feelings for him.

◆ ◆ ◆

After one particularly heart-breaking day trying to signal a two-masted schooner, only to see it race off as if scalded, Solomon began to populate his island with imaginary citizens.

Early on Solomon narrated out loud the vicissitudes he faced simply for the sound of a human voice close by. No madness in that. But with yet another rescue whisked away his imagination filled in the gaps created by the loneliness creeping over him.

After a while, his imaginary companions became a tolerable substitute for the emptiness of his island.

He invited all manner of people to join him, inviting those he knew from history, from the Bible, from his days working on the river. He would not, however, speak to anyone he knew to be from story books even if they insisted on making an appearance for dinner. They were, Solomon decided, doubly imaginary and might cause people to think him unstable.

As the sun went down, Solomon lit the torches to keep the insects away, set out his dinner on the mat that was his dining table, and then, reclining by the fire, waved his guests in absentia to come in close and make themselves comfortable.

No matter who Solomon chose to invite to dinner, he always included Lavinia, seating her next to him so he could give her hand a squeeze whenever the notion took him.

Before the meal, he would pour up the fermented intoxicant he'd managed to brew from kava roots. Between sips he would recount the day's activities, embellishing the facts with dangerous adventures to make the ladies gasp and gentlemen swear in amazement.

If he was feeling mischievous, he'd invite Luther and Abigail, serving them raw tree slugs that he'd caught fresh that day, just to see the expression on their faces as they spooned up the squiggling brutes. It always made him laugh.

Lavinia, on the other hand, never failed to do him proud, politely eating whatever he served, down to the last morsel. She never failed to offer him thanks for being a most thoughtful host in the face of such scarcity and adversity.

The next morning, Solomon would be back out at the lagoon, spearing fish and watching for sharks.

So it went, until the tally of hash marks numbered one year. Solomon's calculation included the number of days between Luther shooting him and the whale yanking him out of the boat, plus another three days for the time tangled up with the whale. He couldn't be sure how much time he actually spent snared to the whale, but if three days was sufficient for Jonah of the Bible, it was a good bet the Almighty would not require more days from Solomon.

By Solomon's arithmetic it was time for Griffin to make good on their bargain.

To mark the occasion, Solomon prepared a special feast of nonu, termites, and coconut, lit extra torches, not sparing the precious fuel. He marked the stars to measure midnight as best he could, not being certain of the month.

While he waited, he drank and ate and played host to all the notables and dignitaries he'd entertained over the previous year. He spoke of victories and setback, challenges and aspirations. Feeling magnanimous, he permitted Abigail and Luther to come in close to the fire, everyone waiting on Griffin.

Solomon continued to drink as the time passed. There was still no sign of Griffin. The talk became difficult, the laughter forced, then all finally dying away. He was alone, and even by his generous calculation, midnight must surely have passed.

He must have dozed and some patch of a dream jerked him awake. The torches were out and the fire burned down to embers.

Solomon roused himself up and staggered away from the clearing, picking up the trail leading to the volcano.

He reached the fork in the trail where the path led up the low, sloping flank of the volcano. He hesitated a moment as if unable to recall which way he'd been headed, then followed the path to the top.

Finally reaching the cone's lip, he mounted the platform and walked to its edge. Breathing hard from the unusual exertion of the climb, his face pinked up and started to bead sweat in the heat. He slipped the token's lanyard over his head and held the metal object out at arm's length, dangling it over the cone.

"If I drop it in, would that be cause enough for you to suddenly appear and catch it?"

Solomon rocked on the balls of his feet.

Below him, the pool seemed angrier, brighter than usual, popping and spitting up through the creases of the crust, his face illuminated, given a sinister cast by the shadows made by the light thrown upward.

How long would the token protect him if he decided to take a swim in that furious miasma below?

In the dark, out on the water, a tiny, moving spot of yellow caught

Solomon's eye. He held his hand up to shield his eyes against the light of the lava below. He followed the bead of flame as it traveled along. An outrigger at this time of night was rare but not unusual.

His fire down on the beach was no more than coals, and he'd never get down the flank of the volcano before the canoe would be out of sight. The spunk was gone. All Solomon felt compelled to do was stand and watch.

As the bright pip came even with the mouth of the breakwater, visible by the moonlit whitecaps striking against the coral reef, the light slowed, then went out.

Solomon slumped. No more than another trick of light played on his inebriated imagination. But as he continued to watch, he saw the moonlight reflecting off the wake-water of something traveling toward the beach.

A darkened canoe. Aiming straight for his beach.

Chapter Sixteen

The Fiji Islands – 1830s

SOLOMON GAVE A SHOUT AND RAN, sliding and scooting, down the foot path, reaching the trail back to his encampment. He loped along, dodging the great leaves, overhanging vines, and roots that tangled the way.

He reached the treeline just as two young islanders drew the canoe up onto the sand. By the moonlight, he saw a tall, muscular young man, the kind of buster who could wrestle bears. With him was a mere smidgen of a girl, petite, shapely, with long hair tied up in a vine of flowers.

Solomon gathered himself to run and hug and kiss and lift them both in elation. But when the Buster pointed toward the ocean at more beads of light approaching the beach, Solomon hesitated. The Smidge flailed about in distress, and the Buster held and comforted her as they hunkered down behind the canoe.

They were fugitives of some kind, that was clear enough, fleeing whoever it was coming on in the lighted outriggers. If Solomon attempted to signal, he'd bring the pursuers down on the young couple. If he did nothing until they were gone, he'd be left alone with the young couple who might not be at all inclined or even able to help him leave the island.

It didn't take long for the four pursuing canoes to reach the shore, beaching quickly and spilling the occupants who rushed to gather around the huddling couple.

Pushing from behind, through the crowd, an angular man of medium build approached the couple still clinging to one another. He pulled the couple apart and in a high, sharp voice scolded the Smidge, making his displeasure obvious by his tone and gestures. Then he turned his anger on the Buster and seemed to plead with the young man to reconsider his actions. But the Buster only reached for the girl, the angular man slapping away the Buster's hand.

The angular man turned, reached into the crowd surrounding the couple, and pulled forward another young woman. She was curvaceous, taller than the men standing around her, made all the more so by wearing her hair tied up off her neck. It gave her the look of a cinnamon Venus with both her arms still attached. The angular man took the Venus by the shoulders and stood her between himself and the Buster.

The angular man lifted a beaded necklace around the Venus's neck, hefting what looked to be a bulging palm leaf pouch. Buster seemed indifferent to the object.

With wide, slicing, and expansive gestures, the angular man made clear the Buster belonged with the Venus by virtue of whatever it was that hung about her neck. The Venus stood motionless, eyes down, as one bearing a great indignity.

The Smidge rushed to the Buster's side and the angular man exploded all over again, repeating his words and gestures.

A good old fashioned family squabble. The Smidge and the Venus were sisters, the angular man was most likely the Daddy, and the Buster was supposed to marry the older sister. But he and the Smidge had decided otherwise, and so had taken matters into their own hands and lit out to run away. Solomon could tell that the Venus was a-cringe with mortification, wishing only for the whole business to be over.

The volcano gave a burst and belch, throwing sparks and smoke high enough to be seen above the rim.

Everyone looked back at it.

Solomon realized his only chance of escape was to sneak past the islanders, commandeer one of the canoes and paddle for the open water while they were distracted, settling their family dispute.

Solomon edged along the treeline, until he reached a natural curve that led him close to the water.

Counting on the glare of torchlight to blind the islanders to anything moving in the dark beyond, Solomon dashed for the canoe closest to him.

Taking hold of the outrigger spar, Solomon strained to lift the canoe and shove it back into the sea. It wouldn't budge.

So he braced his hands on the prow and pushed. And *puuushed*. And *puuuuuuushed*. His feet slipped and slid, his slight build no match for the weight of the canoe. He'd trade a few years of immortality for a mite more muscularity.

He reared back and slammed his hands and shoulders against the prow, levering hard with all his might. Which was mighty little. With another heave against the heavy prow he shoved, running in place for all he was worth, his legs churning, pedaling, spraying sand and moving the canoe—moving the canoe—moving the canoe—not one whit. He slid to the sand. Now in a fury, again he slammed himself against the canoe's prow and pushed, pedaled, and groaned.

It was the gut-deep groan that gave him away. The islanders all turned to see this common, not very good, canoe thief caught in the act of his thievery.

Oblivious, Solomon was churning all the harder when two of the warriors pounced, grabbing him up still pedaling when they hauled him back to the circle of islanders, and stood him in their midst.

Solomon wondered if canoe thieves were treated as harshly as horse thieves back home.

That same old witch doctor stepped into the fire light and examined Solomon, saying something back over his shoulder causing the islanders to flinch back from him.

Solomon was surprised at the small measure of affection he felt for the old gent. Like finding a long-lost schoolmate in an alien land, made welcome by the passing of time and the absence of real friends. He was actually glad the other islanders hadn't fed him to the sharks.

Stepping forward at the word from the witch doctor was the headman, who also studied Solomon up and down. Solomon wasn't at all surprised at the lack of affection he had for that one.

Solomon braced himself for more of the witch doctor's herbal sneezery and that annoying sensation of spear points flung at him. Instead, the witch doctor gave a hand wag at the Daddy urging him to approach Solomon.

The Daddy spoke at Solomon, ducking his head, making little prayer palms with his hands as he laid out the story for Solomon. It was only by the gestures Solomon could derive any sense of the matter and concluded that the whole affair would be resolved if the Buster would marry the Venus and the Smidge would leave the conducting of matrimonial arrangements to her elders.

The Smidge broke in, and made her own case, her voice a passionate stream, tinged with tears, clasping her breast, cupping her heart in her hands.

Solomon realized he had been recruited on account of his supernatural qualities to render judgment in the case being argued before him. It seemed a simple matter, and might earn him a ride off the island.

He looked over where the Venus stood, one knee cocked against the other, her arms folded, not crossed, holding her elbows in her hands.

Seeing Solomon look toward the older girl, the witch doctor gave her a poke with his staff.

She looked first at Solomon, then at the Buster, then back at Solomon. Then she let loose with a tirade that set them all back on their heels. The demure maiden with the downcast eyes was gone, and she let everyone within reach of the torchlight have it. Solomon frowned trying to follow her tone and gesture. She was washing her hands of the Buster, she was leaving him to her sister, and welcome. She didn't care a fig for the men her father was fixing her up with, and if she never had another beau, ending her days as a spinster in a houseful of cats, that was just fine with her. Or so Solomon gathered insofar as he could gather, understanding not a syllable of what she said.

The witch doctor again stepped forward and offered a summation that included the three young people, the Daddy, Solomon, and the volcano above them, which was even now painting the underside of its smoky plume a dull orange. He held out a lei of dark blossoms for Solomon to take, pointing first at the Smidge and then the Venus. Solomon guessed he was being asked to choose the Buster's bride for him, settling this dispute so they could all go home before the volcano got any worse.

The volcano gave out with another burst, a spray of lava sprinkling the cone's rim.

Solomon looked first at the Smidge who was so obviously in love with the Buster. Then he looked at the Venus who had once again bottled up whatever it was she felt, again holding her arms tight against herself. For Solomon it seemed a choice between the grass fire of quick passion or the deep burning coals of a true love. The Venus had it and the Smidge didn't. If they were going to give him the final say, then he'd decide in favor of the Venus. Solomon was confident the Buster would thank him in the end.

Solomon draped the lei around the Venus's neck. There was a gasp among the islanders and a warrior stepped forward raising a cudgel over her head, preparing to brain her with it.

"Whoooooa!" Solomon cried out with a wide sweep of his hands, shaking his head so hard his cheeks fluttered, turning his utterance into an angry warble.

The witch doctor broke in, impatient, pointing his staff at the volcano. Solomon wasn't picking the winner. He was picking the loser who would have her head stove in and then pitched into the volcano to mollify the island spirits for this breach of promise played out on their sacred beach.

Solomon yanked the lei from around the Venus's neck.

The islanders watched him, waiting. These folks weren't going to leave without a proper amen to their ceremony. Looking from sister to sister, he didn't figure either of them deserved such a dunking. The firm sadness of the Venus was familiar somehow, making him wonder if he wasn't doing her a disservice by sparing her, since it was more than likely the Buster would go home with the Smidge when it was all said and done.

Not feeling inclined to consign either of them to a flaming demise just to satisfy a volcano, and being the only person within this congregation who might have a chance of surviving such a swim, Solomon draped the lei around his own neck. This drew an even larger gasp from the islanders, and for a brief flaring moment, a soft look of tender affection from the Venus.

Solomon turned toward the trail that led to the foot path up the side of the volcano. He turned back to the islanders who hadn't moved.

Solomon was a die-hard believer in luck, but not coincidence. By his reckoning the time had run out on his bargain with Griffin. If Griffin had any ideas about welshing on their deal, then maybe a jump into the volcano in front of all these folks would force him out of hiding. It was Griffin always making a big hoo-haw about keeping the blamed thing a secret. Let Griffin do something about it now.

Heck, if Griffin did let him jump and he came through without a scratch, the islanders might throw him a parade and take him anywhere he had a need of going.

With a smile and twinkle he gestured for them to come along and see an island spirit at work. He turned to follow the trail into the jungle. The Venus followed first, then the witch doctor, then the rest of the islanders followed at a distance.

As he climbed, Solomon was more and more convinced Griffin would appear in time to stop him from making a spectacle of himself. If not, he would learn the true extent of his immortality. He'd already been subjected to lightning strikes, pummeling, drowning, and poisons of all kinds. He was entirely confident he could survive the plunge. Griffin was an angel, and he'd said himself Solomon was immortal.

Finally reaching the platform, Solomon climbed up and stepped to the edge. The islanders came up the flank as far as they dared, keeping back from the waves of heat and the intermittent sprinkling of lava flung up and outward.

He took his place on the platform, standing at the very brink, the heat a near-solid wall. Solomon fondled the metal token on his chest, his eyes darting around for any last second sign of Griffin. He closed his eyes, then leapt.

Solomon hit the surface of the lava, knocking the wind out of himself, the molten goo sagging under his weight, but not breaking enough that he might submerge. In an instant his grass skirt, waistcoat and underskirt caught and evaporated in flame, nothing but smoking remains in less than a blink. As the lanyard ignited, he grabbed the metal that had become incredibly hot to the touch. But not untouchable to him.

For Solomon, the heat had a coated quality, like standing against a furnace wall or leaning against a smithy's forge. Just on the other side of his protecting envelope was a heat too intense to stand. But he could stand it. He got to his feet, struggling to keep his footing on the undulating, infirm surface. Old Saint Peter must have felt the same thing under his feet when he went walking on the water with Jesus.

Solomon was panting, his breath coming in quick, shallow bursts, the heat cooking the air before it could reach his lungs.

Light-headed, Solomon squinted to get his bearings, looking for a way out. Geysering lava burped up between the hard crusted spots. Solomon walked slightly stooped over, arms out for balance back to the wall of the cone, just under the platform above.

Behind him the lava broke through the southern wall of the rim and the whole surface shifted, flowing through the breach to fall into the sea below, setting up a terrible steaming hiss that rose up.

The level began to drop, and Solomon had to run for the cone's inner wall. The super-heated gelatin caught at his feet as he ran, until at the last, he leapt for the side. The mass shifted away from underfoot, through the breach, and over the side. The sharp, craggy surface of the wall offered handholds and footholds enough for him to climb out.

Solomon drew himself up onto the edge of the cone, ready to give a triumphant wave.

There was no one there.

He could see from where he stood they were already half-way down the footpath.

He gave a shout and once again slithered and slid down the footpath, this time setting the ground he touched to smoldering, and causing dried grass to flare and smoke, leaving fiery footprints as he ran.

By the time he reached the beach, the islanders had their canoes launched and were paddling across the lagoon.

Solomon cried out, dancing and waving, his body a rosy glow against the dark treeline behind him.

The islanders paddled on.

Reaching the water's edge, the wavelets washed over Solomon's feet, causing steam to rise up.

Solomon could make out the Venus, looking back at him from her perch in the stern of the last canoe.

Jumping into a volcano for a lady ought to be good enough for a canoe ride.

He trudged up out of reach of the water, turning to look at the retreating canoes. He sat down hard onto the sand, drawing his knees up, hugging himself into a ball. Resting his head on his arms, the sand underneath him cooked to a thin, spun-glass film.

Solomon watched until the torches were indistinguishable from the stars low on the horizon, and just as unreachable. Rolling onto his side, pillowing his head on his arm, Solomon went to sleep.

The tickle of gulls pecking at his hair woke Solomon. The sun was high in the sky, and Solomon struggled to sit up, still groggy from all the drink, the exhilaration of rescue, and the gloom of abandonment.

Roused up, Solomon flapped his arms to drive off the gulls. At his feet, he saw the Venus's necklace and palm-leaf pouch.

Solomon jumped up and looked hard about him. But there was no sign of anyone.

He shook the contents of the pouch into his hand. He counted nearly three dozen large black pearls.

The Venus left him her dowry.

He appreciated the sacrifice, but a canoe and a couple of those busters to paddle him back to civilization would have been plenty.

On the other hand, he'd made his fortune within the year. Maybe today would be the day he claimed Lavinia.

Chapter Seventeen

The Fiji Islands – 1850s

"THAT ISLAND WAS TABOO. Me jumping in the volcano just made it worse. No one dared drop anchor. Nothing I could do but kick over my signal fires, move my camp off the beach. Make like the island was completely deserted, hoping some ship'd be desperate enough to land and explore. But no one ever did," said Solomon. "Until today."

"You didn't think to settle down with the girl you rescued? That Venus?"

"No way she could take Lavinia's place. But the Venus did remind me of someone. I didn't see it right off."

Griffin nodded. "Abigail. Blindingly obvious."

"No, not Abigail. Edwin," said Solomon. "How'd you get Abigail?"

"The island girl reminded you of *Edwin*? Solly m'lad, that volcano cooked some of the sense out of you."

"Venus saw how it was between the Buster and the Smidge. She didn't try to steal him away or make her daddy force him to go through with the marriage. She was man enough to leave go. Like Edwin should do, if he has any sort of honest affection for Lavinia."

"That's not what I got out of that story, Solly-boy."

"I'm not surprised. For being an angel among so many of us ordinary folks, you still don't know the first thing about us."

"Apparently so."

"I told you. No matter how long it takes, I'm going back for her. I'll make Edwin see, if he loves Lavinia the way he makes believe he does, he'll stand aside and let her get on with her true, natural life. With me."

"As for that, Solly, it might be a long time before this ship touches civilized soil."

"They're bound to pass by a whaling station or outpost. They can leave me there and I'll buy my way onto another ship."

"I think Miss Nora Samples Garrett will object to that. Especially coming from you. Your first impression on her was not one of your better efforts."

"I'm not asking her. I'm asking the captain. What's-his-name. Creech?"

"What that unerring Durnley luck, you managed to be rescued by a ship that is wandering the South Pacific, determined to find an island where modern man has never once set foot."

"What addle-witted booby would want such a thing?"

"*Miss* Addle-Witted Booby to you. She's looking to start a community of like-minded malcontents escaping the vicissitudes of modern civilization untainted by gambling, tobacco, or liquor. She hired this ship and its master, Creech, to find such an island. They were hoping yours was it. But then you walked out of the jungle. She'll do you no favors. Best you can hope for is a mention in her autobiography. You should read it. All about her efforts to establish an experimental community based on the teachings of the popular communitarians of the day. Going to be a real page-turner, I'll bet."

"What'll it hurt for her to drop me somewhere so I can catch another ship?"

"Ah, m'lad, you belong to that segment of the population that has fallen entirely out of favor with Miss Samples and her pilgrims."

"Sailors?"

"Men. She might prefer to feed you to the sharks just to make a point."

"I have a way with women, as you might recall."

"Your charm will not work on Miss Samples. She is impervious to a charmcicle like you.?

A hatch banged open over the companionway and an even brighter shaft of light lanced through the murk of the bilge lantern's glow. A foot reached down, feeling for the first rung, found it, and was followed by a second foot. A bulky figure backed downward into the bilge, one gingerly step at a time. Missing the last rung, the figure tumbled onto the planking with a cracking thud and a gush of a grunt.

For a long moment the figure lay there, an arm upraised, holding a brandy bottle by the neck.

With another long grunt, Captain Creech sat up, checked the precious bottle for damage and then exclaimed, "I ain't for the knacker's yard yet, by gad! I can still weather a gale and bring m'cargo to port intact!" He took a swig and struggled to his feet.

Creech stooped to avoid the deck beams overhead, with a hand against the bulkhead to steady himself. He moved toward Solomon with a halting step along the half-beams that ran athwartship from rib to rib.

Breathing heavily at the effort, Creech sat down hard, dislodging ballast stones that rattled down to splash in the bilge water. He reclined on one elbow and offered the bottle to Solomon. With thanks, Solomon took a swig, rolling the warm liquid around in his mouth. He was out of practice with the taste and tang of good liquor.

"You were better off staying on that island, mate. Least you was master of yourself. As it is, you'll float around wi' us, like lost Dutchmen, never able to put foot ashore on our own account as long as that harridan bestrides m'decks."

Creech took the bottle, gave a half-salute and knocked back a swallow, then handed it again to Solomon who took another pull.

"Thirty year, man and boy, working these waters. Stood down mutineers, pirates, and storms that'd turn a mainmast to matchwood, and how do I end up? Skulking around my own ship, ordered about by a lubberly female. All on account of money. The sin of avarice, my friend. M'anchor is befouled in its toils." Creech took another slug. "If it weren't for the money, I'd put 'em all ashore on that island of yours and devil take the hindmost."

"Money." Creech took another swallow and stared over the mouth of the bottle. "The root of all kinds of evil."

A shining black pearl floated into Creech's field of vision. It took him a moment to escape the haze of alcohol and focus on the object in front of him. With a cough, he roused himself off his elbows leaning in on the precious drop.

Solomon rolled the nacreous ball between his fingers. "How far you suppose one of these'd take me?"

"A black pearl, by gad."

The pearl, more of a dark, iridescent blue than truly black, fairly twinkled in the lantern light.

Creech's eyes flicked toward Solomon. A smile broke over his puffy, reddened face. He scrambled to his feet with renewed vigor and skill, leaving Solomon holding the bottle. Creech scrambled up the ladder and out the hatch above.

"You may have bought yourself a mutiny, Solly."

On deck, Creech strode toward the steersman at the wheel.

"Prepare to come about," he shouted, "hard a lee!" Creech turned to the first mate. "See to your yards, you lobster! I said come about."

Creech cuffed the steersman. "I said hard a lee," then took the wheel and spun it, slapping at the handles, the tiller ropes purring through the slot and around the barrel.

The ship heeled over hard as it made its turn, the passengers slipping and sliding to starboard as the vessel came around in its turn to port.

From among the pilgrims, Miss Samples hauled herself hand-over-hand along the man-ropes, climbing the ladder to reach the after-deck where Creech stood firmly fixed.

"Where do you think you're taking us," demanded Miss Samples.

"Back to civilization," said Creech, with a leering sort of smile.

"I gave no such order." Miss Samples turned to the steersman. "You will return this ship to its original heading."

"Belay that!" Creech kept his eyes fixed on Miss Samples. "Giving orders when the captain ain't been properly relieved of duty could be considered mutiny, Miss Samples. That could land you in irons until I hand you over to an American consul."

"You forget the sponsor of this voyage, and the source of your income."

"I've decided on a new course."

"You're drunk."

"We shall sail back to America."

"America?" she screeched.

"We're bound for San Francisco," Creech called out to the ship's company.

A cheer went up from the men.

Solomon, now free, climbed the companionway onto the afterdeck. Miss Samples glared first at Solomon and then at Creech.

"I object, Mister Creech," sputtered Miss Samples, "I most stren-uously object!"

"Miss Samples, you will confine yourself to the common areas of the ship for the rest of the voyage."

"You have no idea," said Miss Samples, her teeth clenched, her lip rippling over each word, "how strenuously I can object,"

"I can't possibly imagine, Miss Samples. You will confine yourself to your *cabin* for the rest of the voyage."

"Then I shall object in the strongest possible terms you can imagine in that limited intellectual capacity of yours, Mister Creech!"

Creech's smile broadened.

"That, Miss Samples, I can imagine."

"Mutiny? Mutiny?" Miss Samples' voice wafted up from the bilge, through the open hatch midships.

Standing at the rail with Griffin, Solomon enjoyed the race of wind across his face. "Not sure I feel quite right about a lady chained up like that."

"I paid for this ship!" came Miss Samples' voice.

"For what it's worth, she put up quite a struggle," said Griffin. "Portuguese sailor named Luca drew the short straw to fit Miss Samples with leg irons."

Climbing up from below decks, Luca collapsed on the deck.

"Probably the only time in her life she wished to get her hands on a man's private parts."

The way Luca clutched himself and rolled on the deck, it looked like she might have.

Griffin left the *Samantha* long before they raised the coast of California. Solomon guessed it must have been the boredom. He'd made it plain to Griffin he wasn't ready to give up the metal shard until he'd claimed Lavinia, and Griffin made it plain he wasn't inclined yet to take it by force. Sometimes, Griffin's laziness amazed even Solomon.

With the ladies confined belowdecks, there was precious little opportunity for natural mischief-making with which Griffin seemed to entertain himself. Solomon missed Griffin—slightly—just getting used to him again. He was beginning to see in Griffin a fellow-traveler, a companion who understood the world Solomon lived in now, as an immortal. It stirred in him a sense of alienation from regular folks, and a peculiar vulnerability. All the time he'd spent on the island thinking on it hadn't helped to sort it out in his mind.

When Solomon reached San Francisco, he cashed in another pearl and bought a fine room in the Parker House on the Portsmouth Plaza, across from the City Hall. Solomon's odd combination of ragged dress and ready money didn't seem the least bit strange to people accustomed to sudden wealth plucked up from the earth. It was just that kind of a time.

The town was a milling hive of the men and women swarming the place looking to make their fortunes, either by extracting gold from the earth of the surrounding hills, or extracting gold from the pockets of the miners come down from those hills. The vitality of the town, the gambling, the free-flowing liquor, the women, all of that was a powerful enticement to Solomon.

He ate good meals, drank better whiskey, and laid out a handsome sum for a new suit of clothes. Something he hoped would knock Luther's eye out when he presented himself on the Kantlinghers' doorstep.

Discarding the slops they'd dressed him in aboard ship, Solomon settled on a patterned, broadcloth jacket, dark waistcoat, white shirt, black silk cravat, not too wide, and light brown, almost sandy colored trousers. He bought a pair of half-boots and then spent more than he thought wise on a low-crown, wide-brimmed felt hat. He'd taken a liking to the style after seeing them on the cattlemen selling livestock off the ships crowding the harbor.

Feeling refreshed and re-civilized, Solomon booked passage first on a steamer traveling to Panama at the mouth of the Rio Grande on the Pacific side of the Central American isthmus, then by mule overland to reach Gorgona above the Culebra Cut where the railroad under construction from the Atlantic side had so far reached. From there, Solomon rode the train to Colon on the Atlantic side where he picked up another steamship bound for New York.

During the journey across the isthmus, Solomon hadn't minded the heat, the exotic jungle vermin, the long hours over inhospitable trails before reaching the railhead, or the unceasing rain. What made the five-day journey truly unpleasant was the envious and unrelenting curiosity among the other travelers as to why the blood-thirsty insects of the Panamanian jungles seemed not to bother Solomon at all. Which led to a long and dreary debate among the travelers on whether it was diet, hygiene, or birth order that protected Solomon from infestations. The debate was punctuated by the intrusive curiosity of a missionary doctor traveling with them. He swore a simple examination of Solomon's next bowel movement would settle the argument. From that, the doctor declared, he could prove to the satisfaction of all what made Solomon uninviting to the insect population of the jungle. Solomon was forced to evade the inquisitive doctor whenever the company stopped to answer the call of nature.

Solomon took to slapping at imaginary bug bites for no other reason than to give his traveling companions the satisfaction of seeing him suffer along with them. But it did little to mitigate their envy and annoying resentment toward him that he did not share in their sufferings to the same degree. This, in turn, fed their disdain and their shared contempt for him which continued the whole long way.

Chapter Eighteen

Hudson River Valley – 1850s

SOLOMON SAVORED THE WALK from the river to the front gate of Kantlingher House. Back on the island he'd escaped into this same picture, imagining each step of his homecoming. The kind of homecoming one might expect where the *paterfamilias* of said abode didn't sic the dogs on him.

But here, now, the house in front of him was a decrepit edifice. Much of the fence was broken down, palings missing, the paint weathered away. The trees and grass of the door yard appeared to have been given up to deterioration.

Despite the dilapidation there were a number of horses hitched hip-to-hip at the porch railings, and all manner of wheeled vehicles lined up along the drive. Coming from the main floor was the noise of men at play inside.

This was all Griffin's fault. If he hadn't left Solomon stuck on that island—

"Boy, what a mess, right?" Griffin appeared at Solomon's elbow.

"Would you announce yourself instead of popping in and out like that?"

"You mean like with trumpets?"

"Just stop sneaking up on me."

"Sorry. Out of practice."

Solomon lifted a hand, inviting Griffin to behold his handiwork.

"Now, wait a minute, Solly. You can't put this on me."

The sight for sore eyes Solomon had anticipated so long on that desert island stood reduced to a common eyesore.

"If I'd been here, this wouldn't have happened. You left me stuck on that island while Luther let his son-in-law run this place into the ground. How's Edwin any better than me?"

"You want that list alphabetically or by topic?"

Solomon slapped Griffin's arm. "Look there!"

A woman, lugging a basin of water, came down the steps of the hotel. She carried herself with the same spry and familiar bearing Solomon remembered from the first time he saw Lavinia on the road. The figure was unchanged, her hair pinned up for convenience rather than fashion, and her dress appeared hard used. He didn't need to see her face to know her.

With the carelessness of a common stable hand, the woman pushed through the hitched horses, to dump the water in a muddy patch by the gravel drive.

"Damnation on Edwin and all his kin for putting Lavinia to work in a place like that."

"You don't know what kind of place that is."

From the entrance a man staggered out, grabbing a porch column to steady himself. With the care of a dancer, he planted one foot on the first step, missed the second, and tumbled to the ground. Pulling himself upright, he leaned against the nearest horse to untie it, then tried to mount. The horse turned and trotted down the lane, towing the man still clinging to the saddle skirt, trying to reach his foot into the stirrup. The man danced alongside as the animal trotted down the drive to the road beyond.

"All right. It's clearly not a riding school," said Griffin.

Solomon ignored him and headed for the front door of the hotel.

Inside, the place was all that he'd suspected. The dining room had been knocked into a common grogshop, with a rudely constructed bar taking up one whole wall, tables strewn about, wooden chairs all chipped and scuffed, scattered with no thought of order. Solomon recognized some of them as Esther's best from the parlor.

"There she is." Solomon elbowed and squeezed his way through the convivial crowd of rivermen, carters, and laborers.

The stray curls of her hair blinkered her face from Solomon's view as she handed the basin to the barkeep and took an empty tray from him, continuing through the crowd.

She stopped by a table of men at a game of dominoes, who were braying and slapping tiles each in turn.

As she leaned over the table to gather up their empty glasses, a man of thin mustaches and pomaded hair rested his hand on her backside. She flicked it away and kept her attention on the glassware balanced on the tray.

With a wink and smile to the other men at the table he slapped her buttock, laughing and reaching up to give her a chuck under the chin.

Solomon pushed up his sleeves, forcing his way toward the table where she stood.

"What are you doing?" asked Griffin.

"I don't see Edwin, do you? Someone needs to brace that blackguard."

"You realize he's twice your size. Even with him sitting down you can see that, can't you?"

"I won't tolerate some no-account slickster taking liberties with the girl of my dreams."

Solomon came around behind the slickster and tapped him on the shoulder, hard. The other men at the table stopped laughing.

"I don't take to strangers standing behind me when I'm in the middle of a game." The slickster rested his hands on the table.

"Keep your mind on the game and not on the lady," said Solomon.

The slickster gave a wink to the men around the table, then stood up to face Solomon.

He was indeed larger, but without any of the hardness of body that comes of difficult physical labor. Solomon judged him to be a fancy and a sporting man, more concerned with games of chance and games of evasion and deceit. But—he still had the reach on Solomon.

"You spoiling to fight for the lady's honor?" The slickster cast a grin back at the men around the table. "You look like a fellow in bad need of a drink. How about I buy you that drink? Would that square things?"

"Not for me, and not for the lady, I imagine. You best leave. While you still can."

The slickster pursed his lips and stroked his chin, appearing to give Solomon's proposal serious consideration. "I see. You're asking me to leave."

The men at the table brayed and bawled with laughter, slapping the table and each other.

"I suppose there's nothing for it then," said the slickster, pushing up his sleeves as well.

"I don't suppose there is." Solomon took off his hat and handed it back to where she stood, aware that she'd not moved. What he didn't see was her squint of disbelief.

Solomon stepped back to give himself room to swing.

Koooong!

Struck from behind, Solomon fell forward into the slickster who grabbed him under the arms.

Solomon twisted around to see who'd walloped him. It was Lavinia.

No, not Lavinia, but a face that seemed so familiar somehow. She stared at the beer mug as she rubbed her arm, her face twisted up in astonishment.

Solomon stood frozen, unable to believe he'd mistaken a common grogshop doxy for his precious Lavinia.

Before Solomon could make his apologies and humbly take his leave, the slickster had him by the lapels, lifting him off his feet.

Outside, the horses tied at the rail whickered and snorted at the sound of breaking crockery and cracking wood inside. A bottle flew through the window, smashing onto the porch column, spraying glass. The horses startled and shifted. A hurricane of dinnerware and furniture blasted through the windows, driving the horses into a dancing frenzy, straining against their reins tied to the hitch.

There was a lull, then Solomon flew through the door, hitting the porch deck, and tumbling down the steps onto the hardpacked walkway.

Griffin sat on the porch bannister, reclining against a column. "The science of fisticuffs hasn't improved with you, has it, Solly. It's all that easy island living, don't you know."

Solomon's hat slapped into his chest. He looked up. The girl stood at the top of the steps. She turned to go back inside.

"I mean no discourtesy," said Solomon. "But you're the spitting image of your momma. From behind."

She stopped and turned back, tromping down the steps, unlike anything he'd ever seen Lavinia do.

"I'm sorry. I've completely misjudged you." She stood in front of Solomon, getting in close. "At first, I took you for another lonely drunk in need of attention. I was mistaken." She swept Solomon's legs out from under him, dropping him to the ground again, pulling a hatchet from under her apron. "You're a lunatic." She held the blade under his chin. "You find someone else for your sport, mister, or I'll split you right here and now."

Solomon wasn't afraid of the keen edge under his jaw, but the fury in such beautiful eyes troubled him.

She dragged the blade along his skin as she stepped back, then went up the stairs, two steps at a time, without poise or grace. She was a Kantlingher all right. She had Lavinia's good looks, but she had Abigail's bearing.

Solomon got to his feet, rubbing his hip.

"They say that's Salomé Greene," said Griffin, "Only child of Lavinia and Edwin Greene. Almost eighteen. She's sweet on that greasy fella you let bounce you around the place. Which he owns by the way. You were trying to throw him out of his own establishment. Really comical, if you can stand outside yourself and look on it objectively. Which I can."

"Now wait just a minute. How would *you* know anything about her?"

"We have a sixth sense you mudfoot short-timers seem to lack."

"Like what?"

"Common sense." said Griffin. "I asked someone inside. You'd learn a lot if you tried being a wee bit friendlier."

Back inside, while Solomon was getting a free, professional quality butt-whipping, Griffin elbowed a one-eyed bruiser enjoying the little guy's gymnastical predicament.

"Who is that vision of loveliness?" asked Griffin.

"Over there?"

"Yes."

"Goes by the name a Hatchet. Known to take off a man's toes, fingers, and the occasional ear with a little hatchet."

"I meant the girl."

"So did I. Who'd you think I was talking about?"

"Her, of course."

The one-eyed bruiser leaned over to Griffin. "Her given name's Salomé Greene, but you didn't hear it from me."

"Lavinia and Edwin's little girl? My, my, how she's grown. What is she now? Twenty-five? Twenty-six?"

"She's eighteen. What kinda women you got where you come from?"

"I can tell you we don't have any like her."

"Don't get no ideas, Jack. She's got a fella. That one holding the little squid by his ankles."

The slickster did indeed have Solomon suspended by his ankles, Solomon swinging for all he was worth.

"Mike Scrubb's his name. He owns this place. I guess that's why he don't mind bouncing that little guy off the walls. Since he owns all four of 'em. Ooooh."

Solomon landed against the pillar by the fireplace, knocking the mounted deer head askew.

Back outside, Solomon digested what Griffin was telling him. He slapped his hat against his leg, knocking off the dust, keeping time with the thoughts pounding through his brain.

"If Edwin lost the house and she's still here, where's—where's—" Solomon couldn't finish the thought.

Griffin gave a come-along wag of his head, urging Solomon to follow him.

They walked back along the road where Solomon had first encountered Lavinia. They turned in at that same church, now much larger. They walked past the main building and down the little slope of a hillock to a cemetery enclosed with a fine, whitewashed brick fence.

Solomon didn't hold back, but followed Griffin in, already knowing what he would find.

He stood for a long moment in front of the headstone Griffin pointed out. He'd spun their futures together so often in the smoke of his island campfires.

"Wasn't even three years after I was lost at sea?"

Griffin nodded.

Solomon counted on his fingers.

"You said Salomé was eighteen?"

Griffin nodded again.

Solomon's face emptied. Smoke. Nothing but smoke.

A thought struck him. He counted on his fingers again. Then he counted backward.

A look of fierce anger washed over his face and if eyes could really flash, his would have done so.

He counted on his fingers again, leaving the pinky straight up and damning.

Griffin leaned in. "Math not coming out right? Did you remember to carry the one?"

Solomon held up his pinky.

"You know what that means?" Solomon waved his pinky in Griffin's face.

"An obscure gesture of endearment among Pacific Islanders?"

"That means Lavinia wasn't waiting for me at all. She rushed to do her business with Edwin before the sweat had time to dry on that nag pulling her danged buggy!"

Solomon slammed his hat to the ground and stormed around the headstone.

"Lying, deceiving vixen of vexation. The entire female race. To hell with the whole sisterhood of women! There's not a hair's difference 'twixt her and Eve herself! Luther snapping a cap on me. Not once, but twice. He could've just leave me go. She gave me no thought before or since. And Edwin. Whatever he did, wherever he is, I hope it's hotter'n blazes and Lucifer takes a pitchfork to the seat of his pants."

"There's really no actual practical use for pitchforks in hell, you know."

"If he'd a kept his drawers on, Lavinia'd still be alive."

"You'd just be mad at her some more."

"Where's Edwin now? Where's Abigail? Someone ought to be looking after Salomé. Taking up with those slimy lizards. Can't she see there's not a man-jack among them worth spit? Of course not. She's got her momma's looks, but she's stuck with her daddy's brains."

"Lavinia, Edwin, Luther, women since Eve, and all men with a weakness for feminine beauty," said Griffin. "That pretty much covers everyone."

"Not everybody. I left you out."

"And don't think I don't appreciate that."

"Why didn't you use that common sense you're so dang proud of? Figure out where I got to. Find a way to bring me back. Keep all this from happening."

"But enough about me. What say we complain about Lavinia some more?"

Solomon wasn't listening. He stared at the carving on the headstone.

"I guess it all don't matter in the long run. If you can't trust an angel of the Almighty, then life's about as pointless as lips on a keyhole."

"Does that mean you're ready to give it back?"

Solomon didn't answer.

"You've had a rum go of it, Solly. But it's better this way. Look at the bright side."

Solomon turned, frowning at Griffin.

"All right, maybe not the bright side, but if you think about it, I was actually protecting you. What happened to Lavinia would likely have happened whether you were here or not. Look at all the anguish I saved you. You should be thanking me."

"You have anything, anything at all to do with my being left all alone on that island?"

"At least you shouldn't blame me. There's nothing either of us could do about this."

"I could've given her this damned doo-hickey. Maybe saved her life."

"Then she'd be in the same predicament you are. She'd be watching her loved ones age before her eyes, leaving her all alone. I told you it was one of the drawbacks."

Solomon squatted down in front of the headstone, picked up a stick and drew in the dust around the granite base.

"If it *were* my fault," said Griffin, "I mean if by some perverse stretch of the imagination you could say it was my fault, then I might have been actually saving you from years of heartache. This way, you get it all over with at once. When it comes right down to it, you should look at it that way. That should count for something."

Solomon continued to draw in the dirt, saying nothing.

"Right?"

Solomon continued to brood, drawing with the stick.

"Solly? Right?"

"Guess there's no use crying over spilt milk, is there."

Solomon stood up and threw the stick, watching it spin away in the breeze off the Esopus.

"No, never does any good. Better to get down on your hands and knees and suck it up through a straw. Which isn't dignified no matter how much you need the milk."

"Got to move on, get on with living. Because with this infernal doohickey of yours, I got a lot of it to do, right?"

Solomon turned and headed for the gate.

"What are you going to do?"

"Put this thing to good use."

"You are?"

"Yep. Got me a plan."

Griffin skipped to catch up with Solomon. "Uh, what sort of plan? If you don't mind my asking?"

Solomon stopped and turned to face Griffin full on.

"I plan to get shed of this place. Forget Lavinia. Forget my troubles and join the circus."

"The circus? For the simple, uncomplicated enjoyment of seeing new places and meeting interesting people? I desperately hope."

"Oh, no. For the blood curdling spectacle of seeing a man risking his life every night of the week and twice on Sundays. I'll let them fire me out of a cannon using real cannon balls. Shoot rifle bullets to catch in my teeth. Throw knives at me, feed me to the lions, let crocodiles chew on my head, do a high dive off the highest blamed tent pole into a cup a coffee. I'll be the eighth wonder of the world and everybody from here to Timbuktu will know about the amazing immortalman, doomed to live forever, unable to die."

"That is completely unfair. I am powerless to intervene in the choices your kind makes. I'm not omnipotent!"

Solomon walked away, not looking back as he rattled on. "Angels ought to have pull with somebody. You didn't think to ask around, like, hey, y'all got any idea what's in store for Lavinia, and should I maybe rescue Solomon so he can do something about it because I'm so damned impotent?" Solomon kept walking. "No sir, I've got me a plan and I'm sticking to it."

"Wait. Wait. Jesus, Mary, and Joseph, Solly! Would you just wait!" Griffin clapped his hands over his mouth.

Surprised, Solomon stopped and turned back to Griffin.

They both watched the skies for any meteorological disturbances. There being none, Griffin eased his hands away from his face.

He reached out as if to demonstrate something, but stopped, clenched his fists and chuffed in exasperation. He grabbed Solomon's shirt and yanked him clean out of Time, pulling him along between what looked like high, unending walls of dark rippling water. Solomon couldn't see Griffin, only sensing himself being dragged. It felt a whole lot like being towed behind that damned whale again.

Chapter Nineteen

Hudson River Valley – 1850s

PULLED ALONG, SOLOMON'S BRAIN did the best it could deciphering the information flooding in from all five of his over-worked senses. Passing through the layered waters, he whirled above and along a vast, jumbled, and multi-plane landscape of shadowy features and translucent edifices as if overlaying one on top of the other. Descending, Solomon moved through silent crowds of people, mere shades, indistinct but recognizable as individuals who seemed unaware of his transit through them. He sensed each person as flickers of warmth despite their incorporeality, meshing with the light tap of each heartbeat along his own spine as he filtered through them.

As with dreams, it passed in an instant, but registered so much unfathomable detail. It took several long moments for Solomon to realize Griffin had brought them back to reality, back to a small tavern on the opposite side of town, back on the river.

The stench of stale beer, tobacco, and sweaty men sitting elbow-to-elbow caught up with Solomon's nostrils as his sense of smell re-synchronized in time-constrained reality.

Their sudden arrival drew no response from the other patrons.

The tavern keeper brought two glasses of beer.

"They can see you?" asked Solomon. "I don't want to be sitting someplace, drinking two beers and talking to myself."

"They can see me."

Solomon leaned to the drinker on his right. "Might I trouble you for your walking stick?" Solomon didn't wait for an answer. He plucked it up and swung it through the still insubstantial Griffin, slamming it onto the table.

"I didn't say I was solid." Griffin blew the foam off his beer.

"Hey," called the tavern keeper. "No rough stuff."

"One of these days." Solomon returned the cane.

"That's why I like you so much, Solly. The pure cussed determination. Like me in so many ways."

"I appreciate the drink." Solomon took a long, long swallow, setting down the half-empty glass. "But it won't change my mind."

"You might want to make that last. I'm only good for the one. I'm not on an expense account."

The tavern keeper came over and set a box of dominoes on the table.

"You want to play dominoes for your damned doo-hickey?"

"If you're through feeling sorry for yourself, I'm going to show you something." Griffin poured out the tiles onto the table. "There might be a way to undo what happened to Lavinia."

Griffin flipped the tiles so the pips all faced upward. He cleared a spot on the table and laid down a single tile.

"This is Time, the way you experience it. Time with a capital T. He rested his finger on the tile. "This tile is a reality. A piece of Time. It's happened. All these other tiles here in the pile are probabilities. Some very likely, some very unlikely, some virtually impossible." He picked up two tiles. "I can play either of these two tiles against the one already on the table. These represent eventualities, because I *will* play one or the other. Play this one," said Griffin, laying one down against the tile on the table, "and it is now the present reality. This one, still in my hand, is now a very unlikely probability because there is no place for it." He dropped it back on the pile. "And so Time moves onward. I can anticipate the eventualities because the dominoes are laid down according to the conditions of the game. The rules."

"You said you weren't omniscient."

"I'm not. I see the probabilities and anticipate the eventualities."

"Doesn't that mean you can see the future?"

"I can't see how all of the dominoes will be laid down. I *can* see the eventual dominoes, but they're not the actual future until they happen. Which I can then see."

"You're saying you can see the future after it happens, right?" Solomon gave out with a single snorted laugh.

"You might say I can see when an eventuality, not yet played, has made another probability more likely than any other. I can anticipate how the stream of Time moves toward that eventuality becoming what you would call the Present. But it has to have happened because one of the probabilities prior became an eventuality and made the subsequent probability an eventuality after that. Another domino is laid down and

I can see the probabilities stemming from that brand spanking new reality, and so on, and so on, and so on, happening with blinding speed, until Time reaches its end. If it ever does. Which I'm beginning to think it never will, given how long I've been stuck on this rock, in the hind-end of the universe."

"So, you can't see the future."

"I'm doing you the courtesy of using your inefficient language rather than my own, which would melt your tiny mammalian brain right there in your skull, nothing but gray goo leaking out your ears."

Griffin gave a shuddering shake of his head, then said, "I see the million billion probabilities." He held up a handful of the extra tiles. "Once a probability firms up into an eventuality, but before—" he stopped, seeming to struggle for the right, simple word. Then he smiled, "—before it hardens into fact there's a chance to disrupt it and change the past."

"You don't think the Almighty's going to have a say in me changing the past?"

"Remember what I said about free will? Which, if I may point out, is his idea. Every single mudfoot who ever walked this soggy firmament has the power to completely and utterly change the course of Time and history. Without exception, everyone I've ever met would change history if they could. You actually can, because you don't belong here, in this neck of the woods, Time-wise."

Griffin swept the tiles back into the pile and chose another one. "Luther catches you in Lavinia's bedchamber." Griffin snapped down the tile. "Reality." Griffin picked up another tile. "Probability is that Luther will shoot you. He aims and pulls the trigger. Probability becomes eventuality. The pistol fires. Eventuality becomes reality."

Griffin snapped the tile down on the table and took up another from the pile, holding it up.

"Likeliest probability? Solomon dies in the door yard of Kantlingher House, where there would be weeping and gnashing of teeth." He held the tile, ready to play it, too. "But wait. Solomon is immortal? Oh, no! What ever shall we do?" Griffin pawed through the pile, retrieving a blank-faced tile. He held it up.

"From out of nowhere, the impossible probability of Solomon surviving because he's immortal becomes a plausible eventuality," Griffin snapped the blank tile down onto the table in the line of play, "and thus a reality."

"So. I'm here. How's it make any difference?"

"Because you shouldn't be here. Which means the Time Stream you now inhabit is unstable." Griffin laid down more tiles, none matching suit. "Probability and eventuality aren't matching up the way they should. The artifact that made you immortal also makes it possible for you to leave this stream of probabilities in which you now find yourself and, in so doing, save Lavinia."

"How?"

"Simplest way? You give up that bit of metal, lose its protection, snap back to that point in time when Luther shot you without effect, erasing all of the probabilities that flowed from that becoming reality. That stream of Time ceases to exist." Griffin removed the extra tiles, removing the blank one last.

"You'd get shot, like you did, probably die, given Luther's aim and the quality of medical care available then. But," Griffin laid down another string of tiles running perpendicular to the one on the table, "the probability is very good that Lavinia would be so grief stricken at her culpability she would refuse to marry Edwin, choosing to live a long, unhappy life as a spinster, never know the love of a devoted husband, never enjoy the laughter of her own children, and eventually die a disappointed old maid. And you, Solomon Durnley, will have made that all possible for the woman you love. How does that sound?"

Solomon took longer than he should have before answering. "You know, I don't like the sound of that at all."

"But you save Lavinia. Isn't that what true love's all about? Or am I missing something?"

"If it's all about probabilities, then it's just as probable she marries Edwin anyway and nothing changes."

"I didn't say it was perfect."

"I don't like the odds. At least with me joining the circus, I stay above ground a mite longer."

Solomon stood up. "Thanks for the beer."

"Okay, wait. Consider this. Make sure a non-probability actually occurs, wiping out all other probabilities, changing the eventualities that flow from it, and thus, changing reality."

"How?"

"Do I have to explain everything? Can't you just trust me?"

"No. How?"

Griffin sighed. "Lavinia's flawed decision-making when it comes to men is a trait she will pass on to her daughter, setting a pattern in her eventual choice in the man she takes up with. So, it is highly probable

Salomé will make an equally bad choice."

"Like that Mike Scrubbs fella."

"Him. Or someone like him." Griffin held up the dominoes. "Any number of probabilities. But if you disrupt that, at just the right moment, you choke off that Time Stream and destabilize the event from which it all flowed. Now you can ask."

"How?"

"By marrying Salomé yourself. The eventualities that were laid down by the probabilities so far will hit this completely improbable probability which will create an eventuality that will disrupt Time like waves hitting a seawall, rippling all the way back to the night of the shooting. The past, non-immortal self must now survive, albeit severely wounded for the new probability that Solomon married Lavinia's daughter. Solomon doesn't need the shard to protect him from Luther. The unlikely probability that Solomon survived a point-blank shooting becomes the controlling eventuality, the probability of Solomon surviving to marry Lavinia moves to the head of the line, and the two of them live happily ever after." Griffin spread his hands out to Solomon. "Don't you just love happy endings?"

"Makes my skin crawl, the idea of me marrying Lavinia's own daughter."

"Everything has to be perfect for you."

"Wait. The two of *them* live happily ever after? Who's them?"

"Lavinia and Solomon."

"Me, right?"

"Yes—sort of."

"What'n hell's 'sort of' about it? I'm still me. Aren't I?"

"Of course you are. But it's the mortal Solomon, not the one who became immortal. You, sitting here with all of your memories and feelings from that time to this, cease to exist. The mortal Solomon takes his rightful place in the Time Stream."

"Why can't I just go on—going on?"

"Because your immortality wasn't one of the probabilities. I made that happen."

"You interfered with my free will."

"No, I anticipated the least likely eventuality. You're not in this handful of dominoes. You are a free agent. You enjoy the freest of free will any human being has ever enjoyed."

"I can't say I'm enjoying it all that much."

"Whose fault is that?"

"Well, smart guy, you wink me out, then everybody else winks out with me. How about that?"

Griffin smiled. "Solly, you ever feel like you were living through a moment you already lived through?"

"No."

"Well, some people get that feeling. That's what happens when the Time Stream is disrupted by unnatural manipulations. Nobody *winks out*. They go on, intact, fitting right in with a slightly revised history."

"How often does that happen?"

"It's not like I'm keeping count, you know."

"You're saying the immortal Solomon gets blown out like a used up matchstick and everyone else goes on, fat, dumb, and happy? That's worse than your first idea."

"But it leaves your past self with the girl of his dreams. Doesn't that count?"

"No. And if I had a chance to ask my past self, I know I'd agree with me."

"You don't know yourself quite as well as you think you do."

Solomon pushed back from the table and stood up again. "You'll know where to find me. Just listen for the calliope and follow the smell of the elephants."

"All right, all right, all right! Sit down." Griffin jackhammered his finger at the empty chair. "Indulge me."

Solomon sat.

"I was saving the worst for last." Griffin knocked back the last of his beer. "There is one more way we could try getting you back to Lavinia."

"As me. This me." Solomon pointed to himself, so there'd be no mistake who he meant.

"As your very own self. But it will completely nullify a good chunk of the past and every bit of the future, and that, combined with your surrender of the shard will snap you back to the moment of the shooting, allowing you, the present you, to escape getting shot, and start a whole new branch of time. Same cast of characters, whole different outcome."

Solomon waited.

"Back to our dominoes. Choosing to play this one," Griffin held it out over the table, "and for the very briefest moment of measurable time, it remains an eventuality even though Time is lining up for this one to be reality. We have to disrupt it between the time it goes from probability to reality and, in effect, changing the future as it is in the process of—of—of," again Griffin struggled for a word, "—solidifying into reality."

Solomon stared at the dominoes, his face tense.

"Okay. Just one more before it kills you," said Griffin.

"How?"

"Retrocausality."

"Sorry I asked."

"By changing the spots on the dominoes already on the table."

"If that happens where I come from? Everyone breaks out the firearms and personal cutlery."

"Change the future, by disrupting an eventuality at the moment it's played, which nullifies the probabilities that flowed from the eventuality of Luther shooting you."

"So, I get to keep the doo-hickey?"

"No. You must surrender it. Those two actions will change the future by disrupting the present and so force the past to reorganize in order to line everything up again. Every probability is restored, making possible a whole new bunch of eventualities. Although, it does create an enormous hole in the space-time continuum." Griffin paused, then said under his breath, "Like I'll be able to cover *that* up with a little déjà vu."

"A little what?"

"Just a little reminder to myself," said Griffin. "But if it works, then you'll have had the shard less than a day. They can't complain about that."

"How'm I supposed to know, out of all these dominoes, which one I got to fix?"

"The most obvious. Make sure Salomé chooses the entirely right man of her dreams, after she's chosen the entirely wrong man. Because you shouldn't exist, and you interfere with a choice she's already made? You ensure the most likely probability is nullified, disrupting the previous eventualities all the way back to the night you get shot. But it has to be after she's chosen the wrong man, and before there are children. The moment you make that happen and time starts unraveling, you surrender the shard and ride the deluge all the way back to the night of the shooting."

"How do I know it worked?"

"A great big hole opens up in the space-time continuum and all life is sucked down a drain. You can't miss it."

"What's that look like, exactly?"

"Like all life being sucked down a drain."

"But me, my own self, gets back to Lavinia?"

"Yes. Everything flows backward to that moment. Everything and everybody starts over from that point."

Solomon kicked back his chair. "I've got to find Salomé now."

"Before you go, I should probably mention *why* this idea is the worst of the worst." Griffin began building a tower from the domino tiles.

"Like kittens unraveling your sweater, you can't be a hundred percent sure where it will stop. I mean, we know it will unwind all the way back to that moment you said those fateful words, but, will it keep going, undo anything else? No way to tell. But you can be one hundred percent sure if *two* eventualities are disrupted, the reaction will be like two large angry drunks forcing their way through a single doorway—the fight starts and no one knows what they'll break. So, to be sure we don't do that? You should avoid mentioning the fact you are immortal. Right now, in this time continuum, death is a certainty, and the possibility of human immortality on earth is an impossible dream to every living creature. It is not one of the dominoes."

"But I'm already here, now."

"Like I said, you shouldn't be here. You're traveling in your own lane. The entirety of humanity past and present are moving in the Time Stream where the probability of immortality as a feature of the human condition does not exist on this planet for any of them. Change that while you're changing this one eensie teensie thread, and you could roll up human history all the way back to the Big Bang."

"She won't pay me no mind at all, unless I can prove I'm immortal."

"Fine. You go ahead and do that. But don't come crying to me when all of creation implodes in on itself with a great roaring bang, eradicating all life, crushing every single galaxy with its billions of stars and planets and moons down to a teeny-tiny pinpoint of a cinder so heavy it falls right out the bottom of eternity, and we all wake up tomorrow as pre-animate matter in one great big unfurnished vastiness." Griffin began to arrange the dominoes into a little tower.

"What about the others who had this doo-hickey?"

"Or a piece like it."

"Couldn't *they* have blown up the universe?"

"What do you think? Collecting these is some kind of hobby?"

Solomon didn't move.

Griffin glanced up and then back at his tower.

"You're making me nervous, watching like that."

"The whole universe?"

"Yep. The whole kit-and-kaboodle. The whole ball of wax. The whole nine yards. The whole enchilada. Lock, stock and barrel."

"But—"

"What now?"

"What's to say, me being mortal again, Luther's first shot don't kill me?"

"Until the new eventuality kicks in, you being shot and surviving, you'll remember what's coming. That's more than anyone else in the room will have. That's like having an extra ace up your ass."

Solomon looked around to see who might have heard. "You mean ace up your sleeve."

"I don't play cards much. I just watch."

"Sometimes you're an embarrassment, you know that?

"And you keep looking for an iron-clad guarantee life's going to work out the way you expect it."

"I want to know how it'll work, is all."

"Solly, you have to get it through your thick head there's some things too complex for your thick head."

"I'm a gambler, but I'm not stupid. If I'm staking everything, I need to know if I can trust the fella across the table from me. If I can't trust the fella, I need to know I can trust the cards. Or the dominoes."

"Solly, we've known each other for nearly twenty years. Can't you trust me?"

"When you add up the actual days, I've known you less than two months."

"But doesn't it feel like a lifetime? It does for me."

"I should live so long," said Solomon.

Chapter Twenty

SOLOMON REACHED THE SPOT where the road branched off toward Kantlingher House when he spotted Salomé down the road while she was still far off, heading toward him. She was bonneted, wearing a shawl against the late afternoon chill, and carrying a basket on the crook of her arm. She kept her eyes fixed on the road just in front of her feet, not looking left or right, ignoring the rough beauty of the meadows and trees alongside the road.

For a moment Solomon considered this a divine appointment. He'd settled his mind not to reveal his immortality, and so risk the cosmos. He'd keep that part to himself, though he didn't like giving Griffin his way. Instead, he'd show Salomé the locket, reveal himself to be Lavinia's long lost suitor, and tell her of Lavinia's charge to him to be a blessing to her children wherever he might encounter them on the road of life. Once he got her heart all warm and bubbly, he'd inflame her indignation at Scrubbs—a thorough-going scoundrel—then beguile her with the sunny prospect of a settled life as wife to a fine, upstanding local lad. She'd be so much butter on a hot biscuit. She'd throw over Scrubbs, and fix her affections on the man most directly and dramatically the opposite of that blackguard, Scrubbs.

The flaw in his plan as he saw it, with Salomé getting closer, was the lack of a suitable candidate to whom Salomé might transfer her affections. He wouldn't find such a person among the rapscallions loitering around Kantlingher House.

Surely, somewhere in this whole wide valley, there would be men enough who would count it a privilege and an honor to take a young woman like Salomé to wife. Solomon didn't know any. But he figured they had to be out there. Somebody was responsible for building all the jails and churches.

She was closer now. Without the right object for her deflected affections, he dare not approach her and spend his one good chance. Instead, he stepped off the road into a small wooded patch. Then, realizing his action could be taken for a prelude to waylaying her, he made a great show of examining dandelions along the roadside and admiring the bark on nearby trees.

She walked by. If she'd noticed him or suspected his behavior, she gave no sign.

On the other hand, the sight of a suspicious man on a lonely road wouldn't trouble a woman as handy with a hatchet as Salomé showed herself to be. Any man of nefarious intent should look to his own safety instead.

Once she was far enough up the road, he followed her to the village, keeping well back of her. She still seemed lost in whatever thoughts occupied her the whole long way.

Once they reached the village, Solomon kept one eye on Salomé and the other on the businesses lining the way. He hoped he might draw some inspiration from among the half-dozen or so shops, three or four offices, one hotel, four establishments dedicated to the sale of strong spirits, nine boarding houses, two livery stables, and a wagoner's. Nothing struck him as a ready answer to his predicament.

Watching her among the folks in the village dampened his spirits even further. The women of the village gave Salomé a wide berth, and the men kept their eyes averted, passing without so much as a hat tip. A few would steal a glance back once she'd passed, maybe snicker at her expense. It roused him to anger, an odd mix of jealousy and empathy.

When she turned into Tyburn's Dry Goods, Solomon hurried across to settle himself on a packing case outside by the store front window, to get himself a clear view of the emporium's interior.

Like crabs on a seashore, the other women in the store scuttled out of Salomé's path, keeping their backs to her.

Once or twice, Salomé changed course of a sudden, doubling back, which sent the biddies scurrying like scattered gulls all aflutter. Salomé gave no sign she saw their distress.

Only the clerk behind the counter seemed genuinely delighted to see her. Immediately, the fellow was a disappointment to Solomon. The clerk was a beakish, bespectacled sort of character, wearing an enormous neck-cloth, tied haphazardly, and, in spite of his lanky frame, had buttoned himself into a too-tight waistcoat, revealing a lack of muscularity.

The clerk's smile for Salomé was for something more than the promise of her commerce.

He slipped from behind the counter and came up behind her. He spoke to her, but the glass between them and Solomon reduced the words to a burr.

Other women in the establishment finger-waved and coughed lightly trying to regain the clerk's attention. But he was plainly smitten, his eye entirely fixed on Salomé.

A rather large woman cleared her throat, long enough and loud enough to rattle the storefront glass pane against which Solomon had rested his ear to listen. The clerk paid her no mind, continuing to follow Salomé, continuing to lift merchandise for her consideration, and sneaking great, gusting sniffs of her fragrance when her attention was engaged with some object.

The clerk would have to do, Solomon decided. It was no great stretch for Solomon to see the clerk singing in the church choir, Adam's apple bobbing in time with some ponderous hymn, or frequenting box socials where he'd sit with a plate and saucer perched on his bony knees, or steering clear of anything stronger than elderberry wine, always a sign of good breeding and moral rectitude. Could there be a more distinct opposite to the likes of Scrubbs than this stork of a man?

From behind a curtain at the back of the shop, a short, balding man in sleeve protectors and green eye shade popped out, taking in the situation in a moment. Gesticulating and chirping, he chivvied the clerk away from Salomé and directed him to the large, hacking woman.

The clerk attended to the large woman's questions and complaints, even as he sneaked glances back at Salomé, appealing with his eyes for her to wait a bit longer.

Solomon looked back at Salomé and then at the clerk. Then back at Salomé. Then back at the clerk. Then back at Salomé.

There was no earthly way. Both he and the clerk were deluding themselves.

Salomé turned on her heel and walked out of the emporium.

The move surprised Solomon and his practiced speech fled his brain as she walked past, paying him not a whit of attention.

She was a dozen steps beyond him when he started to follow, seeing her turn into a slender alleyway between Sisler's Boarding House and the office of Dibble and Douglas, attorneys-at-law.

Solomon, catching up, had just turned in at that same alley when the cold blade of her hatchet was again under his chin, setting his skin tingling.

"You've come a mighty long way today, haven't you?" Salomé studied him through narrowed eyes.

"Miz Greene," was all he could manage, afraid she'd try to use her little hatchet and discover she couldn't break the skin. Her resulting confusion would make it impossible to gain her trust. It might even set time rolling backward long before he was ready.

"You didn't get your fill this morning?" The hatchet didn't move.

Despite all that might go wrong, Solomon couldn't help but admire her. In her cool fierceness, she was less like Lavinia and more like her aunt Abigail. He could easily imagine Abigail teaching Salomé the use of edged weapons where men were concerned. Salomé's gaze was firm and fearless. It endeared her to Solomon all the more.

He carefully removed his hat, hoping to buy a little time with the courtesy she so rarely seemed to receive around here.He'd spoke slowly. "Lavinia sent me."

Salomé's fingers tightened on the handle and the pressure of the hatchet edge along his jawline increased. He raised himself ever so slightly on his toes.

"I am here on Lavinia's behalf."

If the neck and shoulders of a woman ever looked like a water moccasin coiling to strike, it was those on Salomé.

He held up his hand, his fingers clenched, so she could see.

Her whole being seemed to tighten. Solomon could see in her eyes, she was choosing where to strike—until the locket dropped from his fist, dangling at the end of its chain.

A sneer curled her lips. "I don't take gifts from addle-witted men." Then her eye fixed on the pictures in the locket. She took hold of the open case and lifted the pictures closer.

"Lavinia." She glanced up at him. She continued to hold herself in a terrific tension.

"I gave one just like it to Lavinia on her w-w-wedding night." Solomon stumbled over those wicked words.

"I've seen it." She lowered the hatchet.

"Lavinia kept it?"

"No. It was among Abigail's things when she died."

"What was she doing with it?"

"I don't know. She died when I was a baby." She pointed at his picture. "This is you?"

"Of course it's me. Who else could it be? I'm supposed to carry around the picture of my beloved with some other fella?"

"You're the one Grandpap had to chase away the night Lavinia was married?" The skepticism returned to her voice.

"I gave her the locket and promised I'd watch over her ch-ch-children," the word leaving a bad taste in his mouth, "wherever I might find them."

"Why show yourself now?"

He was about to tell her of being lost at sea, dragged half-way round the world by a whale, washed up on a deserted island, lived like a Hottentot for all these years, then finally rescued by a passing ship. But he could see how the details might strike her as a mite far-fetched and undermine any scrap of trust he'd managed to build with her so far.

"I'm here now. I've come a long, long way, and for Lavinia's sake, I've got to speak my mind about that Scrubbs fella."

He could see her goodwill evaporating.

"Lavinia was the finest, dearest, sweetest, kindest, most good-hearted woman ever drew breath, and I know she'd want me to tell you, straight up, Mike Scrubbs is no good. You'd do well to have nothing to do with him."

Solomon paused. It sounded better in his head when he'd practiced it.

"Because he gave you a thrashing in front of God and everybody?"

"Because he's a scoundrel and as big a rascal as you'd ever hope to meet. Not that you'd hope to meet a scoundrel or a rascal." This wasn't going as he'd planned.

"You might have saved yourself the train fare. He's asked me to marry him, and so I will. Tomorrow, as a matter of fact. And if that don't strike every single living soul in this tiny town right in the eye, I don't know what will."

"Tomorrow!"

"Tomorrow. And then I'll be done with this place for good and all."

Solomon's grim concern melted off his face, brightening into a great smile of delight.

"Then I'm just in time."

"Just in time? I don't think you should show your face anywhere near him."

"This is as good a piece of news as I've had in—ever."

"Good news? After telling me to have no truck with him? You're moonstruck." She edged around him, back onto the sidewalk, her hatchet at the ready.

Solomon hustled to follow her, catching her by the arm.

"It means your choice is made and the time is set. It's become an—an eventuality," said Solomon, remembering the word Griffin used.

"Now, if you don't marry him, it'll fix everything."

"The only way everything is fixed is if I *do* marry him."

"You don't understand. It'll set everything right."

"No, *you* don't understand. Let go of me!" She took the hatchet in her left hand and raised it.

"Mike Scrubbs keeps a wife in Kingston!"

She stopped struggling. "What did you say?"

Scrubbs might not be an actual bigamist, but Solomon knew his type. It wouldn't be wide of the mark "He's got another wife in Albany." Might as well pile it up high.

"He does not." But the look on her face told him she could easily believe it was so.

"A man of Scrubbs' character is not a man Lavinia would want you to marry." The look of dismay on Salomé's face gave Solomon a twinge of regret. Still, it was for the good of all.

"He has to marry me. Now." Her breath had become choppy, shallow panting. The dismay became fury.

"A girl your age? There's plenty a time for settling down."

The clerk appeared behind Salomé.

"Is this—gentleman annoying you, Miss Greene?" he asked, already flinching away from the expected rain of fists.

Salomé ignored the clerk.

"I have to get married," she said, as if that was all the explanation Solomon should need.

But Solomon, more intent on his own scheme than her predicament, babbled on. "Fellas are like horsecars. There's always another coming along right behind."

"Who—in this whole town—who would that be?" Salomé was not expecting an answer.

"Him." Solomon pointed at the clerk.

"Me?"

"Him?"

"He's quite the fellow of quality," said Solomon. "Aren't you?"

"I don't drink, chew, or play cards—maybe a little whist, but not to excess," said the clerk.

"I know for a fact, this fella sings in the choir, is good to his mother, won't spend on horses. What more could you want?"

"No man of quality in this town—"

"Wait." Solomon held up a hand to Salomé and turned to the clerk. "Are you married?"

"No."

"You want to be?"

"To whom?"

"To her."

As one, Salomé and the clerk spoke together. "I do."

Salomé yanked him along, hauling him down the street, the clerk bounding, trying to get in step with his bride-to-be.

Satisfied, Solomon watched them disappear down the street, weaving in and out of horse and foot traffic. He could, if he put his mind to it, charm an alligator right out of its skin.

Solomon looked up at the sky to see if the cosmic chaos had begun.

A little cloudy with a slight breeze coming off the river, but nothing out of the ordinary. Certainly nothing like Griffin described.

Solomon returned to the tavern and stood over Griffin who was still at the table, having re-built his castle of dominoes.

"So. How'd it go?"

"I don't see all life being sucked down a drain yet."

Griffin raised up and looked toward the windows. "Me either."

"I stood out there waiting. I didn't see anything."

"Hmmm. Whatever could the hold up be?"

Outside, the rattle of speeding wheels racing along, the whinny of horses, the cursing of men, and the shouts of women exploded just beyond the tavern doors. Men leapt up from their chairs and crowded the door and windows of the tavern.

"Maybe that's it." Griffin hopped up and joined the gawkers in the doorway. Solomon followed, pushing past them, out onto the sidewalk.

They were just in time to see a buggy flash past, Salomé a wild-haired madwoman at the reins, cracking the whip at the horse's hind-quarters for all she was worth. The clerk gripped the footrest and side bar, holding on for dear life.

Bootsteps pounded along the sidewalk of boards. An old man waving his hat came at them, calling out as he ran along, "Willard Wertz shot Mike Scrubbs in the back! Willard Wertz shot Mike Scrubbs in the back!"

"Wertz? Who's Wertz," asked Solomon.

"Willard Wertz. He's the clerk you fixed up with Salomé," said Griffin. "You didn't think to get a name before marrying her off to him?"

"How is it you know his name?"

"I told you. I see all one hundred million billion of the probabilities. His name popped up in there somewhere."

The drinkers grabbed at the old man, demanding to know what just happened.

"Somebody told Mike Scrubbs that Hatchet Greene was at the Justice of the Peace marrying Willard. He dragged her out, kicking and screaming, and Willard shot him in the back. Then Willard went and cleaned out the safe in Tyburn's Dry Goods and high-tailed it for Californy! He took Hatchet Greene with him. A posse's being got up to chase them down."

The men, well-liquored up and in need of a diversion, ran to join the posse.

"Well. Now we know what the hold up is."

"But he was a fine, upstanding fella."

"You need to watch where you're pointing those arrows there, Cupid. Look before you let fly."

"You could've warned me."

"That clerk might turn out all right—unless they hang him."

Solomon wasn't listening to Griffin. "They'll say it's my fault."

"Who?"

"The whole lot of them. Sitting on their clouds looking down on me, like I'm some kind of scoundrel, selling Salomé that pig in a poke."

"Well. You kind of did."

"You're the one who said it would fix things."

"I made some suggestions. Oh, come on. Look at it this way. Now she won't go through life blaming herself for her bad luck with men. She's got you."

"How's it going to look, Lavinia asking me to be a blessing and the first thing I do is saddle Salomé with that chicken-necked miscreant?"

"You're off the hook. You never agreed to be a blessing."

"I most certainly did."

"No, you did not. You suggested they get a dog instead."

"I have to find her. I have to tell her."

"About the dog?"

"I have to tell her it's not my fault."

"You know, if you do manage to roll back time, that little fact of you screwing up her life would evaporate with everything else as reality re-sets itself."

"I don't want Lavinia thinking it for one single minute. I won't give anyone the satisfaction of saying 'we told you so.' "

"Yeah, well, good luck getting close to Salomé after this. Wouldn't you rather quit while you're behind, and take your chances with Luther again?"

"You know what I've come to appreciate about you?"

"My sunny disposition?"

"Your singular knack for being useless and unnecessary in so many clever and original ways."

Solomon left Griffin and bolted down the street after the buggy.

"Thank you, Solly. That means a lot coming from you," Griffin shouted after him.

Chapter Twenty-One

California – 1850s

SOLOMON SET OUT FOR THE CALIFORNIA GOLDFIELDS, the most logical place for someone on the run, someone looking for a place to disappear.

Griffin, having made it plain that all available modes of overland transportation were unsatisfactory, left Solomon to find his own way west.

Solomon headed down to Philadelphia by schooner, then westward by rail, stage, canal boat, steamer, and sometimes foot, until he reached St. Joseph on the Kansas-Missouri border. He arrived bone-weary and irritable, his immortality doing nothing to relieve the dull ache and mind-numbing monotony of cross-country travel.

In St. Joseph, he joined up with a wagon train of settlers headed for Utah and latecomers to the gold rush headed for San Francisco, facing more miles of heat, dust, jouncing, and the pervasive smell of draft animals worked to a slow, marinating lather.

Once he reached San Francisco, he headed straight up the Sacramento River to the gold camps.

Having no clear plan how to find Salomé, Solomon figured to go from camp to camp looking for the clerk's familiar beak, or asking if anyone heard about a newcomer by the name of Willard something-or-other, traveling with a young woman named Salomé.

Seemed easy enough. That is, until he made the first camp. Every man he saw was bearded, sun-baked, dirt-streaked, and wearing a face of dogged hope scarred by work-weary reality.

All Solomon got from the miners in the way of answers were scowls, growls, and pistols pointed at his vitals. The miners were a hard-fisted and closed-mouthed lot.

At yet another small camp of a dozen or so tents, Solomon studied the miners working their claims, strung out along the water's edge.

Most worked in pairs or threes, with cradles and sluice boxes, with rifles or pistols close at hand. Solomon spotted one lone miner away from the others, squatted down, swirling water and gravel in a pan. He had no sidearm or long gun within reach. Solomon decided to approach him.

Solomon stood over the miner and tapped him on the shoulder.

"Pardon me, friend. I'm looking for a skinny fella and his wife, a woman by the name of Salomé."

The miner stood up and turned to face Solomon.

"Then you've come to the right place," said Griffin.

Solomon stumbled backward.

"I told you not to go sneaking up on me!"

"Hey, who tapped who on the shoulder? Who snuck up on who, Solly? I was here first."

The miners around them stopped to look at Solomon.

"Oooh, better smile and make nice. They think you're a claim jumper."

Solomon smiled for the miners.

"Now say you're sorry for sneaking up on me."

"No," said Solomon, incensed at the excess.

"What's that, claim jumper? I couldn't quite make out what you're saying?"

The miners grabbed up pistols and pickaxes.

Solomon gritted his teeth. "I'm sorry for sneaking up on you, *friend*." He stretched his lips into the approximation of a smile.

"No harm done." Griffin picked up a bit out of his pan, holding it up to the sunlight "I don't see the appeal. This stuff's worthless where I come from." Griffin flicked the bit back into the river, dropping the pan, and heading downstream, as the listening miners swarmed the spot.

"You know where they are?" Solomon trotted after Griffin.

"Of course I do. You certainly took your own sweet time getting here."

"Where are they?" Solomon stumbled on the broken earth, trying to keep up.

"They're not here."

"Then what're you doing here?"

"They *were* here."

"Where are they now?"

"They're not here anymore." Griffin spoke more slowly, enunciating carefully.

"So then where are they?"

"Which one?"

"Salomé and that clerk of hers!"

143

"Make up your mind."

Solomon grabbed for a handy length of wood, an impulse of his frustration.

"All right. They were both here before, but they're not here now," said Griffin. "Willard staked a claim just about a mile up around that bend there. Worked it until the little girl was born."

"Little girl?"

"I think it was a little girl. Yeah, a little girl. Did I mention that Salomé was in the 'family way' when she came west with Willard?"

"No, you did not."

"She was. It was all too much for Willard. He went barking mad. Ran around wearing nothing but a night shirt, passing out acorns saying they were gold nuggets."

"Where is she now?"

"She headed downriver for San Francisco."

"I was just there."

"Then what are you doing here?"

Solomon marched past Griffin. "You might've told me before I came all this way."

"Oh. Hadn't thought of that." Griffin followed Solomon. "Where are you going?"

"Back down to find her."

"What for? Willard turned out to be as bad as Scrubbs. Which she has you to thank for, by the way. It's over. Time marches on. You lost your chance."

"I still got some cards to play."

"What cards."

"You said there was a daughter?"

"Right."

"Still a Kantlingher, right?"

"Aren't you tired of your quest for lost love? I know I am."

Solomon whirled around to face Griffin. "It's more than that now. I don't want Luther, Abigail, and Lavinia—especially Lavinia—sitting on their clouds scowling down on me for wrecking the lives of their kin."

"Solly. There's something important you need to know."

"What?"

"You can't actually sit on clouds."

"You know what I mean. Wherever they are, the whole blessed family is watching me, thinking I'm some kind of monster."

"Oh, no, Solly. Not a monster. Arrogant, yes. Self-centered, yes.

Indifferent to the suffering of others, maybe. But not a monster."

"Indifferent? How?"

"Willard, for instance. Had a nice little career ahead of him, until you came along. Or how about Nora Samples Garrett, who might still be in the brig back on the *Samantha* for all you care."

"Fine, fine, all of them, too. I may not have done so good a job convincing Salomé. But, she's got a daughter, you said."

"So?"

"So—Salomé's just as likely to pass on that same bad judgment about men as Lavinia did. You said."

"I suppose. If I said it."

"You did. So. I still got me some cards to play."

"That'll be years from now."

"I can wait. Thanks to your doo-hickey. Unless you got any better ideas how I can put things to rights."

Griffin didn't answer, so Solomon continued down the mountain, Griffin following as if yanked along with a rope.

Solomon and Griffin parted company over the purchase of a mule.

Solomon bought beans, dried beef, tinned peaches, a little bit of flour, salt, and a twist of tobacco for the journey down out of the hills. He also bought a mule, figuring that once he reached Sacramento he'd sell or trade it for passage on one of the steamers that made the trip to San Francisco.

He and Griffin were just up from the river, out back of the wood-and-canvas structure that served as a store selling supplies to the prospectors still coming into the goldfields.

"Buy me that one." Griffin pointed to a large beast at the end of the string of animals tied to a rope secured between two trees.

"Buy your own."

"We don't carry money. You keep forgetting that."

"I'm not spending good cash money on a mule for you. You don't need one."

"You think I'm going to run alongside you all the way down the mountain?"

"I won't go faster than a trot on the flat. Satisfied?"

"After all I've done for you."

"Oh, don't get so pouty. You can ride behind. You don't weigh anything when you put your mind to it as I recall."

"You won't catch me riding double on some old mule, looking like a farmboy coming in from the sticks for a hoe-down."

The skinner came back leading the mule, so Solomon didn't say anything more. The skinner handed the reins over to Solomon. When Solomon turned back, Griffin was gone.

As Solomon traveled, alone with his thoughts, he decided to tell Salomé about Griffin.

He was convinced she'd never understand all that business about Time Streams and dominoes and changing eventualities and snapping backward through history—he hardly grasped any of that himself.

Griffin was slippery, for an angel, and Solomon didn't trust him any further than he could pitch him. But it made sense for Solomon to keep the immortality a secret. She'd never trust a word he said if he came off sounding like a lunatic.

But—angels, on the other hand? No great secret there. Everyone knew about angels. Griffin never said a word about keeping that part secret. Solomon figured the word of an angel would carry more weight.

Solomon stepped off the steamer at the Green Street wharf on the northeastern shore of San Francisco. He walked to the head of the dock past the passenger shed and stacks of cargo heaped for loading, making his way to the foot of Green and Vallejo streets.

Looking up at the town that had bloomed in only a few short years all over the hills overlooking the bay, Solomon wondered how in blue blazes he was going to be able to pick out one soul from that mass of humanity. Much less in a town where anonymity could be as precious a commodity as gold?

First, Solomon needed a place to hole-up, alone, away from the scrutiny of the insatiably curious, which, as he'd learned on the whaler, wasn't likely to serve him well.

He steered clear of the tents and shanties that proliferated every which way he looked. He avoided the floating hulks in the bay which had been abandoned by masters and crews smitten with gold fever, and commandeered by squatters for cheap lodgings. He needed to be anonymous, but he didn't have to be miserable while he went about it.

He would have preferred the ease and convenience of the numerous hotels that sprang up to serve the flood of cash customers bent on digging their fortunes out of the hills or out of each other. But in public accommodations of that sort he'd have to put up with the curiosity aroused by any new face with money.

So he kept to the boarding houses in and around the Embarcadero, losing himself among the sailors, longshoremen, carters, and warehousemen working the docks along the bay. He might be a stranger, but he'd be an unremarkable stranger.

Figuring he had the means, he insisted on a room and a bed to himself.

By mid-afternoon, Solomon resigned himself to sleeping under a wagon or in a woodpile. Privacy was simply not to be had, at least not on his terms.

The sun was low over the water, and a chill was moving in off the bay. He'd decided to try one last house before settling down to snooze al fresco. As with all the others, the landlady stood in the doorway, her palm under his nose for the first week's rent, in advance, in gold coin, nugget, or dust. She would see the color of his money before she let him set foot inside, and he wasn't about to hand over his money without being certain of a room and a bed to himself.

"Well, I am danged sorry, your highness," said the landlady. "Nobody told me Prince Albert was in town."

"I don't cotton to sleeping in another fella's pestilence," said Solomon.

"I run a clean house, mister!"

"You're telling me there's no place a man can have a bed to himself?"

With a shift of her silvery blue eyes and a cool twist of her hairy lip, she sized him up again, then said, "There's one place you might try. Hudson's. Up on Vallejo Street. North side. Big old porch and a double stair. Can't miss it. I'm sure they'd make a place for a delicate fella like yourself." She leaned in at him. "You say Lotti Bumstead sent you, and they'll fix you right up." She smirked, closing the door hard in his face.

Before Solomon stepped back from the door, an old man sitting on a bench against the railing, reading a paper, hissed at him.

"Mind yourself," he said, not lowering his paper. "That house's a rough place. Mostly sailors and miners, where a fella too much in his cups might find himself shanghai'd by crimps stealing men for ships bound for China."

"Much obliged, neighbor. I've had my fill of the sea." Solomon started down the steps.

"If the landlady at that house don't feed you to the crimps, she's just as likely to brain you as look at you. Terrible temper. She's lightning quick with that hatchet of hers. She'll use it if a fella so much as looks crossways at her."

Solomon stopped.

"That landlady got a name?"

"They call her Hatchet Ann, but not to her face."

"How do I get there?" Solomon hoped there didn't exist two such women favoring hatchets.

"One street over and three up." The old man and went back to his reading. "Don't say I said anything."

It was a short walk, over unpaved and mostly dry roadway to reach Vallejo, a graded dirt stretch of road running uphill, a high row of houses on the north side and a low row on the south. A boarded walkway ran along the line of buildings to the north.

After about fifty or sixty paces he saw a likely structure, with a porch larger than its neighbors, reached by a narrow flight of stairs running up from either end of the frontage and meeting in the middle of the porch at the top.

He'd paused at the foot of the steps. If it turned out Hatchet Ann was Salomé, he granted that she might still be smarting over the advice he'd given her about that clerk.

Reaching the doorway, he considered maybe it wasn't her. Then, again, maybe it was and maybe she wouldn't recognize him.

But it was. And she did.

The hatchet flashed across the room and landed in the door frame, biting deep into the wood.

Salomé howled, frustrated.

Every other man in the place, dropping newspapers and smokeables, made haste for the door, crowding out around Solomon, leaving him standing alone. Salomé kept to the other side of the room, having put the horsehair sofa between herself and Solomon.

He pulled the hatchet from the woodwork, rubbing some of the splintered wood back into place. He held it out to Salomé, handle first, then pulled it back.

"Lemme say one thing."

"I don't want to hear a single, solitary word out of you."

"I admit that clerk fella might've been a mistake."

"Not a blessed word!" She leaned over the back of the sofa, trying to reach the hatchet handle with a swipe of her hand.

"It wasn't my fault." He inched the hatchet handle out toward her.

"So help me, I'll cleave you top-knot to navel." Salomé grabbed the hatchet from him.

"I was led on by this angel, see?" He shut his eyes against the coming blow.

But it didn't come.

"What?"

He opened his eyes and straightened up. She was still standing there, hatchet poised.

"If I'm going to brain a man, the least I can do is make sure I heard his last words rightly."

"There's this angel."

"An angel, now?"

Grateful for the opening, Solomon rushed on. "This angel told me how I could set right all the bad that's happened to Lavinia, to me, to you, everybody since that night she ran off with Edwin."

"I'm sure he did."

"He explained it all. Using dominoes." Solomon warmed to her reasonable attention. "Even with the dominoes, I didn't understand it all."

"Who can, when you're talking to an angel."

"His name's Griffin."

"You can't help yourself, can you?" Salomé folded her arms, resting the hatchet on her bicep. "I was so mad for what you did, I could've chewed iron nails. But seeing you again, now, it's all clear. You can't help yourself."

"There's a chance for me to make things right."

"Lost at sea," she went on, not listening. "Turning up after all these years."

"The angel said—"

"I don't know if you're flesh and blood," she went on.

"—if I change who you're fixed to marry, I can set time rolling backward—"

"Or a ghost, or a creature from Hades itself got up to look like that two-faced scoundrel. But it's plain, whatever you might be, you're doomed to walk the earth spreading misery. Nothing but a hex."

"His name's Griffin, by the way—hex?"

"If you're flesh and blood, maybe you could use a drink." She pointed behind herself with the hatchet, toward the archway curtained off from the rest of the room. "Sit yourself down and rest a spell." She held back the curtain.

He moved through the arch, keeping an eye out behind himself, but she had tucked the hatchet away into the folds of her skirts.

Once through the arch, she let the curtain drop, flicked her hand toward the chair set against the wall underneath a light sconce. She went to a cabinet and poured up a small whiskey.

He sat down, dropping his haversack by the chair.

"What's all this about a hex?"

She handed the short glass of brown liquor to him.

"You show up unannounced, laying claim to Lavinia as your bride. Not so much as a how-do-you-do for Abigail. Luther, fed up with your audacity, shoots you right before her eyes. You run off to sea and get yourself pulled overboard by a whale, never to be heard from again." She hiked skirts up over her knee and putting her foot up on the arm of the chair, taking hold of the wall sconce above his head to steady herself.

"All I ever meant to do was set things right." He took a quick drink.

"Bad things happen because of you. Wherever you go. Whether you mean it or not. For your lost love." She sneered at those words. "Maybe you are flesh and blood. Maybe you're not. Either way? I don't care to know."

With that, she yanked down hard on the branch of the wall sconce, shoving against the back of the chair with her foot, flipping the chair backward through the hole that opened up in the paneling.

Solomon fell down a short shaft and landed in the coal bin, hard, flat on his back.

Solomon laid there in the dark, staring up at the small light above disappearing as the panel closed.

What in hell was Salomé thinking? Solomon knew for a fact, just looking at himself in a mirror, he hadn't changed a whit. She knew the locket. She'd seen his picture. It should be obvious he was who he said he was. He was not some shade or specter out to haunt her. How could she not see he was as solid as herself? Certainly no hex.

Solomon sneezed hard, the coal dust tickling his nostrils.

Hard hands yanked a burlap gunny sack over Solomon's head and snugged it tight around his neck.

"This un's still squiggling," said a great big dullard of a voice. "The fall didn't knock him out."

"Then hit him again," said an oily weasel of a voice.

There was that familiar *kloong* as a solid wooden object connected with Solomon's skull bone.

"Not so hard!" said the oily weasel.

"He's still squirming," said the big dullard.

"We're out our ten bucks, you stove his head in. You want Hatchet Ann carving her share outta your hide? Hunh? Do ya?"

Unconsciousness being the better part of valor for the moment, Solomon flopped over, his limbs splayed.

"That's some hard headbone," said the big dullard. "Took him a whole minute to realize he's out cold."

The big dullard flung Solomon over his shoulder, carting him through the back alleys to a wharf of the Embarcadero. Solomon recognized the smell of the brackish water around the docks and the sounds of wood, canvas, and rope in cacophonous movement along the quay.

As soon as he felt the sway of the gangplank under the man toting him aboard whatever ship they'd found, he slipped his folding knife from his hip pocket, pulling the blade open with his mouth through the gunny sack, and then slit the man's belt. The man's britches dropped to his ankles, tripping him headlong, dropping Solomon into the murky water of the bay with a splash.

Solomon struggled to cut himself free of the wet bag over his head as the two men used boathooks to probe and fish for him. Their burbled curses reached down through the water to him. Finally getting free, he swam the length of the vessel and bobbed up between the ships, keeping close to the hulls until they were out of sight.

Solomon paddled under the dock and hauled himself up out of the water, then made his soggy way back to Hudson's.

But Salomé was gone, and from what the men watching said, she left in a panic. She, along with her little tyke, Edith, had vamoosed.

"Took only what she could throw in a valise," said one fellow.

"Good riddance," said another.

No one had any clue, nor any desire to know, which way she went.

Solomon retrieved his haversack from the room behind the curtain and left the men standing there, swapping their worst Hatchet Ann stories, now free from the fear of her reprisal.

Solomon took the steps two at a time, bounding down to the street, the night having finally closed in, the moon not yet high enough to light the way. To catch her, he would run all night if he had to. Problem was, he didn't know which way.

Solomon walked downhill toward the lit part of the town, where they'd just started lighting the streetlamps. He figured she'd want to put as much distance between herself and him as quickly as she could.

From the waterfront he could hear the churning and chuffing of the steamers still working the waterways after sundown.

She wasn't likely to have booked passage for a sea voyage. She'd still be sitting in the passenger shed waiting to go aboard. She'd be too impatient for that.

Nor would she head back to the goldfields. It was a good bet she had her fill of that. So it seemed likely she wasn't on a steamer heading west to Sacramento or south toward Stockton.

That left the stage lines. Anything heading north or west would have to cross the bay on one of the ferries. That wouldn't be fast enough to suit her. So it would be something headed south, and right away.

He made for Portsmouth Plaza where he'd found transportation eastward the last time he'd been here, after being rescued from that island in the Feejees.

From the clerk selling tickets, Solomon learned there had indeed been a stage headed south for San Jose. It was long gone on the roughly nine-hour trip. And, yes, the agent remembered the woman Solomon described, asking which-a-ways to Yuma. Paid in gold dust, he recalled. She'd been lucky to find something leaving today. There was nothing more to be had until tomorrow afternoon. Which left Solomon stranded at least until next morning when he could buy a horse and take up the chase again.

"You could still catch her," said the ticket agent. "There's bound to be breakdowns between here and San Jose. Bandits between Monterey and Los Angeles. And between San Diego and Yuma, who knows? Add Indians to all the other troubles. They might raid a depot or waylay one of the coaches. Everything stops until the army can sort things out. So you've got plenty of time." The agent looked from side to side, checking to see if he'd been overheard. "But don't tell anyone I said that."

All Solomon could do now, was wait for the next stage leaving San Francisco.

Chapter Twenty-Two

The Territories – 1850s

SOLOMON WAS ON THE NEXT STAGE out of town, more than a day behind. The trip was long, but unremarkable. Of course there was the bad weather, the road grime covering everyone and everything, the constant bone-shaking, the changing of the teams every fifteen or twenty miles, being told to get out and walk alongside to lighten the coach while the mules rested after a bad stretch, or pulled the empty vehicle up or down particularly steep hills, not to mention the occasional mudhole or gully into which the driver had steered the coach, requiring all of the passengers to help push it free.

Solomon couldn't figure why Griffin didn't want to come along. They were making such good time.

Until they got to Yuma.

Primarily an army post guarding the river crossing for freight and the mails, there was no longer the great number of passengers making their way to the goldfields. Even fewer passing through, heading back east.

The stock handler unhitched the mules from the arriving coach even as the passengers were stepping off. Solomon, first down, ran to the relay station's common room as the worn-out animals were led to the corrals for feed and water.

Inside, the station agent had been sweeping around the tables, and setting chairs for the arriving passengers, few of whom would take advantage of the meal.

"Did a young woman traveling alone with a little girl pass through here?" asked Solomon.

The station agent stopped, chewed, spit a long string of tobacco juice, then said, "Quick tempered cuss? Ain't grateful for the food put before her? Likes to settle disputes with a hatchet?"

"Yes."

"Through here two days ago, headed for Tucson, and good riddance." He spit another long string, barely getting it clear of his bottom lip. "You hungry?"

Solomon had watched the black dollop arc and land on the well-sprinkled floor between the tables.

"Won't be for a long while yet," said Solomon. "When's the next stage east?"

"Ain't." The station agent kept sweeping, smearing tobacco juice and dirt around the floorboards. He didn't offer anything more, so Solomon went back outside. He checked the board by the door to the relay station's common room for himself.

The only departure time chalked on the board was the stage back to San Diego for the day after tomorrow. Nothing scheduled to leave for Tucson or El Paso. Yuma had been the last stop for the other passengers. Solomon was the only person looking to continue east.

The coach sat unattended now, its shafts drooped in the dust.

Solomon spotted the driver, a burly man they only knew as Asa, taking his ease on the porch, foot on the rail, smoking a twisted cheroot. He'd hung his corduroy coat on the back of the chair, pushed his gloves into the hip pocket of his denim britches, and tilted his battered black derby down over his eyes.

"When's the next stage leaving out for El Paso?" asked Solomon.

"Could be some time, sonny." Asa lifted the brim of his derby to look up at Solomon. "Fella riding shotgun for me up and quit. No'n else is fool enough to take the job."

"Don't people have places to get to?"

"Between the Mexican banditos, the Apache war parties, and yer run-of-the-mill American desperadoes, no place east of here seems worth getting to anymore."

Solomon had a worrisome thought.

"What about the last stage that left here heading east?"

"That's how we got wind of all the trouble. Dispatch rider brought word. Ol' Tom was driving the mail coach headed for Tucson. Said he had to run his team near to death when a bandit tried holding him up in one of the passes 'tween here and Tucson. A few lead balls in the rear boot but no great harm. Ever'body safe and sound. But they told us to hold up until the army sorted it out."

"You just need someone to ride along for shotgun?"

"Not just anyone, sonny." Asa pulled the derby back down over his eyes.

"I'll take the job."

Asa lifted his derby again to study Solomon.

"Kinda scrawny. When'd you eat last?"

"There's enough of me to handle anything you're likely to run up against."

Asa snorted and stood up, looked Solomon over once more, and snorted again.

"Come on, sonny." He walked over to the abandoned coach, stepping up onto the front wheel hub to reach into the boot under the seat. He pulled out a short-barreled scatter gun.

"You ever shoot something like this afore?"

"Sure." The scatter gun went off, blowing away the toe leather from Solomon's right boot and raising dust. It made him shiver, his toes wiggling at the tingle.

Asa studied Solomon's foot, switching his cheroot from side to side as he ruminated.

"You mean to do that?"

"Yes," said Solomon. "I like to try out the action of any firearm I handle."

"Sonny, I got government mail that has to get through or I'll lose my contract. I can't handle the team *and* fight off trouble, so I need an hombre that can hit what he aims at, live on no sleep, bad food, and don't mind a little pain every now and again."

Asa looked at Solomon, then at the bare toes between the shredded leather.

"You'll do. Th'ow that warbag of yours in the boot and I'll have Cimarron fetch us a team so's we can be on our way."

Solomon held the scatter gun out to him.

"Keep it, greenhorn. You're gonna need it."

They set out and drove straight on through. And sure enough, in one of the small gullies winding through the hills west of Tucson, they were stopped by a gang of six bandits.

The mules had slowed, struggling to pull the coach up a steep incline with a sharp turn at the top. The bandits ranged themselves across the road, blocking their way. The leader, wearing a sweat-stained sombrero and crossed bandoleers, rested on the pommel of his saddle.

"Dang," said Asa. "That varmint's El Niño."

The stage had been traveling too slow to drive on through the bandits. They'd have been easy targets for that many guns. Asa had to haul up on the reins and bring the coach to a halt.

Asa shouted at them, "Stand aside, Niño, we ain't carrying no passengers worth robbing nor money box worth taking."

"That's what I like about this country," said El Niño. "Full of such honest people. Of course I will believe you. So, we'll be on our way," he said, but stopped and leaned down as if listening to his horse. "What's that? But they seem like such honest fellows. Oh, if you insist." El Niño straightened up. "Señor, I would gladly be on my way and leave you the road. But, you see, my horse, he is a simple creature. Not so trusting. He insists we see for ourselves." El Niño pulled his large caliber pistol from its holster and aimed it at Solomon. "Throw down the mail sacks and the strong box. I would gladly let you pass, but," he shrugged, "who can argue with a horse?"

Solomon, impatient at yet more delay, swiveled in his seat and pointed the scatter gun at the bandits.

"Stand aside and let us be on our way so no one gets hurt."

Asa scrambled to the ground, taking shelter behind a rock, away from the deadly array of firepower.

"This is your lucky day, señor" said the bandit chief. "I was going to let one of my men shoot you. They need the practice. But I will do you the favor of shooting you myself. You will be famous. Shot dead by El Niño with his very own pistol."

The bandit chief took aim with the big pistol and fired. When the smoke cleared, Solomon was still sitting there, the scatter gun resting on the arm rail of the seat, its barrels still pointed at the bandits. Solomon shivered.

El Niño looked at his pistol, then at his men, then at Solomon.

"I think your head is too small, señor," said the bandit chief. He aimed his pistol, sighting along the barrel at Solomon's chest, and then fired.

The smoke cleared and Solomon was still sitting there.

"You missed," said Solomon.

The bandit chief cursed and with a sweep of his sombrero waved his men to action. They all let fly a fierce fusillade at Solomon, their horses dancing, agitated by the rapid gunfire.

Bangbangbangbangbangbangbangbangbangbang—clickclickclick-clickclick—click—click. Click.

The air cleared. Solomon's clothes were pierced with smoldering holes, his eyes screwed shut against the irritation of the acrid smoke.

El Niño looked at the men on either side of him.

"He is too skinny," said the bulky bandit on El Niño's right.

"We're used to shooting wider men," said the buzzardy bandit on El Niño's left, holding his hands out to show how wide a proper target ought to be.

El Niño holstered his sidearm and rested on his pommel again.

"I have to tell you," said El Niño, "and I don't often get a chance to say this to someone I have just shot—you are one lucky sumbitch."

"Do I get a turn now?" Solomon lifted the scatter gun, squinting one eye to sight down the double-barrels at the bandits. "Seems only fair."

"Of course, señor," said the bandit chief. "This is the West. We're all about fairness out here in the middle of nowhere."

Solomon pulled back the hammers on the scatter gun.

"Ah, but—you have to wait until somebody says 'go.' " El Niño turned in his saddle and looked back over his shoulder. "Hey, Antonio, you will stay here and say 'go.' "

Antonio didn't seem all that keen on the job.

"When Antonio says 'go,' señor, you may take your turn." With that he wheeled his horse and rode like the dickens with the rest of his gang to the top of the grade. He turned back and shouted, "Any time now, Antonio. Adios, señor." His horse reared up, pivoted, and pitched down the grade out of sight, his men following, leaving behind nothing but horse dust and the echo of hoofbeats.

Antonio was right behind them, riding hard, legs slapping against the sides of his mount until he too rode up and over the crest and down out of sight.

Asa raised up from the rock behind which he'd taken shelter and clambered back up onto the seat. He studied Solomon a long while.

"You just sat thar, like you was made a smoke," said Asa. "Them lead balls passing all around you. Nothing but holes in your duds. Goldangedest thing I ever saw," he said, grabbing up the reins and lashing the mules for the run on into Tucson.

"Lucky Smoke," said Asa, cracking the big whip over the heads of his mules.

The name stuck.

So, as Lucky Smoke, Solomon criss-crossed the Arizona and New Mexico Territories trying to pick up Salomé's trail once again. Riding shotgun mostly, since driving was more physical labor than he cared to do, handling the four-up or six-up teams that were used to pull the coaches. He'd learned to do it so he could be ready any time a regular driver was too drunk, or green, or just plain incompetent to handle the team or the terrain. But riding shotgun meant he was pretty much his own man when they stopped at one of the towns, relay stations, or homesteads along the various routes. It gave him time to roam about asking after the young woman who was quick-tempered and carried a hatchet as easily and natural as a lady's parasol.

But the trail had gone cold. There was no word of her, or anybody who answered to Solomon's descriptions of her or the little girl, Edith. All he could do was keep searching, a bloodhound running his nose back and forth over an old trail, fixed, determined, indifferent to a master's whistle, in hopes of picking up her scent again.

Lucky Smoke, in his slouch hat with its large eagle feather stuck in the beaded band, plaid coat, red wool shirt, neckerchief, denim britches with rolled up cuffs, and low-heeled Army-style boots, became an enigmatic fixture of the landscape. The most anyone knew or remembered about Lucky was his extraordinary ability to survive a gunfight, whether it was a showdown, bushwacking, or back-shooting. He was, as many a stage driver, passenger, and bandit behind bars readily admitted, just so danged lucky. He did seem impossible to hit with powder and shot, and he encouraged everyone to believe it was his unassailable luck.

He was also an abysmal marksman, even with a scatter gun. Just as it was said of him that the only shot that ever found its mark with Lucky Smoke was in a glass filled with rot gut rye, so it was also said that good old Lucky Smoke couldn't hit the door of a one-hole outhouse sitting inside it.

Nevertheless, road agents and highwaymen, alone or in gangs, let any stagecoach carrying Lucky Smoke as shotgun guard pass unmolested through their ambush. He was quick to return fire when the need arose, but never actually shot anybody, as far as anyone could recall. But he'd been so unnaturally lucky that no hold-up gang wanted to be the first when Lucky Smoke finally found his aim.

Adding to the mystery of Lucky Smoke, he never spoke of any kin, or part of the country he'd admit to calling home. It was certainly characteristic of his nickname—a smoke that doesn't settle in one place, but lingers awhile then disappears.

When war between the states broke out, Confederate raiders were added to the many dangers, so the run between El Paso to Yuma was abandoned and Solomon was out of a job. He moved north and found work on the California Trail, again riding shotgun on the stages and mail coaches that ran east and west through Nevada and Utah to California, all the while looking for sign, for any clue left by Salomé by which he could track her.

It was that nickname of his, Lucky Smoke, that fetched him the first good clue to Salomé's whereabouts that he'd had in ages. He hadn't kept track of the exact number of years that he'd been looking, but it had been considerable if he stopped to tot them up.

Carson City – 1870s

Solomon was the shotgun guard on a stage passing through Eagle Valley, Nevada, headed for Sacramento. They'd stopped in Carson City to change teams and give the passengers a chance to stretch their legs before bundling them all back inside and heading on, cutting south around the foot of Lake Tahoe and then westward, on to Placerville.

The passengers had tumbled out of the coach pausing only for a moment to flex, twist, stretch, and bend their abused frames back into a semblance of normalcy before dashing for the depot's dining room. Solomon remained by the coach, and stood with his arms folded, his foot up on the hub of the front wheel. He watched the people like he always did, looking for Lavinia's likeness among the faces and figures around him. He drew on his pipe, blowing smoke out the corner of his mouth.

When there was to be a stopover, Solomon would go poking around, having himself a whiskey, chatting up the barkeeps, gamblers, and dance hall girls—all those folks whose stock in trade were the secrets people let loose in such company. Sometimes he'd chat up the old timers idling about, men with enough time and curiosity to keep tabs on strangers passing through, or keep up with the gossip carried from place to place.

He'd been through Carson City maybe half a dozen times already, the last time no more than a week or so earlier, so he was content this trip to stand and watch the world go about its business.

"Sure as I live and breathe, that's Lucky Smoke, standing big as life right in front of me," said a brittle voice of some culture.

Solomon heard the dirt crunch underfoot as someone approached him from behind. He kept his eye on the commerce in front of him.

A hard finger tapped his shoulder.

Solomon didn't move. He ruminated up a considerable load of spittle, intending to hawk a long string at the intruder's shoe, and then beg pardon for not noticing him.

A hard finger tapped his shoulder again.

"You look and tell me," said the brittle voice, now with a hand attached, waving in Solomon's face a copy of The Saturday Journal, a magazine of popular stories and questionable news.

Solomon turned, cheeks loaded, lips pursed.

But the picture the man waved in front of Solomon's face stopped him. Solomon spit wide of the man's brogans, not taking his eyes off the image before him. On a page folded back was as near a likeness of himself as he could think possible, given that he never sat for any sort of portrait. It was a picture of him standing up in the front boot of a running stage, facing the rear of the coach, his pistols blazing as the banditos riding alongside the coach fell before his gunfire, dying in poses of contorted agony.

The man waving the magazine was duded up in a Tyrolean walking hat, lederhosen, and a gamekeeper's jacket. His sideburns were fashioned into enormous muttonchops, with a sweeping handlebar moustache. Over the smoked lenses of his half-glasses, the man goggled at Solomon, with his silvery, almost watery blue eyes. The man had the look of an easterner traveling for the sheer indulgence of soaking up frontier atmosphere. There was a keen familiarity about him to Solomon. But the man was not one of the passengers from the stage. Maybe Solomon had by this time seen so many faces that complete strangers struck him as familiar.

"I knew it was you by the feather in your hat and your neckerchief." The man admired the picture as he held it up for Solomon to see. Then he tucked the magazine under his arm, grabbed Solomon's hand in his own and went to levering it like a pump handle on a dry well.

"I just have to shake your hand so's I can say I did it," said the brittle voiced man. "The missus won't believe I had the dash of it." He fairly giggled at his own audacity.

"Lemme see that paper of yours." Solomon reached for the gadfly's magazine.

The man handed it over and sidled around to look over Solomon's forearm as he studied the likeness. "You're taller in the picture, ain't you?"

Solomon was fixed on the gruesome tale of bloody violence and Lucky Smoke's audacious good fortune in the worst of circumstances. Sheer entertainment. None of it true. The violence fairly glowing on the page. Solomon flipped through the magazine. It was chock full of stories about big city corruption, women lost to the vice of men, and frontiersmen who were a beguiling mixture of virtue and violence.

Solomon read a few such periodicals, finding it convenient to adopt the taller tales as his own to share when he found himself in occasional company, passing the night with cards, corn liquor, or communal music-making with his concertina. It was a handy way to join the pastime of swapping such stories without giving anything of himself away. But here was a whole catalog of exploits, at the core of which was his uncanny and unexplained ability to escape every ambuscade set for him. A bald challenge to every sure-shot and gun-hand in the territory who might be looking for a way to make a name for himself.

Work-a-day bandits were inclined to avoid trying Lucky Smoke's hand. He was to them an occupational hazard, and if they could minimize their risk and maximize their profit by steering clear of him, all well and good. But sidearm specialists keen on building a reputation and seeing their own name and exploits in print could take it into their heads that facing down Lucky Smoke would be a quick way to popular notoriety.

Lucky Smoke's peculiar ability was pointed out there in black-and-white on cheap newsprint paper, circulated to the thousands, just begging to be tested. Solomon felt exposed, a lizard caught lazing on a rock. He could already sense the hawks nosing down on him from above.

He continued to flip through the periodical, reaching the last story. Printed above an advertisement for concoctions to address the female complaint was a story about a cantankerous woman, Hatchet Jane, who ran the Silver Locket saloon in Iron Hill, Kansas. She was notorious for her temper and her hatchet made of silver, given to her by a lover killed in a duel for her favors. She now used that hatchet on every sort of man who might cross her, no matter his color, creed, or size.

Solomon handed back the paper without another word. He pulled his warbag out of the stage's rear boot and went off to find himself a way east. Solomon was done with shotgun guarding as an occupation.

He was headed for Iron Hill.

Chapter Twenty-Three

Iron Hill, Kansas – 1870s

SOLOMON STEPPED DOWN FROM THE TRAIN before it came to a complete stop at the Iron Hill depot. Solomon could see the cattle pens and the loading ramps just beyond. The air carried the aroma of livestock gathered for shipping. In the other direction, away from the pens, stood the livelier part of town that catered to the trail hand's commerce with its saloons, outfitters, eateries, and hotels.

Scores of people, excited by the occasion of the train's arrival, gathered at the depot. Conveyances of all sorts were clustered around the depot and strung out alongside the roadbed of the open track.

Solomon slung his bag over his shoulder and walked through the milling crowd, the ringing chuff of the idling engine behind him.

He was no longer Lucky Smoke. He'd given up that garb for a pair of gabardine trousers, black braces over a white shirt missing its collar, a long, dark coat, and a vest all buttoned up. His topper was a hat made of fur felt, broad-brimmed, its tall crown pinched to a point with a four-finger crease.

Iron Hill was brand-spanking new in just about every way. Less than two years ago it was nothing more than a log hut and water tower for the new railroad. The pipe dream of aggressive land promoters, Iron Hill struggled to win the cattle transport business away from its neighbors. There was Salina just to the west, Abilene a few miles to the east, and Wichita and Newtown further south.

The arrival of longhorns, stockmen, and cowboys with pockets full of cash brought in a rush of entrepreneurs eager to capitalize on all that ready money. In addition to the substantial railroad depot, the town now had a wide main street of packed dirt, fronted on both sides by emporia constructed of raw, unpainted wood, carrying wares to be sold to the herdsmen, cattle dealers, and grangers of the region.

Iron Hill had five saloons, which were mostly large, canvas tents, with fronts and verandas made of raw wood, and four hotels, which were of a slightly better construction, being entirely of wood and in most cases whitewashed.

At one of the town's intersections sat two of those saloons—the Kalamazoo on the northeast corner and the Silver Locket on the southeast corner. It was not nearly as opulent as the picture in the magazine made it out to be.

Solomon pulled on the brim of his hat to obscure his face as he walked toward the Silver Locket.

He'd not gone more than a few steps when a lanky young cowboy in chaps, vest, and leather wrist cuffs came tumbling out of the saloon, landing all a-crumple in the street. Heavily freckled, the cowboy was tolerably handsome despite his long, stringy hair and dirty face. His hat sailed out of the saloon's darkness, plopping down beside him. He staggered to his feet, and felt around for his holster, flapping empty on his backside. He spun around, trying to catch up to it, first one way, then the other.

Out of that same darkness marched Salomé waving the cowboy's pistol by the barrel, like a hammer. Older, Salomé was—sturdier, to put it delicately. Much, much sturdier. But Salomé, sure enough. Solomon could see the silver hatchet hanging in her sash.

Faces appeared in the door frame and window cutouts of the saloon. On the street, people collected at a distance as Salomé and the cowboy now faced off.

The cowboy reached for the pistol, but Salomé jerked it back, ready to brain him with it.

"Ain't right for a woman to take away a man's sidearm like that." The cowboy yanked at his vest in frustration, straightening himself, running his fingers through his hair.

"I told you what I'd do if you tried shooting out the eyes of my elk head."

"It was all just fun." The cowboy snatched up his hat, slapping it hard, watching her.

"What's the trouble, Miss Jane?"

Solomon had to remember Salomé went by Hatchet Jane.

A tall, strapping figure in a frock coat, vest, white shirt, and narrow string tie, pushed his way through the gawkers. A lawman, by the badge he wore. He stood back to see both combatants.

"Him." Salomé pointed at the cowboy. "And you, for not locking him up in the first place."

"Miss Jane, I can't go locking people up on your say-so."

She fixed a squint-eye on the cowboy and then on the lawman.

"How about for discharging firearms inside the city limits?"

"I didn't hear anything," said the lawman.

Salomé, never taking her eyes off the lawman, pointed the pistol at the cowboy, sending the gawkers diving out of the way. She fired, blowing his hat off his head before he had time to cringe.

"You heard that, didn't you? Now lock him up!"

"All right, all right. Give me the gun."

She hesitated.

"For evidence."

She handed over the still-smoking pistol.

The lawman took the cowboy by the arm and walked him down the street.

"That's going to break poor little Edith's heart." said a voice just behind Solomon's ear.

"What will?"

"Seeing her fiancé locked up like that," said the voice.

Solomon spun around. Griffin stood there, bobbing, hands up, ready to box, a big smile on his face. He was dressed in a white shirt with sleeve bands, a black vest, checked trousers, and a long, white apron.

"By gum, it's good to see you, Solly." Griffin plucked Solomon's hat off his head and pushed it over his face. "You here for the wedding?"

Solomon jerked his hat away from Griffin, resetting it on his head.

"What wedding?"

"What wedding! You come all this way, and don't know about Edith and that cowpoke? You're pulling my leg. You knew, right?"

"No."

"You've only missed the bachelor party so far. That's the guest of honor being carted off to jail."

Solomon watched as the two men reached a small, squat, mud-daubed structure next to the tent serving as the office for the town's law enforcement.

"When're they getting married?"

"If Salomé has her way? The day after hell freezes over. It'll be quite a day. Everyone's looking forward to it. The wedding, not hell freezing over. Because that's nothing to look forward to." Griffin rolled his eyes. "Listen how I'm babbling. It's just so good to see you. It feels like only yesterday. If I had any sense of what a yesterday actually felt like."

Solomon looked back at Salomé as she watched the lawman close and lock the metal grate on the cowboy, stooped over to fit in the little jail. Then she whirled and went back into the saloon.

"I would not have known it was Salomé, but for that hatchet of hers." A thought struck him. "How long's it been?"

"Beats me."

"Don't seem all that long ago."

Salomé came back out onto the veranda.

"Griffin! Get your sorry carcass back in here." She spun around and went back inside.

Griffin started toward the saloon.

"She can see you?"

"Got me a job. It's not like I'm planning on settling down or anything. But it was something to do until you showed up."

"Wait." Solomon stopped. "How'd you know I'd show up here?"

"I didn't *know* know. Given the circumstances, chances were that you'd show up. Remember? Probabilities? You're going to make me explain it again, aren't you?"

Solomon's blank look was answer enough.

Griffin sighed. "Edith was going along, easy as you please, not a care in the world, until that cowpoke caught her eye. Handsome. A real popular kind of guy around here. Free-spending. Always getting into mischief. She's been heart-over-hindcicle ever since. She set her cap for him and thus, circumstances being what they were, there was a good chance you'd be along to intervene, in your effort to change the course of history."

"I barely found out where Salomé was. I came right on when I did."

Griffin hooked hold of the column as he stepped onto the veranda. He paused and looked back over his upper arm at Solomon, his eyes hooded.

"Amazing coincidence, don't you think?"

"More dumb luck, I'd say."

"That, too."

"I came as soon as I got wind of her. But I sure didn't realize Edith was all grown up."

"Maybe you should carry a calendar. Make little tick marks. Keep track of the days."

"Griffin!" bellowed Salomé from inside.

Griffin went in, Solomon trailing him.

Inside, the saloon was lit with kerosene lanterns giving off a weak light, the glass chimneys all dirty with soot. Men sat around tables, drinking, playing cards, and dealing in cattle. The smell of tobacco, stale alcohol, sweat, and wet sawdust strewn all over the floor, mixed with the odor of horseflesh and cowhide blanketing the town.

Solomon tipped his hat to Salomé, tucking his chin to hide his face.

Griffin went to work behind the bar, setting up drinks as the men crowded around for service.

Solomon wedged between the press of drinkers at the far end of the bar.

"Seems unnatural, an angel tending bar," said Solomon.

"You know what's great about this? The beer!" Griffin filled another glass, twisting away to take a sip before turning back to set the glass in front of Solomon.

"What's Edith see in that stringy-haired galoot? What's wrong with that lawman, as a for-instance? He might be just the ticket to change the course of history."

"Funny you should mention him. He is awful sweet on her. Gainfully employed. Good to his mother back in Omaha. But Edith, or little Edie as she's known around town, inherited her mother's aversion to law enforcement professionals. Once they made him marshal, he cleaned up the town, cut down on the drunken shootouts, the crooked gamblers, the darlings-of-the-dark fleecing the cowboys fresh off a cattle drive. He's given this town the first law-and-order its ever had. Everybody agrees. He's a real kill-joy." Griffin went on serving up beers. "Edie gave him the brush-off. Salomé can't stand the idea of her little Edie marrying that no good saddle tramp. But her distaste for lawmen goes deeper."

"So that cowboy's the one she's got her heart all set on? I mean, really set?"

"Every inch of her. They'll be married tomorrow. Well, once she makes bail for him."

Solomon took another long slug of beer and slammed down the glass, wiping his mouth on his sleeve, leaving the rest of the beer rocking in the glass.

"I've got me some work to do."

"You coming back to finish this?" Griffin pointed to the swallow of beer left in the glass. But Solomon was gone. Griffin took up the glass and twisted away to drain it.

Outside, Solomon made for the jail, where he saw a young woman already standing toe-to-toe with that lawman.

"Edie," the lawman was saying, "Edie, just listen, please."

Edith was tall like her mother, dark-haired, with an almost golden complexion. Whatever fair skin she might have inherited from Lavinia had been lost in the hard frontier sun.

"What would you have me do? Just let these fellas shoot up the town because you happen to be sweet on one of them?"

"Oh, I see. For spite. Plain old spite. That's why he's in jail."

"It's for his own good. Just 'til he sobers up."

"Is locking everyone up the only thing ever comes to your mind?"

The lawman's eyes ranged about. Her voice carried, and people within earshot dawdled to enjoy the lawman's discomfort. He leaned in at her. "If it keeps a lazy, good-for-nothing saddle tramp off the street? Yes."

"Don't worry, darlin'." The cowboy smiled through the grate at Edith. "I'll be out in plenty of time for our wedding."

"How much to let him out now?"

"Fifty dollars."

"Fifty dollars!" Edith stormed about, her fists swiping the air. "Nothing but spite. Pure, mean, low-down spite."

"He's safer locked up. I could've let your mother shoot him instead."

She exhaled hard, eyes closed, then turned, marching back toward the Silver Locket.

"That's some feisty female, hunh?" Solomon approached the lawman.

"Yeah," He watched her go. "Runs in the family."

Solomon watched her as well. She didn't have that same sway and swivel he'd so admired on Lavinia. More like the hard gait that Abigail displayed when she was roused over something, which seemed to be all the time as he recalled. Still. She was a Kantlingher through and through.

"Why'd a fine upstanding fella like you let a girl like that go?"

"Why, indeed," asked the cowboy, still clinging to the grate. "Why, oh, why indeed?" And then he laughed, moving back from the metal slats.

"You shut up."

"Why don't you come in here and make me." The cowboy lunged back at the grate, giving the lawman a monkey-faced grin. "Oohoohooh! Ahh! Ahh!" He cackled like a chimpanzee, jumping around in the tiny mud calaboose.

"Maybe she don't fully understand your intentions?"

"She understands right enough."

"And you're just gonna let her marry him?"

"It'd take a pry bar to unmake that woman's mind." The lawman turned away from the still giggling cowboy.

"Woman wants a man that'll fight for her. Make her feel she's worth fighting for." Solomon studied the cowboy grinning out at them. "You know, sometimes a woman pays attention to a fella just to get the goat of some other fella she's really got her cap set for. Maybe that's all this is. I've seen it before."

"Hey, tin star!" called the cowboy. "I don't want to be late for my very own wedding. How about we play cards for my bail. What'd'ya say?"

"Seeing you behind bars is kinda growing on me." The lawman kept walking.

"Hey, I know. How about we shoot for it? Yeah, how 'bout that? You and me can shoot it out like good Christians. Settle it once and for all."

The lawman stopped, not looking back.

"How many times have you and me shot it out before?"

"I don't keep count."

"How many times've I beat you?"

"You didn't beat me that time with bows and arrows."

"How many?"

"You're chicken, you know that." The cowboy tucked his hands in his armpits, and went to cackling, flapping his elbows.

"Momma was right, you are a sorry, wicked cuss."

"Momma told me the same thing about you!"

"Your momma?" asked Solomon.

"Back in Omaha," said the lawman. "It's a danged good thing Momma's stuck in Omaha so she can't see him like this." He called back over his shoulder at the cowboy, "It'd break her heart!"

"What's Edith see in this bla'guard?" Solomon jerked a thumb at the cowboy.

"Tell him about the monkey, why doncha?" The cowboy pushed his lips through the grate. "Tell him about the monkey." The cowboy leaped around in the cell, laughing and hooting like an ape.

"You hush up or I'll throw you in the stock tank 'til you're swole up like a barrel cactus." The lawman's red face took on a hard grimace.

"Train came through here," said the cowboy, "and there was this Eye-talian had this monkey all dressed up in pants, vest, and a derby. Had him a wooden pistol." The cowboy paused, catching his breath. "Well, that monkey got loose, snatching hats, grabbing purses, and waving that little wooden pistol around like he was a regular Jesse James."

"I told you to shut up."

"Mister Law-and-Order here thought it was a midget." The cowboy, gasping with laughter, pointing at the lawman. "Tried to arrest him for armed robbery, didn't you? Went up a tree after him, didn't you? Didn't you?"

The lawman grabbed up a fire bucket and heaved the water at the cowboy, who scampered back away from the dousing.

The cowboy, still laughing, flinging water from his sleeves, came back.

"There he was, dangling from a tree limb, calling out, 'Halt in the name of the law.' And don't you know, that little booger stole his badge, his gun, and his necktie right off'n him, right there in front of God and ever'body. He goes and locks up that Eye-talian and his monkey. But— you know the best part?"

The lawman flung the empty bucket at him.

"Hatchet Jane bailed out the monkey. Bought him a beer. Made him toast of the town." The cowboy caught his breath. "You're right, I don't know what Edie sees in me, 'cause he's the one that makes her laugh." With another fit of laughter, the cowboy fell onto his back, his legs kicking, fit to bust.

"All right. All right." The lawman grabbed the padlock, stabbed in the key, and twisted it open. He swung the grate wide and took the cowboy by the collar, hauling him out of the jail.

"Boy're you gonna be sorry," said the cowboy. "I've been practicing."

"Sure."

"You gonna give me my sidearm?"

"When we're in the street."

The gunplay was unexpected. Solomon thought there'd be something more of a romantical nature between Edith and the lawman. It didn't seem likely to Solomon a fella could shoot his way into a woman's good graces.

The two men made for the middle of the street, the lawman walking steady, upright, and full of purpose, while the cowboy danced and jigged like the monkey, ready for a sport.

Solomon left the two brothers and made for the Silver Locket to warn Edith that he'd accidentally arranged a noisy end to her fiancé. He hoped to make her see it was best for all parties.

Behind him, word of the coming shootout flashed through the town. People cleared off the streets, ducking for places of safety from which to watch the boys bang away at each other.

Solomon stepped into the saloon just as a boy in knee-britches pushed through behind him. "There's gonna be a shootout! Jake

Cleaver's gonna shoot it out with his brother Mose!" The boy disappeared, running to spread the word.

The men in the bar stampeded out, flowing around past Solomon, who snatched off his hat to hide his face as Salomé followed the crowd out to see the gunplay.

Edith had gone deathly pale. She whirled to dash out with them, but Solomon caught hold of her arm before she was through the door.

"Let me go!"

"Hear me out a minute," said Solomon. "If you choose that cowboy, you'll end up just like your mother, and her mother before that. I've got it on the sacred word of an angel how everything can change back, and we can all start over."

Edith stopped struggling. She stood stock-still, mouth agape, aghast, eyes fixed on Solomon.

He fished out the locket and opened it up, holding it so the light would pick up on the two portraits inside. Edith squinted, looking hard at the locket, then at him, then lifted out her own locket. That very same locket. She opened it, studying the pictures.

"It's you."

"It's me. I'm Lavinia's dearly beloved Solomon. Parted from her by that no good snake-in-the-grass, Edwin Greene. Now I'm trying to make my way back to her," said Solomon. "If you change your mind right now, on the very eve of your wedding, marry that lawman instead of that cowboy, everything'll snap back to the beginning, everything starts over, and all the bad, all the trouble, all the problems you ever had'll vanish. Everything'll be set to rights. We'll all get to live the life we were supposed to have."

The saloon was empty. There was no sound. Edith seemed not to breathe. Then she inhaled hard, finding breath enough to speak.

"Momma told me about you."

"She did?"

"She told me what to say if I ever did meet up with you."

"She did?"

"Only trouble is—" She paused, reaching behind herself. Then started again, "Only trouble is—"

"What?"

"I don't use language like that."

The porcelain spittoon shattered as Edith brought it down on Solomon's head, with a resounding *kee-rash*!

That all-too-familiar bell tone echoed inside Solomon's skull, followed by the tingle that reached right down to his toes. Shards of china and dust dribbled onto his shoulders. And, of course, everything else inside the spittoon.

Edith dashed into the street.

"You've been busy, haven't you?" Griffin held out a whiskey, giving Solomon a coy smile and a cock of his head. "On the house. Helps reduce the indignity."

In the street, both men were already squared off against each other.

"It's a trick!" shouted Edith, dashing between them. "Momma's right. There really is a hex. Don't do it!" She took up a position, stretching her arms out, palms up, ready to stop the pending gunfire with her bare hands.

Both men drew. Edith crouched, fingers in her ears, not moving from between them.

"Dang it! Move, woman!" shouted the cowboy.

"Edie, get yourself out'n the way!" shouted the lawman.

The two men had no clear field of fire with Edith crouched between them, unwilling to give way and let them shoot each other.

They danced around, trying to get clear of Edith who shifted and sashayed trying to stay between them, still keeping her head ducked and her ears plugged.

The lawman and the cowboy caught each other's eye and with a nod they faked left. Edith followed, but they stepped back to the right, and were finally clear to shoot each other.

Both guns blazed.

"Yeow!" The cowboy dropped his pistol and hopped around, holding his gun hand.

"No fair! Y'spoilt my shooting hand," he cried, still dancing and hopping, holding out his injured hand.

"Momma's gonna whale the tar outta you!"

There was a very strange silence surrounding them.

Edie straightened up and unplugged her ears. She looked around. Salomé was square in the middle, and mighty relieved. But behind her the townsfolk looked awfully solemn, staring at Edith.

"You hussy," shouted a woman from the back.

"Me?" Edith cried out.

Salomé whirled around, hatchet in hand. "Who said that?"

Suddenly, several of the dolled-up girls from the Kalamazoo broke out of the crowd and enveloped the wounded cowboy.

"Tramp!" the Kalamazoo girls shouted.

"Jezebel!" the respectable ladies shouted.

"Spoilsport," the gambling men shouted.

"This is what comes of toying with a man's affections," said a tubby woman in a sunbonnet, gingham dress, and broken-down clodhoppers. She wrinkled up her nose, giving Salomé a defiant nod, pushing past her to join the general stroking and petting on the wounded cowboy.

Edith slapped her arms against her sides, exasperated.

"Edie," said the lawman. "I know this is all out of the blue, but—darlin'—would you marry me? This hard country's no place for girl like you."

"Run the trollop out of town!" shouted the tubby woman in the sunbonnet, which sounded like a good idea to the rest of the crowd, so they chimed in, chanting, "Tar and feathers. Tar and feathers."

Salomé twisted this way and that, unable to decide who she should whack first.

"When you put it that way, yes," said Edith. "Can we leave now?"

The cowboy held out his wounded hand, looking all pitiful, which made the crowd that much angrier.

"I swear on my Momma's gray head I'll make it up to you," said the lawman. "First thing I'll do is give you the biggest gol-danged wedding ring this town ever saw." He took her hand and hooked her arm over his. "I'll just go get me a little money together" He led her up the street.

"Could you possibly move any slower," asked Edith, glancing back over her shoulder at the grumbling crowd, washing around Salomé, and moving toward them. She commenced to dragging him along, not knowing where he was headed, but figured that elsewhere would do just fine.

In the saloon, Solomon knocked back a second whiskey just as the shots fired. It seemed a good sign there being no general uproar.

Until the same boy ducked his head in again.

"Jake Cleaver asked Little Edie to marry him right there in the middle of the street and she said yes!" He dashed off, his news delivered.

Solomon slammed down the empty glass and ran to the door, so as not to miss the time-space continuum beginning its roll backward.

Suddenly from up the street more gunfire erupted, followed by the pounding hooves of running horses as the lawman rode by, hell-for-leather, followed by Edith, skirt billowed behind, showing her bare legs slapping against the horse's flanks. They leaned into the turn and rode hard for the open country beyond the town.

Griffin came up behind him. "That didn't look good."

"Maybe they're in a hurry to set up housekeeping?"

Galloping behind on foot came a fat cattle broker, shouting, "She stole my horse! She stole my horse!"

The busy little boy ran past again, crying out, "The sheriff and Little Edie just held up the Drover's Bank!"

"You've been quite a blessing today, haven't you?" said Griffin. "Transformed a blushing bride into a horse thief, bank robber, and fugitive in, what? Less than an hour? Have you ever thought about bottling whatever it is you've got and sell it?"

"Anything you didn't tell me about that lawman?" said Solomon, slowly, steaming.

"Let's see," said Griffin, frowning, thinking. "I mentioned he was the town marshal. That he was sweet on Edie. That his brother's a trigger-happy saddle tramp."

"I found out that last part myself."

"Oh. Well, he is. That he's good to his mother back in Omaha." Griffin snapped his fingers, recollection lighting up his face. "She's in *jail* back in Omaha."

"*That's* the part you left out."

"At least I remembered it was Omaha."

"Why was she in jail, Griffin?" Solomon watched as Edith and the lawman disappeared in the distance.

"Armed robbery. Grand Larceny. Petty Larceny. First, second, and third degree burglary. It's her kleptomania. Runs in the family."

"Kleptomania?"

"You know. That natural urge to steal everything that's not nailed down."

The thundering of hooves rattled toward them.

"That'd be the posse," said Griffin. "Again."

A dozen or so riders went by, raising dust and flinging stones.

"Yep," said Griffin. "You think it's true about the apple not falling very far from the tree?" Griffin watched the disappearing posse. "So. Any more bright ideas?"

Solomon slammed his hat onto the ground, hopping hard on it, then danced around, finally giving it a kick, sending it sailing.

"I assume that means no."

Solomon stood, hands on hips, staring out.

"Ready to give up? Admit I'm right and you're wrong?"

"About what?"

"That you can't sweet talk a complete stranger into changing their life goals on your say-so."

"You never said that."

"I didn't?"

"No."

"Okay. I'm saying it now. You can't sweet talk a complete stranger into changing their life goals because you want a second chance at true love."

"It's more than that."

"Oh, right. You get the willies thinking how everyone is sneering down from heaven at you for mucking up their lives. Again. For which they now have Exhibit B. Or C." Griffin gestured toward the horizon, now empty of Edith and the posse. "Maybe we're on D."

"It's way more than that."

"Now what?"

"Salomé said I was some kind of supernatural freak."

"She said hex."

"I don't care how she said it. She thinks I'm not natural."

"Well, you're not."

"I'm still me."

"No, you're not. You haven't been *you* since Luther's bullets failed to kill you."

Salomé passed by, ready to bite somebody in two. Griffin and Solomon both turned to admire the workmanship of the iron tire on a buckboard's wheel, like it was a holy relic. When she'd gone into the saloon, they straightened back up.

"Time to make yourself scarce, Solly."

"I oughta be here if that posse brings Edith back. She may need a character witness."

"You do know the difference between character witness and character assassin, right?"

The crowd broke up, the dust settling, the wind a mere whisper. Beyond were the sounds of men back to work, moving cattle.

Griffin took the apron off over his head. "Time to mosey along. Give me a whistle when you catch up with Edith again." Griffin draped the apron over Solomon's shoulder.

"So that's it, you just pop back up into the air and disappear for another twenty years?"

"You miss me already." Griffin winked and gave him a punch.

"I don't miss you. I just thought you'd want to see how this thing ends. Maybe get your doo-hickey back."

"I have a day job out there in the cosmos, you know."

"Don't seem to me you've got all that much to do."

"Being seen with one particular mudfoot too often draws unwelcome attention. There are hideous creatures itching to get their hands on that shard. Not one as good-natured as me."

Solomon kicked at the dust.

Griffin sighed, then looked at his wrist, which did not have a time-piece on it. "What say I check in on you again this time next year. If the weather's nice. Sound good?"

"What if I set everything to rights before then?"

Griffin wrinkled his nose, thinking about it. "Mmmmm. I'm betting not." And with that, Griffin was gone.

Chapter Twenty-Four

FROM THAT DAY ONWARD, Kantlingher women were on the run—from the law, from failed marriages, from more bad choices than seemed possible for a woman to make in a single lifetime.

But every Kantlingher woman took comfort in one indisputable fact. No matter how bad things got, how often a marriage imploded, a debt turned sour, or a jolly jaunt with a beguiling young man turned into a crime spree that sent them both hot footing for the state line, each Kantlingher woman knew deep down, it wasn't really her fault. Each woman could point with confidence to the single source of all her misfortunes—the Kantlingher Hex.

The story, as it often appeared in sworn testimony, was how any criminal charge she faced should be blamed on the hex bedeviling the Kantlingher women down through the years, beginning that first night he showed up to claim old Lavinia Kantlingher. Driven off by Luther Kantlingher, the hex, bent on revenge, began to show up on the night before a Kantlingher was to be married. Sometimes before she herself knew of any such thing. He'd show her a locket nearly identical to the one her mother passed down to her. He'd claim on the sacred word of a bona fide angel she had a once-in-a-lifetime chance to erase all the years of disaster and put everything to rights for herself and all the Kantlingher women. All she had to do, the court records often read, was throw over the man she intended to marry for some other man he'd picked out for her.

If she had her wits about her, she knew to find something sharp, heavy, or fully loaded, and use it on him. Because, mothers would tell their daughters over the years, once the hex appeared it was a good bet she'd be on the run or in jail by sundown the next day.

Of course, that excuse never seemed to stand up at her arraignment. Best she could hope to get for it was an overnight stay in the drunk tank, minus her shoes.

There were two pieces of advice a Kantlingher woman always got from her mother. First, it's just as easy to love a rich man as a poor man, and second, when the hex appears aim for the knees, it's the only head start she'll get in life.

Iron Hill – Still 1870s

Solomon waited for the posse to return. When they rode in, worn out and empty-handed, Solomon knew he had to follow the trail himself. He stopped in at the Silver Locket to have himself one last drink.

He kept to the shadows and watched Salomé. The starch had gone out of her and Solomon felt a twinge. He knew he could make it all up to them by changing everybody's fate.

Once he finished his drink, Solomon bought himself a sturdy horse, rolled up his few possessions into a rain slicker that he'd tied up under the saddle's cantle. He pointed his mount in the same direction he'd seen Edith and that lawman vanish.

He trailed the Sweetheart Bandits, as they'd come to be known, through scrub country, green hills, mountains, towns, and solitary homesteads. Along the way, he'd meet someone who swore they had a real live encounter with the Sweetheart Bandits and, boy, did he have a story to tell, yessireebob. Then they'd launch into anecdotes filled with bold holdups, lots of gunplay, rich takings, and daredevil escapes. They'd swear it was all the God's honest truth and point off in the direction the pair took to make their escape. Solomon would thank them kindly and follow whichever way the finger pointed.

Those tales, and the occasional wanted poster, kept him in pursuit.

It was natural their trail at first led north to Omaha. That lawman might take Edith home to his mother. But the trail veered east and then south, through Iowa, down through Missouri into Arkansas, cutting back west into Oklahoma then down into east Texas.

All along the way, depending on the person telling the tale, the Sweetheart Bandits were a beneficent rain upon the land, only robbing those who deserved it or could afford to lose it, never keeping more than what they needed to cover the few incidentals their life on the run from the law might require. They would, honest-to-pete, give the rest to widows and orphans they'd met along the way.

Or they were no better than a plague of locusts, a pestilence of biblical proportions who took special delight in robbing those very same widows and orphans.

The degree of affection or animosity for the Sweetheart Bandits depended entirely on how much the witness lost in the encounter.

For a good long while, Solomon never seemed to be more than a few weeks behind them. But after a handful of seasons on the trail, the stories dribbled to a stop. Finally, even the wanted posters, with Edith's simpering face and dandy hat, disappeared, giving way to the faces of new desperadoes.

The trail evaporated entirely in east Texas.

Solomon continued traipsing the highways and byways, chatting folks up, reading newspapers, and flicking through the handbills and circulars. He took on menial jobs that wouldn't draw attention as he roamed the country. A wandering man of means often provoked curiosity and suspicion, so he kept his fortune tucked away and took gainful employment to fit in. Nothing too stressful, nothing that would prevent him moving among folks, something where a man's mystery might be tolerated, and a man's history was nobody's business but his own.

Solomon could still make himself a fine addition to a night of drinking and gambling, merry-making and music-making when he could find it. He'd tell stories of women over-fond of hatchetry, the Sweetheart Bandits, and gold-mad men with their wives on the American River, all in hopes of sparking a memory, rousing a recollection, and maybe tease out a new clue to follow. When it did, he'd pick up and move on.

He'd decided that anonymity might serve him better in his search. He quit giving out his rightful name in case Edith caught wind of him on her trail. Instead, he'd take on the nickname given him by the locals wherever he spent any good stretch of time. He found such nicknames to be a handy way of erasing himself from the landscape of history and avoid the questions that followed a man of his peculiar qualities.

When he left one part of the country for another, he'd leave that nickname behind.

Once in a while, as had happened with Lucky Smoke, his nickname turned into a beacon of notoriety.

Like when Solomon took a job working the sweeps on a flatboat along the Red River. That lasted until a water moccasin appeared to have sunk its fangs deep into Solomon's thigh. Too far from help of any kind, the flatboat's pilot offered Solomon whiskey for the pain and help ease his transition to the afterlife. When nothing came of it, and Solomon seemed no worse for the encounter, the deckhands, a wild and quarrelsome but highly suspicious lot, wondered what sort of nefarious associations it took to shrug off a man-killer like that. Some of them had caught glimpses of the peculiar metal object Solomon wore on a leather lanyard around his neck. That led to speculation it was an Indian fetish given to him by a Pawnee medicine man. Others were certain it was Lakota Sioux. Without a good look, no one could be certain. And in any case, everyone had long since learned that Solomon was mighty quick with that bowie of his if pestered about the thing-umma-bob around his neck. So it stood to reason it must be devilish.

They took to calling him Injun Tom. Nights around the campfires weren't as hospitable as before.

Solomon moved on. Long memories and local lore made it necessary for Solomon to change his appearance, growing or shaving beards, cutting or growing out his hair, affecting an eye patch or glasses or whatever.

Griffin's annual visits, all the while, were as lively, chatty, and useless as ever. He seemed to have no difficulty finding Solomon, wherever he lit or how he changed his appearance. Solomon would never admit it, but Griffin's visits were about the only thing he looked forward to, since rolling back the space-time continuum remained as elusive as ever and each visit was a reminder of his greater purpose. It could be a struggle to keep it in mind as time rolled along.

Not being a creature of calendars or time pieces, Griffin made what seemed to Solomon a bare, half-hearted effort to show up every spring with any kind of punctuality. A few days early, a few weeks late. Never the same day of the month two years running.

Not that Solomon had anything good to report. Just a string of failed leads in his search, a few hair-raising escapades that raised the hair on neither Solomon nor Griffin, and the occasional observation about life and purpose that didn't resonate with Griffin, being truly immortal and unfazed by so remarkable a state of being.

Griffin didn't seem all that curious about how Solomon occupied his time between failures either. He acted like he'd seen it all before.

Still. Solomon looked forward to the visits. It meant he could talk to someone about the real things, and not pretend a caution he didn't really feel, or bless a luck he knew he didn't really have, or bemoan the aches and pains of an all-too-brief existence he didn't really share.

On each visit, their conversations would eventually dwindle to a stop.

"See you next year," Griffin would sometimes say. Or not. And he'd be gone until the following spring. Or thereabouts.

Chapter Twenty-Five

Mississippi Valley – 1890s

FOR A WHILE, SOLOMON WORKED as the brakeman on a passenger train running between New Orleans and Cairo. One night, on the run down to New Orleans, the southbound number three stopped in Warrenton, a few miles south of Vicksburg, for passengers, mail, and a new flagman. They'd just pulled out, rolling into the darkness, the lights of the passenger coaches and the red lanterns of the end car flickering through the trees.

Solomon, dressed in his blue serge railroad uniform and hard-brimmed cakebox hat, passed through the coaches. He'd stopped on the vestibule of each car, standing on the bottom step of each platform to lean out and have a look up and down both sides of the train, to catch any signs of fire or mechanical trouble.

Finished with his inspections, Solomon retired to the forward baggage car where the train crew could take their ease. Solomon barely got his pipe lit and going good when the conductor, whom he didn't recognize, came in and stood over him.

It wasn't old Morrissey, who'd taken charge of the train when it pulled out of Cairo yesterday morning. Nor had they picked up a new conductor in Warrenton, Solomon was certain about that.

This fella was pale, his blond hair a thatch that sprayed out from under his cap. He wore his glasses down on his nose, snugged his considerable paunch into his buttoned-up blue uniform jacket.

"By yiminy, I tink we pick up a cardsharp," said the new conductor, blowing out his moustaches with an impatient puff. A danged Minnesotan. "Yew get out dere and catch her wit her pigeon and we put her off next stop, you betcha."

The conductor was boss of the train, so Solomon was obliged to go.

Solomon and the conductor walked to the end of the second baggage car and out onto the end platform. Solomon was about to step across the gap over the couplings to the next car when the conductor caught him by the elbow.

"She tink we tumble to her tricks and she'll hide away dem cards. We'll never catch her out no how." The conductor gestured upward. "Peek in and catch her before she sees yew."

As a brakeman, Solomon often walked back and forth over the tops of moving freight trains in all kinds of weather. However, the roofline of a passenger coach made that impractical. But getting a quick look in through the small ventilator windows of the monitor roof to catch out a cardsharp would be very little effort for Solomon.

Cardsharps, especially lady cardsharps, were a common enough nuisance on the passenger trains, preying as they did on businessmen making the long, boring runs between big cities. Some fellas, once fully fleeced, didn't take their losses like a man, but would pester the conductor, blaming them for the cheats being aboard. It was as much self-interest as railroad policy to put a cardsharp off as soon as possible.

Solomon hiked himself up and stood on the end railing, held the roof apron to steady himself, then pulled himself up the roof's duckbill slope onto the upper deck of the clerestory that ran the length of the car. Once he got his feet under himself, he stood, shifting his weight with the motion of the coach to keep his balance.

"Half-way back, on d'near side," called up the conductor.

Solomon walked along the narrow upper deck of the roof to the middle of the car. He checked with the conductor, pointing to the spot. The conductor nodded, looking grim and blowing out his moustaches.

Solomon got onto his hands and knees, his backside in the air, and leaned down so he could peek through the narrow upper windows of the clerestory's deckside.

This coach, one of the train's two parlor cars, was laid out with padded swivel seats and small tables. On the outboard side of the coach he could see three men seated around a lady shuffling a deck of cards with a mastery beyond any simple ladies' games. She fanned, she cut, she cascaded, she riffled, working the cards, and showing off a well-practiced dexterity. Solomon figured the fellas had it coming if they chose to sit down with so fine a hand at the cards.

"So?" he heard the conductor call across to him.

Solomon leaned down a little farther to get a better look at the lady and her pigeons.

He nearly slid off the roof. There in the coach, not eight feet from his nose, was Edith Kantlingher. Or someone exactly like her. Solomon could see she wore a tight-fitting jacket with wide lapels and gathered sleeves, her floral blouse rising up right to her jaw line, and all topped off with a brimmed, flat-crowned hat sprouting feathers, and a veil of dark purple netting over her face.

So caught up in marveling at this chance discovery, Solomon failed to notice the train entering a cut in the right-of-way overgrown with trees.

The right-of-way was usually kept trimmed well back. But this narrow stretch, with the hillside close on the left and the sudden drop-off on the right to the creek way down below, had been neglected for some time.

The first branches knocked off Solomon's cap, catching his attention. He realized he could be swept off the train. It would be a long walk from wherever he landed. And he sure as heck-fire didn't want to lose track of Edith now that he'd spotted her.

Before he could flatten himself out on the roof, the point of a sturdy branch ran down the back of his collar, slitting his jacket at the seam along his spine. The end-point of the branch ran down the back of his trousers, ripping out through his seat. Speared, his britches full of small limbs and leaves, he scrabbled for a handhold, his fingers squeaking along as he tried to grip the flat surface of the coach roof rolling along right out from under him. In a very few cars, the train would be gone and he'd be left suspended twelve or fifteen feet above the track if he didn't do something and soon.

Twisting from side to side, he struggled to unbuckle his belt, trying to get loose before he reached the end of the train. He'd worked the buckle free just as the last car scraped along underneath him. Letting go of his belt, he grabbed the coach's stove pipe, straining for all he was worth, the tree limb flexing until the branch pushed his trousers down to his ankles, slit the seat and finally sprung free. He was left dangling down off the end of the car, gripping the tin chimney, the trap-door on his red long-johns flapping in the windstream.

Suspended there, hobbled by his trousers around his ankles, he was unable to swing a free leg back up to the roof. His split jacket now a pair of blue serge wings fluttering, he found himself hanging in full view of two ladies taking the air outside on the little platform at the end of the coach.

"Indians!" they shrieked, and fled back inside. Running through the cars, from one end of the train to the other, they cried out their alarm, alerting everybody to the horde of savages who must have dropped from those trees and were now swarming over their very heads ready to scalp the men and bother the women.

Solomon managed to pull himself back onto the roof and taken only a couple of hobbling steps when every coach of the train seemed to erupt in a blaze of random gunfire, thoroughly peppering the night on either side. The muzzle flash of flaming light flick-flickered along the landscape as the passengers banged away, firing through the roof at imaginary moccasin steps overhead and out at the hillside alive with fierce, war-bonneted shadows.

Grabbing at his ripped trousers, Solomon galloped toward the front of the train, hobbled by the tangle of fabric knotted at his knees and refusing to budge.

Shots dwindled away as the passengers used up their ammunition. Solomon flopped down and rolled over onto his back, undulating to inch-worm himself back into his torn britches. He stood up, swaying as he tried to fasten the front fly. But with the buttons gone and the buckle of his belt sheared off, he had to hold onto the waistband to prevent further indecency. He was a scarecrow of tattered fabric, fluttering in the windstream.

He scrambled down off the roof of the parlor car and yanked the door open, dashing in.

Everyone was up, guns still drawn, staring out the windows into the night, the car filled with the acrid, faintly sweet odor of gunsmoke.

A woman seated closest to the doorway, near to fainting, got one good look at Solomon and realized one of those rascals had broken in on them. She shrieked, fainted dead away, sliding out of her seat like a loosely-packed sausage.

The men aimed and clicked away on empty cylinders.

Ignoring the dumbshow fusillade, Solomon strode up to the young woman in the purple veil.

One of the three men Solomon had seen at cards with her stepped between Solomon and the young woman. He was a rather tall, well-muscled traveler in checked suitcoat and pants, high celluloid collar and wispy moustache. He put his hand out, checking Solomon in his approach.

"I'm looking to speak with the lady, if it's any business of yours," said Solomon.

"You might want to come back when you've sobered up," said the checker-suited traveler, then turned to the others. "A drunk. Completely bushed," he said, which set the men to laughing at Solomon's vegetation-pierced garments.

"You kin to her?" asked Solomon, deciding how much damage he ought to inflict on this impedimentiary fella.

"I've only just met the lady," the traveler protested. "However. I'm sure any kin of hers would appreciate my standing in for them with the likes of you."

"Then I'll make my own introductions." Solomon pushed passed the checker-suited traveler.

Before the traveler could accost him again, Solomon asked her straight out, "Was your mother the Sweetheart Bandit? Name of Edith? Rode with a renegade lawman out of Kansas?"

The young lady's posture never tensed or changed, offering no apparent reaction. But Solomon could see how her eyes darted about, watching for the impact his words might have on the other travelers.

Solomon went on, "I'm Lavinia Kantlingher's long lost sweetheart, and I have a message for you."

Before Solomon could get really good and going about angels, the space-time continuum, and putting things to rights, the young woman spoke up. "If you are truly Lavinia Kantlingher's long lost sweetheart," she said, "I have a message for *you*."

Fortunately for Solomon, he landed in a large, leafy beech tree when the young woman's companions braced him and pitched him off the train.

Chapter Twenty-Six

Mississippi Valley – 1890s

UNFORTUNATELY FOR SOLOMON, that big, leafy beech tree grew on the bare, open slope running down to a creek, some hundred-twenty feet below.

He hung there in the tree, the lights of the coaches strobing away into the night, until he was left in darkness, springing and swaying on a none-too-sturdy branch. He kicked up his leg, trying to hook his heel on the limb.

A flickering glow of a light appeared along the track in the distance, coming back from where the train had gone. Would it be too much to hope that knuckle-headed conductor noticed Solomon getting the heave-ho and stopped the train to come look for him?

It would, indeed, be too much to hope. There was an unpleasant familiarity about the light as the blue-white glow came nearer.

Griffin. Ambling along the middle of the track in Solomon's direction.

Solomon held on, figuring he might as well wait for Griffin to get right below him. He could use the light of Griffin's portable luminescence to see the roadbed and gauge his swing to avoid the drop into the creek below.

Griffin came even with the tree where Solomon dangled.

"Not a good time?" asked Griffin.

"What are you doing here?"

"Probabilities suggested you might get thrown from a train right about now in this general vicinity. Thought I'd check."

"If you're here for your doo-hickey—"

"Wouldn't think of it, Solly-boy. You look like you've got your hands full."

"Did you know she was on that train?"

"Who?"

"You know dang good and well who."

"Solly, this part of the world is teeming with mudfoot short-timers. You'll have to be more specific."

"Edith!" Solomon shouted, more in frustration because at that moment the bough broke and he fell from the tree. Hitting the bare slope, he went tumbling down the hill, rolling, bounding through the brush, somersaulting all the way to the bottom, landing in the cold, shallow water of the creek with a flat splash.

He rose up on his hands and knees and remained motionless for a long moment. Then, of a sudden, he gave himself a mighty dog's shake all over, finally sitting back on his haunches.

Griffin stood on the other side of the creek at its widest part.

Sloshing about, Solomon got to his feet and slogged toward the opposite shore, lifting his feet high to clear the rushing water of the creek, squishing and splashing.

Reaching the shore, he sat on a large stone and pulled off his shoes, dumping out water and sand.

"I've worked all over, up, down, and sideways, poking around every nickel-and-dime hotel, every saloon, barrel-house, gambling joint, and bawdy house, and never once laid eyes on her until this very night."

"Whoa. You look terrible. Good thing I brought these." Griffin held out Solomon's satchel, overcoat, and derby. "Saw them there, and no Solly. Knew you couldn't be far. Thought I'd come looking."

Solomon stripped off the shreds of his trousers and jacket, threw off his shirt and left it all in a heap on the rocks. He was done with railroading, that was for sure.

He took his satchel from Griffin, plopped it on the ground and pulled it open, taking out his old salt-and-pepper.

"You know anything about where she was headed?" In pants and shirt, Solomon stepped back into his waterlogged brogans and laced them up.

"Who?"

"That card sharp on the train. Looks exactly like Edith."

"Edith now or Edith going on twenty years ago."

Solomon stopped and looked up at him.

"I *told* you to get yourself a calendar. Little tick marks? Remember?"

"Okay. It's someone who looks exactly like she did back in Iron Hill. Is that her daughter?"

"How should I know? I told you. I'm not omniscient."

"You managed to find Iron Hill easy enough. Got there before me."

"Lucky guess."

"All I can say is it's one helluva coincidence you showing up just as I lay eyes on her. The first good sighting I've had in years." Solomon shrugged himself into his jacket and ran his fingers through his hair, flinging water and dislodging more leaves. "You could help me find her."

"Remember what I said about free will?"

"Then do me a favor." Solomon bundled his overcoat into his satchel.

"Of course, old buddy," said Griffin, then held up his finger. "If I can."

"Get lost." Solomon took up his derby and slapped it on his head.

"Nothing would make me happier, Solly. But I am incapable of getting lost."

Solomon trudged through the soft sand and loose gravel of the shore, making for the narrow footpath that led away from the water's edge.

"I did fetch your luggage for you. That should count for something."

But Solomon was already fading into the dark of the footpath.

"Do you have any kind of a plan?" Griffin called after Solomon.

Above, Solomon had reached the dirt farm road that paralleled the tracks, rising to run level with the roadbed, the ravine with its creek in between. He stopped and looked back down along the path where Griffin still stood.

"Unless you brought along a horse or a magic carpet, or something useful-like, I guess I'm walking to New Orleans."

Griffin followed, whistling a tune he'd picked up from some years ahead.

Figuring himself to be somewhere north of Baton Rouge, Solomon would have to walk all night and all day to reach New Orleans, unless he managed to find a vehicle. Solomon didn't want to misjudge the young lady, but she had a big city look about her. She must be headed for a place that would appreciate her gifts and have more to offer than any of the small towns along the way. That made it a good bet she was headed for New Orleans. Picking up her trail ought to be mighty easy. He'd be standing back on Lavinia's front porch before sunset tomorrow.

Solomon was no stranger to New Orleans. He had all the confidence in the world he knew a thing or two about the place. There couldn't be that many handsome women having an extraordinary felicity with the playing cards, whose specialty was fleecing passengers between Cairo and New Orleans.

NEW ORLEANS – 1890S

He'd arrived at the muddy outskirts of the city closer to midday than mid-morning, riding most of the way on top of a cotton wagon piled high with bales wrapped in burlap headed for the wharves of New Orleans.

It had saved him a long walk, but it was anything but restful. The driver walked alongside the horse-hitched team of four scrawny oxen, and it was no effort to guess why. It was a rough and rocking ride over a road cut by rain run-off that had slashed the dirt into hard-pack, sun-baked ruts running catty-corner shoulder to shoulder. He'd been on boats with less pitch and yaw.

For nearly the whole way, Solomon was hungry and tired, immortality being no proof against the all-too-natural gnawing in the belly and the ache in the bone.

Griffin turned up part way through the trip to ride along. For the sheer humanity of the experience, he said. He'd arrived just about the time Solomon's belly was rumbling its discontent.

"You are a grumble-guts." Griffin showed no mercy, pontificating on food the whole long way. For someone who didn't need to eat, Griffin knew more about food than was humanly tolerable.

It was late in the day when Solomon reached that part of the Crescent City he knew best, where Bienville Street intersected Liberty, Franklin, and Basin Streets. It was a place of sporting houses, saloons, and bagnios. The young woman from the train might not make her living by the cards in this particular part of town, but her reputation must surely reach this far.

Unable to concentrate with Griffin constantly pointing out food at every turn, Solomon gave in to hunger and had himself a hasty meal of chicken and sausage jambalaya, finished off with a glass of beer. Then, ignoring the local enticements, Solomon began his inquiries, acting for all the world like a young sporting gent looking for a good time, very particular in his tastes, but amiable, so as not to give the wrong impression. He would not get one word out of a single soul if he came off like some arm of the law, bill collector, or irate *pater familias* hunting a wayward scion among the fleshpots.

But after several hours in and out of the palaces of desire, low, mean, and rough, or high, grand, and refined, he was no closer to picking up the trail of that young woman than when he'd started.

That was not to say there weren't women of every age, complexion, and size who could be called skilled at cards, and every one of them ready to sit down to a game or two, if he'd be so kind as to show them his bankroll, dearie.

But there wasn't a single woman to be found who matched the woman he recalled from the train, with her fresh, luminous face, fit with sparkling, mischievous eyes, and a tall figure of willow and steel, in a silk brocade.

When he'd finally worked his way as far east as Iberville, he decided to sit a spell on the wooden curb of the planked sidewalk, in his shirt-sleeves, his waistcoat unbuttoned, his jacket off and draped over the satchel placed beside him. His derby was pushed back, and he was having himself a bottled tonic beer. He wasn't in the mood for anything stronger just yet. The sky was overcast, there wasn't much of a breeze, and the damp heat was almighty oppressive. While there was still day-light left, it was looking more and more like he wouldn't be rolling back time and spending the night at Lavinia's this evening. He resigned him-self to staying the night here.

Griffin stood over him, looking out on the people, the mule-drawn omnibuses, the *marchandes* with their baked goods, fruits and candies, the hawkers of housewares and hand-made cigars, the occasional chim-ney sweep, the itinerant handymen crying their skills, and the panhan-dlers moving up and down the street. There were sporting men, dandies, drudges carrying the day's groceries or paper-wrapped parcels. There were women in pairs, in singles, accosting men, some nodding to each other, extending professional courtesies, others evading each other with a hiss and a spit, all stepping over the trash and spill that flowed along the shallow channels on either side of the street, carrying runoff and refuse.

"Girl like that," said Solomon, "ought to have made some kind of mark. Ought to stand out. This is just the sort of place that would ap-preciate skills like that."

"Not that I go in for that kind of thing, but wouldn't a card sharp keep her skills to herself so as not to scare away their pigeons?"

"Ha! A fella wouldn't show off such skill. But a woman? She's nothing but a challenge in a flowery hat. No matter how poorly a fella might play? Every one of them would think themselves fit to put her in her place."

"You know this town pretty well, don't you."

"Yes."

"Then maybe you can help me for a change."

"With what?"

"You could tell me where I can get beignets and coffee."

"I'm trying to find the woman that'll turn back time for all of humanity and you're thinking about coffee and pastries?"

"Beignets. Big difference."

"You beat all, you know that?"

"You know what I think? I think you being so helpless is an excuse. That's all it is. An excuse to hold onto that shard. Because, truth to tell, you don't care if you ever go back."

Solomon popped to his feet squaring around on Griffin. "You know what *I'm* thinking? *I'm* thinking if you wanted this doo-hickey so bad, you'd help. Give a shake of those dominoes and point her out to me. Put an end to it."

"I can't do that," Griffin barked back at Solomon. "Students, want to tell him why?"

They both shouted at each other, "Free will!"

"I think it's your excuse for being lazy," said Solomon.

"Lazy? Lazy? Just for that, you know what I'm going to do? Do you? Hunh? Do you?"

"What?"

"I'm going to find my *own* beignets and coffee." Griffin launched himself off the sidewalk toward Canal where he caught up with a passing omnibus and stepped aboard, stopping next to the coinbox. Solomon followed, dropping in coins for himself. Then remembering angels didn't carry pocket change, he dropped in coins for Griffin.

As the last coin rattled through the slot, Griffin said, "They can't see me. But I appreciate the thought."

Sometimes, Solomon could just kill him.

When the omnibus reached St. Charles, Griffin hopped off, with Solomon right behind.

Solomon followed along, becoming more and more angry at Griffin's frivolous meandering among the toggeries, groggeries, booteries, hotels, and storefront offices.

"You smell that?" Griffin sniffed the air, hard. "Must be along here somewhere." Solomon smelled nothing but an overcrowded, overheated, overcast city.

"Once you get past the gagging stench of raw sewage hanging in the air, the rot from the river just over yonder, and the horse manure that permeates everything," said Griffin, "You can pick out some of the most delicious aromas. There's coffee and chicory, boiling sugar turning into caramel, toasting pecans, sweet fragrances of piled up fruit, crawfish just starting to boil." Griffin stretched out his arms to embrace the very air above their head. "Doesn't it make your nose hairs quiver?" He stopped, turned back, but Solomon wasn't there. "Where'd you go?" Griffin made a show of missing him. He seemed truly surprised to discover Solomon three doors back, standing stock still, staring into the window of a shopfront.

Solomon stood fixed on the framed photograph displayed in the window of the Beaux Arts Studio and Photography Emporium.

It was a large, black-and-white photographic print of a young woman seated at a table. She held a hand of five cards resting on her lap, an ace high flush. She stared off into the distance, seeming spent. She was alone, a pile of money in the center of the table, and cards dashed down by the other players, all now absent, suggesting they'd lost and left her in possession of the winnings.

"That's her," said Solomon, intent on the face.

"Who?"

"The girl from the train."

"Why merciful heavens." Griffin slapped his hands aside his face. "What lagniappe is this? You go hunting for a snack on the other side of the city, and look what turns up."

Solomon went inside, the bell over the door tinkling their arrival. The space was arranged with photographs of all shapes, subjects, and sizes, some of which were hung by velvet cords, but mostly they were stacked upright four and five deep against the walls. A long table held an angled display case, showing off smaller pictures with handsome, well-gilt framing. At the back stood two large, wooden cameras on tripods surrounded by a clutter of potted plants, short pillars, earthenware jars, flags, and draperies, behind all of which was a backdrop painted with a wild garden landscape.

The photographer came out from the back, through a doorway hung with tasseled velvet swagged back from a sheer lace drape. He was in a long, rubberized apron, wearing sleevebands, and wiping his hands on a scrap of toweling.

"Come to have your portrait made. Let me call my assistant and if you would, give us a few minutes to get everything ready." He spoke as he untied his apron. "Willem!" he shouted back over his shoulder.

Solomon started to speak, realizing that Griffin was still at his elbow. "Can he see you?"

"Sure. Why not?" Griffin stepped forward.

"By damn," said the photographer. "Didn't see there were two of you." He adjusted his spectacles down from his forehead where he'd pushed them. He stepped in close to study Griffin's face.

"I'd be obliged immensely if I could do a Greek study of you, sir," said the photographer. "Something tasteful. You won't be disappointed at the results."

Griffin turned his smug twist of a smile back on Solomon.

"You the one made that picture? The one in the window?" asked Solomon.

"Of course, of course." The photographer spoke as if dismissing the question, intent on Griffin's features, bobbing in close, then hauling back, examining Griffin from every which way.

"You make the one of that girl?" Solomon asked, a tad louder.

"Ye-e-e-s." The photographer nodded, more for Griffin's physiognomy than Solomon's question. Then seeming to recover, he asked, "Which one exactly?"

"The girl holding the playing cards."

"Ah. Miz Hudson. What about it?"

"Who is she?"

"That's Amelia Hudson." The photographer went back to Griffin's out-thrust chin as it caught the amber-gold light of the lowering sun. "Elmira Hudson's daughter."

"I've been all over this town. Never heard a single word about her. A woman of her ability with the playing cards ought not to have escaped notice."

"Cards? Amelia Hudson, playing at cards? Ha. Ha-ha. Hahahahaha!" The photographer laughed so hard he had to lift his glasses and wipe his eyes. "That, sir, is a rich one. The daughter of Elmira Hudson playing at cards?" It set him off again, laughing and shaking his head.

"That picture was Amelia's idea of a joke," he continued once he'd caught his breath. "She doesn't know the first thing about cards. My assistant, Willem, had to show her how to hold the pasteboards. When her mother, Elmira, saw the photograph, she was scandalized. Yessir. Wouldn't let Amelia bring it home. Refused to pay for it. So it's mine to do with as I will. Makes her madder'n a hornet seeing it in my shop window every day. But there's not a lovelier girl anywhere on the delta. Don't you think?"

"Seems like a lot of stuff and nonsense over a little card playing."

"Oh, not for Elmira. She is, by far, the straightest of the straight-laced women around. One of the Reformers. Pillar of the community. Founding member of the First English Lutheran Church. Does needlework for the poor, bakes cakes for all kinds of charity do's and raffles.

Makes you wonder whatever brought her to New Orleans. Amelia's always had a bit of a rebellious streak. It was her way of twisting the lioness's tail, having her likeness made sitting at a gambling table. It tickled her so. But I'll bet Elmira came down on her like a hod of brick when she learned of it."

Solomon was the very picture of a downcast treasure hunter standing over an empty hole. Elmira—if she really was Edith—didn't sound anything like the spirited young woman who rode out of Iron Hill on a stolen horse to make her living as a notorious outlaw.

"Where'll I find this Elmira Hudson?"

"Across the street. Elmira's Empire of Fashions for Ladies. Painted right on the window. Can't miss it."

"Do we have time for me to get my picture done?" Griffin continued to preen for the photographer.

But the tinkle of the bell told him Solomon was already gone.

Outside, crossing the street, Solomon was deep in his own thoughts, walking slowly, indifferent to the traffic that flowed around him, and the curses and catcalls of irritated drivers.

Griffin caught up with him.

"If Elmira *is* Edith, and if she's made herself over entirely, and her daughter Amelia's almost half-way to being some kind of nun already, why didn't everything snap back of its ownself? I mean, it stands to reason, don't it?"

"The improbability would be if someone who should not exist, which is you, convinces someone who does exist, which is her, to unchoose a fixed choice. There's nothing says a person can't change for perfectly normal reasons."

"I thought the same thing at first. But I caught up with her. I had my say. She changed. Amelia's turned out to be a sensible girl. There's no good reason time shouldn't snap backward, snatching me right out of my shoes."

Solomon almost walked into the horse pulling the hack coming to a stop in front of the line of buildings on the west side of the street. The driver seemed not to notice nearly running him down. Solomon was about to tear a strip off him, when he spotted Amelia stepping down from the hack.

"That's her," said Solomon, peering over the horse's backside.

"Who?"

Before he could answer, the traveler in the checkered suit, stepped out of the hack, right behind her.

Solomon and Griffin lingered at the horse's head, out of view as the traveler gave instructions for the driver to wait.

Griffin and Solomon ducked under the horse's neck and scurried into the narrow alley between the buildings, still watching Amelia and the traveler who started to follow Amelia into the dress shop. She planted her hand in his chest.

"No. You wait with the hack. Momma finds out I'm running off with a professional gambler she'll stick me in a convent quicker than you can say Jack Robinson. You stay here and I'll have Dalmatia bring down my things."

"You be quick about it, because Ma-*mah* or no, I'll come up and steal you right from under her nose."

"Don't you worry about that. I can tell Momma I've seen the hex. She swears there's nothing for it but to fly once you've laid eyes on him. She'll probably give me money to go."

"We can use the stake."

Amelia went inside the shop as the traveler lit his cheroot and paced the wooden sidewalk out front of the emporium.

Griffin and Solomon looked at each other.

"I guess now we know why."

Chapter Twenty-Seven

New Orleans – 1890s

"THAT FELLA WAS WITH HER on the train. He said flat out he didn't know her at all. They're working together. Fleecing the passengers." Solomon thought hard a moment then broke into a smile, a man restored, a busted gambler given a fresh stake and another roll of the dice. He leaned out to check on the traveler, still pacing in front of the shop.

"Can't go through the front door." Solomon looked around the alley where they stood. A gate behind him led to a small, inner courtyard overgrown with flowers, vines, and shrubs in small pots. There were two wooden benches, the back slats of which were broken loose. On the wall, near the gate leading back to the street, was a rain spout running up to the gutters fixed to the eaves of the slope-shouldered roof. He could climb up, cross over the second-floor gallery and sneak in through an open window above.

Solomon glanced around to make sure he wasn't observed, then dragged a bench over for the extra reach. He shinnied up the pipe, using the brackets for footholds. Staying crouched over to keep his footing on the slope, he made his way across the roof.

The shutters of the nearest window were closed and locked from inside. Keeping himself hunched over, Solomon moved to the next window, its heavy wooden shutters partially open. He could tell the sash was up, the curtains billowing outward in the lazy breeze.

Peering in, he could see the parlor was all a-clutter, with two small divans, a square grand piano covered with a drape on which a multitude of ceramic figurines sat. Across from the window stood an iron stove, a glass-front bookcase, and on the walls framed pictures hung by tasseled cords from the picture rail that encircled the room. To the right, in front of a side window, were placed two wing chairs. A tall electric floor lamp stood behind the chair on the left, and a small table lamp on a mahogany stand beside the chair on the right.

And no guns.

In one chair sat a woman Solomon recognized right off as Edith, despite the years she was carrying. Whippet thin and wiry, her skin tanned and mottled, she wore dark satins and a white underblouse, her hair neatly arranged and pinned up. She sat upright, with a twist of her lip, perhaps a frown. Amelia was seated in the other chair, leaning in, her hands clasped in her lap.

"Maybe it *was* the hex. So, if you give me the money, I could go live in Chicago. At least for a while."

"How could you be sure?"

"He asked me in front of everybody if you were the Sweetheart Bandit and rode with a renegade lawman out of Kansas. I didn't say anything back. So he went on and said he was Lavinia Kantlingher's long lost sweetheart, and had a message for me."

"Did he show you the locket?"

"No."

"Did he mention the angel?"

"No."

"Then, it couldn't be the hex. Probably someone who used to ride with me and Jake. Some saddle tramp down on his luck, trying to shake you down."

"He didn't seem at all old enough to be one of that gang."

"The hex shows itself the day before a wedding. You're not planning to marry anyone, are you?"

"No. Of course not!"

"Yes, she most certainly is." Solomon clambered over the window sill into the room.

Edith was on her feet in an instant, recognizing Solomon.

"You again," said Amelia, more fierce than fearful.

"He's the one you saw on the train?"

"Yes."

"There's a fancy fella downstairs waiting for her this minute."

"A—a—a buyer. From Chicago!"

"He's a card sharp and a shill. Fleecing passengers riding the railroad. I watched it all with my very own eyes and I've come to tell you." He turned to Amelia. "That fella you're fixing to run away with is no fit match for you or for any good woman."

"Wait. Are we talking about Lloyd Llewellyn? That dandy I've seen hanging around the shop front?"

"He's down there now, waiting for her to come with her things."

"What have you to do with him?"

"Not a thing, Mamma! Not a blessed thing! This—creature accosted me on the trip down from Chicago and some very nice men whom I didn't know at all put him off the train."

"While it was moving. Forty mile or more outside the station, thank you very much."

Edith glanced at Solomon then back at Amelia.

"Did you know this about Mr. Llewelyn?"

Amelie's eyelids fluttered a mile a minute. "Of course not! You think I'd take up with—with—gamblers?" Amelia's arms wagged for emphasis.

"You handle cards better than any woman I've ever seen," said Solomon. "And that's saying something. That fella's taking advantage of you." Solomon turned to Edith. "He swore he'd come up and carry her off, will you or nil you."

"Amelia!" Edith's voice was a husky mix of maternal indignation and fear.

Amelia kept her wounded face on just a moment longer then gave way, her story played out.

"All right, all right. It's true." Amelia stuck her tongue out at Solomon, shucking off all pretense. "I feel so caged in. You can't possibly know what it's like, Mamma! Lloyd Llewellyn wants to show me the world, which I will never see all cooped up here!"

"You can't," said Solomon.

"I forbid it," said Edith.

"I promised!" Amelia shouted, then wilted. "I owe him money."

"How?"

"Cards." Amelia's arms dropped, her shoulders drooping as she turned and paced about the room.

"Gambling?" Edith sat down again, the starch gone out of her.

"No! I hate gambling," said Amelia. "I was cheating. He caught me. But he wasn't mad. He said he'd never been taken by any woman at cards. Said he didn't think there could be an angel in heaven who could manage a deck of cards or shuck a sucker faster than I could." That fact seemed to please her.

"I know one angel that'd give you a run for your money on that," said Solomon.

"Lloyd really, really, really wants to marry me, Mamma."

"For the money you'll rake in."

"When you think about it, doesn't it seem like an investment in our future happiness?"

Edith twisted in her seat, rustling the fabric of her bustle. She twisted the fingers of the one hand in the other.

"I have us a way out of this pickle," said Solomon, seeing as how the ladies might be ready for an extreme solution or two.

"You?" asked Amelia. "How?"

"Don't ask him," said Edith.

Solomon took a deep breath and with as much reasonableness and conviction as he might muster said, "I'm Lavinia Kantlingher's long lost sweetheart, charged by her to be a blessing to her children wherever I might encounter them on the road of life, and," he paused to inhale, "I have it on the solemn word of an angel right out of heaven that everything can be set to rights if you foreswear this Llewellyn fella, and rightly marry someone worthy of the husbandly calling." Solomon gave a snap nod of his head to end his speech.

Amelia stared at Solomon. Edith straightened the tools by the iron stove, a seeming nervous tic, adjusting them just so.

"Seems there's nothing else for it."

Amelia turned now to stare at her mother.

"Mamma!"

Solomon pulled the locket from inside his shirt and popped it open for Amelia to see.

Edith stood up, removing her own locket, opening it for Amelia to see the likeness. Then she settled it on Amelia.

"He says he's Lavinia's long lost sweetheart. He's got the locket. He says he's taken it as his charge to be a blessing wherever he finds us. Coming all this long way to warn you against running off with Mr. Llewellyn and set your eye on marrying a man worthy of you. Isn't that what he said?"

"Yes," said Amelia, realization seeming to sweep over her, a reluctance to agree with her mother.

"So. You understand what that means." Edith lifted Amelia's chin with a tender hand, looking her in the eye, and handing her the coal scoop from the scuttle by the stove.

They were quiet for a moment, and Solomon was already feeling the cool breeze off the Esopus on his face as he made his way back to Lavinia's.

"He really is the hex?" said Amelia finally, in a very small voice.

"He really is the hex," said Edith, and whipped the drape off the piano, flinging it over Solomon, the figurines gone flying, shattering everywhere as Amelia klonked him as hard as she could with the scoop.

By the time Solomon untangled himself from the piano drape both women were gone.

Wasting no time, Solomon climbed out the window onto the roof.

Griffin sat, his legs dangling over the roof's edge. "Time for coffee?"

Down below Amelia and Edith piled into the waiting hack. Llewelyn scanned the roofline, pulling a pistol from inside his coat. Spotting Solomon, he fired.

The wood of the shutter frame splintered behind him.

"For a peaceable sort, you sure draw an awful lot of gunfire."

Another bullet hit the window frame, throwing splinters.

Solomon ran, his arms flapping to keep himself upright on the slanted surface.

"I'll just catch up with you later, okay?" shouted Griffin as Solomon reached the end of the gallery roof and leaped to the gallery of the next building over. Llewelyn followed right along, banging away at him from the street.

Solomon ran out of roofs, forced to launch himself onto the net of wires strung pole to pole over the streets. He caught one, and springing to a halt above the street, sagged ever so slowly until the wire parted with a bright blue arcing spark. Solomon fell, swinging on the end of the wire down to the street, slamming hard onto the cobbled paving.

Struggling to his feet, still holding the live wire, Solomon's hair stood on end, and he fairly hummed as the electricity flowed through him. Throwing off blue arcs, he set up such a buzz that ladies swooned, men swore, and little boys poked him with sticks to see if the wood might catch fire. The wild current set his shoes to smoking and caused his trouser cuffs to catch fire.

Solomon had to stand on the cable to pry his hands loose, locked on as he was. When he broke free he shivered hard, gave his scalp a mighty rub to dispel the hum that filled his skull and shook his arms to rid himself of the worst case of pins-and-needles he'd ever had in his life. He felt like he'd been knocked on his funny bone, all over. He shook so hard he nearly threw himself off his feet.

If that hadn't been enough, a bullet whinged over his head.

Llewelyn closed in, reloading.

Solomon planted his feet and cocked his fists, ready to meet Llewelyn head on.

"Hey, Solly." Griffin was at his elbow once more. "Now that you've got everyone's attention, what'll you do for your next trick? Hmmm?"

"I wanna bust him one then I'll be on my way."

"I always tell you, it's not a good idea."

"Give me one good reason why I shouldn't settle his hash?" Solomon slowly windmilled his fists, ready, as Llewelyn got closer.

"I'll give you two. Only charge you for the one. First, the coppers are on their way already."

Solomon spotted the blue bullet helmet of a city policeman heading for them.

"And, two, if they don't put you in jail, they'll put you in a zoo and charge folks a nickel to come and gawk at the Amazing Electrified Man." Griffin looked at him. "Just saying."

Llewelyn was nearly on him. Solomon spun suddenly and dashed headlong down the street.

"Oh. And you'd be a real hit with the voodoo set around here," Griffin shouted after him. "That's three!"

Solomon ran down Gravier Street, finally reaching the wharves at the river's edge, with Llewelyn right behind him, nearly cornering him among the bales of cotton waiting to be loaded. He was up onto the bales and running along the tops, Llewelyn still firing when he had a clear shot, cursing his bad aim, while Solomon, pricked and pinged, cursed Llewelyn's amazing ability to hit a moving target.

He reached the end of the long stretch of stacked bales and leaped to the ground. To the right were steamboats loading passengers, and to the left steamboats loading cargo.

A bullet struck the bale just behind him, throwing up a cloud of cotton fiber.

Solomon headed straight for the middle, up to the pier edge, and dived into the muddy brown water of the mighty Mississip'.

Llewelyn ran right up onto the edge of the loading pier, windmilling his arms to keep from falling headlong in after Solomon. He took careful aim at Solomon's bobbing head as he swam for all he was worth toward the middle of the river. Llewelyn smiled and pulled the trigger. The hammer fell on an empty chamber.

He shook his fists at the sky and cursed a blue streak.

When Solomon judged he'd reached a distance sufficiently out of pistol shot, he stopped and tread water so he could look around to see how far he'd reached.

A good twenty yards ahead of him was a side-wheel steamer maneuvered by a pushboat away from the dock and toward the middle of the waterway for the trip upriver. A figure was seated on the fantail, legs dangling over the stern.

"Over here!" the figure shouted.

Griffin. Of course. Solomon swam for the steamer that hadn't yet engaged its engines and started the paddle wheels turning.

Solomon reached the steamer's gunwales and pulled himself aboard.

"You might want to consider taking your chances with Luther. Your ability to evade gunfire seems to have improved immeasurably."

"Not hardly." Solomon stretched out the tail of his shirt, showing the charred holes peppering the fabric. He rubbed his face and flung the water from his hands, then ran his fingers through his hair. He leaned back, bracing himself with his arms behind himself. "You never gave me cause to say it before, but this time, you give me no choice."

"That's completely uncalled for, Solly," said Griffin, jumping in, "How could you even begin to think—"

"Thanks."

Griffin shook his head. "Excuse me?"

"Thanks. I might never have latched eyes on Amelia, if you hadn't pointed her out to me."

"Whoa, there, Solly. In spite of your flowery, well-crafted expression of gratitude, you're mistaken. All I said was let's go find some beignets and coffee. Which I never got. Don't go jumping to conclusions. That would be a gross violation of your precious and inviolable free will."

"Still."

"I can't *help* help."

"You said."

"But there's no law against me giving you a teensy bit of advice."

"What sort of advice?"

"Just spit-balling here, but popping out of nowhere, announcing yourself to be Lavinia's long lost love, saying all their troubles melt into air if they do whatever you say, doesn't instill a lot of confidence."

"What am I supposed to do about it?"

"Don't spring it on them right off. Earn their trust. Get them to like you. *Then* spring it on them."

"First I got to find them."

"Yes, there is that."

"Like I said, it don't seem you want your doo-hickey as bad as you say you do."

"I do. But. It's in a safe place. No one knows you have it."

"You don't think I'm going to make it back to Lavinia, do you."

"Anything's possible."

Griffin vanished just as two deckhands grabbed up Solomon. Sitting on the fantail, scorched and soaked as he was, he didn't seem a regular passenger to them. Short of cash, his satchel gone, they carted Solomon off for a stowaway. The deckhands carried him kicking and thrashing, down to the coal bunker and stuffed him in until they could put him off at the next landing.

Which they did about thirty miles upriver, the spot no more than a stretch of dock jutting out from a patch of bare ground. The steamer's pilot didn't bother to guide the boat in close, but kept well off, not willing to risk any snags mired under the muddy waters just to be rid of a stowaway.

It took four good-sized deckhands to carry Solomon to the rail and fling him overboard into the mighty muddy river with a mighty big splash for such a mighty average-sized fellow.

Treading water, Solomon caught sight of Edith and Amelia under the lights of the upper promenade among the passengers watching the fun. They gave no sign of recognizing him, since he was little more than a soaked head and shoulders against the dark water.

The steamer steered back for the river's middle as the paddle wheels set to churning again.

Solomon swam hard but it was futile from the git-go. He gave up, turned for the shore, and breast-stroked his way in until he could stand up and wade onto dry land.

Griffin was standing there. Yet again. With his things. Yet again. Which he dropped to the ground. Yet again.

"So. Same time next year?" Griffin asked. "Mind what I said about earning their trust."

Solomon gave himself a shake and swiped away the water from his face and hair.

"I could've been spared another dunking and still be on that steamer with Edith and Amelia if you'd a left these behind when you vamoosed."

"I do always seem to be picking up after you, don't I? Force of habit. You'll make a guardian angel of me yet."

Solomon took up his satchel.

"You have any idea where they're going?"

Griffin shaded his eyes with his hand as he studied the river, studied the starry sky, studied the surrounding landscape, studied Solomon.

"North?"

"I could use a little more'n that."

"You know what they say. Sometimes the journey is more important than the destination."

"Them that say it don't know where they're headed or how long they'll be in the going of it."

Griffin was already walking away, saying over his shoulder, "Or they come to realize the destination wasn't worth the trip." With that, Griffin walked toward the woods, whistling, evaporating before he reached the stand of trees, taking with him what little light there'd been.

Left in the dark, without any settlements nearby, Solomon kept to the worn path that ran up from the river to the road and then followed it north.

Part Three

Chapter Twenty-Eight

Oklahoma – 1980s

YEARS ON THE ROAD BROUGHT SOLOMON to the outskirts of a good-sized carnival, set up in a dirt field behind a large mall set back from the highway. A little bit before eight in the morning, the sun was a low disk on the eastern horizon, throwing a muted orange glow across the silent rides, closed concession vans, and game booths snugged down under canvas.

Only the airplane ride was running. The mechanical arms lifted and lowered the little, battered biplanes, circling full-tilt with a single rider aboard.

Solomon stood behind the short, portable barricade that encircled the ride. He'd shaved his head and wore a seaman's knit watch cap with a rolled hem, pulled low over his ears. He wore a touch of clown-white at his temples, and a carefully tended scruff of beard, hoping it made him look older.

Watching the biplanes as they circled, Solomon considered how the only thing left in the world sure to irritate him was the mere chance Griffin might be right about anything. It didn't happen often, but when it did, it made him squirm. Griffin's godawful arrogance didn't need vindication.

Solomon scratched at the burring itch of his whiskers, freshly irritated at what Griffin told him the very first night they met.

"Next thing you know," Griffin had said, "you're on the run, hiding, pretending you never were the person you used to be."

The one rider, a girl about three or four years old, sat in the open cockpit of the little biplane while a young woman stood at the controls of the ride.

Here Solomon was again, aiming to pass himself off as someone else. All for an ever-receding hope of escaping his reputation as a hex and going back to who he was.

But all these years gone by, trying to gain the trust of suspicious women, turned him into—something else. A damned hard thing to consider Griffin being right about anything. Least of all that.

After getting himself pitched off the steamboat, Solomon followed the river north, heading for Chicago, and asking at every landing about two women from New Orleans. He could never get a decent answer because the only thing people up and down the river wanted to talk about was the Amazing Electrified Man. It seemed every newspaper ran the same picture, a remarkably clear half-tone of him taken by that same photographer who'd put him onto Amelia. Any mention of New Orleans anywhere along the river got them talking about how much Solomon looked like the fella in the paper.

With no word of Edith or Amelia, he pushed east. Solomon got the idea of joining up with a traveling circus to avoid all that curiosity. He painted himself up as a clown, calling himself Shotwad. He took seriously Griffin's warning about the cosmic disaster that might follow any discovery of his immortality but decided there'd be no harm if he traded on it just the least little bit.

So he took to eating fire, juggling nine-pins, and riding a unicycle. But it was his antics with gunpowder packed into everyday objects that first won him the job. Trying to light his cigar with a burning stick of dynamite, wearing a necktie made of exploding firecrackers, and setting off a box of TNT that blew him twenty feet in the air made him a crowd favorite.

East Texas – 1910s

In the late spring, a handbill tacked to a fence post on the outskirts of Texarkana led Solomon to Amelia's daughter, Theodora. She was doing a bicycle act in a rival circus outside of Waco. He hired on with them for the rest of their tour.

Since Amelia may have given Theodora the locket with his picture in it, Solomon stayed behind his greasepaint mask. It allowed him to be the sort of benefactor he promised Lavinia.

More than a time or two Solomon stood up for Theodora in her run-ins with the local farm boys or cowhands driven to romantic excess by that fresh face of hers, haloed by those raven-black curls, and her long, shapely figure in pink tights and short skirts. She came to look on

Shotwad, as a kind of clown in shining armor.

That is, until Solomon learned she was running off with the avaricious old ringmaster.

While the roustabouts loaded the box cars for the jump to Albuquerque, Solomon took her aside and revealed his true self.

She seemed to take this startling news quite well, coming as it did from someone she'd grown to trust so thoroughly.

Until she pulled the pin from the hasp on the lion cage door and set the big cats on him.

The last she saw of the Kantlingher Hex was him with his head in the lion's mouth, getting chewed on. The last Solomon saw of Theodora, between the slathering tongue and yellowish fangs, was her pedaling for Mexico.

Theodora escaped in the resulting pandemonium, leaving Solomon to take the blame for releasing the beasts. His face, painted up and bewigged, adorned wanted posters for the rest of that decade.

Having no choice, he went back to working the railroads, now as a switchman and living in a switchman's shack north of Memphis, where the locals only knew him as Hey Fella. Solomon planned to stay out of sight until all that circus folderol died down.

Which lasted until the day a closure rail at a switch point snagged Solomon's foot the same day a near-blind signalman sent a freight train loaded with gravel, sand, and quarried slate southbound straight for a northbound freight train carrying timber, turpentine, and cotton to meet head-on at the very spot where Solomon stood pinned.

The engineers first spotted Solomon stuck on the tracks, then each other barreling for a head-on collision. The crews jumped and the locomotives smashed into each other right where Solomon stood, with a crunching, screeching, booming, crumpling, cascading crash. Freight cars rolled up over each other, thrown this way and that, snapping trees, and gouging up the hillsides, spewing dirt, and strewing timber, stone, cotton, and trade goods everywhere.

Solomon's shielded body squirted out like a greasy bean in a high, arching flight, then landing in a billowing cloud of dust.

The crews, amazed at finding him alive, demanded to know how he'd managed to escape.

"Well, sir," said Solomon, looking at the oil he'd wiped from his face, "when I saw the direness of my predicament, I doused myself with oil from my oilcan and trusted to its lubricative properties. The impact squeezed me right between them two locos, spitting me out like a watermelon seed, clean out of harm's way."

In clearing away the wreckage, workmen found one of Solomon's boots still caught in the switch, the steel curled upward. The crushed oil can nearby made it official. Proof enough of Solomon's claim, at least to the romantics among the railroad fraternity. Old Squirt, as they took to calling him, passed into railroad legend. Which ended Solomon's railroading days for good.

Moving on, Solomon took such work as he could and kept looking. He made his way in a meandering loop, going from job to job, a few days here, a season there, herding cattle, stringing telegraph wire, and the like. When he reached the Gulf of Mexico, he took work on vessels fishing the waters along the coast from Galveston to Pensacola. Being a new face in a new place, he'd gone back to joining the merry-making and storytelling with crewmates when confined aboard, and with the locals all along the coast when ashore. He was always careful to give no offense or provoke any wonderment at his past.

Gulf Coast – late 1920s

Theodora turned up in the Florida Keys, winter of the late 1920s or so, with her daughter, Hester. She operated the charter boat, *Drifter*, for sportsmen, fishing for marlin, sword, amberjack, and mackerel.

Solomon donned an eye-patch, soaked his hair in a bucket of peroxide, and painted his teeth with marine varnish to pass himself off as Bucholz, a Swedish brass-hat diver between jobs. His knowledge of boats and seamanship was a godsend to Theodora when she ran into hard times the year of the stock market crash and took up rum-running rather than lose her boat.

It was Solomon who taught her how to navigate in the dark, to rig a boat for running in on a beach without waking up nearby residents, and to offload illegal liquor and cigarettes with barely a footprint in the sand. There was no one she and Hester trusted more than Solomon in his guise as Bucholz.

Until he confronted Hester about her plan to run away with the handsome first mate on the *Jolly Bender*, a notorious rum-running schooner working out of Jamaica.

Catching Hester as she gassed up Theodora's boat for a run out to the three-mile limit, he revealed who he was, proving it with his locket.

Hester stood transfixed, gas pouring out onto the dock, her brow furrowed, confused, betrayed. She dropped the hose and leapt onto the boat, threw off the lines, and slapped the throttle hard against the stops, roaring away from the dock. She turned to look back only long enough to fire a flare into the puddled gasoline around Solomon's feet.

The wooden dock went up in flames, taking the gas pump and tanks with it. The last Hester saw of the Kantlingher Hex was him standing silhouetted against the roaring, exploding, rising fireball. The last Solomon saw of Hester was her cutting a high wake, aimed for Cuba.

Solomon stayed close to the Florida coast, packing fish, loading freighters, working oil platforms, and renting beach umbrellas. He'd do just about anything if it allowed him to avoid attention and keep a watch out for the two women and their boat.

His longest stretch came as a deckhand on a fishing boat working the Gulf. That lasted until the skipper sent Solomon over the side, harnessed and tied off, to clear a net fouled in the rudder.

Solomon wasn't in the water more than five minutes when the biggest damned shark anyone ever saw clamped down on Solomon and swam in furious circles, spinning the boat on its keel trying to pull him loose. The men managed to spear the beast and haul the shark aboard, with Solomon still gripped in its jaws.

When the fishermen pried open the shark's mouth to free Solomon, they stood amazed to find the monster didn't have a single tooth in its head. None to speak of anyway. How lucky, they all said, to be struck by the only toothless shark that ever swam God's great oceans.

Solomon figured that it was more likely the shark had lost all its teeth trying to saw through him. So he was just as glad to call it luck and drink his own health when the skipper shared out a cup of whiskey to each hand and saluted this sign of divine favor.

They took to calling him Gummy, and his fame spread all along the Gulf Coast. Again, finding himself celebrated in song, story, and drunken toast, Solomon gave up fishing and headed inland, back to drifting from job to job, working as a pinsetter in bowling alleys, mowing grass in graveyards, and riding dynamite trucks.

For a time, Solomon went by the name of Axel and drove for a moonshiner out of Immokalee. Solomon's fearlessness on a dark road in the middle of the night at high speeds won him a terrific admiration. It was a fearsome thing to watch, and no one in their right mind ever rode along with this Axel kid making runs to Tampa, Fort Myers, or Miami.

On a run down to the Florida Keys , Solomon spotted Theodora's boat, *Drifter,* tucked away in a slip on Key Largo. The boat's owner, an old gent in a linen suit, two-toned shoes, and wide-brimmed panama, told Solomon he bought it for cash from two women who said they were in a hurry and needed money right away to move as far west as they could to get the stink of fish out of their nostrils.

Solomon left the Keys, bought a used motorcycle, gathered his few belongings, and rode westward, mastering the idiosyncrasies of the two-wheeler as he went.

Twin Falls, Idaho – 1950s

A bubblenose Freightliner hauling livestock ran Solomon off the road and into a ditch, just outside Twin Falls, Idaho. The semi's driver gave him a wave and a blast of his airhorn as he whizzed past.

Solomon pushed his bike into Twin Falls looking for a filling station with a garage and found Hester managing a drive-in restaurant right next to the filling station where he'd brought his motorcycle.

Hester was on her own, with a sixteen-year-old daughter, Bonita.

Solomon took a job pumping gas at the filling station and helping out around the drive-in, working for little more than burgers and fries.

Solomon still went by the name of Axel, but kept his dark hair close-cropped, trimmed his whiskers into a goatee, and always wore his leather aviator's helmet with the goggles pushed up on his brow.

Most days, as Solomon tinkered with his motorcycle, Bonita was right behind him fascinated with all things vehicular. She had little use for girlish tales of romantic adventure and true love, soaking up Solomon's stories of driving moonshine and evading law enforcement. She would linger, listen, and inhale the hot road-iron smells of the motorcycle.

Bonita showed herself to be in a hurry to grow up, to pick out the fastest boy from among her many admirers hanging out at the drive-in and take to the open road.

She had her heart set on a wannabe outlaw in a shiny red roadster and Solomon knew time was running out for him to have his say.

His chance came the morning she asked him to show her how to ride a motorcycle to impress the kid in the red roadster. In between explaining the clutch and the throttle, and how to balance the machine, Solomon revealed his true self to Bonita, pulling the locket from inside his grimy tee-shirt.

Bonita seemed genuinely touched at his concern. Just when he'd convinced himself he'd managed to win her sympathy, she twisted the motorcycle into a low-rev spin turn, swatting Solomon to the ground. She leaped into the saddle, throttled it wide-open, and rode for the highway.

The last Bonita saw of the Kantlingher Hex was Solomon sprawled in the dust. The last Solomon saw of Bonita was her fishtailing his motorcycle, spraying gravel, disappearing down the open road.

Word got around that Bonita, being a wizard on two wheels or four, was the getaway driver for a string of bank robberies across five states. It caused the locals to wonder where she picked it up, working in her momma's drive-in. She turned out to be the slipperiest wheelman anywhere from Bakersfield to Boise. Nothing that ran on gasoline or rode on rubber could touch her.

On the Road – 1960s

Nameless once more, Solomon was back to roaming the country, following up on rumors that Bonita finally got shed of her bank robbing boyfriend and settled somewhere around Northfield, Minnesota under a new name.

Travel was harder for Solomon by that time, relying on commercial transportation to get from place to place. Having a driver's license meant proving who he was, which he couldn't, and if he could, he might accidentally annihilate the whole of creation—assuming Griffin was to be believed—all because he was living proof of human immortality. For Solomon's money it wasn't worth risking the unravelment of all creation just to stand in line to get a driver's license. Griffin could add that to his long list of inconveniences associated with his doo-hickey.

Downtown after a week working as a turf-cutter, Solomon ducked under a movie house marquee to avoid a sudden rain squall. He found himself staring at the most astonishing likeness of Bonita he could imagine.

It was only a gaudy, four-color movie poster, with her playing some sort of hot-rod honey. But, damn, if that wasn't Bonita just as he remembered her. She couldn't still be that young, but for sure those features don't grow on trees.

He could make out Lavinia's locket around her neck, with its distinctive shape and peculiar color. He slipped out his own and held it up just to be sure.

The lettering splashed across the poster said she was Loralee Twayne. Solomon asked the lady in the box office where he might find the girl on the poster. The lady winced at his ignorance and pointed in the general direction of Hollywood.

Solomon went looking for the very next bus headed westward.

Hollywood – 1960s

Solomon stepped off the bus at Vine Street in Los Angeles and spent three days roaming from place to place, asking at every studio where he might find Loralee Twayne. He tried passing himself off as a messenger with a telegram, a deliveryman toting flowers, and finally a blacksmith sent to shoe a horse.

He struck pay-dirt standing outside the gate of a large studio off Santa Monica Boulevard. A harried assistant director in inch-thick glasses swept him up with a score of other men waiting to board a bus full of extras for a World War One movie starring Loralee and shooting at a private airfield.

Costumed as a doughboy and marched onto the field, Solomon spotted Loralee, playing a wartime aviatrix, next to a wood and canvas biplane. She stood in the company of a slim and lanky fellow with a thin moustache and short, unruly hair, and wearing dark glasses. Her private pilot and driver, some said of him. Her lover, said others. A fugitive and blackmailer whose got the goods on her, still others said.

Tightly corralled by that assistant director, and protected by that mystery man, Solomon saw no way to reach her.

Then right after lunch, the assistant director lined up all the dough-boys. He needed someone to play the ground crewman who would hop up on the wing of Loralee's plane, wipe the windscreen, and then hop down. Maybe throw a salute. "Someone small," he said, "who won't put his big foot through the canvas wing." He hauled Solomon out of line, and said, "You'll do."

Now dressed in coveralls and a fore-and-aft cap, Solomon stood next to the aircraft with a rag for wiping Loralee's windscreen. The mystery man, dressed as a pilot, helped Loralee into the front cockpit and then climbed into the rear cockpit.

The pilot switched the engine on and called out contact. Another crewman swung the propeller. The engine caught and the propeller spun, a coughing, burping rattle of pistons firing.

Solomon hopped onto the wing and went to wiping the windscreen.

Seeing this might be his only chance, Solomon launched into his speech at Loralee.

"I'm Lavinia Kantlingher's long lost sweetheart," he shouted over the propeller's wind stream.

The airplane engine revved up.

Solomon turned to appeal to the pilot for another moment to finish what he had to say.

He wouldn't get the chance.

It was Bonita behind a greasepaint moustache. She shook her head and shouted, "You are one determined cuss." She pulled her goggles down and throttled up the engine, hard.

The airplane rolled forward faster and faster, the film crew chasing along, Solomon clinging to the strut as the tail lifted and the wheels left the grassy runway.

Airborne, Bonita jinked and rolled the airplane, swooping and diving, stunting to shake Solomon loose.

There wasn't much Solomon knew about aviation, but he knew there'd be no chance of Loralee and Bonita surviving a crash in this crate. If he knocked out a strut, stepped through a wing, or fell into the propeller, they'd be done for.

Aiming toward a nearby lake, Bonita pulled up hard again and then pushed over for another spiraling, wing-tearing plunge. With his eyes on the lake, Solomon thrust away from the aircraft into freefall.

He missed the lake, landing smack in the middle of a cottonwood tree, splitting it right down to the roots with a long, tearing crack.

He laid there for a moment, pierced with hundreds of long, raw splinters, then gave out with a piercing banshee yell that rattled around the hills.

"Daaaaaaaaaaaaaaaamn!"

The last Bonita and Loralee saw of the Kantlingher Hex was Solomon howling at the sky, a bristling porcupine. The last Solomon saw of the Kantlingher girls, for as long as he could bear to look, was their aircraft coming out of its spiral, waggling back on course, and then disappearing into the far-off clouds.

For the next few weeks, news reports were full of Loralee's astonishing disappearance with her mystery man and the morbid speculation about the role of the clumsy extra who'd disappeared along with them.

A blurry frame of movie film showing Solomon's face was blown up to wanted-poster size and hung in the post offices and police precincts for years.

Nameless once more, Solomon roamed the southwest, scouring every airfield and landing strip in his hunt for any wisp of gossip about the odd and unexpected appearance of an old-fashioned warplane flown by two women. A retired airplane mechanic in Utah hinted at just such an airplane having been abandoned in a nearby alfalfa field. But he couldn't recall what happened to the aircraft or its pilot.

Denton, Texas – 1980s

At a truck stop outside of Flagstaff, Solomon hitched a ride with a long-haul trucker headed for Denton, Texas, forty miles north of Dallas. The driver said he could use a helper to unload when he made his delivery, saving himself the cost of hiring warehouse lumpers out of his own pocket at the end of the run.

It was as much to stay in motion and avoid curiosity as it was to pick up some clue to the whereabouts of Bonita or Loralee. Not like the old days when he could show up someplace, find work, ask questions, and move on when it suited him.

As they rode along, Solomon let the trucker tell his stories of driving the old Route 66 and lecture him about grabbing life while he was still young.

"Ah, youth," said the trucker, "wasted on you kids, right? No offense."

When they parted company outside Denton, Solomon didn't have any good ideas which way to head. He started walking along the highway toward town, considering that Bonita might be inclined to go back to New York where there might be some of the old family still.

A sudden rain squall with its curtains of rain and pulses of lightning forced Solomon to take shelter in a motel just off an access ramp.

The rain swept over the motel, the wind shimmying the neon sign out by the road, the pool water whipped up to white caps. And the lightning, reaching down under the cloud cover, seeming to feel around for him. Not that he was overly suspicious of the natural elements.

The room clerk handed Solomon the key and said there was a ten-percent discount because the television was out of order. Which suited Solomon. He'd never acquired much of a taste for it.

The room was a simple, lightly plastered plywood box of a place, with plastic covered mattresses and thin sheets, and a television that was indeed out of order. A bullet hole in the upper corner of the screen created a starred pattern of cracked glass.

Solomon stared out at the clouded dark, wondering why it was such storms seemed to search him out. Was it one more ill-tempered feature of the natural order? Or some unnatural conductive quality caused by the doo-hickey?

For being so all-fired important according to Griffin, why did Griffin let him go so damn many years holding onto it?

Despite the lightning, Solomon liked the gray clouds and enjoyed watching the rain stroke over the landscape, like brushing a horse. There was a kind of peace about it.

He'd be the first to admit there was much he didn't know about creation, out where he couldn't see. He'd admit, for all his Bible reading, there might be something he'd missed when it came to the nature of angels. Something not apparent to the casual reader of holy writ.

Checking the drawer by the bed, he pulled out the Gideon Bible. Maybe there was something to explain Griffin and his indifferent pursuit of this doo-hickey. He cracked it open, not sure where to start.

The television blared to life behind him, loud and bright.

"I guess the rain surprised all of us, too, didn't it? You may want to re-think your career as a weatherman, Phil. Ha! I'm just kidding. Phil's our weather-guesser. Better luck next time, Phil," said the anchorwoman on the screen, giving out with a squint-eyed, wide-mouth laugh. "May want to call the Weather Service, get your money back on that forecast. Ha!" The anchorwoman was broad-shouldered, horse-toothed, with a high forehead and big, Texas hair. Her voice sounded like it'd been stropped on leather to give it that keen edge, sharp enough to slice flesh.

"It don't bear thinking about what all this rain's doing to the alfal-fal-fal-fal-fa. Woo. That's one of those words you get started and you don't know when to stop, do you? Alfalfa. Right? Cacaphony's another one, isn't it. Ca-ca-ca-caphony. Just keeps on going. Well, once this rain passes over it's all just mud anyway. And that's easy to say. Mud. But that's not Phil's fault, is it? Of course not."

Solomon had a rudimentary understanding of television sets, but not a lot of experience. He went about twisting knobs and pushing buttons to make it quit.

"Since there's no sense going out in all this bad weather," said the anchorwoman, "why don't you sit right back and lets you and me take a trip down memory lane."

Solomon reached behind the cabinet on which the television sat and yanked out the plug. The box kept on squawking.

"Isn't there someone'll cross your mind and you find yourself asking, where are they now?" Those words flashed up onto the screen, between the dark fingers of broken glass.

Solomon tore the blanket off the bed to muffle the beast.

"Loralee Twayne and her mysterious pilot boyfriend disappeared twenty-one years ago. Just flew off, never to be heard from again. Left a budding movie career and a whole passel of fans that must be wondering—where are they now?" The words flashed up on the screen again. "Of course they do. If they didn't, we'd have to move on to the cattle buyer's report from the Department of Agriculture, and that'd bore a squirrel to tears, right?" She gave out with another hard, shoulder-shrugging laugh.

Solomon lowered the blanket to stare at the screen.

"We recently tracked down Loralee Twayne, once a rising young movie star, now a down-and-out denizen with a traveling carnival where she's still flying, but these days it's a kiddie ride."

A little carnival carousel of airplanes filled the screen. Off to one side, watching the kids and parents queued up for the ride, was Loralee. Or someone who looked a lot like she might after twenty years.

"No sign of the mystery man. But then, isn't it always the way, girls." The anchorwoman gave out with another toothy laugh.

"She'll be appearing daily through Labor Day outside of Norman. What? And give up show business?" The anchorwoman was wiped from the screen as a lightning strike overloaded a transformer, knocking out the electricity to all the businesses on the motel's side of the road. Only the sound of rumbling thunder and pelting rain remained.

Chapter Twenty-Nine

Norman, Oklahoma – 1980s

SOLOMON STOOD WATCHING the little airplanes circling in the Oklahoma morning.

"Bank left!"

The voice of the young woman in the ride operator's booth came from the speaker, a tinny jangle in the morning air. The little girl leaned hard left, growling out her engine noises, adding to the new-morning musicale of day-breaking sounds.

"Bank right!"

The little girl leaned hard right.

"Loop-the-loop!"

The little girl threw herself back, her arms into the air.

"Keep your arms in the cockpit! You don't want to fall out, too!"

"Ditch the hex! Ditch the hex!" the little girl shouted, then pushed her stick forward. "Dive," she shouted, motoring her lips as she circled by Solomon.

"Barrel roll!"

The little girl leaned hard left again, then righted herself.

"Okay. Let's land the plane and get ready for work."

The ride came to a stop with a clank of machinery, humming gears, and the knock of fiberglass.

The young woman lifted the little girl out of the airplane and onto her hip, walking past where Solomon stood resting on the steel barrier.

"If you're looking for a ride, too, you'll have to come back when we're open," the young woman said to Solomon.

"I've had my fill of aero-planes. Thanks just the same."

"Then if you're looking for work you should check over at the boss's trailer. The green one with the striped awning." She disengaged the little girl's exploring hand from her hair.

"Your little sister?"

The young woman snorted.

"Francie!" a woman's voice shouted from among a cluster of trailers behind the fence at the back of the carnival.

Even after all this time, Solomon recognized Loralee as she stood in the doorway.

"Come try this on!" She held up the skirt and bodice of what looked like a wedding dress. "Hurry up! We don't have all day!" She disappeared back inside the trailer.

The young woman, Francie, again pointed Solomon toward the striped awning while she headed off toward her own trailer.

Solomon worked a few carnivals before, finding them a quick and easy means of melting away, making a little money, having a place out of the weather if you weren't too choosy. Where you were tolerated no matter how wild, impractical a story you might concoct about your origins.

This carnival was more like the kind he'd worked on before, carrying a sideshow as well as the usual games, rides, and food concessions.

Sideshows appealed to Solomon, with their outrageous acts and magical mysteries and the occasional human oddity thrown in. These were outsiders and kindred spirits. Add in the flashing, colored lights pulsing in time with the calliope music, and it was easy for Solomon to forget the hard-packed surface of a life lived on the road.

Solomon headed for the green trailer to ask for work.

The boss took him on as general labor and was glad to get him. It was work Solomon knew, and the boss was desperate to replace someone who'd been picked up by federal agents for embezzling back in Montana.

"Can't trust nobody, can you?" said the boss, watching Solomon fill out a paybook as Skeeter Martin, then sign it. He handed Solomon a key and pointed out the little trailer where he'd bunk.

The work was pretty much what Solomon expected. When he wasn't spelling the man on the ring-toss, an old-time carny named Clyde, he was picking up trash, toting ice for the concession wagons, and cleaning up the accidents of kids overstuffed with corndogs and cotton candy, spun, twisted, and shimmied to projectile velocity under the mad, driving musical excitement of the carnival.

A few nights later, with the carnival closed down and the parking lot cleared out, some of the carnies gathered in lawn chairs circled around an oil drum fire next to the picnic tables. Fireflies mingled with the sparks floating upward from the licking flames that lit the faces circling the fire barrel. They smoked, drank, and talked, trying to peel the bark off their fellow carnies.

Carnival people don't change much it seemed, hiding like they do behind the quick smiles, outrageous claims, and rapid-fire patter. Solomon couldn't say he ever got to know folks all that well, but he could do them the courtesy of knowing one from the other. Sometimes all he could do was latch on to some odd trait or peculiar bit of history to fix each one in his mind, if only for a season.

Bonita sat out with them for a while, and Solomon kept his cap pulled down over his eyebrows. But she paid him no mind, turning in early. Loralee was still in the trailer, working on the wedding dress. Francie sat on the ground, bare-legged in a pair of scant, cut-off denim shorts and rubber beach thongs, leaning back against the bench of the picnic table, sipping a soda. Marjorie sat drawing in the dust, wedged between Francie's legs

There was gossip about romances, about townies versus carnies, law enforcement, marks and dolls. Solomon was happy to sit quiet and take in what he could learn about Francie and the little girl.

Solomon's discreet distance didn't last.

"Hey, Skeeter!" called out Clyde, the old ring-toss guy who was pure carny and no known country of origin. "Show us your fingers."

Solomon frowned and gave a shake of his head.

They all knew the story. Solomon's first day on the job somebody's hat fell into the chain on the coaster. The coaster guy called Solomon over to help work it free. They left Nevin, the college dropout trying to decide between show business and the Army, to watch the coaster. But he set the coaster in motion before Solomon got clear, and sent the whole string of cars rolling over Solomon's hand. Everyone knew without looking he'd lost fingers. But he didn't.

"Don't be shy. I'm trying to make a point."

"Looked worse than it was." Solomon didn't want to make anything of the accident, nor did he want to invite too much curiosity. So he touched another match to his pipe, using both hands. If they cared to check.

"See that? Skeeter's going to make a great carny. High tensile steel," said Clyde. "Keep the kid greased up with unreasonable hope the next day's gonna be a little better and he'll last you a lifetime."

That resonated with all of them. It turned their focus off Solomon and back on themselves.

"Unreasonable hope," said Sasha, the buxom, narrow-faced farm girl from Iowa who billed herself as a warrior princess and dressed in an armored skirt and breast plate to juggle battle axes. She turned to Francie. "Hey, Francie, whacha hear from your Texas oilman?" Sasha snickered into her beer can as she took a swig, the coal of the cigarette between her fingers reddening her cheek.

"Come on, Marjorie. It's way past your bedtime," Francie got to her feet, lifting Marjorie. "Say good night."

"G'night." Marjorie gave a little, clam-finger wave as Francie carried her beyond the light of the fire barrel, back to their trailer.

"Sorry. Didn't mean to run her off. But—I am so glad I don't have to hear about her rich Texan again tonight."

"If I got a millionaire back home waiting for me, you wouldn't catch me grab-assing with you losers," Dolores found a home as the carnival's mistress of funnel cakes after too many years in the Navy. "No offense."

"You can leave lying around so many millionaires back home?" Zhanna, the Ukrainian contortionist, seemed older than her attractiveness and severe makeup suggested.

"If there really is a Texas oilman back in Amarillo waiting for her, you can grill me up for a catfish," Gunner, the Tilt-a-Whirl guy, always wore a neckerchief to hide his prison tattoos.

"Maybe," said Clyde, "that hex of hers finally got him."

"I don't believe there is hex," said Zhanna

"I don't believe there is Texan," said Sasha, mimicking Zhanna.

"Lulie's in there making the wedding dress. Right now." Donnie, the skinny, tattooed sword swallower, was notorious for his crush on Francie. He was, to Solomon's thinking, way too insecure and immature for someone who made a living by putting sharp objects down his gullet.

"Lulie's playing along with Francie." Sasha took another drag on her cigarette.

"He sends her presents all the time. Bought her a watch, a necklace, couple of rings. Got her mom a food processor."

"A food processor. If that don't say true love, I don't know what does."

"She's not buying them herself, Dolores. With what we get paid?"

"I've handled mail this whole trip," said Sammie, the college kid waiting out academic probation. "Only mail I've ever seen for them comes with a big red "past due" stamped on it."

"Doesn't the post office swear you to secrecy handling our mail?"

"Don't be jealous, Donnie."

"Maybe," said Gunnar, "If the hex did get hold of her Texan then the way's clear for Romeo here."

They could tell, even in this dark, Donnie was blushing.

"Shit! Francie's gone in, and we're all still sitting here talking about her rich Texan." Sasha stood up. "I'm off to bed. You losers need to get a life."

That seemed to end the night for everyone. They tossed cigarette butts into the fire barrel, knocked back the dregs of whatever was left in their beer cans and soda bottles, and headed off for their bunks.

Solomon stood up on their going, there being women among them. It was a reflex, a habit he found hard to break. So he covered by fishing in his pockets for another match, then sat back down to repack his pipe and stay for another smoke.

When the flare of the match dissipated and Solomon's eyes adjusted again to the twilight, he saw that Donnie still sat there, hang-dog, leaned over, his arms resting on his thighs, his hair, long and somewhat stringy, hiding his face.

Solomon wasn't in camp more than one full day before he'd learned all about that rich Texan back in Amarillo waiting to marry Francie, and this sideshow kid Donnie right here with his heartstrings tuned tighter than an idiot's banjo, mooning over her.

It didn't seem much of a contest to Solomon. A Texan with money and family, or a kid earning a paycheck by skewering his innards to the delight and horror of young and old alike? Which of the two would do more to violate the cosmos in its fixitude and cause it to unravel all the way back to Lavinia? This'd take some studying. Solomon drew on his pipe.

"Skeeter?" Donnie studied the dirt between his shoes. "You ever have someone eat a hole in your heart, and they don't even bother to stop and taste it?"

"I learned from day one with this outfit all about how Francie DeSoto ate your heart out without doing you the courtesy of putting it between two slices of bread." Solomon blew out a smoke ring. "You tell Francie herself? Straight out?"

"I've said every whichaway I can. Songs. Poems. Straight out."

"Maybe you're coming on too strong."

"No. It's not that. She says it's not meant to be."

That made sense to Solomon. Kantlingher women could be fiery and reckless, strong-headed and wrong-headed. But they weren't ignoramuses.

Solomon must have grunted in a way that sounded judgmental to Donnie.

"Not because of me or anything. She says on account of the hex. A full-on, no-joke, real, live hex."

Solomon kept his face aimed at the fire, barely flicking his eyes over at Donnie.

"There's no such things as hexes."

"Hey, I'm a full-blooded Carpathian, and we know all about hexes."

"You're born and raised in San Diego. I got that part of the story first day, too."

"You can't hide from who you are. Start talking about hexes, it's like something goes off inside me. I can't help believing it."

"Sounds like too many corndogs, you ask me."

"She says it was the hex that broke up her and some motorcycle guy she was seeing."

That made Solomon turn to look at Donnie.

"Lulie and Bonnie had a crop-dusting business somewhere south of Phoenix. Chandler, I think. Francie was seventeen. Ran off with some guy on a motorcycle. But he dumped her at a truck stop near the interstate outside of Decatur. That's in Illinois."

"I know where Decatur is, Donnie. She told you this hex was the cause of it?"

"She swears it. When she told the motorcycle guy she was pregnant, he said, like out of nowhere, he had this vision how he had to join a commune and they didn't allow women. So he left."

Solomon sprung to his feet and took to pacing. Not that he remembered getting to his feet.

He hadn't even known Francie had been born, much less that she rode off with some guy on a motorcycle, and certainly didn't meet up with her in Decatur. And here she was blaming him for something he didn't even do.

"She said it was the actual, Kantlingher Hex?" Solomon's tone was downright peevish.

"Just said it was the family hex. Didn't give it a name or anything. Said it happens to all the women in her family. She finds a guy, everything's going along great and then the hex shows up for no good reason and her whole life falls to pieces."

"No good reason?"

"No, no reason."

"'Never said anything about being Lavinia Kantlingher's long lost sweetheart? Or being charged by her to be a blessing to her children wherever he might encounter them on the road of life? Nothing about having the solemn word of an angel right out of heaven he could change the past and set everything right?"

This was just dandy. Kantlingher women being so keyed up, on their guard against him, they'd taken to blaming their own natural shortcomings on him. He wasn't even in the same part of the country, damn it.

"Which one said that? About changing the past? The hex or the angel?"

Solomon stopped and looked over at Donnie. He'd forgotten himself. Forgot there might be someone listening.

Solomon flopped back into the lawn chair, wishing he'd kept his mouth shut. "You don't believe any of that malarky, do you?"

"I've got family goes all the way back to the Carpathian Mountains."

"So you said."

"It's in my blood."

"It's malarky."

"If that guy in Amarillo had any real feelings for Francie, would he leave her working in a place like this?"

Solomon stretched out his legs toward the fire, making a show of relaxing.

"You know what I wish?" Donnie flung back his hair and gazed up at the stairs. "I wish there really was a way to change the past, fix the mistakes. Do something that'd make somebody like Francie see me differently."

"Even if you could do that, what makes you think you'd wind up in the same place as before? Or there'd even be a Francie waiting for you at the end of it?"

"Some things are meant to be. Others, not so much, I guess."

They both stared into the reddish gold embers glowing through the perforated barrel. Fireflies glittered around them. Then Solomon roused up and knocked the ash of his pipe into the fire.

"One thing's for sure. Marjorie believes it."

"Little Margie?"

"First thing Marjorie wants to know about you is if you've ever seen an angel."

"Hasn't asked me yet."

"She will."

"When she does, I can for sure tell her they're not all they're cracked up to be." Solomon started to walk away, then turned back. "Or so I hear."

Chapter Thirty

Norman, Oklahoma – 1980s

MARJORIE HAD AN UNSETTLING WAY of studying Solomon. Like she was biding her time, looking for the right moment to ask her question about angels. Maybe catch him off his guard.

Marjorie would turn up, silent as sawdust, to watch Solomon at the ring-toss, skinning marks with the rope rings rigged by using a couple of six-penny nails to throw it off balance. Or watch him handing out burlap sacks to the riders on the Super Slide, playing matchmaker by sending kids down too close together, to land in each other's laps. Or watch him taking tickets at the Manic Monkey, using graphic patter of head-spinning thrills and stomach-churning spills to induce the queasy and vomitous to forget about riding, or provoke them to go ahead and puke before they befouled the ride. Or she'd watch him brushing down the ponies in their paddock at the end of the day's work, talking to them about who knows what-all.

Solomon enjoyed the ponies most of all. It was one of the few smells that took him all the way back to the Hudson Valley, to Saugerties, and what he'd come to think of as home.

Still, he'd keep an ear out for the little rustle that would signal him she was standing there, hanging over the fence rail. Watching.

The Good Book says their angels were on close speaking terms with the Almighty. That had to give them a lick of insight adults didn't have.

One early morning, before the carnival opened, Solomon took his concertina and walked just beyond the camp, into the middle of the broad, vacant lot south of the carnival. He found himself the stump of an old fence post amid the patches of short scrubby weeds and sat down to play.

He'd left off playing for a long while. It had become too lonely a sound for Solomon, there being no one to sing along or dance to the music. But the old tunes could stir memories in the same way the ponies did. It refreshed his connection with Lavinia. Oh, how she loved to dance. He'd never been any kind of a hand with a fiddle, guitar, or piano, but he could set her to whirling with his concertina.

Back before Luther tried to shoot him, Solomon had been invited to a musicale being given at the Kantlingher home. The invitation came by a special messenger to Missus Monroe's rooming house where he was staying. Not used to receiving mail of any kind, it had peeved him at first, having to drop the two pennies' tip in the messenger boy's hand before he'd hand over the envelope.

When he saw it was from the Kantlinghers, he was more than a little perplexed. Luther couldn't abide Solomon under the same roof with him. Esther wasn't likely to cross Luther by inviting Solomon. And it was a sure thing that Abigail wasn't willing to take Solomon's part. It warmed him, thinking of Lavinia wearing down Luther with her impassioned pleas for permission to invite Solomon. He could see her glee in taking up her pen, writing out the invitation in her own fair hand.

He turned over the page to look for her signature, but it was Abigail's name at the bottom. Formal, not warm. Simply "I am in expectation of your reply, Miss Abigail Kantlingher."

At first Solomon was let down, then thrilled to the idea that Lavinia must have put Abigail up to it. A sisterly subterfuge to evade Luther's watchful eye. Oh, how it must have galled Abigail to write his name anywhere on this very excellent stationery. He breathed in the lady-like fragrance and imagined Lavinia stroking her perfumed wrist over the paper when Abigail finished.

The evening was filled with music of all kinds, with familiar hymns, sentimental ballads, and tunes from popular operas, with dances for groups and for couples. The Kantlinghers played and sang, with Esther on the tall cabinet piano, Abigail on the fiddle, Luther on the jaw harp, and Lavinia, tinging away on the triangle.

The whole gathering joined in singing and dancing as the Kantlinghers played their entire stock of melodies, delighting everyone.

To give themselves a respite, they invited folks up to take a turn playing the piano or whatever instrument the impromptu musicians happened to have brought along with them.

Everyone took their turn. Everyone but Solomon.

He'd joined in with the singing in a fine, clear tenor voice. He joined in with the dancing, whether in lines or paired off. When the whole houseful of musicians took up a tune, whaling away on their instruments, Solomon would keep right up with them on his concertina.

But he hadn't yet been called up alone to play with the family.

Toward the end of the evening, Abigail called Lavinia to the piano. Lavinia fluttered and demurred, but Abigail took her by the arm and led her to the piano.

Then she turned to the gathering and searched as if not having thought about who she might call up to join them, only just now deciding to spot Solomon as if for the first time that night. Solomon had to smile, thinking of her having to write that invitation, wishing him in the farthest reaches of creation.

Abigail summoned him and pointed to the chair between herself and Lavinia now seated at the piano.

Solomon had proved himself a nimble dancer and a fair singer, but he had yet to show himself a magical musician with his concertina. He wiped each of his wet palms on his thighs, convinced Abigail had tapped him in hopes of seeing him make a fool of himself.

Lavinia and Solomon watched as Abigail waved her fiddle stick to clear the center of the room. They were going to play one last reel, a Norwegian *gammeldans* and she wanted to give the dancers plenty of room.

Everyone pulled back chairs, edged to the far sides of the room and then, with a bob of her head Abigail drew her bow across the strings.

But Solomon was ready.

Abigail took off, sawing and weaving, her ringlets alongside her face dancing with the music, her chin clamped onto the instrument, jaw tight, like it would fly off her shoulder if she let it.

Lavinia was only a fair hand at the keyboard and struggled to keep up with her sister.

Solomon was bound and determined to match Abigail note for note, and if he had to leave Lavinia in the dust, well, this was a race worth the effort. He was doing it for Lavinia.

Like runners who out-pace the pack, the competition between Solomon and Abigail turned into a deep and mutual connection, keeping close to each other, stride for stride, measure for measure, melody and harmony, their breathing synchronized, hearts no longer stroking as two, but now a single beat shared between them, each keenly attuned to watch where the other would step and an eye-blink moment to decide where their own step would fall, secretly enjoying the chance to shine against so worthy an adversary.

The music soared, the dancers capered, and Abigail and Solomon played, lost to the dancers, lost in each other.

Left behind by a mile, Lavinia had finally thrown up her hands, laughing fit to bust. The dancers, spent and perspiring, could only stop and watch Solomon and Abigail finish out the tune, passionate and harmonious play, oblivious to the rest of them, until the crescendo and climax that set the whole gathering on their feet, cheering and applauding.

Solomon hopped up, panting and smiling, and did a spin before sliding onto the bench with Lavinia, telling her that she'd been wonderful. She laughed and pushed him off for a flirt and a flatterer, saying that she couldn't keep tempo.

Abigail laid her instrument on the lid of the piano, her face aglow in the bright candlelights, but her manner still icy, telling Solomon he wouldn't be half-bad on that contraption if he could learn to play it with a finer hand than some farmboy milking a cow gone dry.

Solomon had been squeezing out that same tune, not realizing he'd been playing just as hard as he'd played all those many years ago, head thrown back, eyes closed, his knee jerking and foot stomping to keep time as his mind's eye took in that scene in the Kantlingher home once more.

At the crescendo and climax, all he could see was Lavinia's face at the piano. But it was Abigail's fragrance that he recalled, from the invitation, made all the more pungent by the sweet glow of perspiration.

Abigail's fragrance. Not Lavinia's.

His eyes popped open.

Marjorie was standing there in front of him. A wisp of dust floating about her legs, carried off by the wind blowing across the vacant lot.

That mysterious piercing gaze of hers was pure Kantlingher. The kind of gaze Abigail had honed fine with constant practice, and Lavinia would let loose only when supremely vexed. He could see their stormy looks in Marjorie's little face all the way back to Salomé, and not a trace of Edwin Greene in her features.

The dirt around Marjorie's feet had been all kicked up.

Solomon squeezed out the first few measures of another little tune. Marjorie took to whirling and kicking, first one way then the other, sending dust to flying.

He stopped. Marjorie stopped.

"Ever see an angel up close?" asked Marjorie.

"Not that I recall. Ever see a sailor dance?"

"Not that I recall." Marjorie gave him a quick smile and a hunch of her shoulders.

Solomon stood up, leaving the concertina on the fence post stub. He drew himself up, arms folded, then threw himself into the steps, kicks, and turns of an old-time sailor's jig, like he'd danced on decks when his watch was done. He ended with a grand hop and a click of his heels, then gave Marjorie a solemn bow.

Solomon took up the concertina and sat back down. He gave a little flick of his hand to her, motioning her to get ready, then held his concertina set to play.

Marjorie folded her arms in front of her, cocked her knee like she'd seen Solomon do, and when he started to play the notes to a hornpipe, Marjorie followed his steps as best as she could remember, ending with the kick-up of her heels.

"Not bad. You're a natural born sailor."

"They say momma's hex was a sailor once."

Solomon continued to squeeze the concertina, playing a slow, soft tune.

"You think there's such things as hexes?" Solomon studied his finger placement on the buttons.

"Sure." Marjorie tried a few steps to the drifty measures he played. "Can't be any fun for him, can it? Having to follow momma around?"

"Is that what he does?"

"Not all the time. Maybe he can't help himself. But I guess he has to."

"One way to look at it, I suppose."

"Nan-nan says he oughta be nailed in a box and sent over Niagara Falls." Marjorie stopped her dancing. "Where's Niagara Falls?"

"Nowhere around here, I'm happy to say. Maybe he's a guardian angel."

"He's not an angel. But he says there's one." Marjorie tried clicking her heels again.

"Marjorie!" Loralee came up from the camp, wading through the short, stemmy weeds.

Solomon didn't turn quite the whole way back to watch her coming.

"Let's show your Nano what you learned." Solomon squeezed out the tune, which set Marjorie to whirling and kicking as much of the dance as she could remember, ending with a click of her heels.

Loralee applauded and Marjorie ran to her. She gathered her up, shifting her to her hip.

Solomon went back to squeezing out that soft tune.

"How's that dress coming?"

"Almost finished."

"That Texan. He a good fella for Francie?" Solomon kept his tone light, intent on the music.

Loralee turned back, seemed to consider Solomon for the barest moment, then said, "Good enough." She flicked a smile at him, then let it fade as she walked back to the camp with Marjorie riding Loralee's flank, watching Solomon as she went.

Marjorie continued to keep a close eye on Solomon, watching him work the ring-toss, shepherd riders on the Super Slide, and brush the ponies at the end of the day. She would even appear out of nowhere when he'd go off to play his concertina. She chitter'd away, peppering him with questions and opinions. But not another word about the hex.

There'd been a few more nights around the fire barrel, but nary another word out of Francie about that Texas oilman back in Amarillo. Like he dropped off the earth. No amount of baiting from the rest of the crew could draw her out about him. Let them think what they would, Francie seemed through with him.

Watching the way Francie, Loralee, Bonita, and even little Margie, all clammed up, made Solomon wonder if they'd somehow caught wind that the true hex was nearby, there being a real wedding in the works now.

Then Solomon shook his head hard.

Damned if they haven't got him thinking of his very own self as a hex right along with them. Insidious daughters of Eve, using their wiles to turn a man's own mind against him.

Chapter Thirty-One

Norman, Oklahoma – 1980s

WITH LABOR DAY COMING ON, they were all looking for one last big weekend before tearing down and breaking up for the winter.

But rain started early on the Friday morning and got harder as daylight came on, hidden as it was behind the thick cloud cover. There was no sign of a let-up and the grounds were already a muddy slough.

There was nothing to do but snug down all the canvas tarps, lay out straw over the muddy places for clean walkways and write the day off as a loss.

While everyone else bundled into vans, pickups, and cars to head for town, Solomon stayed behind. The rain was a warm, heavy drizzle, and did nothing to cool the air.

With no sound of thunder and no threat of lightning, Solomon sat out under the awning of the trailer where he bunked. Having shucked his work shirt and relaxed in just his work pants, boots, and sleeveless undershirt, Solomon figured with everyone gone there'd be no one to mind his immodesty.

Being left alone gave him the opportunity to pour himself up a little something strong to drink, which he'd taken to calling pickle juice ever since Marjorie caught him swigging straight from the plastic jug. It was as much to shelter his young charge as any good guardian might do as it was to keep to himself the fact he preferred buying homemade liquor of dubious legality from the locals, to spending on pricey store-bought.

The pay phone on the pole outside the boss's trailer rang. Solomon let it ring, there being no way any phone call would be for him.

The door on the DeSoto's trailer banged open and Francie crossed the wet ground in a series of syncopated stag-leaps, her bare white legs flashing, toes pointed as she stretched for the dry spots, to catch the telephone before it quit ringing.

He was up and back inside his trailer before she could look around and see him there. He hadn't realized she'd stayed behind, and he didn't want her to go thinking he'd done so just to keep an eye on her. There seemed suspicion enough without adding to it.

Inside the trailer Solomon watched out the window from between the curtains as she talked on the telephone, hunched against the rain. She was too far away for him to hear anything, but it was clear she was delighted with whomever was on the other end.

When she finished the call, she did her stag-leap race back to her trailer.

Solomon waited to see if she'd show herself again. When she didn't, he slipped out to fetch the drink he'd left on the ground beside his chair. He'd have to stay inside to avoid Francie catching sight of him.

He'd picked up the drink, keeping an eye on the DeSoto's trailer when he saw the cloud mass beyond the camp begin to rotate, then reach down for the ground, starting to form a wide, dark funnel. Lightning flashed back of it.

Solomon dropped his drink and ran, sloshing through the mud, making straight for the DeSoto's trailer.

He pounded hard on the sheet metal door.

"Francie! Francie!" He pounded with the flat of his hand, rattling the glass panes in the jalousied windows.

She threw open the door, surprised and scared. "What!" She stood in the open doorway, barefoot, wearing her wedding dress, the veil in her hand.

"Come on!" Solomon reached for her. "There's a tornado coming!"

She'd pulled back but Solomon grabbed her by the wrist and pulled her out of the trailer, catching her around the waist and setting her on the ground.

"My dress!"

"I'll buy you a new one. We got to go before it sees us!"

She hauled him to a stop.

"Before it *sees* us?"

"You never hear about the eye of a storm?" Solomon pulled her along. This might be a bad time to tell Francie about nature's personal animosity toward him.

"Marjorie and momma! I gotta call them!"

"They're in town. There'll be lots of places for them to take shelter."

In the distance the warning siren could be heard underneath the wind and the rattle of blowing canvas and pelting rain.

"Where're we going?"

"This way." He pulled her toward the equipment trailers, unhitched and parked close together.

"We'll hide under here. If the tornado's aiming away from us, we'll be safe enough from the hail and flying trash it'll blow. If it looks like it's aiming toward us, we'll make a run for it."

The hard winds were flinging dirt, rocks, and sticks.

Francie gave out with a mournful moan, gathered up her skirts as best she could, duck-walking under the cargo trailer as pieces of broken plywood slapped against the sides.

Donnie was already hiding there.

"Why didn't you go to town with everybody else?" Solomon shouted over the rising noise, peeved at having to look out for two people now.

Donnie flinched with every loud *ba-lang* as heavier and heavier objects were picked up and hurled against the sides of the empty cargo trailers.

For a fella who didn't seem to mind the risk of lancing his liver every couple of hours, every day for a whole summer, Donnie sure was a scairdy-cat.

"If there really was a way to roll back time and put things to rights, now'd be the perfect time," Donnie shouted back. A sheared section of picket fence palings slammed against the trailer side with a ringing boom, making Donnie press his face back down into his forearm.

"What did you say?" Francie had one hand pressed against the trailer's undercarriage, the other gathering up her skirts to keep them out of the mud.

"Maybe it's not the hex's doing at all. Maybe it's your guardian angel. He means for us to be together. Not you and some guy in Amarillo. That's why you're here. Why you're in your dress under here with me. It's a sign."

"Donnie! This ain't the time to go Carpathian on us. You're scaring the girl." Solomon wished Donnie would go back to hiding his face in the dirt. Or, barring that, he had more headroom to swing a two-by-four with just enough impact to relax the boy for a while.

Donnie looked over at Solomon, "If I had the word of an angel that marrying someone like me would give us a clean start and put the world to rights, I wouldn't even stop to think about it. I'd just do it."

Another resounding *bah-boom-ba* made Donnie slap his face down on his forearm again.

Solomon kept watching Francie.

"Don't—" Solomon could see Francie comparing dangers—under the truck with a madman who might be the Kantlingher Hex in the flesh, or a tornado bearing down on her, hurling debris at ninety-miles an hour. "There's no such a thing," said Solomon.

"Wouldn't now be a good time to consider what that angel said?"

Francie reared up, screaming, cracking her head against the under-carriage, knocking her down onto her hands and knees. In no more than a blink, she was up on her toes and fingertips, doing a fast raccoon-wad-dle out from under the trailer.

"No, Francie!" Solomon lunged for an ankle or handful of fabric, anything to hold her back.

Donnie didn't hesitate, scrambling up after Francie, in spite of his lily liver. Solomon followed, duck-walking out from under the trailer and chasing after the both of them.

Francie was running west, away from what looked to be the storm's path, with Donnie right behind her.

Amazing, Solomon couldn't help but think, watching Francie run. Just amazing the speed and agility she had with that dress caught up in each arm.

Then the tornado seemed to make a hard change of direction, aim-ing for Francie and Donnie.

"You gotta be kidding me." That thing decided—*decided*—to fol-low after Francie.

The last thing Solomon wanted to do was invite the undivided at-tention of a twister chock full of lightning and loose auto parts. He ran toward Donnie and Francie.

By now Donnie had reached Francie, catching her up around the waist and dragged her, kicking and flailing, toward the turnoff where the service road joined the access ramp to the highway.

Solomon could see Donnie was making for the drainage notch on the side of the road with its large concrete culvert below grade level.

It wouldn't be enough. If the twister passes over them, it's likely to suck them out of the culvert and right up into the vortex. Or beat down on them with all the junk it's picked up by now. Or fill up that notch with a flash flood of runoff from the rain.

"Damnation." Something drastic and unpleasant had to be done.

"Hey!" he shouted into the storm. "Hey! You looking for me? There's nothing for you over there!"

Solomon danced around, waving his arms and throwing himself up in the air in giant jumping jacks trying to catch the tornado's attention before it reached where Donnie and Francie had taken cover.

"You won't find me over there, you —" But he stopped. How's he supposed to rile up a whirling vortex of wind, water, and flying trash any worse than it already was?

"Your nothing but a bag of gas!" Solomon flinched and dodged the flying debris. "Full up with nothing but cow chips and horse apples!"

The howling funnel paused and then appeared to lean toward him. That storm was eyeballing him. Plain as day.

Solomon turned and jogged in place a few steps, making as if to flee, but watching to see if the storm followed.

It whirled, not seeming to make headway in any direction.

Maybe it's worn itself out and ready to break up. They can't last forever.

The storm started toward him. Almighty fast.

Solomon ran as junk and jetsam whipped by him.

He'd have to lead it away from the shopping plaza where people were likely hunkered down, and away from the carnival where it would tear the place to matchwood.

He angled back toward the open field, running for all he was worth, all ankles and elbows flying. But the funnel was gaining on him, and in a wink it swept over him, snatching him up in its cloudy coils.

Solomon was airborne along with everything else the tornado had picked up along the way. He twisted and flexed, a gymnastic aerialist try-ing to avoid the fenders, tires, metal signage, twisted bicycles, tree limbs, steel fence stanchions and broken sheet rock flung about with him.

A section of cyclone fencing folded over Solomon, wrapping itself around him as he rocketed along, pinning his arms at his sides, sausage tight.

Solomon had his eyes squeezed shut against the whizzing gravel and splinters, so didn't anticipate his sudden arrival headfirst at the cinder block wall of the Dandy Dollar discount store, piercing it and leaving him stuck fast in the neatest hole ever created by a tornado using a man for an auger.

Done with its nefarious business, the tornado broke up, leaving noth-ing but a hard rain behind. Solomon wiggled in the steel mesh wrapping of the cyclone fence, looking from inside the store like a well-mounted wall trophy. With his hindquarters hanging outside, the rain ran down into the backside of his britches, pouring out the pant legs. A flash of lightning gave him one last lick on the seat of his pants for good measure.

"Son of a—" Solomon struggled all the harder, his face clenched with the effort.

Opening his eyes, breathing hard, he saw Griffin standing there looking up at him.

"What're you doing here?"

"I happened to be on your side of the universe, thought I'd stop in, see what you were up to," said Griffin. "So. What *are* you up to?"

"What's it look like I'm up to?" Solomon gave himself another mighty useless wiggle.

Griffin's face twisted up to one side, and his cheeks filled out, working air from one side to the other as he concentrated. "Recreational taxidermy?"

"You jackass!"

"Did I get it right?"

"Get me out of this! I'm stuck."

"I've told you, I'm no guardian angel."

"You get me out of here, or when I do get loose, I'm going to whupp your angel heinie!"

"That's the kind of faith that moves mountains." Griffin came in close. "So, how should I get you unstuck?"

"Pull on something. Grab my shoulders, or get a hold of this fence."

"That looks like way too much work." Instead, Griffin reached both hands into the wall and pulled loose a cinder block.

The whole side wall collapsed with a roar, down on top of Solomon. The dislodged roof beam-ends fell, canting the ceiling, knocking loose acoustical tiles, struts, brackets, steel conduit, and light fixtures down over the pile of rubble.

Griffin used his toe to scatter the debris until Solomon's face was visible.

"You want help with that, too, I suppose."

Solomon lay still a moment, then thrashed and waggled hard, growling rage through gritted teeth.

"I'll take that as a yes." Griffin started bending back the steel mesh of the fence.

"You know what they don't have anywhere in heaven?"

"You, I'm thinking." With his arms freed, Solomon could push against the metal mesh.

"Fences," said Griffin.

"That was going to be my second guess, if I needed one."

"No need for fences. Wouldn't do any good. You go where you want."

"Saint Peter stands at the pearly gates counting noses, don't he? If there's a gate, there's got to be a fence."

"Nope." Griffin unfolded a section caught around Solomon's ankles. "So, there's a chance for me after all?"

Griffin stopped. "Oooh, I wouldn't go that far." Griffin straightened up, dusting his hands together. "But that's not for me to say."

Finally freed, Solomon stood up and brushed himself off, knocking away bits of cinder block and acoustical tile, clambering over the wreckage aiming for the doorway.

Solomon forced open the door blocked by a layer of mud.

Outside, the rain had moved on and there was that crystal yellow brightness that seemed to follow a hard storm passing.

The National Guard showed up and Solomon let them drape a thermal blanket on him, but declined their offer to take his blood pressure and check his vitals. Then, while survivors wandered through the destruction, Solomon drifted away.

Back at the carnival, there wasn't a whole lot of damage. Carnies stood marveling how the tornado passed between the shopping mall and the carnival, missing both by a hair.

The DeSotos' trailer was gone. Tangled in the wires of the telephone pole right next to where they'd been parked, was Francie's wedding dress.

It was a relief to Solomon she wasn't still in it. Once that tornado turned to follow him, Francie would have been safe. So the tornado didn't shuck it off her. She took it off and left it behind. Maybe as a peace offering to the hex, or maybe a talisman against the hex following them.

A breeze flicked at the dress. Damned if they won't blame him for all this mess.

Asking around among the carnies, Solomon could get no word where the DeSotos were headed when they took off. Amarillo, most likely. But that was just guessing. Didn't even bother to break down their airplane ride. Just left it.

Solomon went back to the trailer where he'd bunked to pick up his things. Griffin, always the obliging cuss, already had them out on the ground.

"How far's it to Amarillo from here?"

"Angel miles or mudfoot miles?" asked Griffin.

"You gonna give me a ride?"

"I've done my good deed for the day."

Solomon shouldered his seabag and hefted his valise, heading for the access ramp to the highway. Griffin walked alongside.

"So. Given any more thought to taking your chances with Luther?"

"You know what gets my goat?"

Griffin slipped him a sidelong look. "No. What?"

"Why nature would treat one of God's good creatures like me that way."

"No idea." Griffin blew a little sigh of relief.

"A prince of a fella. Like me."

"Boggles the mind."

"I'm the salt of the earth."

"A real head scratcher."

"Nobody as true blue."

"Does make you wonder."

"Are you even listening to me?"

"More's the pity—wait—what did you say?"

"I thought so." Solomon walked on.

"No, really. What'd you say? Come on, you know I'm not omniscient."

Chapter Thirty-Two

Amarillo, Texas – 1980s

WHEN BONITA AND LORALEE DISAPPEARED with Francie and Marjorie right after the tornado, Solomon figured they might be headed back to Amarillo where they kept a mobile home parked for the off-season. He wasted no time heading for Texas.

It took Solomon a while to locate the trailer park once Solomon reached Amarillo. When one of their neighbors saw him knocking at their door, she let him know the DeSotos wouldn't be back from Oklahoma for a quite a while. Solomon asked how long that might be, and the neighbor said one to three years. Or sooner, with time off for good behavior.

Oklahoma state troopers picked up Francie at the state line for passing bad checks. Loralee called the neighbor, asking her if she could look after the place for another couple of years.

Turned out there really was a Texas oilman in Amarillo whom Francie had been expecting to marry. The problem was, he wasn't expecting to marry her. He kept a half-dozen or so women on the jangle, women who had to travel for a living. The Texan had a particular fondness for flight attendants, semi-pro athletes, forest rangers, truck drivers, and carnies.

He must've had an even softer spot for Francie, because she was the only one he'd given a book of checks for her very own. She'd used them to buy herself gifts and tell people they were from him. Because, in a way, they were. Until a sharp-eyed clerk telephoned the bank and the bank telephoned Amarillo, getting Missus Texas Oilman on the line. She happened to be rummaging through Mister Texas Oilman's office looking for evidence of infidelity, so she was happy to take a message for her husband.

Rather than face the wrath of Missus Texas Oilman, Mister Texas Oilman denied giving Francie the checks.

State troopers carted Francie back to Norman where she was convicted of check fraud and the judge threw the proverbial book at her. There were only two things the judge couldn't stand—he let it be known as he pronounced sentence—out-of-staters who defrauded the good people of Oklahoma and carnies. Since Francie was both, he gave her the maximum. Go ahead and have your mail forwarded to the Mabel Bassett correctional facility, he'd told her, you're going to be there awhile. The family parked their travel trailer in nearby McLoud and settled down to wait for Francie.

There was nothing Solomon could do for her. It was all on that Texas Oilman for letting Francie take the blame, but she'd likely see it as the hex's doing. It would only raise more suspicions against Solomon if he showed his face in McLoud trying to make himself useful.

So he did what he could by renting the DeSoto's mobile home and taking a job tending the grounds of a cemetery west of town. He told the neighbor he was a retired goldminer named Cyrus hiding from greedy relatives. It was, he told the neighbor, the reason he paid in cash, not trusting banks or snoopy estate lawyers.

He also learned to ride a bike. He hadn't bothered about it before but getting around Amarillo wasn't going to be easy. A driver's license was out of the question and hitchhiking brought on extra special attention from law enforcement.

Once Francie served her time the family headed back to Amarillo. Solomon moved out before they got back and took a room in a residence motel that catered to long-haul truckers.

Solomon developed a fondness for talking Texas football over shots and beers at Outlaw Maud's when he wasn't working or checking in on the Kantlingher women. Occasionally, he'd let himself be talked into a game of pool, but regulars knew not to invite Solomon to the table if they wanted to hang on to their rent money.

Talking Texas football grew out of following the sports teams at Marjorie's high school where she marched with the Rifleers, a drill team of girls whose routines were as much dance as drill. They dressed in stylized military uniforms dolled up with sequins, and carried rifles painted metal-flake blue that made the weapons glitter something fierce under the lights.

Watching Marjorie gave Solomon a kind of pride at the small part he had in her graceful mastery of movement.

Still, keeping a low profile meant that he could only watch from a distance as she walked the aisle at graduation, then when she took up with Skip Perisch, a transplant from Orlando who ran a fitness studio. They snuck off and got married in a civil ceremony without telling anybody and Willa was born a little less than a year later. It didn't take long for Skip to get his fill of domestic life and head out for New York, failing to alert his wife and new daughter of his plans on setting himself up in a more independent lifestyle.

New York City – Present Day

Marjorie followed, and Solomon followed right after.

When she took an apartment in Manhattan on the Upper West Side, Solomon managed to get himself a place in the same building, just down the hall from her, keeping out of sight while she got settled. It helped that the place was cheap.

Hoping to make himself seem older, he took to using a cane, whitened his hair and mustache, donned a ratty cardigan sweater over a two-toned shirt tucked into a pair of over-sized, high-waisted trousers. A narrow-brimmed fedora completed his disguise. Fully acting the role of an old, retired gent he tipped his hat to her in the hall and kept to himself, blending into the wallpaper.

Solomon's disguise made him invisible until the day he couldn't help but hold the door for her as she struggled to get the stroller and Willa out onto the sidewalk.

She stopped, looked at him, hard. "Skeeter? Skeeter Martin?"

"Marjorie? Little Marjorie—" He made a show of grasping for her last name, snapping his fingers.

"DeSoto! Right. I'm Perisch now." She wiggled her wedding band at him. "Skip. He's traveling. For work."

"How's it you found me? You didn't come looking for me, did you?"

"No! This is a complete surprise! What're you doing here?"

"Retired. That tornado took the love for carnival life right out of me. Finally made it back here. It's where I'm from."

"Carnies always seem to be from nowhere. Hard to imagine them having a real home someplace." She rolled the stroller back and forth, soothing Willa. "You seem ageless. Not at all the type who needs a cane."

"I'm a whole lot older than I look."

"You want to come down to the park with us? I need to let Willa run wild for a few minutes."

Solomon was glad to oblige.

They spent a good long time together, sitting on the benches, watching Willa toddle about, investigating sticks, candy wrappers, and the other kids in all their climbing, swinging, and dashing around the playground.

While she kept a half-eye out for Willa, Marjorie caught Solomon up on the carnival, dancing, the tornado, and the story she'd heard about him getting carried off by the twister.

"Pish." Solomon flicked a wave of his hand.

"Oh, I know. That wasn't anything but Francie and her carny talk. But it sure makes a great story."

Marjorie was honest about the time Francie spent in jail, about her own marriage, about Skip being long gone and not just traveling for work, like she'd first said, for which she apologized. That led to a little more honesty about the struggle to make a go of being a dancer in the city and her money troubles.

Solomon took it as a chance to help out her and Willa. Marjorie shrugged it off.

"Thanks. But I never met a carny with money saved back. Maybe there are. But I don't know any."

"I came into a little money a little while ago. A nest egg. From an admirer."

"Oooh. A ladies' man. I better warn my girlfriends."

She gave him a pat on the wrist, and danged if he didn't blush, feeling the warmth in his face.

"But thanks. I'll keep it in mind if things ever get too tight." She glanced at her watch. "I have to get to work. It's a restaurant down in Chelsea. You should stop in."

"I have to see a man about a dog, but maybe sometime soon I can come by."

"It's so good to see you. Like old home week. Speaking of—do you still play the concertina?"

"Not been much reason to for a long time."

"Well, we need to fix that." She planted Willa in the stroller and pushed off, heading up the inclined path to the street.

There were times after that, he would encounter Marjorie in the hall or around the neighborhood, sometimes with Willa, sometimes alone. They would stop for a word or two, but Solomon took care to keep his distance and give Marjorie no cause to think he was looking out for her.

Solomon took to waiting up for Marjorie to get home from working late, listening for the sound of her keys in the door. It meant good money, she assured him, when the restaurant stayed full right up until the kitchen closed, taking longer to clean up and close down her station.

He'd given her a large metal key fob after the last time she'd misplaced her keys and needed to borrow the set she'd left with him for emergencies.

"Hard to lose these," he told her at the time, "and handy for self-defense." It also had a distinctive, brassy rattle that let him know she was home safe.

A week or so after that, Marjorie was especially late getting home. Solomon waited up, reading through old National Geographics he'd picked up in a church thrift store off Amsterdam Avenue. A way to catch up on what he'd missed over the decades.

When he finally did hear her keys downstairs at the front door, he put aside the magazine and listened.

He heard her keys again as she stepped off the elevator. But she didn't open her front door right away, like usual. In fact, not for a long time.

Concerned, Solomon was about to go see if anything was wrong. But he didn't want her to think he'd been watching for her. So, he grabbed a grocery bag, filled it with some newspapers, a few empty cans and a soda cup, then stepped into the hallway.

Marjorie stood well back of her door, daubing her eyes with her sleeve.

"Oh! Sorry. Didn't mean to wake you." Marjorie sniffed, stretching her nose and lip to get control of her runny nose.

"Emptying the trash." Solomon lifted the bag for her to see. "Better late than never." He shuffled around her and reached for the elevator button, looking back at her.

"Everything all right?"

"Of course. Everything's fine. That's the problem." Then she gave out with a little laugh. "I guess that doesn't make much sense, does it."

"I wouldn't hold myself out as a judge of what makes sense and what don't." Solomon kept his eye on the elevator's annunciator.

"That's refreshing." She sniffed and squared up her shoulders, throwing back her head, looking dead on at whatever it was that had her worked up. "There's a guy. A guy at work I like. Kurt, and, I think, likes me back. Not the usual loser, you know?"

"That's good."

"No, that's bad."

"That's bad?"

"You remember all that talk of a hex on the women in my family?" Marjorie daubed her nose again.

"I recall something like it going around the camp."

Marjorie sighed. "At first, I blamed the hex for Skip leaving me and Willa. But Nano and Nan-Nan both said I'll know for sure it's the hex when he says how he's got the solemn word of an angel right out of heaven that there's a guy for me who'll make everything right. *Then* your life blows up in your face. So, it means the hex hasn't paid me a visit yet. Now there's this guy at work, and I'm wondering do I have to ignore him so the hex'll leave me and Willa alone?"

It tore at Solomon, watching Marjorie struggle.

"Believing in hexes seems a little much for a city girl." Solomon smiled, hoping she'd see it as a gentle tease. "Can't say I ever gave much credence to such things."

"Oh, there is one. Nano and Nan-Nan both saw him. Nan-Nan saw him when she was just out of high school. Then when Nano was like seventeen or something, she and Nan-Nan both saw him at the same time. Mom says she saw him, too. She blames him for Dewey."

"Dewey?"

"That Texas oilman. She also blames the hex for my father. Sherman. The one with the motorcycle? Told her he had to join a commune that didn't allow women?" She snorted. "Yeah. For her being a hardshell carny, Mom could be really gullible."

"What'd Francie say he looked like? The hex, I mean?"

"For a long time, she thought it was Donnie. The sword swallower? Can you imagine? But Nano and Nan-Nan both said it wasn't Donnie. They both told Mom that Dewey was her own fault. I think he married the axe juggler and now he's teaching high school biology. Donnie, not Dewey."

"Could be—if there was such a thing as hexes—maybe he's done with you."

"You think he'd get tired, right? Tired of following us around. When I was a kid, I felt sorry for him. It's got to be as much a curse on him." Another sniff and another daub at her eyes. "When I married Skip and the hex never showed, I hoped I broke the curse. That it ended with me. Then Skip left us, never saying a word. The jerk. So, okay, I said to myself, I had the one hex for my lifetime. I got through it. Nan-Nan said, oh, no, not by a long shot. Until he looks you in the eye on the night before your wedding, you're still due a hexing, and the next thing you know you're married to someone who seems wonderful then turns out to be awful. Or running from the law."

Her face squinched up hard, her breath coming in staccato chu-chu-chuddering. "I don't want to be an outlaw."

He felt her blame falling hard on him, without her knowing it. Then he remembered.

"Loralee—your Nano—your grandmother—she wasn't planning to get married the day she saw him—the fella she says was the hex. Was she?" Solomon spoke before realizing he'd never heard that part from Marjorie or Loralee directly. He held his breath hoping Marjorie didn't notice he knew more than he ought.

"That's what proves it's a hex." Marjorie sniffed hard. "After Nannan put them down in that onion field in Utah, Nano married the crop duster who'd seen them land their plane and went to help. Of course, he turned out to be another class A jerk. It just took longer. Mom was twelve or thirteen when he disappeared, leaving the two of them. Flew off one day and never came back."

Marjorie gave one last sniff, blew out a sharp puff, releasing tension and relaxing her shoulders, resuming a calm, pleasant attitude. "So. I don't plan to be an outlaw and I don't plan to marry. He might as well move along."

"The guy at work?"

"The hex. He can bark up somebody else's family tree. Now all I have to do is convince Willa to be a nun when she grows up."

Marjorie fished into her purse for her billfold and got ready to open her front door.

"I've wondered if he believes there really is a way to make up for what he did with great-great-great grandmother? Or however many greats she is. Was. I can never remember."

"Beg pardon?"

"The hex. Bet he never thought he'd end up spending eternity trying to make up for a hot, one-night stand."

It jarred Solomon to the core hearing Marjorie joke so free and easy about something he never put into words for himself. True, he had no clear memory of what happened the night he snuck into Lavinia's bedroom, but he trusted it had been a sacred thing shared between them. When she denied it to his face the night Edwin stole her away, Solomon could only imagine whatever happened was powerful and intimate and it shamed her.

Now, here's little Marjorie joking as if the secret of that encounter was common knowledge passed around and made light of from the beginning. But who else could have known? Who else could speak of it, except Lavinia herself?

If she did speak of it, why wait until he was lost at sea? Why pretend nothing happened while he stood right there in front of her, willing to do anything for her?

"That's quite a notion," he managed to say. "Where—where'd people get such an idea?"

"Abigail, of course," said Marjorie, as if that explained it. "But it would have been pretty obvious, even if she'd never said anything. If you know what I mean. Which is why Luther shot him. Thank God for Edwin."

That's how. Lavinia told Abigail and Abigail couldn't keep her yap shut. "That how they tell it?"

"Scandalous, right? Times were a whole lot different back then."

Being thought a thief of Lavinia's virtue was bad enough, thinking he was nothing more than a vexatious hex set upon Lavinia's descendants was worse still. But worst of all for Solomon was seeing little Marjorie trying to protect herself from any hope of making a life with someone because of him.

"I think you should give that guy at work a try."

"Why bother? I get a babysitter, I get dressed up, and he turns out to be a dud. Or he turns out to be wonderful and the hex shows up and turns him into a dud."

"Go ahead out with him. Don't let this talk of a hex whup you."

"You'll protect me? Because if he does show up, I'm telling him it was your idea."

"If that hex shows up, you point him out to me, and I'll settle his hash."

"Seems a lot of trouble."

"Start out easy. Like—let this fella walk you home."

"From the restaurant? In Chelsea? At two in the morning?"

"Won't be a bother to the right kind of fella. Heck, if he's any good for you, he'd carry you."

"That's—pretty old fashioned." She laughed and opened her front door. The babysitter was waiting. Marjorie handed her the cash, then turned back to Solomon. "I guess I could risk splitting the cost of a cab ride with him."

"Fella ought to pay. Always."

"Come on. You are not *that* old."

Solomon smiled, turning back to his own door.

"You were taking out your trash?"

"Oh. All this scintillating chit-chat put it right out of my head." Solomon got on the elevator and rode down to the basement.

Chapter Thirty-Three

WHAT MARJORIE SAID ABOUT THE HEX going along making a mess of things without even knowing it, kept Solomon sitting up all night, brooding on just who was running things. He was still in his chair the next morning when a knock at the door startled him awake.

It was Marjorie, with Willa in the stroller. She knew him to be an early riser, and worried when she hadn't seen him up and about.

"Thought I'd return the favor," she said, "for you listening to my troubles."

"Got busy tidying up and forgot what time it was."

"I know you're not much for company, but I hope you don't mind my checking in on you."

"I do have one visitor, drops in about this time every year. That's about all I can stand."

"From back in your carny days?"

"Further back than that. We spend a few minutes lying to each other about how well we're making out, that kind a thing. Then he goes his way and I go mine."

"I'd like to meet him. Hear the stories."

"Wouldn't have much good to say. He's known me too long."

"Well, as long as you're okay."

"I appreciate you calling on me."

She left him standing there, watching her muscle the stroller back into her apartment. He closed his door before she could catch him watching.

Solomon went back and sat in his chair, refreshing his pipe, and refilling the glass jam jar he used for drinking.

That was sometime before noon. Since then, Solomon had sipped and smoked a little more, ate some, read quite a bit, and considered what he'd read. He'd kept on through the day and on into the dark, with only the coal oil lamp for light. A blue-white glow creeped over the floor toward him. He kept on reading, not looking up.

"Got your nose in a book? Solly, you are just full of surprises, you know that? Most times I drop in on you, I might find you in a fistfight, or in the burning wreckage of some vehicle you've borrowed but haven't quite mastered, or passing time teaching street urchins how to pitch pennies. Instead, here you sit enjoying a quiet pipe, a bit of intellectual stimulation. Which doesn't require sharp edges or doctored dice." Griffin picked up Solomon's drink, "An adult beverage." He took a whiff. "Whoa. All right. Homemade. But still, it is in a glass. You're turning into quite the respectable gentleman."

"You're early."

"You know how it is, I'm wandering around your part of the cosmos and thought I'd look in. See how what's-her-name was getting on these days."

"Marjorie."

"Marjorie? I thought her name was Francie."

"Francie was her mother."

"What happened to Loralee?"

"Loralee's *her* mother."

"Marjorie?"

"Francie."

"Which one was in Oklahoma?"

"Francie was from Amarillo, worked a carnival in Oklahoma, got herself arrested and spent time in jail there, then she went back to Amarillo."

"Where was Marjorie?"

"Marjorie lived with Loralee."

"In Amarillo, right?"

"In Oklahoma while Francie was locked up. Then back to Amarillo."

"You know, it's easier to keep a litter of barnyard kittens straight than it is to keep track of you mudfoot short-timers."

Solomon went back to reading.

"Any chance I got here in time to see you match Marjorie up with another Mister Right?"

"I'm out of the matchmaking business."

"Probably for the best, Solly. You can play poker with Beelzebub himself, but as a matchmaker, you're a dud. If you don't mind my saying."

Solomon could hear it coming, the way Griffin sighed and cocked his head trying to catch Solomon's eye. He was ready for it.

"Does this mean you're prepared to let Luther take another shot at you?"

Solomon exhaled and took a long, hard look at Griffin, like in the old days, trying to read the player across the table to divine what cards he might be holding.

"Thought you'd never ask." Solomon lifted the lanyard over his head and held it out to Griffin, closed his eyes and tensed for the rubber-band snap Griffin said would come next. He didn't want to see what was coming if he'd guessed wrong and bet it all on the wrong horse.

But—nothing.

Solomon opened one eye a wee bit, peering through his eyelashes still laced together over his eyeball.

Griffin was no longer sitting across from him. The shard still hung from his hand.

Solomon looked around.

Griffin stood at the window, bent over, his hands clasped behind his back as he gazed out onto the narrow breezeway between the buildings.

"What a lousy view. Did you even look at the place before you moved in?"

"Don't you want this damn thing?"

"Of course I do. But it cuts me to the quick if you think I'm capable of taking advantage when you are clearly not yourself." Griffin remained bent over, looking out the window. "That guy across the way could do us all a really big favor and pull the curtains while he's in the shower."

"This is what you've been after all this time, isn't it?"

"Of course it is." Griffin said without looking at Solomon. "Hey! Butt ugly! There's people trying to eat around here!" Griffin sprung upright and spun himself away from the window. "The nerve of some people, right?"

Solomon stood up and moved in on Griffin holding out the artifact.

"What's your hurry. I just got here." Griffin moved away from the window, making a casual tour of the apartment, his hands on top of his head, his fingers laced together. He jigged and spun to avoid any contact when Solomon tried to touch him with the shard.

"Come on, Solly. You dropped it in something icky and now you want to get it all over me." With his hands still on his head, Griffin walked up over the arm of the sofa, across the cushions, over the other arm and onto the floor. He sidled around behind the tattered club chair, reversing when Solomon doubled back to meet him on the other side.

"That's it, isn't it? Something icky-sticky." Griffin backed into the small kitchen alcove and pulled the refrigerator door open to block Solomon's advance.

"You pester me year in and year out for this damnable doo-hickey. Here I am offering it to you on a silver platter. Now you can't be bothered to touch it?"

"I smell a rat." Griffin took a big sniff. "Yep. It's you. No offense. Have you ever thought about using a topical deodorant?"

Solomon stepped back, lowering the artifact to his side.

"Or—could be these eggs. How about I scramble us up some eggs?"

"Angels don't cook."

"I've been meaning to learn. Put that thing away and you show me."

"I thought so." Solomon slipped the lanyard back over his head, tucking the artifact into his shirt.

"I am one mighty ignorant cuss. Thinking I was being oh-so-clever, tracking them girls across time and territory, and every time, when it looked like I'd lost their trail for good, lo-and-behold, I'd catch me a pinch of my natural born luck and practically trip over one of them. Gawd, I was awful high on myself."

"Whose trail?"

"Which ever one of those women you'd care to mention."

"You're going to make me name them all? Do they have to be in order?"

"Wasn't any luck to it. Just you. Johnny-on-the-spot. You had me going. I'll give you that. You had me thinking I was in a game with a handful of cards that couldn't lose. I'd return and take my rightful place with Lavinia and all the troubles that followed those poor girls around would vanish when the cosmos rolled back and restarted."

Griffin closed the refrigerator door and came out of the kitchen.

"Okay. We wait on the eggs. You're not looking all that hungry."

Solomon took up his drink and drained it, not that it would do him any good.

"Living a half-life for more than a hundred-fifty years—can't use my rightful name, can't get a regular job. Can't get a driver's license. Can't do anything that might bring the law down on me. And if I do, I got to high-tail it for some other part of the country. Can't join the army. You know there've been at least a half-a-dozen wars from back then to now. I should've done my part. But no. You had me going with all that bilge about how the cosmos'd roll up right back to the dawn of creation if anyone found out I was immortal. So—I wore an eye-patch. I limped. I'd go around coughing like a buffalo with a cattail caught in his craw, because I sure couldn't join up." Solomon picked up a magazine off the pile, waving it in Griffin's face. "Hell, I can't even get a library card, thanks to you."

"Thanks to me?"

"You fixed me good. You and your doo-hickey. Got me doing all of your dirty work! I'm nothing but a mine pony, hauling away in the pitch dark, all used up, doing your job."

"My job? Really? *My* job?"

"Ignorant fish that I am, I took the bait, hook, line, and sinker."

"Solly, I hope you'll take this in the spirit in which it's intended—but in the coherence department, your brain went on a long holiday and didn't bother to leave you a note. You may want to go have a long lie-down until it gets back from wherever it went. I'll wait."

Solomon picked up the Gideon Bible from the little table by the chair and waved it under Griffin's nose, expecting that to be explanation enough.

"You be careful. You could put someone's eye out with that thing." Griffin retreated up onto the big chair, tumbling over the back and onto the floor behind it. He rebounded, looking for all the world like he'd meant to do that.

Now with the chair between him and Griffin, Solomon opened the Bible up, licking his thumb and fingertip to turn the pages, while Griffin appeared to be looking for a handy exit through the masonry behind him.

"Right here." Solomon held the open Bible out to Griffin, then angling it so he could read to him, Solomon's finger tracing along under the words, " 'No one born of a forbidden union may enter the assembly of the Lord. Even to the tenth generation, none of his descendants may enter the assembly of the Lord.' "

He snapped the Bible closed.

"There it is. In black and white. The book of Deuteronomy. Chapter twenty-three. Verse two."

"Solly, Solly, Solly. You're using a known language, but you're not making any sense. I've seen this before. That first day right after the Tower of Babel? You couldn't even order a cup of coffee."

"You used this blasted thing to turn me into an instrument of the Almighty's wrath!" Solomon held out the shard on its lanyard. "Following those poor women around generation to generation."

Griffin straightened up, head cocked, eyes narrowed, watching Solomon. "And just why would I do that?"

"Because you didn't want your wing-tips dragging through the mess."

"Uh—I don't have wings, Solly."

"You didn't want to get any honest dirt under your pearly pink fingernails."

Griffin gave a quick, surreptitious glance at his fingertips, then buffed them on his hip.

"So. You roped me into it. Figured you'd leave it to some sinner already besmirched."

"Be-cause—why?"

"Because of that forbidden union."

"Which one? Exactly? You've had so many."

"It was something Marjorie said about the hex."

"Which is you?"

"Which they *think* is me. Which they think, so she says, is some fella who had his way with Lavinia."

"Had his way? Like sold her a used car that turned out to be a lemon?"

"Knew her. In the Biblical sense." Solomon's mouth was a fierce, tight bow, holding in what he would not say.

"Knew her?"

"You just want me to say it."

"It'd help." Griffin gave Solomon the widest, most innocent silver-blue eyes.

"Had us a moment of personal intimacy. Damn! You can be so blamed ignorant when you put your mind to it."

"Ohhhh. You mean fornication without benefit of clergy."

"Which we didn't."

"I clearly remember you insisting you did."

"Well—I was wrong."

Griffin ran to the window.

"What?

"Checking for flying pigs." Griffin turned back from the window. "Solly, you're admitting you might be wroooooong?"

"I come to realize that nothing happened between me and Lavinia. She's too good a woman for the likes of me. That's why she didn't answer me when I spoke of it there in front of Esther and Abigail."

"So, I don't see the problem."

"Marjorie said Abigail was the one told the story on me. Abigail was there that night. She heard me. Then, when Abigail lost her sister, when I wasn't there to defend myself or Lavinia, she filled the ears of everybody around with that story how I'd taken liberties. Now you've got me chasing after every Kantlingher woman since then, mother to daughter, on down the line, on the word of a snippy old spinster."

"All this time. Nothing?"

"If something like that'd happened, I'd have it burned in my memory for all time."

"Then, I'm amazed."

"I'll give you the lack of omniscience, but don't you check on something like that before consigning people to torment?"

"You had me convinced."

"Well, Mister Know-It-All, turns out Lavinia knew better than to trust herself to someone like me. Not only that, she didn't call me a cad and villain to my face when she had the chance. Shows you just how kindhearted a girl she was."

Griffin exhaled hard. "You know, I told them it didn't sound like my old buddy Solomon Durnley. Come on, I said, he wouldn't do that with the one true love of his life. But I was outvoted."

"That's a lie."

"It is?"

"A bald-faced, black-hearted lie. That isn't how it went."

"It isn't?"

"You said, sure, why not? A good-for-nothing like Solomon Durnley? Sounds like just the thing he'd do. Leave it to me, you said, I'll snare him and I'll have him dancing right up to Judgment Day, you said."

Griffin stared at Solomon for a long moment, then shook himself. "Amazing. Like you were right there in the room with us."

"Well. I'm finished with all that. You get someone else to do your dirty work."

"So, you're serious about giving it back to me and taking your chances with Luther?"

"Not by a long shot. You think I'm going to give all of you the satisfaction?"

"What about Lavinia? What about undoing the trouble you've caused all up and down her bloodline?"

"I told you. I'm finished being your agent of vengeance."

Solomon caught the sound of Marjorie's keys as she stepped off the elevator. He'd been so worked up at Griffin he hadn't paid attention to her coming through the door downstairs.

"It's an okay place to work," he heard her say to someone getting off the elevator with her. "The money's decent. But once I've made enough, I'm heading back to Texas."

Solomon leaned his ear against the door, listening.

"Thanks for sharing your taxi with me," came a male voice.

"It's not my taxi. Yet. I'm still making payments on it. Twenty dollars a night for three thousand nights. I've only got another twenty-six hundred and nine payments to go."

"I'd love the chance to help you pay it off."

"You own one official half-share. But I don't give out certificates."

Solomon felt a breath on the back of his neck. Griffin had his own ear to the door.

"Remind me again which one this is."

"Be quiet!" hissed Solomon. "It's Marjorie. The fella must be Kurt she talked about."

"You and Skip won't get back together?" the male voice asked.

"Not as long as the hex is out there waiting."

"That's quite a story."

"So. This is my door. Thank you for seeing me home. Now. I have to go to the other side and leave you on this side."

"I've come all this way."

Solomon eased open his front door, peering through the crack.

Marjorie stood with a young man, nicely dressed in black trousers, white shirt with an open collar, his tie slack around his neck, the knot slid down. He had his arm around Marjorie's waist.

"This is as far as it goes, Kurt. It's late. I'm tired. You're tired."

"Not me. You did invite me up."

"To see me to my door. Which is this one right here."

"What about that business with the corkscrew? Table eighteen? You slipping your corkscrew in my apron?"

"You were serving wine. You had a full tray. It was a help, not a mating ritual."

"And the way you can't stop talking sex when I'm around." Kurt put his nose to Marjorie's neck.

Griffin squeezed in over Solomon, putting his eye to the crack, watching.

"He seems nice."

Solomon twisted his head to look up at Griffin. "This is how you do it, isn't it? Get me to put my foot in it."

They both put an eye back to the crack, watching.

Kurt appeared to be winning the magic hands game.

"Yep. I could see how a true romance starts out just like that. But—what do I know?"

"Kurt!" Marjorie rasped.

"Is real true love two out of three falls? Or just for whoever gets pinned first? I'm curious."

Marjorie gave out with a sigh of exasperation.

Solomon stepped back and looked around the bare apartment.

Griffin was right there, holding up Solomon's bowie knife. "Use this. It won't wake the baby."

Solomon grabbed the bowie away from Griffin. "You'd like that, wouldn't you." Instead, Solomon flopped onto the sofa and took up a magazine, pretending to read.

Marjorie gave out with little yip.

Solomon tipped up the glass jar, trying for the last bit of moisture in the bottom, making a show of disinterest.

There came a louder yip.

Solomon squeezed his eyes shut.

Marjorie saw over Kurt's shoulder when Solomon stepped out of his apartment into the hallway, holding his camera, the strap around his neck. He seemed not to notice the wrestling match, but approached them, studying the camera.

"Either of you know anything about cameras?" Solomon looked up, giving them a half-smile.

"Get out of here with that," growled Kurt.

Solomon fired the flash in Kurt's face.

"Shit!" Kurt flinched, squinting against the flare.

"See? That's my problem. Thing keeps going off before I'm ready." He switched in another bulb and fired another flash in Kurt's face. "Oops."

"Cut it out!" Kurt held up a free hand against the painful flash.

"Let's do us a proper picture. I'll straighten your tie for you." Solomon let the camera dangle on its strap as he grabbed Kurt's tie, sliding the knot snug up against Kurt's larynx, choking him.

"There. Brings out the color in your cheeks." Solomon gave Kurt's face a pat.

"Don't, you asshole" Kurt struggled to loosen his tie.

"You're right. Better without the tie." Solomon pulled out his bowie and slid the gleaming blade between the knot and Kurt's naked Adam's apple. Kurt's eyes went wide, as Solomon cut the tie free with a quick slice and stuffed the pieces into Kurt's shirt pocket.

Kurt wormed out from between Marjorie and Solomon, bolting for the stairs.

Solomon flashed another bulb at him, then turned to Marjorie.

"Those pictures'll be spoilt. Fella just wouldn't stand still long enough. Fidgety sort, isn't he?"

"I suppose I'm lucky you have a hobby that keeps you up late." Marjorie straightened her top.

"Is that the fella you mentioned?" Solomon swapped in another bulb.

"Yes."

"Sorry for driving him off." Solomon aimed the camera at her and snapped off another flash. He looked up, twisting the knob to advance the film, then closed the view finder.

"Working fine now. Kind of funny."

"Bet you didn't realize how busy you'd be when they gave you the job being my guardian angel."

Stung, Solomon fixed his face in a smile for her, then turned back to his door.

"Thanks, Skeeter."

Solomon gave a goodnight wave back over his shoulder and went into his apartment.

Inside, Solomon closed the door, and put his camera on the bureau.

"See all the good you're doing? You're a hex in shining armor, you know that, Solly?"

"I told you I'm through doing your dirty work."

"Then you're serious? About giving it back?"

"No. I plan to do some real good with this thing. Be useful for a change. Maybe spend the rest of my days righting some wrongs. World could use a fella like me."

"Do you even know the difference between right and wrong?" Griffin raised his hands in mock surrender when Solly spun around to face him. "Just asking."

"Can't be any worse than it's been."

"I've said it before. You'll end up locked away for a monster. Or they figure out you're immortal and all of time rolls up all the way back to the Big Bang."

"I've had over a hundred and fifty years of practice living life without leaving a footprint. Nobody's noticed me yet." Solomon headed for the bedroom.

"They just need to know where to look."

Solomon stopped just at the bedroom doorway.

"Beg pardon?"

"I said, 'it'd be keen if you wrote a book.' "

"Do me a favor."

"Anything, Solly, mi amigo."

"Turn yourself off so I can get some sleep."

"You know, Solly, that joke never gets old."

Solomon went into the bedroom and shut the door.

The smile dropped off Griffin's face. "Because it was ancient about the same time Cleopatra was in diapers." Griffin melted away into the dark.

Chapter Thirty-Four

ONE THING SOLOMON LEARNED early in life about gambling—when it's clear you can't win, put down your cards, leave the table, and find another game.

Unless—the player sitting across from you is an arrogant, over-confident angel, who is easily bored. A fella like that could be ripe for a fleecing.

For someone who navigated eternity as easily as Griffin seemed to do, he sure seemed easily vexed when he had to wait for anything.

That might be Solomon's only decent card left to play.

Solomon went about his morning, as he often did, playing chess with Morton Dunne at one of the stone checkerboard tables on the shaded promenade of the monument overlooking the Hudson River. Mort, a retiree and long-time resident, spent *his* mornings challenging all comers to as many chess games as they could handle. It passed the time for Solomon until Marjorie brought Willa out to the playground for a few moments before heading on to work, or dance class, or tryouts for a stage show.

This morning, Griffin reclined on the nearest of the big black cannons aimed at New Jersey, staring up at the sky as Mort and Solomon concentrated on their pieces spread across the board.

"Did you know, if you stare at a cloud long enough," said Griffin after a bit, "your teeth hurt?" He ran his tongue under his upper lip, as if feeling for damage.

Solomon kept his eye fixed on the game board.

Griffin let out another loud, pitiful sigh, then raised himself up on one elbow.

"I have to tell you, Solly, after last night I expected you to fill up your days with brash acts and ill-conceived adventures."

"I'm studying on it." Solomon kept his eye fixed on the game board.

"Eh, what?" Mort had a habit of turning off his hearing aids to shut out the whine of children and the harsh, grinding sounds of the skateboards the older kids rode all over the plaza.

"I said, I'm studying on it," Solomon repeated, louder for Mort.

"Don't take too long. My idiot son-in-law is counting the days 'til probate."

Griffin flopped back onto the cannon, his arm thrown over his eyes, a pitiable picture of long-suffering patience.

If Griffin had any inkling what Solomon was up to, he made no sign. It would be a handy thing if Griffin wasn't omniscient, as he liked to insist.

Solomon kept his attention fixed on the game as Griffin let out a piteous groan.

Last night, Griffin's reaction was enough to convince Solomon the game had been rigged against him. Griffin didn't mean for him to win back Lavinia. The dice were loaded. The cards marked. The horserace fixed. Reason enough to tell Griffin he could find himself another patsy because Solomon was through playing matchmaker.

Which wasn't quite true.

Now more than ever, Solomon wanted to clear Lavinia's name and do whatever he could to put Marjorie and Willa back on course to better days of some kind. But—anything Solomon might try was fixed to end badly. Hadn't Griffin said as much?

If he hoped to have any chance of success, he had to trick Griffin into taking charge. Because Griffin, being an angel straight out of the Almighty's throne room, couldn't help but make the right choice for her. All Griffin had to do was look at them dominoes of his to figure out the future.

It didn't matter if it unraveled time or not. If it did, Solomon was ready to give up the doo-hickey and take his chances with Luther again. If it didn't, at least he'd seen to it Marjorie was fixed up right. He'd keep the doo-hickey and find himself enough adventure to tie up Griffin and out of Marjorie and Willa's hair until the crack of doom.

The tricky part would be getting Griffin to think it was all his own idea to play matchmaker for Marjorie and set her up with someone who could break the Kantlingher Hex for good and all.

What Solomon needed was a solid gold opening.

With his head down, Solomon let his eyes range around the monument plaza.

The place was busy with joggers, nannies pushing strollers, dog walkers, kids on their skateboards, and snack vendors with their carts.

Marjorie and Willa could be along any time now, and no good ideas jumped out to bite him.

"Honestly. Is this how you plan to spend the entire first day of the rest of your life?"

"Like I said, I'm studying on it."

"Check mate," said Mort.

"Aw, too bad," Griffin rolled off the cannon, landing with a squat on the ground and popping upright. "So—what's next for funsies?"

"Got time for another?" asked Mort.

"More time than you could imagine," said Solomon.

Griffin did a slow flop backward athwart the cannon, his arms splayed out. "This is not the Solly we've all come to know and love. Where's the fire brand? Where's the lover? Where's the gambler who's wormed his way into our hearts and minds?"

"Getting ready for another game with my old friend Mort here." Solomon gave Mort a great big smile.

Griffin slid off the cannon and came up to stand behind Mort.

"Look around. I'll bet right here in this very park, this very minute, there's someone that'd be the perfect fit for what's-her-name."

"Marjorie."

"Right. And you're just going to sit there, letting the cosmos roll on by you, letting her miss maybe her one chance for real happiness?"

"Marjorie's made her choice. No going back now. At least this time I didn't wind up in some nearby body of water."

"Anything that undoes the future by changing the present would change the past."

"You said once they choose, their future's fixed, and they're stuck just like their mommas before them. Or can't you remember that one day to the next?"

"I didn't say that."

"You did."

"Do you have that down in writing somewhere, because I don't remember it that way."

"You're telling me an angel can be forgetful?"

"Excuse me for having a brain filled up with billions more memories than you do."

"Doesn't change what you said."

"Use that native mudfoot intelligence of yours. Anything that undoes the future by changing the present would change the past. Wouldn't it?" Griffin smiled as if willing Solomon to grasp that. "So?"

"So, what?"

"So, what are you going to do about it?"

"I think I'll—be white this time, if you don't mind." Again, Solomon smiled at Mort as he set up the chess pieces again.

"Solly, don't you understand? There's still a chance the whole future would break down, history would roll up like Christmas wrapping paper, and you'd have your second chance with Lavinia, if you could get her to make the right decision this time."

"And end up with Luther's pistol aimed straight at my heart. I'll pass." Solomon appreciated Mort having his hearing aids turned off. It meant that he didn't have to explain his peculiar, apparently one-sided conversations.

"I can't believe you're serious about giving up any chance of getting back to Lavinia."

"Damned serious. I'm through getting myself knocked on the head for my troubles. I told you. I'm retired. I'm out of the matchmaking business."

"Matchmaking?" Griffin gagged back a burst of laughter. "Can I give you a little constructive criticism about your so-called matchmaking?" Griffin blew a big, wet raspberry at Solomon.

"Like you could do any better." Solomon concentrated for all he was worth on straightening the chessmen, doing his best to ignore Griffin.

"That goes without saying."

"Oh. Then let me be the first to say it. You couldn't do any better."

"Better *and* blindfolded."

"Don't embarrass yourself. You don't have a clue what's going on inside a woman where her heart's concerned."

"Don't kid yourself. I've had to watch you mudfoot short-timers for aeons. There's no mystery left in a single one of you."

"You wouldn't know where to start with a girl like Marjorie."

"Piece of cake. I fix it so she bumps into someone who's a little bit good looking and a little bit clumsy, she feels the need to take charge and," Griffin snapped his fingers. "Game over."

"That's just meddling. Meddling is not matchmaking."

"Your matchmaking is not matchmaking, Solly, my lad."

"Okay, then you go ahead and have a go at it. Show me I'm wrong."

"I would but I can't."

"I figured as much. Big talk."

"You recall that I am duty-bound not to interfere with you mudfoots, no matter how much you may deserve it?"

"Yeah, and if I wasn't duty-bound to be respectful of God's divine creatures, I'd whup your heinie, and make you eat dirt."

"That's bold talk for somebody wearing a two-tone cardigan and suede hush puppies."

"I'd whup you buck naked if it'll make you feel any better."

"I'd like to see that. In fact, there's a whole legion of my compatriots who'd pay cash money to see that."

"You keep telling me how angels don't have money."

"With that many of us, we'd figure a way to get some." Solomon could see Griffin getting pink around the ears. "For a chance to see something like that? You bet we would."

"Like I said, big talk."

"Wanna bet?"

"What have you got to bet with? Pixie dust?"

"You name it." Griffin's ears were full-on red now.

"Okay, I will. If you match her up, I hand over the doo-hickey, free and clear, and I'll take my chances with Luther. But—if you don't, I keep it, long as I like. And no more of your dirty work."

"Done." Without a flicker of hesitation, Griffin spit in his hand and held it out for Solomon to shake.

Solomon spit in his own hand and was about to shake—but stopped.

"Now who's all talk," said Griffin.

Solomon took hold of Griffin's hand but didn't shake it.

"You're not afraid I'll unwind the whole blamed cosmos with it, if you lose?"

"First, I won't lose, and second, I know you, Solly, you're too selfish to take that risk. You like you. You're a big fan of you. You think you hung the moon. And I'm betting you wouldn't do anything to put the one thing you love most in jeopardy."

"You're forgetting Lavinia."

Griffin studied him only a moment, then said, "No, actually, I'm not. Deal?"

"Deal." Solomon gave Griffin's hand a single hard pump, not wanting to seem at all eager.

"To make it sporting, I'll let you choose the guy I match her up with."

That caught Solomon off-guard. "You figure you got me coming and going, don't you?"

Griffin smiled.

"I choose a loser, it'll be my fault all over again. If I choose a winner, you get your doo-hickey back and maybe I get shot for real this time."

Griffin shrugged, about to speak but something on the plaza behind Solomon caught his eye.

"Uh-oh."

Solomon looked to see what had wiped that smug smile off Griffin's kisser.

Two officers stepped out of a police cruiser parked at the curb. They crossed the promenade to where Solomon and Mort sat. The officers weren't moving all that fast, but they were aiming right for Solomon.

Solomon looked down at the table. Kurt probably called the cops on him for holding a knife under his chin last night. He seemed the type, even though the rascal ought to be the first to admit he deserved it.

Solomon figured he could outrun the shorter officer, a woman with stubby legs and a low center of gravity. But the taller officer, a young man having the longer legs, would make a race of it. That would end Solomon's masquerade as an old man.

The officers were much closer, taking their time. Of course they would. They thought he was a geezer.

The short cop wore a veteran's service stripes on her sleeve, and commendation ribbons on the tab above her badge. She seemed no-nonsense, with her hair colored to a rusty auburn, tied back in a tight bun. She'd be a mite tough to hornswoggle.

The tall cop was more of a middling height, his skin a working man's tan over a ruddy complexion, with short black curly hair. He was most likely a rookie, seeing he wore no hashmarks or commendation ribbons. Still, he had too bright a look about him to trust that he could be flim-flammed by any of Solomon's fast talk either.

Solomon turned back to the table again, as if studying the board, while his eyes were ratcheted over watching for them to come up on him.

"Hey, pops," called out the tall officer.

Solomon didn't have to turn his head to feel them both right next to him. He looked up, smiling innocence.

From this close, Solomon could read their name plates. "Wood" on the short cop, "Lighter" on the tall cop.

But they weren't looking at Solomon. They were looking at a disheveled old vagrant in an ill-fitting overcoat, his back to them as he struggled with something at waist level.

The vagrant looked back over his shoulder at the officers, his silver-blue eyes wide as he chewed his tongue at the effort.

"You can't do that here," said Lighter.

The vagrant squared around to face them and Lighter hopped backward to avoid whatever unpleasantness he imagined was about to happen.

The vagrant gripped a soda bottle in both hands, trying without success to twist off the cap. He held the bottle out to the cop.

"Sorry," he said in a gravelly, whiskey voice. "Drinking soda illegal in the park now?"

Wood laughed and put a knuckle to her nose.

Lighter took the bottle from the vagrant, twisted off the cap and handed the bottle and cap back, wiping his palm on his trouser leg. The vagrant saluted his thanks and then took a long swallow, his Adam's apple bobbing. He wiped the bottle's mouth with the lapel of his grimy overcoat and offered a swig to Lighter.

"I'm good, thanks."

"That's some nose you've got for crime there, Ray," said Wood.

The vagrant weebled across the promenade, as he tried to drink and walk at the same time, disappearing down the street.

The officers leaned against the railing, watching the plaza.

Solomon didn't want to press his luck. He slipped away from the table, leaving Mort asleep in the seat, his chin on his chest.

"So, all you need now is a girlfriend." Wood wiped her forehead and then the sweatband of her duty cap.

"I'm looking."

Solomon stopped, pivoted slowly around, and sat down again.

"Wish I had a rich aunt to leave me a vacation in Hawaii. Two weeks? Sweet."

"A senior citizen package. Good for five years. Aunt Tulla expired before it did."

"When're you going?"

"I don't know. I may not. It's not like I'd be out any money."

"You'd skip a freebie Hawaiian vacation because your fiancée dumped you for a banker? There's a couple EMTs out of Yorkville would love to go."

"You can't take just anybody. To Hawaii? You save something like that for a honeymoon."

A big brown Labrador dragged its walker over to smell Lighter's shoes. The dog walker, a brunette in spandex pants and a hooded sweatshirt gave him a half-smile of apology.

"Sorry." She hauled at the dog's lead, pulling him away.

"That's okay," said Lighter. "You ever happen to get out as far as Queens?"

"Seriously?" The smile was gone. "No."

To the other side of Solomon, a slim blonde in embroidered overalls and a long-sleeved tee-shirt stopped to crouch down by a stroller. She thumbed dry cereal bits into the palm of a toddler who slapped the pieces into his mouth with gusto.

A bedraggled teddy had dropped out of the toddler's stroller. Lighter picked it up for him. Handing it back, he smiled at the blonde nanny.

"Ever been to Queens?" he asked.

The blonde nanny squinted up at him, shading her eyes with her free hand, shook her head, and said something that might have been German or Dutch about *polizei* then smiled to show there were no hard feelings.

Lighter bobbed his head in a good-natured sort of agreement as he turned back to join Wood.

"What makes you so chatty today?"

"Something I was thinking about at my Aunt Tulla's funeral." Lighter scanned the park. "I don't want to be sitting around when I'm old and alone wondering if some girl might've been the one, and I missed out because I didn't open my mouth."

"Talking to women has never been your best thing."

"Yeah. Painful. I keep listening for a voice that says, this is the one you should talk to. So I don't keep embarrassing myself."

"C'mon. A trip to Hawaii? You tell any one of them that and you'll snag a fiancée in plenty of time before the offer expires."

Solomon leaned back, took off his hat to fan himself as he looked around for Marjorie.

He spotted her just coming onto the plaza with her friend, Gayle, both of them pushing strollers.

"I'm looking," said Lighter, as they walked away from the monument.

Solomon eased himself up from the table and found Griffin back on the cannon, his arms across his eyes. Solomon tapped him, causing Griffin to rear up.

"Gosh, that was exciting." He rubbed his face and stretched. "All done?"

"I got one for you," said Solomon. "That lawman." He nodded toward Lighter and Wood walking away.

Griffin hopped down, clapped, and rubbed his hands together. "Prepare to eat your words."

Then he stopped and laughed. He turned back to wag his finger at

Solomon.

"Ahahahah. I see what you're doing. You thought you had me, didn't you?"

"What?" Solomon kept his face as blank as he could manage.

"Solly, Solly, Solly, Solly, Solly."

"You don't get a move on, he'll be gone." Solomon could see his scheme breaking apart.

"Kantlingher women hate lawmen. You think by choosing some random cop she'll refuse, I lose the bet, and you go on your merry way."

Solomon worked his face into what he hoped would pass for sheepishness, biting the inside of his cheek.

"Can't blame a fella for trying." Solomon watched as Lighter and Wood had almost reached their cruiser.

"I see right through you."

"If it's too hard for you, okay then. But—you lose." Solomon turned back to the table. "Thanks for the doo-hickey. Now get lost."

"I didn't say that. I'm saying you don't fool me."

"Well, you just keep standing here jawing."

Griffin smiled, shook his finger at Solomon one more time as he trotted away toward the police cruiser. He melted into the figure of a kid on a skateboard, bumping into the hot dog man as he passed, light-fingering the hot dog man's wallet out of his pocket, then riding hard to catch up with the officers.

"Officer?" shouted Griffin, his voice an adolescent crackle, "Did you see that lady dropped her wallet?"

The officers both looked back at him as he pointed toward Marjorie heading toward the path down to the playground.

"Take it back to her," said Wood. "She'll give you a reward and you can get yourself a popsicle."

"Which one?" asked Lighter.

"The brown-haired one," said the kid.

"Pushing strollers? They're both probably married," said Wood.

Lighter nodded and said, "Knock yourself out, kid," and turned back to the cruiser.

"I didn't see her wearing a ring," said the kid, then chuffed, "You don't want to be sitting around when you're old and alone wondering if some girl might've been the one, and you missed out because you didn't open your mouth."

Lighter stopped. "What did you say?"

But the kid now had his finger up his nose, intent on whatever solid object he'd found up there.

Lighter looked to where the kid had pointed, but Marjorie had already gone down the path.

"You need some pick-up lines?" the kid asked, studying the tip of his finger. "Great for meeting girls."

"I don't need advice from a twelve-year-old."

"You're just going to hand it back to her and say, here's your wallet, lady? You'll be on your way to Hawaii in no time. Sheesh."

"Who are you, kid?"

But the kid was back to examining his fingertip.

Lighter pivoted hard on his heel and strode off after Marjorie.

The kid followed him as far as the top of the pathway to watch. When Solomon came up behind him, Griffin had already ballooned back into himself.

Lighter sped up to a jog down the path, dodging strollers, leaping dog leashes, and dancing around cane-walking pensioners as he headed for the playground.

"This is better than billiards. It's a one, two, three-cushion shot. Come on, let's go see if he can sink it."

Down near the entrance to the playground, Lighter caught up behind Marjorie and Gayle.

"Why did you let Kurt come up with Willa there?" Gayle asked Marjorie.

"I didn't think he was going to suck out my sweat glands. I'm waiting my whole life for an angel. All I ever get are men. At least he split the cab fare before Skeeter choked off his air supply."

"Pardon me—ma'am—uh—miss," said Lighter, with a glance at her ring finger.

"You—uh—dropped your wallet—lady?" He seemed unable to decide between a grimace and a smile, holding out the dark brown, heavy leather billfold. Which could not possibly belong to her.

Marjorie and Gayle looked at the wallet and then at him.

"Seriously?" asked Marjorie.

"Points for originality," said Gayle to Marjorie.

"Your—dad's maybe?" Lighter waved it. "Or yours," he said to Gayle. Gayle smirked, flashing her wedding band.

Marjorie reached down the front of her sweatshirt and lifted a small money clip on a chain. She waved it under his nose.

"Excuse me. May I?" He took hold of the clip and waved it under his nose again. Then he sniffed the wallet. Then sniffed her money clip again. He let go of the clip.

"I'm never going to make police dog. I keep flunking the physical."

Marjorie smiled, but turned to go.

"You know—as part of the precinct's community outreach, we treat citizens—random citizens—totally random citizens—to a cup of coffee—at random. On me. Us."

"Already had my random morning coffee. Thanks."

"Oh. Maybe you could have your afternoon coffee early. Think of the time you'd save."

Marjorie was about to refuse, when a faint gleam of panic flashed across her eyes. She turned to Gayle. "What if I say no and there's no hex?"

"What if you say yes, and there is?"

Marjorie turned back to Lighter. "You ever been to Oklahoma?"

"No. You ever been to Queens?"

Marjorie turned back to Gayle. "But what if there's no hex?"

"But what if there is?"

Willa, impatient with all the jibber-jabber, was struggling to slip out of the stroller and get to the playground.

"I—um—thanks, but I don't have a babysitter. Really. Thanks. But, sorry. Tell the New York Police Department thanks for me. Maybe some other time."

"Then, again," said Gayle, studying Lighter, "what if there isn't?"

"You're no help," said Marjorie in a low hiss.

"Just thinking out loud." Gayle covered up a smile.

"Bring her along," said Lighter.

"Really?"

Willa squirmed free of the strap holding her in.

"Sure. We all carry handcuffs, remember? Let her run off some of that energy, then I could meet you at the Fatty Starbuckle's up on Broadway?"

"When?" asked Marjorie, lifting Willa back into her stroller.

"What's good for you?"

"In about an hour?"

"Sure. Sure. That'd be great. An hour." Lighter backed away, moving up the path toward the monument, nearly taking out a Scottie on a long leash behind him.

Officer Wood waited for him at the top of the path.

"So?"

"Wasn't hers."

"Did you look inside it first?"

Lighter opened the wallet. The picture on the license was of a heavy-set man with a mustache.

"I'm guessing she doesn't look a thing like her picture."

"Come on."

"So. She the one meant to be?"

"Have to get through coffee first." Lighter scanned the faces on the plaza, then walked over to the hot dog man and held out the wallet. The hot dog man patted his pockets in a panic, then grabbed it from Lighter, opening it to check the contents.

Wood was still laughing when they got back in the cruiser and headed up town.

Down at the playground Marjorie turned Willa loose, then stood next to Gayle.

"That'd be a first. Someone in my family on the right side of the law."

"It's just coffee."

Solomon watched from his spot on the bench just up from the playground. Behind him, Griffin reclined on the slope of grass, sweeping his arms and legs in great arcs.

"I'm glad my destiny doesn't hinge on a couple of sixteen-ounce cappuccinos," said Griffin.

"Don't you need snow?"

Griffin hopped to his feet, leaving a yellowed angel pattern in the green turf.

"Helps to transcend the laws of nature."

Chapter Thirty-Five

WOOD SAT BEHIND THE WHEEL of the police cruiser parked at the curb next to Fatty's on the corner. Marjorie stood next to the cruiser. Willa sat in her stroller, shaking Lighter's handcuffs for the jingle.

Lighter backed out of the coffee bar, juggling three tall, top-heavy cups of coffee.

"Here you go." Lighter held out the cardboard carrier to Marjorie. She twisted one of the cups out of the carrier.

"Thank you, NYPD," said Marjorie, raising the cup.

"Ditto," said Lighter, saluting with the carrier, nearly toppling the other two cups.

Recovering, Lighter held the carrier out for Wood, then took his own coffee, leaving the carrier on the hood of the cruiser.

"What did I tell you?" Lighter nodded at Willa infatuated with the shiny metal cuffs. "Nature's perfect babysitter."

Marjorie smiled and sipped.

"So," said Lighter, sipping and watching Marjorie. "Is the hex a person or more a state of mind?"

"Definitely a person."

"Playing matchmaker?"

"Fixes you up with some guy who turns out to be a crumb, and your life explodes."

"If it means anything, I was voted most likely to help old ladies across the street."

"Yeah, well—present company excluded, you know."

They both took deep swigs from their sixteen-ounce cappuccinos.

From across Broadway, standing in between the fruit and vegetable bins of the bodega on the corner opposite Fatty's, Solomon watched Lighter and Marjorie. He had a couple of avocados in a death grip.

"You going to buy them or pit them?" asked Griffin. "Regretting our wager already? They haven't sipped past the foam to reach the coffee yet."

"No, I'm not regretting our wager." But Solomon put down the avocados and took up a bag of grapes.

Two teens on skateboards raced through the intersection, riding down Broadway, close alongside the parked cars, weaving between pedestrians in the crosswalk.

"Will you know him if you see him?" asked Lighter, the sound of the skateboards catching his attention.

"I sure hope so. Makes it hard to meet guys, though. I have to be so careful about guys who seem nice but are really jokers he's tricked me into meeting."

"I'm totally safe, then. This was my own idea."

"You *and* the NYPD, right?"

"Them, too."

"It doesn't mean I don't still have high standards."

"Of course. Like—avoid anyone with in-laws who wind up in prison or on wanted posters, right?"

Marjorie's smile froze. She squeezed out a toothy little laugh.

From across the street, seeing Marjorie laugh caused Solomon to squeeze hard on the bag of grapes.

"You should have a nice table wine any minute now." Griffin held out an apple. "Try this. It'll take you longer to squeeze it into cider."

Solomon flinched away from Griffin, dropping the grapes and took up his grocery sack. He stepped from between the bins, trying to get a better look at Lighter and Marjorie.

"So," asked Lighter, "are there any clues you can look for to spot him?"

"No, but he must be, like, a total oddball," said Marjorie. "Freakish, don't you think?"

From uptown, a heavy-set guy on a skateboard careened down the sidewalk, zipping along, dodging people, sending them scattering. Dressed in a blue jumpsuit and sunglasses, his gray, frizzle-haired ponytail streaming in the wind, he shouldered past a very large lady wearing a tracksuit and electric green running shoes, dragging her little dog. She shrieked as Ponytail Guy hopped over the leash and landed again on the skateboard, riding on, aiming straight for Solomon.

Hearing the commotion, Lighter looked across the street just as the Ponytail Guy slammed into Solomon, a starburst of arms and legs, and exploding groceries. The collision carried both of them into the side of the car parked at the corner.

"Excuse me." Lighter handed Marjorie his coffee and trotted toward the mayhem.

On the ground, Ponytail Guy wiggled and squirmed on top of Solomon, patting him all over whispering, "I wanna live forever, I wanna live forever" as he wormed back onto his feet, then catching Solomon under one arm to help him up.

"Get your hands off me, you clod!"

"Jeez, I didn't see you, old timer," said Ponytail Guy, more to the gathering gawkers.

Solomon slapped at Ponytail Guy's wandering hands. He pulled Solomon in close, continuing to dust him off, whispering harsh and low, "I wanna live forever, I wanna live forever, I wanna live forever!"

Solomon, spooked, grabbed Ponytail Guy in a maximum torque headlock, his arm across the guy's mouth.

"All right, all right, break it up," Lighter reached in to lever them apart.

"I had another coconut just about this same size," said Solomon, looking at the exploded groceries. "Any you seen it?"

Ponytail Guy popped loose from Solomon's headlock, falling backward, sitting down hard.

"Animal cruelty! Animal cruelty!" shouted the lady in the tracksuit pushing through the crowd, grabbing Lighter's sleeve. "Arrest him! Arrest him," she cried out, pointing at Ponytail Guy. "Stop him before he rolls over some helpless dog." She turned to the others gathered around. "You saw how they go! Whoosh-whoosh-whoosh! Just like that. Whoosh-whoosh-whoosh!"

Griffin, on his hands and knees and crawling backward holding a doggie treat, enticed the little pooch to weave its leash around Ponytail Guy's ankles.

Solomon put his hat back on and looked around at his groceries scattered about. He bent to pick up one of his cans lying stuck between the car's tire and the curbstone.

Ponytail Guy lunged for it, but the leash around his ankles tripped him up, throwing him headlong onto the sidewalk. The little mutt yelped, dragged after the collapsing Ponytail Guy, toppling the lady in the tracksuit backward into Lighter's arms, carrying them to the ground.

"Assassins!" she shouted, lying back on Lighter, waving her arms and legs, trying to right herself.

Officer Wood steered the police cruiser to the curb, touched the siren for a half-warble to clear the gawkers, then parked and got out, leaving the emergency lights spinning.

Scrambling to his feet, Ponytail Guy grabbed up his skateboard and ran.

"Hey!" Lighter, pinned under the large woman, swiped one free hand at the retreating suspect.

Ducking between cars, and out onto the street, he dropped the board and mounted it with a hop, paddle-footing up a side street and out of sight.

"He's getting away," shouted the lady in the tracksuit. As Lighter struggled to get out from under her, she squealed, "Don't drop me!"

Wood helped the lady to her feet as Lighter rolled from under her.

Lighter took a few steps after Ponytail Guy, but he was long gone. He turned back to help Solomon gather up the scattered groceries. Then he picked up and handed Solomon his cane.

"He might have done some serious damage, causing a fall like that. We can run you over to the emergency room, have them check you out."

"Not but a few scratches."

Lighter and Wood exchanged looks. They didn't see any scratches.

"Then how about a lift home?"

"You live in the neighborhood, right?" asked Wood.

"I can walk from here."

"What's it hurt for us to take you home? It's not like you two guys faked an accident to shake down the store for some insurance money, and then got spooked when we showed up? Right?" said Wood.

Solomon chewed on that a long moment, studying Wood, then jabbed his cane at the police cruiser. Lighter opened the rear door and Solomon slid in. Griffin sat on the other side of the back seat.

"At least it doesn't have a meter, right?"

"Shut up."

Across the street, Marjorie, still holding the two coffees, watched the police cruiser disappear into traffic.

She knocked back first one, then the other, dropping the empties into the trash with a flourish, then wheeled Willa up the street.

Solomon unlocked the door to his apartment and pushed in backward, his cane hooked over his wrist, his arms clamped around the busted sack and loose groceries. He let everything spill out onto the kitchen counter, corralling the oranges to keep them from rolling off the edge.

"You weren't much help out there," said Solomon.

"I've told you, I'm not the guardian angel type." Griffin brought one runaway orange to a halt with his fingertip and flicked it back toward the others.

"Can't say much for your handiwork as an avenging angel either."

"I did give your assailant a little kick in the pants while he was down on all fours. I thought you'd appreciate that. You maybe didn't see it."

"I'd like to think you're just acting ignorant for my benefit. But it comes so natural to you, I wonder how on earth it could be a put-on."

"Am I missing something here, Solly?"

"You couldn't see what he was doing? You may not be omniscient, but you sure as heck got a pair of eyes in your head. You didn't see him frisking me like I was carrying contraband? Kept saying 'I want to live forever, I want to live forever,' like he knew about this doo-hickey of yours?"

"Oh. That." Griffin stroked his cheeks and ran his hands up over his head. "I've been meaning to tell you about this guy."

"You know who he is?" Solomon slapped his thigh. "Of course you do. You're a blamed angel. Who is he? And what's he doing putting his greasy paws on me like that?"

"He's turning out to be a real menace, that's who."

"I gathered that while I was laying there on the sidewalk after he bounced me off a car! Who in hell is he?"

"Alvin Shortwick, a man who will stop at nothing in his search for immortality. This guy is two-hundred forty pounds of pure mayhem. Two-sixty after lunch. He arranges accidents for short-timers hoping one of you'll turn out to be an immortal."

"He knows something, doesn't he. He didn't just take it in his head one day that someone somewhere on God's green earth had the power to live forever."

"Who knows where these screwball notions come from? People have been chasing eternal youth since the Garden of Eden when Lucifer told Eve about cellulite. And we both know how that turned out."

"You're saying he just happened to pick me out of all the millions and millions of people walking the earth?"

"Sure seems that way, doesn't it?"

"With that kind of luck he ought to play the lottery." Solomon ran his hand over the back of his neck, rubbing away the sudden hot breath he felt there. "If he finds out for sure I can live forever, doesn't that mean—" Solomon snapped his fingers.

"You need to vamoose and not give him the chance."

"Just like that? Up and run?"

"This is a guy who will stop at nothing to find someone, anyone, who possesses the secret of immortality in the here and now."

Rubbing his jaw and looking toward his front door. That would mean leaving Marjorie and Willa. "Maybe now he's had a go at me, he'll be off to try out some other dumb sap."

"Oh, no, he'll be back."

"Why would he?"

Griffin gave Solomon a sickly grin and shrugged.

"Why would he keep after me? Nothing happened when he bounced me off the sidewalk that'd make him think I was anything special."

"What say we talk about it on the way out of town." Griffin held out Solomon's empty duffel bag. "I'll help you pack. Quicker that way."

Solomon cocked his head, eyelids no more than slits. "How'd he find me? Really?"

"How can you expect me to explain the mental processes of a mud-foot short-timer who is clearly deranged?"

"You might as well tell me." Solomon grabbed the duffel bag from Griffin and threw it on the floor. "I'm not moving one inch out of this room until you do."

"Well as you yourself said, quite rightly—" Griffin wandered the room, licking his lips and wiping the corners of his mouth, "—and with astonishingly keen insight for being a mudfoot, I might add—" Griffin backed away as Solomon pushed his face close in on him.

"How?" demanded Solomon, trying to lock on Griffin's shifting eyes.

"You've had more than a hundred-fifty years of practice living life without leaving a footprint, which is an impressive skill to have mastered in this particular century—" Griffin continued to keep his distance from Solomon.

"How!" shouted Solomon, hopping around to cut him off.

"I gave him a hint."

"A hint!"

"Just a tiny, itty-bitty, little hint!" Griffin held up the tippy-tips of his fingers.

"You fingered me, you stool-pigeon?" Solomon grabbed his pistol and aimed it at Griffin, thumbing back the hammer.

"Mind the breakables!" Griffin held out a sofa cushion between them.

Solomon stopped. He tilted the pistol barrel upward and eased the hammer down to rest on the charged cylinder. As much as he would have liked to pull the trigger, if only for the smoke and noise, it wouldn't do a bit of good. He tossed the pistol onto the shelf, then rounded on

Griffin who kept Solomon at bay with his own cane. Solomon snatched it back from him.

"For the good of the cosmos, can we leave now?"

"Is that your big answer, you gave him a hint just to get me to high-tail it for parts unknown? Why let him find me in the first place?"

"Because you are so good at hiding. I figure if we can get him to waste his days chasing after you, he won't bother looking for any of the others."

Solomon reared back, looking full on at Griffin.

"Oops."

"You said I was the only one out there."

"I did?"

"I asked you if there was anyone like me still out there, and you said—"

"—you're one of a kind. I meant it for a compliment."

"So, there are others out there like me."

"Not anymore."

"But there used to be? Where? How many?"

"It's not like there was a credit union. Aw, come on, Solly. What do you want from me? Can't you see I'm trying to keep the cosmos together with just these two hands."

"Why the Almighty would leave you in charge of anything beats the living daylights out of me."

"So. Are you satisfied? Can we leave now?"

"No. I want you to tell me who this Albert Shuckwit—"

"Shortwick."

"Albert Shortwick—"

"Alvin. Alvin Shortwick."

"Don't bandy words with me. Tell me who he is. Why he thinks I'm his ticket to immortality. And why the hell you decided to rat me out to him."

Griffin sat on the sofa and sighed.

"You want the long version or the short version?"

"Short version. So you don't have quite so many places to hide the truth."

Chapter Thirty-Six

Minnesota – Present Day

FOR THE LONGEST TIME, ALVIN SHORTWICK made a living sponging off rich old women. You wouldn't know it to look at him, but he could be quite charming. He managed to worm his way into the good graces and sizeable bank accounts of quite a few such women. It wasn't pretty, but he totally avoided the whole, nasty workplace experience.

Until he met Philippa Waverly.

He'd learned of her from reading an article in some local shopping circular about the oddballs and eccentrics of Minnesota. Described as an elderly recluse, Philippa lived alone—as far as anyone could tell—in an enormous, two-hundred-year-old house set on a bare hill, without so much as a runty shrub. The great, encircling lawn had grown wild because Philippa could not abide the sound of power mowers and weed wackers.

She never entertained, and only the occasional tradesman ever called. Most of them never laid eyes on her, all of them taking their instructions from notes she pinned to the door, along with their fee in an envelope of cash.

This made her a prime candidate for the old Shortwick charm. So he tied up his wispy, graying hair, put on his uniform of youth, and called on Philippa to pitch himself as a lawn boy.

He arrived on her great front porch, stuffed into his lady-killer jeans, white shirt with the turned-up collar, black leather vest, and motorcycle boots. Banging the great knocker on the front door of the antiquated mansion, he stood back to let her get an eyeful of him. When a second and a third knock failed to rouse her, he slipped a note under the door, offering his services.

Philippa's reply, slipped out to him from under the door, written on thick stationery paper and in fine penmanship, accepted his offer, and settle himself in the gardener's cottage until the job was done.

Using only a push reel mower and sling blade, the job took Alvin a week. In all that time, he never saw any sign of Philippa.

When he'd finished, Philippa appeared on the great porch and summoned him up to the house. He tried not to wheeze as he trudged up the long, winding walk. Lawn work did not agree with him.

Philippa was quite the vision, dressed in figure-hugging black, gold high-heeled sandals, and a turban that barely corralled the scattering of gray hair. She draped her neck and wrists in a burdensome load of jewelry. Most of it would seem fairly rich-looking to someone like Alvin, well-practiced in covetousness. Only the bauble holding her turban together looked out of place.

Of course, it was like nothing Alvin had seen before. An odd metal in the shape of a hand-forged bolt head. Could have been old barn hardware or petrified elk droppings for all Alvin cared. He was in a hurry to cash in on the richer stuff.

Philippa was, like so many of the others he'd preyed on, withered with advanced age, and appeared to be easy pickings. But as she led him through the house, and into the parlor for a sherry, she showed an unexpected vigor, with quick, sharp movements and keen eyes that studied him closely.

Whatever Philippa saw in Alvin as he tamed the wilderness of her unruly landscape, it was enough to win him a longer stay.

Sitting and sipping her sherry, eyeing him closely, the room filled with the radiance of promise.

Only the portraits of ancient ancestral relations hung on the walls, and nothing to suggest any immediate family to interfere with Alvin's scheming.

Giving her a sly look, Alvin asked her outright, "Won't your family be scandalized, a strange man living under the same roof with you?"

She barked a laugh and said, "There's no one left to be scandalized."

There being no further disagreement to the living arrangement, they toasted their decision with another sherry, and set up a chaste sort of housekeeping.

As with all the others, Alvin fixed his eye on the payoff to take his mind off the withered features of his latest hostess.

He spent the next few months making himself charming and amiable, appearing to dote on Philippa, making every effort to seem servile and attentive. All the while he cataloged the contents of her house to be sold off when the undertakers finally got their chance to carry her away.

Philippa would tease compliments out of Alvin, and he would oblige her, waxing eloquent about her youthful skin, fulsome hair, and graceful movement. Alvin was an accomplished liar.

This went on for nearly six months. Philippa seemed as vigorous as the day she'd invited him up to the house. She could outlast him in whatever physical activity she dreamed up to fill their hours, no matter how strenuous.

She was inventive, and inexhaustible. The strain was telling on Alvin. So much so, she chided him for his lethargy. Sponging off old women had never been such hard work before.

So Alvin did the only thing a red-blooded gigolo could do when faced with a vigorous, indefatigable patroness.

He started arranging little accidents for her.

Soap on the floor beside the tub. Loose carpet at the head of the long, winding staircase. Electric bug zappers accidentally knocked into her bathwater.

She was impervious.

At the sound of her hitting the floor, or tumbling down the stairs, or sizzling in electrified bath water, he'd rush in to find her—absolutely fine. No broken bones, no third-degree burns. Not so much as a scratch or bruise or blister. She wasn't even winded.

He moved on to poison. Likewise, ineffective. He spooned arsenic into every morsel of her food and drink, even going so far as to slip it into her tooth powder.

Nothing. Except complaints about the flavor of his cooking. That, and the funny taste she had after brushing her teeth.

Over the customary sherries at the end of a day, Alvin, after downing several, smiled hard and remarked on all her—vigor.

Philippa must have seen it as a romantic prelude because she lit up, assuring him she was as vigorous as anyone he might ever hope to find.

Alvin, with a snootful of liquor, couldn't hide his skepticism.

So, in a moment of weakness and vanity, she told him about the artifact and its marvelous power. Something she'd been strictly warned never to do.

It came about, she said, while she was on her deathbed, advanced in age, surrounded by her greedy relations. She wanted some way to deny them her fortune. With her last breath she rasped out, "I want to live forever." Immediately, invigorated as she had never been before, she rose up, fully restored, a miracle.

"I haven't aged a day since that moment," she said.

All Alvin managed to say was, "Do tell." He was not impressed.

She leaned in close to him and said, "That was four-hundred twenty-two years ago." With a smoldering look of invitation aimed at Alvin, she leaned back to let that little tidbit land.

Clearly, to a rational, gold-digging Lothario like Alvin, this woman was not simply some vain, addle-witted old woman. She was crazy.

But she didn't stop there. She told Alvin about the angel's visit, the shard as one of many such pieces from an ancient heavenly battle, the angel's plea that she give it up, the supernatural creatures hunting for it, the dire consequences of keeping it. When she realized it couldn't be taken, only surrendered, she refused, and ignored every warning she'd been given.

A man desperate to live forever will, if presented correctly, believe anything. He'll work overtime to convince himself. Alvin was just such a man, and it didn't take long.

But he needed time alone to think.

So he topped off his glass, slugged it back, and then pretended to slide out of his chair, dead drunk. He laid on the floor, until he heard Philippa storm out of the parlor and up to her room. When he was certain she was gone, he went to hide in his own room, locking the door. For good measure, he wedged a chair under the doorknob.

Alvin might not believe she was over four hundred years old, but there was no denying she survived every mortal wound he'd tried to inflict. He was determined to discover her secret.

The next day, with Philippa in her bath, Alvin ransacked her rooms.

She caught him, standing in the middle of the shambles he'd made of the place. He pleaded with her to show him the object, to let him share it with her. Instead, she accused Alvin of being a fortune hunter and ordered him out of the house.

He grabbed up her jewels by the handful, demanding she tell him which one.

"Of course, you'd think it was some precious stone or metal," she said. "You looked at it every day and wouldn't have the sense to recognize it if you saw it again."

He flung her to the bed and ran from one end of the house to the other, grabbing up objects, saying over and over, "I want to live forever. I want to live forever," trying to recall which object he'd looked at every day.

The smell of smoke is what finally stopped him. Philippa had set fire to her own house. The flames spread quickly and drove him out of the house onto the sloping lawn.

As Alvin watched the roaring conflagration engulf the house, Philippa stepped onto the porch, her clothes burned off her body. She laughed at him, her hands on her hips, in no way harmed by the flames.

Then turning as if arguing with someone Alvin couldn't see, she shouted "Take it, and damn you!" What she said next was lost in the roar of the flames, and then Philippa was sucked out of existence.

Someone must finally have noticed the blaze and called the fire department. By the time they reached the top of the hill the house had burned to the ground. As the firemen ran out their hoses, Alvin set up a caterwaul and a keening lamentation, so everyone would get the picture he was mourning Philippa's demise.

Alvin was long gone by the time they found the kerosene can in Philippa's bedroom, and the five-pound bag of arsenic, nearly empty, in the gardener's cottage. Locals identified Alvin as the only other person being in the house with Philippa as far back as anyone could remember.

On the run from the authorities, Alvin was in despair. The secret to longevity had been within reach, and disappeared along with Philippa.

Brooding on it constantly, Alvin finally realized the one thing he'd looked at every single day was the brooch that fastened her turban. Of all her jewelry, that brooch was the one thing she wore every day.

One of many such pieces, Philippa had said. But he couldn't remember exactly what it looked like. That didn't stop him. From that moment on, Alvin made it his life's work to find another such immortal, man or woman, adult or child, learn the secret of their immortality—and take it from them.

Brooklyn – Present Day

Nowadays he works nominal jobs and spends every waking moment searching for any unusual artifact that resembles what little he can remember of Philippa's brooch.

Alvin's small, spare, and somewhat squalid apartment is the nerve center of his search for immortality.

The building is dilapidated, and the neighborhood is home mostly to first generation immigrants and a motorcycle gang. Some tenants call it Early War Zone.

Alvin's rooms are cluttered with the tools of his search. Picture albums, computer disks, flash drives, old newspapers and magazines spread out everywhere. Binders and file folders of articles about longevity, medical cure-alls, and dietary alchemy guaranteed to bend the facts of aging into the reality of immortality or at the very least a tolerable approximation.

In the years he'd been at it, Alvin gathered an amazing wealth of information on people who survived death and destruction, or exhibited longevity out of all proportion to the norm without artificial aids or dietary supplements.

On one wall against which he'd pushed a battered dining table was an expanse of flattened cardboard boxes he'd nailed up for a makeshift bulletin board. Alvin used this to pin a large map of the United States. Being a person of interest in the disappearance of Philippa Waverly meant he had to rule out Europe, Asia, and Africa. Technically a fugitive of sorts, he couldn't risk getting a passport to travel outside the country.

With color-coded pushpins and yarn, Alvin tracked every occurrence of miraculous survival or unexplained longevity. He collected census records, church, court, and cemetery registries, newspaper files, and city archives of birth and death certificates, compiling genealogies, and cross-referencing those against his collection of catalogs and brochures from estate sales, auction houses, and dealers in antique jewelry. If the subject was still alive and living within the continental United States, he'd gas up his van, and take a road trip to seek them out. If they looked unnaturally healthy or possessed an object that looked anything like Philippa's brooch, he would arrange an accident for them.

When the target failed the test, he'd take flight and head back to his haven to plot his failure on the map board. Alvin would unwind all the yarn, pull down the notes, remove all the pushpins, and throw them on the floor, stomping and wailing in rage until the neighbors pounded on the wall, yelling at him to shut up.

There were lots of empty holes in his map board where there had once been push pins.

This couldn't go on. Even Alvin knew that. What he needed was a lucky find, something that would cause everything to fall into place for him, focus his attentions, and stop the scattershot search that would in the end draw the attention of some very disagreeable creatures.

New York City – Present Day

That lucky find turned up in another of the tiny, hole-in-the-wall bookshops he prowled, this one in the East Village. A bookshop that was rank with the smell of damp rafters, decaying plaster, and old paper. Alvin combed through the unruly and unsorted stacks.

Shifting a pile of books, Alvin stepped on the shop's mouser, a one-eyed tabby cat, who just happened to be ambling through the aisles at that same exact moment. Alvin went headlong into a stack of magazines that came tumbling down on top of him.

Alvin grabbed his arm and let out with a moan loud enough to bring the clerk and at least one corroborating witness for the personal injury lawsuit.

The moaning didn't last long.

Among the magazines scattered over his lap was a vintage copy of Methuselah Monthly, a periodical prominent in the late fifties and early sixties for immortality enthusiasts. It happened to flap open to an article that fairly shouted up at him. *Are There Immortals Among Us?* in bold letters. *Does Amulet Bestow Immortality?* in slightly less bold letters.

Alvin sat up and skimmed the article, his pain forgotten.

The clerk, a boxy, big-boned, broad-faced goth girl, stood over him and asked if he was, like, you know, okay?

But Alvin wasn't listening. He hopped to his feet, paid the twenty-dollar price stickered on the cover, and fled the shop.

Alvin sat in a bus shelter reading the article more closely. The excerpt that caught his attention was taken from the autobiography of Nona Samples Garrett, that obscure nineteenth century utopian philosopher and misanthrope, published sometime in the 1890s. Of particular interest to Alvin was the castaway Miss Garrett encountered during her search for the perfect uninhabited island on which to plant her pristine, male-free community. The castaway, Solomon Durnley, swore he'd been snatched off the whale ship, *Mary Hoppe,* by a rogue whale in the 1830s. This castaway insisted he'd been dragged half-way around the world until he washed up on the very same island where she found him. Describing his outlandish garb, Miss Garrett remarked on the only artifact of civilization he seemed to possess: an amulet of worked metal, a peculiar obsidian-like substance, infused with flecks of some remarkable metal.

The writer of the article confirmed that according to the log of a whale ship christened the *Mary Hoppe,* a sailor by that name had been dragged overboard by a whale. The writer also found church records of a memorial service for the missing sailor conducted in the home of a prominent local businessman by the name of Luther Kantlingher of Saugerties, New York.

Alvin wasted no time getting uptown to the main branch of the library to find Miss Garrett's book and see for himself.

It was right there among the open stacks.

Alvin flipped through the book until he found the part about Solomon Durnley. He didn't plan on returning the book, so he discarded the anti-theft tag, to evade the metal detectors when he left with it. He slipped the volume down his pants, and limped out through security, making himself a pathetic figure, more to be pitied than patted down.

Brooklyn – Present Day

Back in his apartment, Alvin pulled Miss Garrett's book out of his pants. He tore out the pages where she mentioned Solomon and tossed the rest of the book in the trash. He highlighted in yellow marker the description of the amulet.

Back to his map board, Alvin plotted this new information with pushpins and more yarn. He found nothing on Durnley, but a lot on Kantlingher.

It didn't take him long to see how often a Kantlingher turned up near an open case of miraculous survival. Lucky Smokes out of San Francisco. Old Squirt near New Orleans. The clown named Shotwad outside of El Paso. That deep sea diver named Bucholz in Key West. Skeeter Martin who'd been carried off by the twister.

Every single time, he'd find a descendant of old Luther Kantlingher somewhere nearby.

What he needed was a living relative of Luther.

Finding Francie DeSoto led him to Marjorie in Amarillo, their last known whereabouts. Doing the math, Alvin figured Marjorie would be in her twenties now.

Expanding the search circle, Alvin got a hit when he'd reached New York City. A snippet from two years back, out of a local paper about an original musical review that mentioned Marjorie Perisch. A dancer. From Amarillo. He did a search on Marjorie. Dancer. New York City.

He got another hit. This one a cabaret advertisement, listing a Marjorie DeSoto as a dancer. In New York City. Just across the river.

Alvin jumped up and danced around the living room until the neighbors pounded on the walls, yelling for him to shut up.

So he popped one of those high octane energy drinks and jazzed himself up for another trial by aggravated assault.

New York City – Present Day

Alvin rolled along in his van, dressed in a blue jumpsuit, sunglasses, and ball cap. At the corner of the avenue, he avoided eye contact with the officer behind the wheel of a police cruiser parked next to the Fatty Starbuckle's.

Once through the intersection, he slowed to get visual confirmation of his target, the guy squeezing fruit to death at the produce bins of the bodega. Satisfied, Alvin circled the block.

He waited for the two kids on skateboards to race past, then climbed down out the back of his van, holding a skateboard of his own.

Alvin careened down the sidewalk on his skateboard, zipping along, dodging people, sending them scattering. He shouldered past the very large lady wearing the tracksuit and electric green running shoes, dragging her little dog. She shrieked as Alvin hopped over the leash and landed again on the skateboard, riding on, his target in sight and in the open.

"I'm painfully aware of what happened next," said Solomon. "What kind of angel turns himself into a cat?"

"Wait—why is that important?"

"You'll turn yourself into a cat for no good reason, but won't bother to warn me what that knucklehead planned to do?"

"You had to look genuinely surprised. He can't know you're onto him."

"He knows now."

"Oh. That did not occur to me."

"You beat everything, you know that."

Chapter Thirty-Seven

THE JINGLE OF MARJORIE'S KEYS caught Solomon's ear.

"That's Marjorie." Solomon stepped into the hallway just as Marjorie reached her door.

"Glad to see it's you. I was over at the market, and it looked like you were having a run-in with the law. Had me wondering if you'd need somebody to come bail you out."

"No. Just a little community outreach. I was the lucky one that got outreached."

Solomon grunted. "Don't have much use for lawmen myself."

"Momma never had a good word about them either. But—"

"You don't see it quite the same way she does?"

"He seemed, like, real, you know? Like, under all that cop stuff, he's okay with being a little bit good looking, a little bit clumsy. Not trying to be superman."

"Well. Not that I give them much thought, but what I could see, under that badge and gunbelt, could be he's an upstanding sort of fella."

"Hunh. That upstanding fella upstood me. Left me holding two sixteen-ounce cappuccinos. Couldn't have been all that interested. He didn't bother to come back."

Willa gave a jangle with the handcuffs.

"Looking on the bright side? I got a pair of handcuffs out of it. And a caffeine buzz that'll take all day to shake. Hah. Shake."

"Any chance something'll come of it?"

"He never asked for my phone number, so I'm guessing not. Saves me having to explain the felons in my family tree. He let me know how he felt about that." Marjorie stabbed her key at the lock. Then she stopped, her shoulders giving out under the weight.

"Carnies are my family. Maybe it screwed me up. But I don't want to be hiding Momma in a closet just to meet someone, you know?"

"You might want to give the fella a chance, see how he is with it."

Marjorie let out a sigh. "Who're we kidding? We both know that me and the law don't mix. It's in my DNA."

"DNA?"

"My blood?"

"Ah."

"No matter how far you go, they're always right there to knock everything out from under you. Don't get me wrong, I love them. But I wouldn't mind being a little more like you."

"How's that?"

"You don't seem the type who ever had to worry about anyone like that."

"That fella I mentioned? The one that drops by once a year?" Solomon glanced over his shoulder. "He's a lot like that. A pain in the—well, wouldn't want to say it in front of you-know-who." Solomon winked at Willa, who was taste-testing the handcuffs.

"We should run off, the three of us. Some place they'd never find us."

"I know just the spot. An island. Smack dab in the middle of nowhere. You feel up to a long sea voyage?"

She smiled and gave a toss of her head. "If I didn't have to work tonight, I'd take you up on it." Marjorie got her door unlocked. "Rain check?"

"Always. Unless the volcano blows up and buries it."

Marjorie laughed and wheeled the stroller through the door.

"Hey." Solomon laid a finger aside his nose, then pointed at her. "Don't give up on that lawman just yet."

"Whoa. That's a big deal, coming from you." Marjorie smiled, then closed the door behind herself.

Solomon stood for a moment, seeing little Marjorie, dancing in the dust. He turned and went back into his own apartment.

Griffin held out Solomon's duffel and valise, already packed. "It'll be just like old times. The hum of tires, the smell of asphalt, the struggle to master a motor vehicle without embarrassing yourself."

"I'm not going anywhere."

"May I remind you about the danger of Alvin learning you are an actual immortal? You did get that part when I told you, right?"

"You should've considered that before giving him your hint. I'm taking my chances here."

"*Your* chances? And the rest of us? Scattered throughout creation, who didn't get a vote in making you the supreme chances-taker for the rest of us?"

Solomon unpacked his duffel. "If you're giving up on our bet, I win. I expect you to pay up."

"You're putting the entire cosmos at risk just to win a penny-ante bet with me? You know, Solly, that kind of gambling is an addiction. You might want to consider therapy."

"Then fix Marjorie up. Get back your doo-hickey. Save the rest of us."

Griffin watched out the window as Alvin's white utility van whipped in behind a roll-off dumpster full of construction debris and parked.

"If Shortwick learns immortality is an actual fact in the here and now," said Griffin, watching Alvin, "she and that lawman won't even have time to pick out curtains."

Alvin slipped out of the van and did a quick glance in both directions. He was dressed in a light tan jumpsuit with a hand-drawn delivery company logo. He wore a utility belt with a cellphone holster, telephone lineman's handset, a tool pouch, and a claw hammer. He carried a large manila envelope and a digital track pad. He straightened up and dashed across the street to Solomon's building.

"Now don't you wish you were more of a guardian angel type?" said Solomon.

"You need to do something so the entire rest of us don't—" Griffin grabbed the edge of the roll shade in the window and gave a yank. In a cracking snap flash, the shade rolled up on its spindles.

Solomon considered the shade wrapped tight around its roller. "I guess there's nothing for it then but to take me a whole 'nother bath. Thanks to you and your friend, Shortwick, I'm covered with street grime and who knows what else."

"Take a bath? Okay, fine. You have a relaxing soak while the rest of us just wait here for the cosmos to evaporate. Take your time. We'll wait." Griffin flopped onto the sofa, putting his feet up on the arm, crossing his ankles. "Maybe I'll read a magazine and wait for everything to go *pffft!*"

"Okay by me. Just don't dog-ear the pages. I hate when people do that." Solomon went into the bathroom and closed the door.

Below, Alvin ran his finger down the button labels of the intercom panel by the door, checking the names printed next to each button. There was only one blank label. 5D. Alvin pressed that one.

Up in Solomon's apartment, the rusted contacts of the ancient intercom buzzer made only the slightest of electric clicks.

Griffin shifted his glance from the intercom to the door of the bathroom where Solomon was still running the water, then to the front door.

Alvin leaned hard on the button, stretching to see into the lobby.

A clacking connection rattled the speaker.

"Who is it?" Solomon's metallicized voice sing-songed through the speaker.

"I'm looking for Skeeter Martin," said Alvin.

"What do you want?" the voice lilted.

"Are you Skeeter Martin?"

"Who wants to know?" the voice continued, roller-coastering.

"I have a package for Skeeter Martin. He has to sign for it."

Alvin held his breath.

There was a buzz and snap as the lock opened up. Alvin scrabbled to get through the door before the buzzing could stop.

On the fifth floor, the elevator door slid open. Alvin edged out and along the wall, up to Solomon's front door. Keeping to one side, he reached out to knock.

Nothing. As Alvin eased himself closer, putting his ear against the keyhole, the door behind him opened. He jumped, whirling to face the threat, holding up the package and track pad to protect his face.

Marjorie, dressed for class and carrying a large dance bag slung over her shoulder, spotted Alvin as she locked her door.

Alvin peeked out from behind his defenses. Seeing Marjorie, he stuttered out a laugh.

"I'm just looking for Skeeter Martin. He doesn't answer his door."

"He's there," said Marjorie, reaching for the elevator call button.

"I know. He buzzed me in."

"Keep knocking."

"I've come a long way and now he doesn't answer."

"Oh." She turned back to face him. "You're him, aren't you?"

Alvin tensed up, ready to run.

"He told me about you."

"It wasn't me, it was him. He came out of nowhere."

"Aren't you the one he's expecting?" Marjorie smiled at him.

"Expecting?" He managed to smile back at her.

"The visitor Skeeter's expecting."

"Right. Yes. He's expecting me. Me. Of course. We haven't laid eyes on each other in forever—"

"Since last year, isn't it? Don't you together once a year?"

"Ah—ah—amazing how twelve months feels like forever. I meant that." Alvin stuttered out another laugh. "This is his door?"

"Right." Marjorie turned back to the elevator and the door opened.

"Nice meeting you."

"Wait!"

Marjorie stopped, holding the door.

"Umm—could—could you do me a favor?" Alvin skipped over to lean in close to Marjorie. "You know how it's been a whole year since he's seen me, and you know how old guys are. He might not recognize me after so long."

"Skeeter's pretty sharp."

"Okay, I've changed a lot since the last time. Just come here, okay?"

Inside the apartment, Solomon out of his bath, had put his trousers back on and was buttoning his shirt.

Griffin whirled away from the door where he'd been peeking through the peephole.

"Ah. Feel better now?"

"I do, thanks for asking. I see the cosmos is still right where I left it."

A soft knock came at the front door.

"Skeeter?" Marjorie called out.

Solomon went to the door and gave a quick look through the peephole.

Marjorie stood there, smiling over at someone he couldn't see.

"Hold these." Alvin handed Marjorie the package and track pad. "I want to give him a big, surprise hug."

"You may not want to open that door," said Griffin, who unfolded a string of paper angels he'd cut out using the pages of the magazine.

Of course, Solomon opened the door.

Alvin launched himself at Solomon, grabbing him up in a bear-hug.

"I want to live forever! I want to live forever! I. Want. To. Live. For. Ever!" shouted Alvin, bouncing and jouncing Solomon off his feet.

Alvin dropped Solomon and started pinching himself, slapping his cheek. He straightened his jumpsuit, adjusted his utility belt, then smoothed his hair and ponytail. Noticing Marjorie still standing in the doorway, he took back the package and track pad. "Thanks. Now get lost." He slammed the door in her face as she jerked her head back to avoid the impact.

Surprised and maybe a bit concerned, Marjorie leaned her ear to the door to listen in.

In Solomon's apartment, Alvin dropped the package and the track pad on the bureau by the door.

"Quick! I need something sharp!"

"I got me just the thing." Solomon pulled out his bowie.

Alvin ignored Solomon, going through the bureau drawers and opening up cabinets.

"Is he here, too? That other guy? That angel, or alien, or whatever he's supposed to be?"

Solomon stopped and looked back at Griffin, who shrugged, then twirled his finger at his temple, giving Solomon the universal sign for don't-look-at-me-I'm-not-the-nut-case-in-the-room.

Alvin grabbed up the fountain pen from Solomon's writing set, braced himself, and then rammed the point into his thigh.

He stood there, nib embedded in the muscle, concentrating on what he was feeling, as if trying to sense his crossover into immortality. Instead—

"Yeow! Jeeeeeez. There's PAIN! Really real PAIN!" He withdrew the pen. "Blood! My own actual BLOOD!"

Realizing this dimwit couldn't be all that much of a danger, Solomon sheathed the bowie.

Alvin caught the movement from the corner of his eye and grabbed out his hammer. "Don't even think of touching that phone."

But there was no telephone.

"In case there's a phone. In here? Somewhere?" Alvin waggled the hammer, searching. "Just don't even think about touching it."

"No telephone. Don't believe in 'em."

"You don't have a phone? No. No, of course you wouldn't. No records."

Alvin grabbed up his package.

"Very clever. Living off the grid, keeping to yourself. Very, very clever. Still." Alvin shook the package at Solomon. "I can prove you're over two-hundred years old. So, don't bullshit me." Alvin prowled the room. "Where's the amulet. The thing that gives you immortality?"

Again, Solomon looked at Griffin who shrugged, eyes wide with amazement.

"You had a few extra helpings of the loco weed salad, didn't you."

"Maybe so, maybe so." Alvin stalked the apartment, waggling his hammer. "No. Wait. You'd like me to think I'm crazy, wouldn't you?" Alvin waved the hammer at Solomon. "Now. Where is it?"

"Where's what?"

"Don't toy with me. I'm a desperate man. It's somewhere in this room, and I want it."

Favoring his wounded thigh, Alvin continued to prowl around the room, pawing over what few objects he found.

"What is it you're after. Maybe I can help you look for it."

"Ha! Sure you could. You know exactly what I'm looking for."

"What's it look like?"

"It's—um—um—I'm not sure."

"I always did enjoy a rousing game of ring-around-the-idiot," Solomon said to Griffin. Then to Alvin, he said, "Whatever it is, you think I have it?"

"I'll know it when I see it. It's—it's very unusual looking." He lifted the cushions on the sofa.

"Oh, why didn't you say so. I threw that out last week."

Alvin whirled on Solomon, looming over him.

"Don't play games with me, pops. I've been at this for too long."

"Then you could use a rest." Solomon hooked Alvin behind the ankle with his cane, gave a yank, and sent Alvin butt-first to the floor, knocking over the chair.

Alvin scrabbled to his feet, arms flailing, taking out a lamp as he struggled to regain his balance, evading Solomon's whip-head cane. But Solomon hooked him again and sent him backward onto the floor once more.

"Stop doing that! I have a bad back!" Alvin rolled over and crawled toward the window.

"A year in traction ought to fix you right up, then." Solomon caught Alvin by the ankle again and gave a twist, sending Alvin flat onto his belly, bouncing his nose off the floor.

Alvin rolled over, his hands out, fending off Solomon's cane point as he jabbed at Alvin's forehead, bouncing his skull off the floor.

"Just break off a little piece," whined Alvin. "I don't need much. Come on! Halvsies!"

"If you plan to live long enough to see the rest of your hair fall out, you skedaddle while the skedaddling is good."

Alvin, struggling for some pocket of safety, crab-walked backward toward the front door, trying to keep one hand up to fend off more nasty blows from Solomon's cane tip.

Still on the floor, Alvin stretched up and pulled the door open, clunking himself in the head, knocking himself to the floor with a satisfying crack.

Solomon reached over and opened the door for him, letting Alvin scuttle into the hall.

Right into the legs of Officers Wood and Lighter.

"I never thought I'd be glad to see The Man," said Alvin, embracing their ankles, an improvised act of worship. He twisted his face up to see Officer Wood looking down on him.

"Persons of the uniformed persuasion." Alvin lurched to his feet.

"How about you tell us what's going on here," said Wood.

"I had a package for this old gee—differently-aged person, and he attacked me. That cane's a deadly weapon. They should make him have a license to carry it."

Wood and Lighter looked at Alvin who was a full head taller than Solomon and carrying a whole lot more bulk.

"Oh, come on. He's making himself look small and helpless. Make him stand up straight."

Alvin spotted Marjorie standing in her doorway.

"She can tell you."

"It sounded terrible in there," said Marjorie. "That's why I called."

Wood stepped through the door, into Solomon's apartment, surveying the ransacked room.

"I was looking for a pen that worked," said Alvin.

Lighter studied Alvin's face and jumpsuit.

"You have some I.D. on you?"

"I.D.? Me? You should ask him. He's the one with the deadly weapon."

"I'm asking you."

"Of course I have I.D. What kind of delivery guy would I be if I didn't have I.D." Alvin pointed to the crudely drawn logo on the back of his jumpsuit. "That's the company I work for. You've heard of them, right?"

Lighter was not impressed.

"There's my name tag. It's—" he blanked and had to look down. "Paul. Right. Paul as in McCartney? Like the Beatles? Funny, huh? I have a concussion, or I'd have remembered."

"Your I.D., please. From the delivery company you work for," said Lighter.

"Sure." Alvin glanced from the officers to the stairs and then back at the officers as he pulled out a thick stack of business cards bound with rubber bands.

Alvin snapped the band. The cards sprayed out, a fluttering fountain. "Oops."

Lighter bent down to help him pick up the cards.

"Don't!" said Wood.

Alvin shoved Lighter into Wood knocking them both backward through Solomon's doorway. He dashed for the stairs.

The two officers untangled, getting back on their feet. Lighter bolted for the stairs, followed by Wood.

Alvin hurtled down the stairs, his feet skippity-skipping as he pinballed off the walls, making the tight turns of the narrow stairwell until he reached the ground floor, slid to a stop, yanked open the front door and leaped the last three steps to the street.

Griffin watched from the window above as Alvin ran toward his van, angling instead for the dumpster, vaulted the side and landed with a crunching crash on the collected debris. He grabbed a piece of cardboard to wave away the plume of dust he'd thrown up, then flopped back, holding deathly still.

He must have finally noticed the nails and wire and broken brick shards on which he'd landed, because he bit his fist, holding back a scream as he lay in all that junk.

Back across the street, Wood and Lighter blasted out the front door, Wood taking a half dozen steps east while Lighter took a half dozen steps west.

There was nothing in either direction. Just empty street.

Wood gave Lighter a back-handed slap on the arm.

Upstairs, Marjorie was still at the door.

"Are you okay?" she asked.

"I'm right as rain. Fellas like that won't get the best of me any time soon."

"I feel bad knocking on your door for him. I thought he was the visitor you were expecting. I could wait around until they get him."

"You go on to your class."

"I can wait. Babysitter's got Willa at the playground."

"Unless you're waiting to give that tall officer a piece of your mind? It's that same fella from this morning, right?"

"Was that him? Lawmen all look alike to me." Marjorie sashayed back into her apartment.

Chapter Thirty-Eight

SOLOMON CLOSED HIS OWN DOOR and went back to the sofa. He sat down hard and laid the package on his lap.

"What did I say? Don't open the door, right? You say you want a guardian angel, then you don't listen," said Griffin.

Solomon opened the package and spilled out the contents. Xeroxed copies of all that Alvin had. All the magazine stories and newspaper clippings. The pages from Methuselah Monthly. Solomon's escape from the desert island. Shipping news of the *Mary Hoppe*. The legend of Lucky Smokes. Shotwad. Old Squirt. Gummy. There were also snippets about Hatchet Jane. The Sweetheart Bandits. Theodora the Unicycle Queen. Loralee. Wanted posters. Payroll ledger pages. Rent receipt books.

"He knows all there is to know about this thing. There's no guessing about it."

"Really?"

"Looks to me like immortality's common knowledge. And this has me square in the center of it."

"Come on. No one reads that stuff. It's full of nonsense about chupacabras, crop circles, and flying saucers. Doesn't exactly qualify as common knowledge."

"First you tell me I'm the only one of my kind out there." Solomon counted off with his fingers. "Then you tell me if I fix it so just one of Lavinia's daughters marry a decent fella instead of the scoundrel she's got her heart set on I stop time and snap back to Lavinia, undoing all the bad that's ever happened to us. Then you tell me if anyone figures out immortality is real, the whole shebang rolls up and—and—and everybody's lost." Solomon waved the three fingers in Griffin's face.

"That's three blamed lies! That I know of! How many more lies have you told me?"

"I can see how the metaphysics would be the weensiest bit over your head."

"Don't give me that. It's lying plain and simple."

"That's a mudfoot short-timer's answer for anything too difficult to understand."

"Angels are supposed to be messengers of the Almighty. Straight from the throne room of Heaven. They don't go around lying to people."

Solomon eye-balled Griffin hard, squinting, shaking his head.

"You're no angel, are you?"

"I never said I was. You did."

"All right, lemme fix that. You were, right from the beginning, a demon from the pit of hell."

"Come on, Solly, it's me, your old bosom pal, Griffin. Think of all that we've been through together."

"All we been through together?" Solomon snorted. "All you put me through! Is there anything you ever told me in my whole life that wasn't a goddamned lie?"

Griffin considered this for a moment, then shook his head. "Nothing of any consequence."

"All I ever wanted was to get back and take my rightful place with Lavinia. And what do I get? You."

"Oh, that's typical. Make me rich. Make me pretty. Give my ex-wife boils. And when you don't get what you want, it's, you stink, you're ugly, you've got a pointy tail."

"It all makes perfect sense now." Solomon rapped his forehead with the heel of his hand. "Only took me two hundred years to figure it out."

"Not quite two hundred."

"Don't bandy words! This whole time, this whole business—it wasn't about tormenting the Kantlinghers for something Lavinia did or Edwin did. It was me. All me. And they just got caught up in it. No wonder you don't want your doo-hickey back. I'm dragging hell around with me, saving you the trouble."

Solomon stopped. He was breathing hard, thinking hard and then swung his fists hard, beating the air.

"You just let me go on thinking this was about a forbidden union? Let me quote the Good Book, never set me straight."

"That's what I love about you mudfoots. No matter how cock-eyed your view of the world is, you've got chapter and verse handy to level it out. If you ever really understood a tenth of what you read, you might actually be dangerous."

"Like you know what's in the Good Book."

" 'The devil can cite Scripture for his purpose.' But I never had to listen to him do it."

"Well, thank you very much, but I'm through. I'm going to find that Shortwick fella and give this doo-hickey to him, he wants it so bad. Sounds like he deserves it. You can torment him throughout eternity and leave me alone. Because I sure'n hell don't want to live—"

Griffin was on Solomon in a blinding, cracking flash of arcing light, his hand clasped over Solomon's mouth.

"Don't—say—another—word," Griffin hissed, his teeth clenched. "Not one single syllable." His eyes were no longer silver-blue, but molten, the pupils a black slag floating on the magma, like Solomon had seen under his feet in that island volcano. Eyes in a face lined with fury, from which Solomon could almost feel the heat of that hellish liquid rock. Actually, he *could* feel that heat. Griffin radiated a warmth that pinked Solomon's skin and made him sweat.

Through Griffin's hands Solomon felt the profound power, a kind of humming envelope of electrical potential that made Solomon certain Griffin could twist his head clean off his shoulders if he was of a mind to do it.

For the first time in a very long time Solomon was afraid, uncertain that the artifact could save him from any dark intentions Griffin might have.

Griffin let Solomon go and flexed his fingers at some unfinished task, then stalked around the apartment, a reddish, glowing hot being of radiant power, the air rippling around him.

"This—this what you all look like? Really?" Solomon asked, trying to square what he knew of Griffin and what he was seeing now.

"You should be very glad I'm *not* a demon." Griffin cracked his knuckles like he hadn't quite given up on maybe crushing Solomon's eggshell skull.

Solomon's curiosity got the better of his self-preservation. "There's more to this whole thing, isn't there?"

"You would throw it all away without a single thought. You mudfoots are all alike."

"If I'm damned for eternity for something I did, I got a right to know what it's all about."

Griffin laughed, a sound that rattled the windows, deep and deadly, and set the dogs in the nearby apartments to barking.

Griffin, his face a twisted smile of frustration and resignation, grabbed Solomon by the shirt front, pulling him toward himself and the welling heat.

Again, Griffin pulled him into that place between the high, unending walls of dark rippling water. In that infinitesimal slice of non-time, his skin crawled with that almost-forgotten sensation, the cold he remembered from being towed behind that damned whale but so much longer, as if eternity had opened up to him and he could feel the tiny tap of a multitude of heartbeats as he passed through silent, shadowy crowds of people, the landscapes ballooning into cities, deflating into flat, rural expanses, folding over into waterways, and rising up as mountainsides before falling away into cities once more, flowing through walls and coming to stand in a large, ornate room as light and sound and temperature resolved itself into a now-ness that Solomon could feel as real once more.

St. Petersburg, Russia – Present Day

Solomon experienced fully the sensation of the journey without the sensation of having traveled any distance. He experienced the departure from where he'd been standing and the arriving to wherever he was now, but no sensation of duration of time passed that would accommodate all he felt during the transit. He arrived and felt flooded-through with the consequences of his transit catching up with him. He'd outrun the speed of thought, and when he'd come to a standstill—wherever he was—everything imprinted itself finally and all at once on his consciousness.

Again, there was that dreamy instantaneousness, of overwhelming detail that evaporated quickly, leaving behind no manageable train of thought or memory to hold and consider.

It was cold. When Solomon could again think about what he was feeling, it was the cold.

Color began to sharpen and sound became crisp again. Not enough to suggest normalcy, but the half-waking from a fragile dream, best grasped as the press of otherness, almost a change in air pressure, scent, and sound.

"Come on." Griffin released Solomon's shirt and moved off into the darkness.

There was no way Solomon would follow Griffin anywhere, now that he's revealed himself for what he was, what he'd been all along.

Instead, Solomon took a good look around himself. He stood in the entryway of a long, grand gallery, dark except for small pools of light extending along either side of the space for maybe one or two hundred feet, as best as Solomon could reckon in the dim light.

Above him the broad lintel of the squared-off archway served as the entrance, supported on eight columns of a reddish-umber stone, polished and gleaming.

The floor—what little Solomon could see of it at his feet—faded into the shadows beyond. It appeared to be elaborately tiled, a regular pattern of stylized starbursts. Along the base of the walls was stonework of what looked to be malachite.

Set into the wall to his right were tall windows, hung with lace shades, and which opened out onto an enclosed and darkened courtyard covered in snow gleaming in the moonlight.

Overhead, the ceiling was carved or painted with complex geometric shapes, mythic creatures, stylized plants and what looked to be heraldic symbols.

Solomon could now see that the pools of light were from display cases of wood and glass along either side of the vast room. The cabinets nearest to Solomon held arms and armor, like storybook knights might wear. Toward the center of the room, on a low platform surrounded by velvet ropes and illuminated with tiny spotlights, stood four medieval war horses, on which were mounted knights dressed in full armor.

Solomon reckoned the place was some kind of museum. Once or twice, when he'd been lonesome enough and feeling out of place and time, he'd visited the museums of the city, looking for the pictures and artifacts that refreshed his connection with the time and place of his past.

Solomon didn't have any fixed ideas about what the Hereafter might look like, above or below, but he was pretty sure Griffin hadn't carted him off to the underworld. Just yet.

Across the room, Griffin seemed the same as always. Still, Solomon glanced around for another way out.

From out of the darkness behind Solomon came the tik-takking of footsteps. He turned, just as a blocky, fireplug of a woman, wearing a red-jacket and swinging a flashlight from side to side, walked through him. The transit of her heartbeat and warmth in one side of him and out the other left him with a chilly, wet shiver.

The woman walked on, giving no sign she'd noticed him, fixed on looking about the room, pointing her flashlight into the darkened corners, then turning around and coming back at him, to leave the way she'd come. Solomon danced aside to avoid her and any repeat of that creepy sensation.

Wherever Griffin had brought him, he was immaterial to those around him. Seeing no other good options, he followed after Griffin who stood in front of a display case set between two of the tall windows that looked out onto the courtyard. The light from the cabinet made Griffin's face appear hard, sculpted.

Griffin gave a nod at the exhibit inside.

In the display case were two suits of armor, along with a few items of military hardware, swords, small shields, and a dagger. The suit on the left was full body armor, of German origin according to the placard written in Russian, French, and English. The steel was highly polished, darkened in the joints and grooves, fitted over a faceless form of navy blue fabric.

The other suit, according to the placard, was of unknown origin, probably Saracen or Persian. It was smaller, fitted onto a much smaller mannequin. It was scale armor, the hammered leaves of which were shaped metal riveted to an undergarment of leather. It consisted of a breast and back piece, shoulder pieces that reached to the elbow. A cowl-like piece that covered the back of the neck, a helmet with a drapery of chainmail, a long skirt of the same metal-leaf construction that reached to the knees, greaves, with extended toe pieces that curled over the end of the wearer's boots.

All of it, Solomon could see, was made of the same dark, translucent substance as the artifact he wore around his neck. The hammered scales of the breast piece were of an identical shape.

Solomon stepped closer to see. The artifact grew warm under his shirt. Griffin threw a stiff arm to block his way and stepped back, forcing Solomon to retreat.

"Lucifer's body armor," said Griffin, lowering his arm.

Solomon glanced at Griffin, half-expecting to see a smirk, but Griffin wasn't smiling.

"Seems a—seems a mighty short fella. He can't be any taller than me."

"We're all thinking that's what set him off in the first place. The Almighty was trying to make a point, if you ask me, and Lucifer completely missed it." Griffin looked up, seeming to scan the vast heavens overhead. "What a mess."

Solomon tried to imagine the lord of Hades inside such a get-up.

"There's a piece missing," said Solomon. "There. Over the heart."

Griffin was still gazing up.

"You're wearing it. Around your neck," Griffin was still looking up. Then he looked at Solomon. "You might want to keep that in mind, next time you get the urge to pull it out and wave it around."

Solomon hopped back. "What kind of dirty work have you got me doing now?" He wanted to rip the shirt right off his own body and throw that damned doo-hickey as far from himself as possible.

"Consider it your small part in postponing the apocalypse. I'd say that's a small price to pay for holding back the end of the world, wouldn't you?" Griffin's eyes glowed again, molten.

"Why'd you bring me here?"

Griffin didn't seem to notice the question.

"Lucifer learned his lesson. He's got it all planned out for next time."

"What next time?"

"You know what he'll tell you? If you happen to catch him in a chatty mood? His problem was going up against the Almighty out there in the middle of a big, empty cosmos. Next time? Won't be out in the open. He's got a place all picked out. Close in, where big swooping fireballs and skull-shattering bolts of energy can't be flung about willy-nilly."

"Where'd that be?" Solomon planned to give any such place a wide berth.

"Here. Not *here* here, but here on this planet. The Almighty has a peculiar fondness for you all and this place. Makes it the perfect battle-field. It's small. You're small. Lucifer's small. There's a kind of poetry in that. Not enough room, cosmically speaking, to swing a cat. This place'll go up like a book of matches. If the Almighty lets it."

"I'd say Lucifer hasn't learned his lesson at all. He got whupped royally the first time."

"That he did. And may again. But look what he accomplished the first time? There's not a lot out beyond your own atmosphere. No life. Used to be a lot more, a whole lot more to the cosmos. Not anymore."

"What makes you think he can get the better of the Almighty the next time?" Solomon worried less about there being any chance of the good Lord losing a rematch with the Prince of Darkness and more about getting caught up in the middle of their donnybrook.

"I don't get paid to think," Griffin seemed to consider that. "I don't get paid. I've never really stopped to wonder what my time is actually worth. Not much call for angelic beings working freelance. There's no real job market. No retirement, no direct deposit, no sick days."

Solomon could see Griffin was starting to feel mighty sorry for himself.

"What's this armor got to do with the next time?" Solomon wasn't keen on listening to Griffin crab about his troubles, which paled in comparison to Solomon wearing a little bit of Hell for a necklace. "Is this some kind of warning?"

"You might call it that." Griffin's brow still bent into a hard scowl.

"What am I supposed to do, then? Warn people? Save humanity.

Go off into the wilderness and eat bugs? Cry doom on the world?"

Griffin laughed. A deep watery laugh.

"Worry about saving me. Saving yourself while you're about it."

"You?"

"Of course, who else? You think I'd waste my time on any of you mudfoot short-timers?"

Griffin looked at the armor in the display case.

"First time Lucifer wore that armor, the Almighty shattered it clean off his body. Pieces went everywhere. Most of it was easy to recover once it could be found. It fell on worlds denuded of life, the floating rock of exploded planetary systems. All we had to do was keep looking until we found all the pieces. Then bring it back and reassemble it."

"That missing piece?"

"Some of the pieces fell onto the earth. Mudfoots found them. Those we couldn't just take back. One of several built-in safety features, so it couldn't be taken from Lucifer against his will. Worked just the same for one of you. Interesting how the self-will of you mudfoot short-timers is just as intense as Lucifer's."

"Not much of a secret if you're keeping it on display like that."

"Until the armor is fully restored, we needed to keep it someplace."

"Here?"

"Here."

"Okay, where's here?"

"Russia. St. Petersburg. The Hermitage. Perfect. Until a few years ago we could trust the Russians to keep it under wraps. They weren't likely to share it, and no matter how little they understood what they had, they weren't about to let anyone else close enough to examine it. Those days are gone." Griffin sighed. "Gone. Now, all it would take is some grad student in medieval studies to get curious and they'd have this thing under a microscope so fast—" Griffin sighed. "That's why he's all in a scratch to recover the last piece and finish reassembling it so he can reclaim the armor and try again to take all of creation for himself."

"Couldn't he just make himself a new one? Save all that time and trouble?"

"You have any idea what it's made of?"

"Nothing I've ever seen before. That's a fact."

"You ever ask yourself, can the Almighty make a rock so big he can't lift it? If he's the Almighty he should be able to make such a rock. And if he's the Almighty he should be able to lift such a rock, which means he's not the Almighty because he can't make such a rock, but if he's the Almighty, he should be able to make such a rock—and you go round and round and round until you need to be sedated? Ever ask yourself that question?"

"No."

Griffin looked over at Solomon. "Figures." Griffin looked back at the display case. "The armor is made from that very same rock. Since it doesn't exist anywhere in your space-time continuum, its properties are what insulate you mudfoots from damage, from aging naturally."

"How did that Captain come by it?"

"Won it arm-wresting an Iroquois Indian who'd found it lying in a creek bed, but never knew what it was or what it did. After the Captain acquired it, by the wildest of chances, he said that very same phrase you did, and activated it. There was no way he was giving it up after that. And that was fine. I could be patient. But he just got to be too much."

"Oh, right. Like you fellas have standards."

"We may not have standards, but we do have limits. I didn't need him creating a war over the piece. There'd be no chance of getting it back and no second shot at taking over heaven."

"So why not take it from me and finish it. And don't tell me free will. I don't see you all paying much mind to that, seeing how you got your start."

"Because I'm not one of those who want it back. I'm not looking for a second shot. In fact, if it stays unfinished until your sun goes nova, melts your sorry little planet, reducing all of you to plasmic goo floating through space, that's just fine with me."

"What's the good of that?"

"Good is such a funny word. You say you read the Bible. You know the lake of fire? Where Lucifer and the rest of us are headed?"

"I suppose."

"I plan to put off taking that everlasting midnight swim as long as possible. To hell with the rest of them." Griffin stopped, considered what he'd said, and gave out with a hard burst of laughter. "Now *there's* a joke that never gets old."

"What's this got to do with me having it?"

"All I have to do is keep anyone from finding that piece and restoring the armor and setting Armageddon in motion."

"Ain't Lucifer in charge?"

"You think we're some kind of organized army? You think we have a chain of command? You think we have a battle plan all worked out, everybody ready to hop-to, do their job?" Griffin had begun to fidget and stalk about, his arms flailing. "How do you think we ended up in this fix in the first place? We're a defeated rabble. One great collection of derelicts, zealots, and malcontents, and we do what the hell we please when we please!" Griffin gripped his head and gave out with a mighty cry, throwing his arms out wide." Then, more calmly, he continued, "But it's the zealots you have to watch out for. The one thing we—they—share is a keen desire to take it all back. By force, if necessary. By guile if not."

"You got me standing less than ten feet from the danged thing! How can they not know you found it!"

"I keep telling you—we're not omniscient. And if you stop waving it around, they won't know. It was by chance that I found it. You know what my job was? Is? How I occupy my time among you mudfoots? Annoying and distracting you from your good intentions, your good ideas."

"I'll give you that. You are mighty fine at being annoying and distracting."

"Thank you. The itch up your nose that causes a great idea to evaporate, or the baby crying in the next room that causes a kind thought to disintegrate, or the corner of the rug that trips you just before some generous act? That's me. That's my job. Who knows how many great works of art, great mechanical inventions, great medical breakthroughs I've derailed just by sticking a long piece of broom straw up your nostril, into your ear, or down your back where you can't scratch without help." Griffin pinched his lip. "I have to laugh. I had a dandelion stem half way up Captain Curtwood's blowhole, ready to make him sneeze, I forget why, when I see the shard hanging on his belt. I dropped everything and followed him, showing up as that lieutenant. Later, I saw my chance to get it away from him when he was playing dice with you. I'd already seen the probability you weren't going to live out the night. That you would be shot and probably die. If you had it, I could take possession of it when you died. So I tinkered with the dice until the Captain lost everything and was willing to risk it."

"What made him risk it, if he knew what it meant?"

"I whispered to him what a good idea it was. Easiest way to fix something firm in a mudfoot's head is to whisper. What I didn't count on was you uttering that phrase so soon after and surviving the pistol shots. But I also saw a slim chance. Slim, but worth it, given the alternative. You were a mild enough kind of guy. Bit of a trickster, but not too outrageous. If I could somehow manage to keep it in your possession, keep anyone from finding out you had it, I'd hold off completing the armor and avoid starting the apocalypse. I had to make you think I wanted it back so you didn't ask too many questions, and to make sure you didn't accidentally set off the safety mechanism."

"What safety mechanism?"

"Something Lucifer engineered to keep it from falling into the wrong hands to be used against him. Emotions radiate mental energy. This thing can sense positive, altruistic mental energy. When it does—*FOOOM!*" Griffin made a great upward sweep of his arms. "Incinerate an entire planet. Just a little piece of it could fry everything within a two-mile radius."

Solomon took a moment to absorb that thought, seeing what that could look like, and him in the middle.

"I've been wearing this thing around my neck!"

"I thought about telling you to keep it in a shoe box. Made of depleted uranium. Lined with maybe two inches of lead. Wrapped up in asbestos. Maybe leave it with relatives. You have any relatives you're not all that fond of?"

"I don't have any relatives, thanks to you."

"Okay, okay. Just asking. Yeesh. Besides—it never went off, did it?"

"You're saying I never had a kind thought or did a good deed?"

"You sound disappointed."

"I may not be perfect, but I'm a hell of a lot better'n some!"

Griffin laughed. "You never gave me any reason to worry." He stopped. "No. There was one time."

"Only one?"

"Closest you ever came was that girl on the island. Had me biting my nails, let me tell you. But since you were trying to steal a boat to get off the island it wasn't entirely altruistic. Scared two or three thousand years off my eternal life."

"What about all those times I tried helping the girls to better fellas and a better life?"

"You'd be surprised how much evil a sincere, meddling do-gooder can accomplish when he's managed to delude himself about his own self-righteousness. And you had it in spades. One thing you were never bothered with was humility. Never once considered the consequences of what you were doing. I knew I could count on that. Not all that much good, not too much bad. As long as you kept telling yourself that what you wanted was what they really needed. You are just the right mix. A real god-send." Griffin winced, heaved his shoulders up and then made an effort to relax. "Which makes me wonder sometimes if I'm not being played and don't have as much to do with holding off the end times as I think. Ah well."

A strapping figure of a man, appearing out of nowhere as far as Solomon could tell, stepped between them to study the armor. He was handsome, smooth-faced, with hair almost snowy white. He leaned in to examine Lucifer's armor. Solomon could feel the man's heat and energy. This was not some immaterial, incorporeal shade like the night watchman.

While the newcomer's face was close to the glass of the case, Griffin reach around behind, pushing Solomon away, shooing Solomon to get lost.

The man looked at Griffin and gave a finger salute. Griffin raised a finger to his own brow and saluted back. It was clear to Solomon that the man could see Griffin.

The man turned and gave Solomon the same slight salute, making eye contact with him.

Solomon, uncertain what to do, looked to Griffin who nodded, his brow furrowed and his face full of warning.

The man squinted, his nostrils flaring, studying Solomon, inhaling him for the smell.

Solomon reached a finger to his brow and saluted back.

The man's face relaxed, looked again at the armor, then moved off.

"You said they couldn't see us," whispered Solomon, once the man had disappeared into the darkness.

"You mudfoots can't see each other. That's one of us."

"One of us?"

"They come by sometimes, have a look at what progress is made, see how much longer we have until Lucifer's ready to have another go at it."

"So, you mean he was one of *you*." Solomon wanted to be on record making that distinction.

"Think of yourself as a sort of honorary member. Don't knock it. If they realized you were a mudfoot, they'd probably tear your head off and eat it. You're not exactly in Kansas anymore, and I don't have a firm grasp of the rules out here. I am breaking them, after all. I doubt that piece of armor would save you. Never had a mudfoot wearing one of those on this side of the veil."

Griffin looked up and across the room over Solomon's shoulder, giving out with another salute.

Solomon turned. A dim shape appeared, highlighted in the small lights of the display cases, his eyes that same molten gold.

"Go ahead, so they don't get suspicious. You might want to get used to it."

Solomon gave the staring creature the salute. Light reflected off his teeth as his lip curled in what for him may have been a smile.

"I have to tell you, I don't cotton to the idea of getting used to it. Not at all."

Griffin stiffened. "Uh-oh. Wait here. I'll be back."

"You're gonna leave me here right next to this thing, with your dad-blamed doo-hickey hanging around my neck?"

"Don't worry. Last place they'd think to look."

"I'm not staying here."

"Have a look around. There's all kinds of things to see while I'm gone. Just don't do anything nice." Griffin backed away, making an explosive burst with his splaying hands and air-filled cheeks, before disappearing into the surrounding dark.

Solomon realized he was alone.

And colder.

Chapter Thirty-Nine

New York City – Present Day

WOOD FOLLOWED LIGHTER out of the elevator and across to Solomon's door.

"The guy on the skateboard? You sure?" asked Wood.

"Or one very amazing coincidence," said Lighter. "Could be how he picks out a victim. Knocks him down then follows him home. Figures the old guy's rattled, disoriented. Maybe injured. Makes him a sitting duck."

Lighter knocked on Solomon's door. "Mr. Martin? Police."

Marjorie stepped out of her apartment, locking the door behind her.

"You lost him? A fake delivery guy in sandals?" said Marjorie. "You can't keep track of anybody can you?" She headed for the elevator.

"Could I ask you something?" Lighter stepped toward her with a quick glance back at Wood still standing at Solomon's door.

"I don't know who that guy was, what he wanted, or where he went," said Marjorie. "Anything else? Glad I could help."

"Could I get my handcuffs back?"

Wood laughed as she knocked one more. "Mr. Martin. It's the police again."

"I'm late for dance class. How about I drop them by the police station?" She punched the elevator call button.

"That would be kind of embarrassing."

"Oh, now I have to." Marjorie stepped into the elevator.

"Only take a minute."

"See you at the police station." The elevator door closed.

"Ray, get over here." Wood knocked again. "Mr. Martin! Police! Are you okay?"

"Maybe he had a heart-attack. The strain was too much for him."

"Greeeeaaat. This time you do the rescue breathing and I do the compression. I hate going mouth-to-mouth on smokers."

The door opened the barest crack, an eye at the door.

"I heard you knocking the first time. So, that fella give y'all the slip?"

Lighter squinted at the face in the crack between the door and the jamb, then whispered to Wood, "I don't remember his eyes being that light a color."

Wood edged Lighter away from the crack. "Mr. Martin, do you know who that was who attacked you?"

"No. Somebody famous? Dagnabit. I should a took his picture. Who was he?"

"We were hoping you could tell us."

"You don't know who he is? Whatcha want his picture for?"

"We don't want his picture. What did that guy want from you?"

"Maybe he wanted *my* picture. But I'm nobody famous."

Wood stepped aside. "You try."

"Mr. Martin, the guy wrecked your place. You want to file a complaint? We'll give you a ride to the station."

"I never was much of a housekeeper."

"You're not getting anywhere, Ray."

"Mr. Martin, that guy looked like the one on the skateboard who ran you down earlier. Did he follow you home?"

"Young fella, you won't make sergeant chasing those rascals. They're like rats. The city's full of 'em." He closed the door in Lighter's face.

Lighter started to knock again.

"Look, Ray, he's not going to file a complaint. Let's go." Wood turned for the elevator.

The door opened again, just a crack.

"You wanna catch something wearing a ponytail, try the gal next door. You don't want to be sitting around when you're old and alone wondering if some gal might've been the one, and you missed out because you didn't open your mouth."

The door closed again.

Lighter frowned, then looked at Wood.

"What's wrong?"

"Ever have a day where it feels like you got people wandering around inside your head? Can see everything you're thinking?"

"No."

Lighter sucked a tooth, considering that, then said, "Me either. Let's get out of here."

St. Petersburg – Present Day

Solomon edged back toward the entry way, keeping his distance from the cabinet.

At the far end of the gallery, two figures stepped from the darkness into the scattered light, making straight for Lucifer's armor. They paused only a moment and then both looked around seeming to sense Solomon's presence, even from across the room. They cocked their heads, hounds adjusting their noses to the scents in the room, trying to pick Solomon's aroma out of the threading breeze of the moving air.

Solomon edged back behind a column out of sight. Once, Solomon had every confidence in his ability to outrun trouble that was usually bigger than him. Looking at those two, he knew that a footrace against a couple fellas who actually could run like hell might not be worth the waste of good shoe leather.

New York City – Present Day

Silver's, a trendy, dimly-lit eatery down in Chelsea, had a good-sized bar area sectioned off from the large dining floor. The ceiling over-head, all black and hung with exposed ductwork and track lighting made up of tiny pin spots, created a cave-like feel, with each table illuminated in pencil beamed flares of light.

The dining area wasn't quite full yet, but soon would be.

The bar, separated from the dining area by vining plants in a narrow, wrap-around planter was filled with the after-work clientele. Two bartenders kept a steady pace, flowing up and down, mixing and serving, cleaning up and cashing out. The ruddy faced one, with a scraggly goatee, and his red hair pushed back with a thin metal hairband, worked the bar crowd. The tall and muscular one, with wavy, straw-colored hair, slicked down, and wearing shades he didn't need given the lack of light in the place, worked the service bar.

Marjorie, now in her uniform of black slacks, glittering blue blouse with a scoop neckline and cap sleeves, waited at the service bar as the tall bartender finished up her order, putting drinks on her tray.

Marjorie heard a hissing at her elbow.

That loopy delivery guy stood just behind her, sausaged into a busboy's uniform and carrying a bus tub under his arm, wearing a name tag that read "Jerome."

"You're that psychopath delivery guy from this morning."

"I'm not a delivery guy."

"So, I got the psychopath part right."

"I'm his nephew!" hissed Alvin. "Really."

"You told the cops you were delivering a package."

"Sometimes he forgets and I have to pretend to be a delivery guy so he'll open the door." Alvin did a quick scan to see who might be listening. "He's actually in the witness protection program. Big drug deals back in the seventies. He's been hiding for years. All those drugs did something to his brain." Alvin wiggled his fingers in front of his face as he stuck out his tongue, giving her a scrambled leer.

"Right." Marjorie turned back to the service bar as the tall bartender pierced each drink with a straw, finishing up the order. Marjorie lifted the tray.

"We're related! We're related. We have the same blood type, see?" Alvin pulled back his sleeve, showing Marjorie his medical alert bracelet.

"I've known Skeeter a long time. He never mentioned having any family, much less a nephew." Marjorie took her drinks and threaded her way through the crowd of drinkers.

Alvin was about to follow when Claude the manager side-stepped to cut him off. He pointed to a table covered with dirty drink glasses and dinnerware.

"Jerome," said Claude, reading off Alvin's name tag, "today, if you would be so kind?"

Alvin kept Marjorie in view as he began to sweep crockery into the bus tub.

Marjorie made her way back to the service area. Alvin weaved along after her, lugging the half-loaded bus tub.

Marjorie punched in a new order at the service terminal. Alvin slid up beside her.

"I can prove it. He's got an old family heirloom. Somewhere in his apartment. It's shaped like a—" Alvin waved his one free hand trying to physicalize the object. "It's about so—actually it's more like—" Then he stopped. "Maybe you've seen it?"

"Nope."

"Waitwaitwait! It's—it's—" Alvin's face clinched up tight in frustrated thought. Then his eyes widened, inspired. "It looks like maple syrup with a swirl of stars in it. You ever see anything like that?"

Marjorie turned to look at him. "He's got a tuxedo made of pancakes. Maybe he keeps it in the pocket." She turned back to the terminal, still shaking her head.

Alvin fairly vibrated with frustration, rattling the bus pan.

Claude looked over from across the dining room. He snapped his fingers and pointed to the table still piled up with dishes.

"*Mange bene*," said Alvin, then turned back to Marjorie. "Why are you protecting him? You're a Kantlingher aren't you? Descended all the way back to those Kantlinghers in New York? You know what's going to happen, don't you?"

Marjorie had stopped, turned, and tilted her drink tray up for a shield.

"There really is a hex," she said, no more than a whisper. She backed away, coming up against the edge of the service bar.

"Of course there's a hex, if that's what you call what always happens to the women in your family."

"You." Marjorie glanced first one way then the other.

Alvin stopped. "Me?" Then he shouted, "No!"

Dining stopped. Heads turned.

Alvin tried to make himself smaller as he moved toward her, keeping his voice low. "Not me. I'm not the hex!"

Marjorie's head pivoted on a gimbal, looking for something—something—

The tall bartender in the sunglasses handed Marjorie a blender jar full of margarita mix.

—something to throw. Of course.

"Thanks." Marjorie heaved it at Alvin's head.

Alvin ducked as the glass container shattered on the wall, spraying mix everywhere.

People were standing up to watch the floor show.

"It's not me!" Alvin shouted again.

The tall bartender handed her another jar and Marjorie heaved that one at Alvin's head, too, shattering it against the wall, spraying more mix over everything.

"Listen to me, just listen to me!" shouted Alvin.

Marjorie turned to the bartender. He shrugged and handed her a glass of cherries.

"All out of ammo," he said.

Marjorie flung it at Alvin, catching him right between the eyes. He grabbed his forehead with both hands. The bus pan hit the floor, dishes and glassware bouncing out, scattering everywhere. Marjorie ran for the front of the restaurant.

Claude stormed toward Alvin, weaving through the tables. Alvin, doubled over in pain, heard the hoof beats of the enraged manager bearing down on him. He jerked upright and bee-lined for the exit, right behind Marjorie, his other hand pushing people and chairs out of his way as he ran.

"Lover's spat," said the tall bartender to the couple at the end of the bar, pushing up his shades and winking a silver-blue eye at them.

Alvin ran after Marjorie who was already out of the restaurant and into the street.

She ran a half-dozen steps, then dived into a cab, pushing in next to the elderly couple just getting settled inside.

"You can drop me," she said, smiling at the man, patting his thigh, giving it a long stroke to the knee. He smiled back.

"Drive!" Marjorie shouted at the cabbie, seeing Alvin barreling down the block at them. She turned back to the old gent. "Could I use your phone?" she asked, doing a finger dance on his thigh.

The cab pulled out and headed down the street.

Alvin staggered to a stop, out of breath, watching the cab disappear into traffic, the tail-lights merging with all the other vehicles in the fading glow of dusk.

Then Alvin heard Claude behind him, closing on him, waving an umbrella.

"This is coming out of your tips," shouted Claude.

Alvin, in no shape for this, jack-rabbited for his van, Claude right behind as Alvin circled it once, leaping over stacked trash bags that tripped up Claude, giving Alvin time to dive into his van, get it started, slapped into gear, and ripping away after the cab, leaving Claude flopping around on the pile of black bags.

Parked in their cruiser down the block from Solomon's apartment building, Wood and Lighter sat, watching the entrance.

Wood checked her watch.

"Ponytail isn't likely to show himself again with us sitting here in a marked car." Wood sipped at her soda.

"I wish I was in plainclothes."

"They wouldn't run a stake out on something this small."

"What's really going on with that old man and Ponytail? Doesn't it make you curious?"

"Because he wouldn't file a complaint? Maybe Ponytail came by to apologize and the old coot thrashed him with his cane. And Ponytail didn't want anyone to know an old geezer like that got the best of him."

"Yeah? What about this?" Lighter waved one of Alvin's business cards.

"The lawnboy card?"

"With the phone number of a pizza place in Minneapolis? All the cards are fake."

"I can't believe you spent your entire break running those down. Did you even taste your burrito?"

"This one phone number connects Ponytail to that rich old woman who went missing in Minneapolis. You see the connection?"

"A possible long-shot, one-in-a-million connection? Sure."

"Louis in Missing Persons says they got a flyer on a guy in Minneapolis passing himself off as a lawnboy." Lighter shook the card. "He moved in with the woman, Philippa Waverly, then torched the place so he could run off with her jewelry. And the old lady? No trace of her."

"She and the lawnboy could be on a cruise somewhere, having the time of their lives. You think of that?"

"Louis said Minneapolis police checked. No sign of her anywhere. I'm betting Ponytail did away with her, and now he's working the old guy. Louis says he'll send me a couple of photos."

"Did you bother to look inside that old guy's place? There's nothing to steal."

Wood stretched and twisted in her seat, trying to make herself more comfortable.

"You do know, don't you, that stakeouts are not the best way to meet women."

"I'm watching for Ponytail."

"Of course you are. We have got to get you married. For the sake of my tailbone."

St. Petersburg – Present Day

Solomon calculated the distance between the two goons sniffing the air and the amount of dark he had for cover if he ran from where he stood, across to the next entryway opposite.

What could have been so important for Griffin to run off like that? It frosted Solomon royally to think how much his safety now depended on a rascal like Griffin, a confessed denizen of the underworld.

Chapter Forty

THE CAB ROLLED PAST the police cruiser, stopping in front of Marjorie's building. Marjorie jumped out, waving thanks at the couple inside. As the cab pulled away, Marjorie ran for her front door.

Inside the cruiser, Wood elbowed Lighter and pointed.

Gayle stood waiting for Marjorie on the sidewalk out front of the building.

"I got your purse," said Gayle, holding up Marjorie's bag. "What is it? Is everything all right?"

"Not out here," Marjorie grabbed the bag, fished out her keys, and unlocked the door, pulling Gayle inside.

Lighter slid out of the cruiser and crossed the street after Marjorie.

Wood called out the window. "You know she could call this stalking, right?"

Inside, Marjorie didn't bother with the elevator, but charged up the stairs and into her apartment, leaving Gayle to catch up and follow her inside.

Marjorie pulled duffel bags out of the closet, filling them with clothing and baby things. Maydell, the babysitter, hefted and jounced Willa who was chewing on a rubber duck.

"What happened, Marjorie? Hey! What happened?" asked Gayle.

"That delivery guy yesterday? Next door? He's the hex." Marjorie kept shoving clothes to the bottom of the bags.

"Hex?"

"Momma was right. There's a hex and I just met him." She stopped and straightened. "I've got to tell you, the women in my family have no taste in men. From the very beginning. Just trying to picture that guy and my great-great-whatever grandmother—gives me the willies." She went back to packing.

"Marjorie, calm down. How about I get something to settle your nerves? Whatever happened, I don't think it's a hex."

Marjorie continued to whirl about the apartment, gathering up things, throwing things aside.

"I heard those hex stories from the time I started playing with dolls."

The buzzer sounded.

Marjorie froze, then hissed, "Don't answer it. That's probably him. I don't want him to know I'm here."

The buzzer sounded again.

"Awfully polite for a hex."

"Just don't answer it." Marjorie continued to pack, gently, quietly.

"Okay. What's your plan?" whispered Gayle.

"Get out of Dodge and never look back."

There was a knock on the door. Marjorie nearly jumped out of her skin.

"Police," said Lighter through the door.

Gayle sighed and went to open the door.

"Don't!"

"It's the police, Marjorie. They can help."

"No! It's that police officer from this morning." Marjorie went back to packing. "I should've seen that coming. Just the kind of guy the hex would choose. Way too nice. Then—*ka-blooey*—there goes your life. He'll turn out to be a walking disaster. He can stay outside until I'm gone."

There was another knock on the door.

"I'm going to let them in. They can hear us. They know we're here." Gayle moved toward the door.

"No! He's part of the hex."

"Some guy out there has really upset you. If he's dangerous, you need the police."

"I tell him I actually saw my hex and they'll lock me up instead."

"If it's a flesh-and-blood guy, they can arrest him. For stalking or something."

"He knew I was a Kantlingher. No one knows that. Not even you. He's been around almost two hundred years. No way they'll be able to put handcuffs on him. He only goes away after I'm stuck with whoever it is he's chosen."

Gayle opened the door.

"No!"

Lighter stepped inside first, taking a quick glance around.

He could see that Marjorie's apartment was a tidy clutter of mismatched furniture, scattered baby things, and a large assortment of angel knick-knacks on most high surfaces, out of Willa's reach.

Marjorie ignored him, intent on choosing which of the angels she could take and which she had to leave behind.

"I hate to leave any of them," said Marjorie, taking a pair of angel salt shakers. "They were supposed to bring me luck." She threw the shakers into the bag and then looked at the rest. "So long, fellas. You're on your own."

"Are you all right," asked Lighter.

"No," said Marjorie stuffing baby gear into a large diaper bag.

"She saw that delivery man from this morning," said Gayle. She leaned closer to the officers. "She thinks he's the family hex. Go easy on her."

Lighter cleared his throat, "Uh—there's a guy out of Minnesota who targets old women. He's wanted for questioning in the disappearance of an elderly woman named Philippa Waverly."

Marjorie stopped and straightened up, absorbing the shot. "Thank you *so* much. I must say, you know how to make a woman feel special."

"I meant the old guy."

"You blush a lot these days," said Wood. "You know that, Ray?"

"You did notice that Skeeter is not an old woman," said Marjorie, then turned to Gayle. "Now tell me the hex didn't pick this one out special for me." Marjorie went back to packing.

"I just meant there might be a connection with Mr. Martin next door. The description on the flyer fits the man we saw yesterday."

"But why pick on Marjorie," asked Gayle.

"Use someone he knows to gain his confidence?"

Crouched on the fire escape outside the fifth floor hallway, Alvin held the pistol grip of a small listening dish, pointing it at Marjorie's door.

"So you could arrest him, then?" asked Gayle, turning to Marjorie. "Right?"

"It's time to give this to the detectives," said Wood. "I'm heading back to the barn. You coming?"

"Gayle," said Marjorie, "I've got to be out of here by morning. Tell Skip he can have the furniture. You can tell him where I hid his guitar, if the gophers haven't—" Marjorie plopped the bags into a pile by the door, then stopped. She stood still for a long moment.

"Marjorie? Honey?" said Gayle.

"Where'll I go to hide from a hex?"

Gayle shrugged at her, stumped.

"Hawaii?" offered Lighter.

They all looked at him.

"But only for two weeks."

Marjorie seemed lost in thought, then turned to Lighter, her chin down, eyes hooded.

"I'm glad you're here," said Marjorie. "You can help me beat the hex."

"Your ex?"

"Hex, hex," said Marjorie, coming toward him. "All you have to do is say you'll marry me."

"Whoa," said Wood. "Okay, partner, time to give this one to the headshrinkers."

"Think of yourself as my tax dollars at work," said Marjorie.

"Sweetie, let's have you lie down."

"I'll go out and pretend to marry a street mime if it'll fool this hex."

"Go ahead, Ray," said Wood. "Wouldn't want to stand between a deranged woman and her wedding day."

"Uh. Sure," said Lighter.

"No. Ask me. Out loud."

"Will you marry me?"

Marjorie brightened, fluttering, "Why, I'd love to. Tomorrow is fine. I'll need a bouquet, a white dress—"

"—a strait jacket," said Wood.

"Now get lost." Marjorie shooed Lighter and Wood out the door.

"It's the end of my shift. I was thinking. Since we're engaged—"

"Bad luck for the groom to see the bride on the night before the wedding. Go on. Get lost!"

"Come on, partner, while she's lucid." Wood took Lighter by the sleeve.

Marjorie closed the door on them, sliding the bolt and setting the chain.

On the other side, Lighter still stood in front of Marjorie's door.

"Think it's too early for you to call in a marriage counselor?" Wood laughed. "Boy, you sure can pick them." She gave him a chuck on the arm. "Leave it to the detectives. Your job here is done."

"You know what they'll say if I mention anything about a hex?"

"It's some kind of insurance scam, that's all. Maybe the old guy's in on it, maybe he's not. Let the detectives handle it."

Alvin, still on the fire escape, pressed himself against the wall as the officers left the building down below him and walked toward their cruiser.

Back inside the apartment, Marjorie leaned against the door, listening to make sure the two officers were gone.

"Can you drive us to the airport. I'm taking the first thing out of here that flies."

"Where are you going to go?"

"Back to Texas," Marjorie whispered.

"Let me break it to Norton that he's got to fix supper for the baby. I'll get the car and meet you and Willa down front. I can drop Maydell off on the way."

Maydell handed Willa to Marjorie and gathered her purse and jacket.

" '*I'm getting married in the morning*'," sang Marjorie, in a not half-bad alto, dancing Willa around the room, stopping to give a quick check out the window, then dancing on.

St. Petersburg – Present Day

Solomon decided that it was time to go, Griffin or no Griffin.

Footsteps started up and were getting nearer. Damn Griffin for putting that damnable image in his head. Solomon could feel the teeth at his neck, the saliva dripping down between his shoulder blades.

If he had a coin he'd flip it, having no good idea which was the better means of escape—stealth or speed.

New York City – Present Day

Satisfied the cops were gone, Alvin jimmied the sash and pushed the window up. He'd just put a leg over, when Marjorie's door opened again and Gayle came out, followed by Maydell. He'd barely gotten back out onto the fire escape and hidden as they'd walked past.

Once they were down the stairs and out of sight, Alvin slid in over the sill and into the building, leaving the sash up.

He tiptoed over to Marjorie's door and put his ear to it. Then he tiptoed over to Solomon's door, knelt down, and went to work picking the lock with a thin sliver of metal. It was not a skill he had.

There was a loud click and he smiled, surprised.

The door behind him swung open.

"Skeeter?" Marjorie stepped into the hallway. Seeing Alvin, she gasped, backpedaling through the door as Alvin leaped up and hurtled toward her, stuffing his foot and fingers into the jamb before she could close the door. Marjorie leaned hard, mashing his extremities.

"AAAAHHaaahhhhhAAAAAHHHH!," he yodeled, then "Shhhhh!" his fingers to his mouth, trying to quiet her. "AAAHH! Shhhhh! AAAAHHH! Shhhhhhhhhhhhhhhh!" he hissed, finally running out of air.

Alvin, trapped and desperate, slammed his body against the door, his weight overcoming hers, forcing her backward. He stumbled into the room, shutting the door behind himself.

He bobbed around the room, holding his injured hand by the wrist trying to howl in pain without making any noise.

Marjorie leapt up onto the couch, an umbrella in one hand and a plaster angel in the other, ready to defend herself and Willa.

"I'm engaged. My wedding's tomorrow. My life is ruined. You've done your dirty work. Now get out of here."

There was a pounding on the wall from next door.

"Turn it down!" The voice rang around the breezeway

"You think I'm the hex?" said Alvin, breathing hard, grimacing in pain. "You think it's me?"

"You knew about me being a Kantlingher. No one else knows that."

Alvin, furious, shaking his finger first at her, then in the general direction of Solomon's apartment, then back to her. Then he stopped. An idea lit up his face.

"R-i-i-i-ght," said Alvin. "Of course I'm the hex. Who else could I be?"

"Why'd you tell me you were Skeeter's nephew? What's he got to do with anything?"

"I told you. He has something I want. You help me get it, I'll quit the hex business. Leave you alone. Disappear forever. That should be worth something, right?"

"Why should I help you?"

"I want to mend my ways. Do a good deed."

"A good deed?" Marjorie didn't sound convinced.

"It was a dying woman's dying wish as she was—dying. On her deathbed, she begged me with her last breath to find that thing I was trying to tell you about. Get it back from the guy who stole it."

"You can't even describe it."

"She ran out of breath. Only had enough air for the part about maple syrup and little stars. Then she croaked." Alvin twisted his face into a death mask. "Doesn't that just break your heart?"

"So—ask Skeeter, not me."

"You saw how he threw me out. He'll hide it. But he'll do anything for you. I just need to get close enough to see if he has it. That's all. The old lady'd be so happy."

"I thought she was dead."

"Of course she's dead!" Alvin strangled a cry. "But not happy! How could she be? She's dead." He exhaled, recovering his calm. "It'd mean so much to her—memory."

Marjorie raised the plaster angel, ready to heave it. "Skeeter wouldn't steal anything from an old woman. He's the sweetest, most kind-hearted man."

Alvin cowered behind his upraised hands. "I didn't say he stole it! Did I say he stole it?"

"Yes. You said stole."

"I meant she *extolled* him to have it."

"If she extolled him to have it, why did she want you to get it back. What good's it to her if she's dead?"

Alvin bellowed in frustration. "How can I think when you keep interrupting me?"

There was more pounding on the wall. "Shut! Up!"

"All right. You thought the hex was bad up to now, you just wait until I get really warmed up!" Alvin kept his hands ready to ward off any more flying objects aimed at his head.

Marjorie looked quickly to Willa then at Alvin. "I help you get this—thing and you'll vanish? Forever?"

"Forever. Help me find it and I'm gone. History. Finito. Via con Dios. Adios, amigo. Comprende?"

"Okay." Marjorie lowered the plaster angel and stepped down off the couch.

Alvin eased his hands down from in front of his face.

"Take me over there right now."

"I knock on his door now, with you standing there, he'll know something's up. Let me talk to him. I'll have him bring it out to you."

"Okay."

"Tomorrow morning."

"Tomorrow?" Alvin was whining again.

"Eight o'clock. In front of the church on Broadway."

"All right. But if he doesn't show, flying off to Texas won't do you any good, sister."

Marjorie's eyes got just a little bit wider.

"That's right. I know everything there is to know about you."

"Be there at eight o'clock. You'll get it."

"Oh. And don't bother calling the police. I see everything because I am everywhere and nowhere. Like fog. On little cat feet." Alvin stepped on Willa's duck, the squeak sending him into a lumbering pirouette, arms flailing, grabbing the floor lamp, spinning, finally righting himself. He eased the lamp back upright.

"Eight o'clock. Sharp. Or else." Then he swatted the shade off the lamp and sent it sailing across the room before backing out of the apartment.

Marjorie set the locks, then leaned her back against the door. She slid down, flopping onto her bottom. She exhaled hard and ran her hands through her hair. Then she took the strands of her hair in her fists, examining them.

Chapter Forty-One

St. Petersburg – Present Day

SOLOMON'S MENTAL COIN FLIP came up heads, choosing speed over stealth. He braced his hands against the column behind him, ready to launch himself.

Then he remembered how Griffin never made a sound when he walked. Those friends of his likely wouldn't either.

From up the stairs came the night watchman again, the beam of her flashlight sweeping across the floor, up along the wall, then down again.

She couldn't see him. Solomon blew out a long, deep breath.

The goons reared up on either side, bracketing him, their mouths open, eyes flaring, claws flexed, reaching for him.

Ready to fight, his fist cocked, Solomon still managed to notice how odd it was that such handsome fellas had such fearsome chompers.

"Hey! Four eyes!" shouted Griffin.

The two goons snapped around to scowl at the interruption.

"That's my snack you're drooling on." Griffin grabbed Solomon by the shirt front, yanking him from between the descending duo of doom.

In an instant, Solomon was in that familiar non-time between the waters.

"You took your own sweet time," Solomon tried to say, but all that came out was a kind of chewy crackling sound, and nothing in the way of words he could recognize.

"Don't try to talk. There's no actual air to make your vocal cords work. You sound like you're gargling walnut shells. Very unattractive."

Solomon tried to ask how it was Griffin could talk, but the effort made Solomon's throat scratch and caused a keen desire to cough away the irritation.

New York City – Present Day

The damp vapor of the transit writhed and curled away from Solomon, leaving him standing in his own apartment again, his throat clinched with the kind of dry-patch tickle that seizes hold of the tonsils and makes the eyes water. He worked his jaw to make spit enough to swallow away the irritation.

There was a knocking on his door. Solomon's gummed-up brainworks took a long time to loosen up so he could realize it.

Solomon looked through the peephole, seeing only hard spikes of blonde hair.

"Skeeter? It's me, Marjorie."

Solomon wiped his face for any residue from his travel and opened the door.

Still rubbing his eyes and trying to get control of the tickling urge to cough, Solomon saw that Marjorie had cut and spiked her hair into a patchy blond, as though she'd run out of peroxide before the job was done.

"I'm sorry. I woke you, didn't I?"

"No, no. Not at all. Come on in. I need some coffee or something. I could get you some."

"I can't stay." But she did step in and lean close. "I've seen the hex. Momma was right. It's a real flesh-and-blood thing."

Solomon leaned back, squinting, not sure how to react.

"Where?"

"He showed up at work, big as life. And then," she glanced behind herself, "he showed up here."

Shortwick. Had to be. Solomon reached for his bowie on the bureau by the door. "Where's that rascal now?"

"He's gone. But I have to get out of here."

"That why the—um—uh—" Solomon plucked at his own hair.

Marjorie flicked her stiffened bangs with her fingertips.

"Part of my brilliant plan."

"You give Willa a flat-top and put her in work boots?"

"Maybe have to." Marjorie tried to smile. "He wants some knick-knack he says you have. It belonged to some old woman. Now he's trying to get it back."

Solomon scratched the back of his neck for no reason but time to think. "Seems a long way round to pick my pocket. If he's so all-fired keen to have—whatever it is—why not come face me like a man, instead of pestering you and Willa?"

"It's a trick. A set-up so I'll fall for whatever bastard he's picked out."

"So what's your plan?"

"Get the hell out of here."

She held out her hand and showed him a small, ceramic angel playing a concertina.

"I picked this up a few years ago. It always made me think of us dancing in that open field back in Oklahoma. I'd keep it, but since it's not likely we'll run into each other again any time soon, I wanted you to have it. So you won't forget about Willa and me."

He hadn't reached for it, so she took his hand and placed the figurine on his palm.

"Margie," said Solomon and then stopped. He couldn't think how in hell to calm her fears about Shortwick being the hex without revealing his true self to her. No words were coming, but he pressed on anyway. "This thing you all are calling a hex—"

"I know, I know. Twenty-first century, middle of New York, and you've got some crazed girl on your doorstep complaining about getting the evil eye. I wouldn't bother you with it, just give you the angel and get lost, but I've always trusted you. Not many guys out there I can trust. I thought you should at least know why I disappeared."

Solomon's courage curdled, and the words evaporated right out of his brain pan.

Instead, he asked, "How about that lawman? Might not be half bad."

"That is the whole diabolical nature of the hex. No matter how good they seem on the outside, you can bet money there's something awful inside waiting to go off. Maybe not right away, maybe years from now, but why chance it? Believe me, they don't make matches in heaven anymore."

"I reckon not, I'm sorry to say." Solomon looked straight at Griffin hovering by the door. "These days they're put together someplace vile, with cheap labor and crappy tools." Griffin shrugged, twisting up his face in a frown of objection and hurt.

"When are you leaving?"

Griffin gave Solomon a questioning looking, pointing between himself and Marjorie.

Marjorie stepped back scanning overhead. "Leaving? Me? Never? I'm getting married in the morning. Just get me to the church on time." She hunched in close to Solomon again, whispering, "I'd already be gone if I didn't know that thing was out there watching."

She checked over each shoulder before continuing. "I made a deal with him to meet me in the morning on Broadway in front of the church. I swore I'd bring you with me so he could get his trinket back. While he's waiting out there for me, I'll be gone. It won't be much of a head start, but I'll take what I can get."

Marjorie straightened up.

"Oh, I forgot all about Gayle." She pulled out her phone as she whispered to Solomon, "She was going to give us a ride to the airport tonight."

"Maybe I should be there at the church. I could give him something to occupy himself while you two take your leave. At least spit in his eye."

"No, you stay out of it. This isn't about you. It's about me." Marjorie thumbed numbers on the keypad. "And Willa. And whoever comes after."

She leaned in all the way this time and kissed Solomon on the jaw, her fragrance something he recalled from some other place and some other time.

"Take care of yourself," she whispered, then put the phone to her ear. "Gayle?"

She gave Solomon a little clam-finger wave goodbye but speaking to Gayle.

Solomon waited until she was back in her apartment before he closed the door.

"I'm going to tell her. I'm going to tell her it's me and not that Shortwick fella of yours." Solomon looked Griffin dead in the eye, daring him to object.

"That's a great idea," said Griffin.

"It is?"

"Once she knows for sure it's you, she won't let you get within a hundred miles of her. If you're both on the lam, the only one Alvin can follow is her, hoping to get to you, because you do such sneaky things when you run. And since she won't have a clue where you are, the piece is safe, you hang onto it for another couple hundred years and the apocalypse remains mere morbid speculation by religious nuts. That's a load off my mind, let me tell you." Griffin smacked his lips, tasting for something. "All this worry made me hungry. What have you got around here to eat?" Griffin went into the kitchen and opened the refrigerator.

"That means you lose the bet."

"I guess so." Griffin stuck his head in the refrigerator. "How sad for me. What's the date on this salami?"

"You had no intention of winning the bet, did you?"

Griffin peered over the door of the refrigerator. "What'd we learn today, class? Don't make bets with the devil. Or any of his known associates." Griffin ducked back into the refrigerator. "You think it'd be any good with this mayonnaise? Whoa! You may need to give whatever's growing in here a name and keys to your apartment."

Solomon came to stand on the other side of the refrigerator door.

"It's indecent to deliberately lose a bet."

"Hey, you won. What do you care how? Wait a minute. Gambling's a sin. Shame on you, Solly. What'll the vicar say?"

"I expect you to hold up your end of the bargain."

"There's no way she'll give that lawman a second chance now."

"Tough, the bet ain't over."

"That's not fair." Griffin stopped. "Okay, that won't work anymore I grant you. Solly, she's hoofing it to the high country. I lost, fair and square."

"Not yet. Not by a long shot." Solomon rubbed his thumb over the ceramic angel Marjorie had given him.

"Would you feel better if I moped around, kicked a pigeon, put on a big old sad face? How's this?" Griffin slapped his hands up against his cheeks, pulling a long face and giving out with a raucous moaning. "Bested by a mudfoot, I can't believe it. I'll be the laughingstock of hell. Oh, the shame of it all." Griffin gave Solomon a hopeful grin. "Better?"

"I'm going to make that meeting with this Shortwick fella." Solomon took up his concertina and heading for the door.

"What'll that accomplish? Solly? What are you going to do?"

"Go play me a little music."

"I mean about Shortwick?"

"Like I said. Spit in his eye. Or I might kick him in the bee-hive. Maybe break a couple of his legs."

Griffin blinked then said, "You're not just saying that are you? Don't get my hopes up. Solly."

"This is going to get tiresome right quick. I can see that." Solomon sighed, his hand on the door knob.

"What is?"

"Having to always think opposite of what you say now so I don't end up like Adam and Eve."

"Hey, that wasn't me. I was totally outside the solar system. Never saw a thing. Solly? Solly?"

Solomon walked out of the apartment and went up the stairs to the roof. He pushed through the short metal door and out onto the tarred roof under the starless sky. The only celestial light was a lonely old moon hanging over the city.

He blocked the door open and stepped between the collection of abandoned brick piles, rolls of tar paper, lawn chairs with rotted strapping, and rusted riding toys.

He took a milk crate and stood it on one end, wiped it off with a couple of quick swicks of his pocket handkerchief and then sat down.

Silhouetted against the rising moon, Solomon squeezed out a tune that rang off the buildings and rattled around in the breezeway. Something, he hoped, would settle Marjorie's riled spirit if she was listening.

Sunrise gave the buildings of the Upper West Side a pale yellow glow, the dusk wisping away as morning took over.

Marjorie, carrying Willa, eased open her front door and did a quick check of the hallway. She and Willa wore floppy hats and sunglasses. She stepped out, pulling the door closed behind her, wincing at the loud snap of the latchbolt in the early morning quiet.

Marjorie shouldered the diaper bag and crossed to Solomon's front door. With only a moment's hesitation, she knocked softly.

"Skeeter?" she called in a low, throaty whisper.

She knocked again. Willa reached out, giving the door a little soft-fisted knock of her own, smiling at Marjorie. Smiling back at Willa, Marjorie took her hand, kissed the knuckles, waiting only a moment more, then cantered on tip-toes down the stairs.

Uptown, Alvin, wearing a light jacket over dark blue coveralls, and hiding behind a mustachioed nose and glasses, stood across the street from a line of idling city buses. The drivers, waiting to start their scheduled runs, stood chatting together, smoking, eating, or checking cellphones.

Chancing a break in the traffic, Alvin, oozing nonchalance, did a fast walk across to the first bus on the line.

Up on tip-toes, Alvin reached through the open window on the driver's side for the door's control. He flinched at the sound of the hissing hydraulics, then scuttled around the front of the bus and slipped aboard.

Once in the seat, he did a quick check to make sure the gear shift, gas, and brake pedals were all where he expected them to be. Then he eased the bus into gear and stomped on the gas.

The bus accelerated away from the line, more slowly—and less quietly—than Alvin expected. Trying to squeeze out a little more speed, Alvin gripped the steering wheel and pressed down so hard on the accelerator pedal that his fanny lifted up off the seat.

One of the drivers, seeing his hijacked bus leaving without him, shouted and hauled out after Alvin. The other drivers followed but lost the footrace as Alvin powered through the turn onto Broadway, the bus canting dangerously through the right-hand turn, then leveling out and roaring onward, scattering pedestrians as he barreled downtown.

Gayle waited by her car, the trunk lid open, standing guard over Marjorie's luggage.

"She's so cute!" said Gayle, seeing Willa's getup and giving her little hat brim a tug.

"It's not cute. It's a disguise."

"I know, but it's still so cute."

"It'd be cute if we weren't running for our sanity." Marjorie dropped the diaper bag into the trunk.

"I wish you'd talk to the police."

"I told you. There's no way it'll work out with him."

"I meant about the stalker. And what *do* I tell Officer Lighter if I see him around the park, asking about you? 'Sorry, Officer, she thought you were such a loser, she just had to leave town.' "

"Don't say anything. Maybe he's not a loser, but I can't take the chance." Marjorie closed the trunk lid.

"If this hex of yours has managed to survive two hundred years and find you after all that time, won't he see through this trick of yours?" Gayle stood by the driver's side.

"He's not very smart and he can't see the future." Marjorie buckled Willa into the car seat in back, then got in the front. "More than one of us Kantlinghers has whacked him with something heavy and he never sees it coming."

Gayle slipped in behind the wheel and started the car.

"Could you do me another big favor? After I'm out of here?"

"Sure."

"Look in on Skeeter. I knocked, but he wasn't up yet and I didn't have the heart to wake him."

"He's up and out already. He was in front of the church when I drove down from the garage this morning. I thought maybe you worked something out with him."

"Oh, shit. He's waiting for the hex! What's he think he can do that we've never been able to do?" Marjorie chuffed and slumped in the seat, her face fixed in a frown.

"What can this hex of yours do to him?"

"I don't know! Give him a heart attack? Drag him off to wherever he goes when he's not ruining my life!" Marjorie's breathing got heavier. "Open the trunk."

"I can't drive around with you in my trunk. What if I get stopped!"

"No, just open the trunk!"

Gayle pulled the lever and popped the trunk lid open as Marjorie ducked out of the car.

Reaching into the trunk, she pushed aside the bags until she found the tire iron.

"What're you going to do with that?" Gayle, now out of the car, watched Marjorie take a few practice swings, improvising a blunt instrument.

"I've always been told it's a sure-fire way to give yourself a head-start against the hex. Maybe it'll give Skeeter and me a fighting chance. Meet me there!" Marjorie took off running, holding her hat down with one hand and hefting the tire iron with the other.

Alvin smiled as he got the hang of steering the bus, weaving between cars, whipping around trucks, nudging taxis out of the way.

He rocketed past bus stops and through traffic lights, ignoring the red lights against him, the shouts and obscene gestures of pedestrians forced out of his path, and the honking horns of cars and trucks he squeezed aside and cut off.

Alvin checked his watch, ducked to check passing street signs, then slid open his cellphone and thumbed a phone number.

"Yeah, I want to report a terrible accident." Alvin gave the cross street. "Looks like an old codger with some girl. And—could you do me a favor? When you pick up the old guy? Check for internal injuries."

The bus roared onward.

Chapter Forty-Two

SOLOMON STOOD ON THE CURB watching traffic, trying to catch sight of Shortwick. Griffin perched on one of the newspaper vending boxes, swinging his legs.

"What could you possibly hope to achieve?"

"A word to the wise, if he's got sense enough to appreciate it. Live with his mortality and leave Marjorie and Willa alone. Won't do him any good pestering them to get to me. I won't have any more to do with them or any other Kantlingher ever again."

"You don't get it do you? The end times are on your doorstep, Solly, and you've got your unmentionables in a knot over one person. Out of billions. I'm telling you, it's better for everyone if he's busy chasing after her and not you."

"No, *you* don't get it. I want time enough for her to see some good in that lawman."

"But—to play devil's advocate here—let's say you have your heart-to-heart with Shortwick, and he doesn't buy it. What then?"

"I'll nick him a mite and give him a reason to appreciate what little mortality he's already got."

"That's so unlike you, Solly. It's so—so—refreshing."

Marjorie danced sideways around the old woman with her walker, and hurdled over the shih tzu's leash stretched across the sidewalk, then she dashed through the intersection a bare moment ahead of oncoming traffic. Marjorie loped along, leaned hard to make the corner, whirling to avoid a man loaded up with groceries, recovered her footing and kept running.

Marjorie, still blocks away, saw Solomon standing curbside in front of the church. He was alone, resting on his cane, looking vulnerable. There was no sign of the hex.

"Skeeter!" she shouted, waving the tire iron, people scattering to avoid the crazed lady with the blunt instrument. "Skeeter!"

Alvin spotted Solomon. Nothing but a few newspaper vending boxes and a couple of street signs between him and the bus.

Now, all he needed was an immovable object to pinch Solomon up against.

Alvin tromped on the gas pedal.

Solomon stepped to the curb's edge. He glanced uptown first, and then downtown, not sure what he was looking for in the flow of traffic both ways along the avenue.

"Didn't your mother ever tell you not to play in the street? You could get hit by a bus."

Solomon kept his eye on Griffin as he took a giant step off the curb into the lane.

"What are you doing?"

"I told you. I'm not about to end up like—"

The bus slammed into Solomon.

"Skeeter!" Marjorie cried out.

The impact carried Solomon through the intersection, ramming a parked step-van loaded with bakery goods on the far corner, driving Solomon through the step-van's rear door. The momentum smacked the step-van into the rear-end of a black town car getting a meticulous dusting by its driver. The step-van's front end crushed the car's rear end and sent Solomon flying through the step-van's cargo bay, blowing bread products out both front doors as he passed on out the front windshield. He burst through the rear window of the crumpling town car, the air bags popping, as Solomon broke out the car's front windshield. He skidded to a stop on the hood, the car alarm warbling.

Solomon melted off the hood and slid down over the front end of the car, onto the street and under the bumper.

"—Adam and Eve." Griffin hopped down. "Right. You did say that, didn't you." He looked around at the mayhem, his hands clasped behind himself. He flexed, looking upward and shook his head. "This is going to be sooooo easy."

Marjorie put her head down and ran, reaching the step-van, wading through the scattered loaves and cakes, climbing in to look for Solomon.

"Skeeter?"

She ran to the town car, still seeing no sign of him, only the Solomon-shaped holes of the shattered rear and front windshields.

Solomon hauled himself up off the pavement, and leaned on the hood of the town car, his shredded sweater and shirt nearly gone, leaving him almost bare-chested, and his pants dangling in tatters as he shook the jagged beads of safety glass out of his hair and his lacerated clothes.

"Never laid a glove on me." Solomon weaved, bracing himself on the hood.

Marjorie edged closer to him, her hand out, not sure what to think, worried for him, but seeing no mark of an injury.

"Skeeter, you think maybe you should lie down?"

Solomon could see the confusion on her face.

"All that bread there must've broken my fall." Solomon spit out a couple of glass beads he'd collected on his travels through the windshield.

Marjorie looked back at the wrecked vehicles and then at his clothing sliced into tatters.

Emergency lights of a police car were already flickering over the scene of the accident. In the distance an ambulance siren warbled its approach.

Alvin stumbled from the bus. Seeing Solomon upright and unharmed, Alvin leaped and capered, "I knew it! I knew it! Finally, finally, finally!" he crowed, his hand up to high-five the bystanders. Finding no takers, he flexed himself into an exalted "X", fists raised to the sky, crying "Wooo-hooo!"

Until Marjorie hit him in the gut with the tire iron, doubling him over. She reared back to deliver the coup de grace to the back of his skull, but a big, burly bystander grabbed hold of her hand before she could get in a good swing.

"Wait for the cops," he said and took Alvin by the collar of his jacket. "I'll hold onto him for you."

Solomon hitched his pants as best he could, then brushed his hair back into place and settled his hat on straight, a dapper if raggedy old guy.

"Thank goodness for them contraptions, right?" Solomon jerked a thumb at the airbags filling the dash in the crunched town car.

Bystanders had their cellphones out, snapping away at Solomon and the wrecked vehicles.

By now the ambulance had arrived and the two EMTs hurried to look Solomon over for damage.

"Don't let him get away! Check him for internal injuries," shouted Alvin.

"What's your name?" asked the blonde tech who handled Solomon, lifting his arms, turning his hands, touching his head.

"My name?" Solomon glanced at Marjorie and decided a little addled confusion was the better part of valor.

"Lemme check my wallet."

"His name's Skeeter. Skeeter Martin," said Marjorie.

"Skeeter, can you tell me who's president?" asked the blonde tech.

"Which year?"

The blond tech gripped Solomon's forehead and held open one eyelid, flicking the beam of a flashlight in his eye.

"I think I see that bright light to the Hereafter you all talk about."

The blonde tech holstered her flashlight.

"Looks like you might have had a pretty bad blow to the head, Skeeter." She turned to her partner. "Get a backboard and brace." She turned back to Solomon. "Just a precaution while we transport you."

"Nossir. You won't be strapping me down. I just need a little room to clear my head a mite." Solomon twisted his neck and rotated his shoulders to work out the kind of kinks a man might get being driven headfirst through two parked motor vehicles.

"Skeeter," said Marjorie, "they need to check you out, make sure there's nothing wrong."

"I won't put you on the gurney," said the blonde tech. "Can you get into the ambulance on your own?"

"Got no need of an ambulance. My house ain't but a few blocks away. I'm fit as a fiddle and fine enough to walk."

Lighter arrived, stepping through the goggling, gaggling bystanders.

"Hey, you okay?" Lighter asked Solomon.

"I'll be fine if they just let me go home."

"They have to check you out. It's an accident involving a city vehicle."

"Crap." Alvin twisted himself, and slipped out of his jacket leaving the burly bystander holding the empty garment.

"Hey!" shouted Lighter as Alvin dodged through the crowd and out of sight.

"Have you thought about another line of work?" asked Marjorie.

"We'll catch him. He's a bus driver."

"He's not a bus driver," said Marjorie, "he's a—he's a—" then stopped, hefting the tire iron, looking for something to damage.

"Could I have that, please." Lighter held out his hand for the tire iron. "I'd feel a lot better."

"I'm fine," said Solomon, eying his own chances of escape. But seeing the shadow of confusion cross Marjorie's face again, he said, "Well, not fine, exactly, since I just got hit by a bus. Kind of shakes a fella up, I grant you." Then he tried indignation as a plausible distraction. "What's the city care if I go home or not? I was just standing there, minding my own business."

"Please, Skeeter." said Marjorie. "You could be hurt worse than it looks. I wish I hadn't said anything about meeting him here."

"Meeting who?" asked Lighter.

"Could you stop being a cop for a minute."

"It's the only reason they let me dress up like this."

The confused looks on the faces of Marjorie and Lighter, as well as the intensely curious crowd, made Solomon realize his stubbornness might be making things worse.

"Come on." The blonde tech guided Solomon to the back of the ambulance. Bystanders leaned in, snapping away at the Amazing Rubber Man.

Solomon felt the lack of something and then patted his bare chest. He still had his locket, but the artifact was gone.

"I lost my—" Solomon looked around at his feet, then stopped. He looked up, scanning for some sign of Griffin, but saw nothing.

"What?" asked Marjorie.

"Nothing. Must've left it at home." Solomon let himself be handed up into the ambulance and buckled into the jumpseat over the wheel well. They closed the ambulance doors and then climbed into the front cab, cranked up the siren, and rolled away.

"They'll take care of him," said Lighter, watching the ambulance leave.

"Oh, go—talk to some witnesses." Marjorie grabbed her tire iron back and walked away.

"I guess I'll just, uh, talk to some witnesses," said Lighter. "Maybe catch up with you later?"

Marjorie had only gone a few steps when she flicked hard at her earlobe to knock away the tickling itch.

"Okay, maybe not, then," called Lighter.

She kept marching and flicking, but the annoying prickle wouldn't stop.

It was Griffin, a hazy, indistinct shape walking in a close lock-step right behind her, working a soda straw around inside her ear.

She stopped to give herself a really good scratch, twisting her head enough that a glimmer in the gutter caught her eye.

Something dark and shiny. A piece of jewelry. Like maple syrup with a swirl of tiny stars.

She picked it up, holding it low against her body, studying it.

Lighter, who'd been watching her, called out to her, "Find something?"

"No. Nothing." Marjorie folded it up against her chest. "Nothing." She kept moving, nearly trotting to get away.

The EMTs took Solomon to a hospital emergency room uptown. Solomon tried to read the signs, get his bearings, and figure out where he was while they were backing the ambulance in to unload him.

The blonde tech spoke to a receiving nurse, and they plopped Solomon into a wheelchair, despite his insistence he didn't need to be babied.

Marisol, the nurse, dressed in what Solomon took for baby blue pajamas and who'd taken over his wheelchair from the blonde tech, told him to quit his belly-aching and let them take care of him.

She wheeled him through the large waiting area, done up in pastel colors, with upholstered furniture, framed prints, and several television screens fixed to the walls. For all the brightness everyone seemed to be waiting for something disagreeable to happen.

Marisol rolled him up to the check-in desk where another receiving nurse waited.

"Name?" asked the receiving nurse.

"Says 'Rosalee' on your tag you got pinned there." Solomon decided to try a little mental discombobulation to buy himself some time. "You can't see it from where you're sitting."

"*Your* name," said the receiving nurse.

Solomon looked down at himself. "Don't seem to have a tag of my own. Nowhere left to pin it."

"Last name Martin. Goes by Skeeter," said Marisol.

"Do you know how old you are, Mr. Martin?"

"Since my last birthday? Or my next birthday?"

"A birthdate is good."

"I like birthdays, too. But not when they run too close together. I prefer them spread out."

"Address?" The receiving nurse flicked a quick roll of her eyes at Marisol.

"No. But a shirt and tie'd be nice." Solomon flounced his rags at her.

"Hit by a bus," said Marisol. "We need to hold onto him until the police can talk to him."

"Isolation three. See if he has a wallet."

"I don't carry a wallet," said Solomon. "Used to carry a chicken. Can't keep eggs in a wallet. Can't keep them in a chicken either, at least not for long." Solomon started whistling a tuneful sea shanty.

The receiving nurse smiled, gave a cock of her head and a wave of her hand at Marisol.

Marisol rolled Solomon around the check-in desk, pushing him past the curtained examination bays, some occupied, some at the ready, all of them chock full of gadgets and doo-dads that made no sense to Solomon. But he was almighty sure he didn't want any of them being used on him.

Chapter Forty-Three

ALVIN PLANNED TO PICK THE LOCK on the front door to Solomon's building, but the super was taking forever to wash the sidewalk and didn't give Alvin the chance.

Then, as if the gods of malefaction heard Alvin's muttered curses, an elderly woman steered her walker to the front door, fished around in a ratty coin purse and pulled out a single key. Then, with arthritic slowness, she stretched up and jabbed her key at the keyhole, sliding off the cylinder, tap-tap-tapping, as she tried to fit the key into the lock.

Alvin, with a whine of impatience, reached to grab it from her. "Here. Let me do that."

She yanked away, glaring at him, her left eye white with cataracts, her right eye a pale silverish blue.

"It's okay, it's okay. I'm the exterminator. See?" Alvin pointed to the hand-drawn logo scotch-taped to the back of his black jumpsuit, and held up a can of bug spray. "I got an emergency call."

"It sure took you long enough," said the old woman. She turned back to the door and aimed her key at the lock. Then stopped. She held the key out to Alvin. As he reached for it, she pulled it back.

"On one condition."

"What!" Alvin strangled a squeal of frustration.

"You come and give my place a good spray-down before you go. Cockroaches dragged off my second husband, Emil, back in the summer of 'eighty-five. I haven't seen anything of him since."

"Okay! Fine!"

The old woman gave a satisfied nod and handed him the key. He opened the door and bolted up the stairs, leaving her on the front steps reviling the super, the landlord, the city, and the President of the United States for every insect, arachnid, and woodland creature she claimed was living in the walls of her apartment.

"Deer," she shouted after Alvin, "I got a deer living under my sink.

An eight-point buck you can hang your laundry on!"

Up on the fifth floor, Alvin knelt down at Solomon's door and went to work on the lock cylinder, chewing his tongue as he worked the pins and twisted on the plug.

The elevator door opened and the super stepped out, pushing a vacuum cleaner.

"Hey!" he shouted, pulling a heavy flashlight out of his tool belt.

"I'm glad you're here. You can open the door."

"How'd you get in?"

"I'm the exterminator." Alvin pointed to the logo on his jumpsuit.

"You're not the regular guy."

"I'm the emergency guy." He pointed to his name tag. "Ringo. Right? Like Ringo Starr?"

"Who?"

"The Beatles?"

"Ain't no bugs here. We keep it clean."

"Got an emergency call for this apartment. Guy sounded desperate."

"Where's your spray tank?"

Alvin held up the can of bug spray, giving it a shake.

"Sounds empty."

"It's an extremely dense super bug killer."

"I'm gonna call the office. They didn't tell me anything about an emergency."

"Come on, man!" Alvin plastered himself into the door frame, his back against the door. "The guy could be dying in there, fighting off cockroaches with his bare hands!" Alvin gave the door a quick kick with his heel.

"You hear that? They've got him on the floor! A guy that old can't hold out much longer!" He drummed the door with his heel again. As the super put his ear to the door, Alvin covered his mouth. "Help me, help me!" The super looked up at Alvin. "That's totally him, man! Quick! Before it's too late!"

The super pulled out his keys and opened the door.

Alvin slipped through and the super made to follow, but Alvin blocked him.

"I'd let you watch, but this stuff is very dangerous. One whiff makes you puke up your appendix."

"I've had worse." The super continued pushing.

"It makes your hair fall out." Alvin pushed harder against the door, then added, "It makes you sterile!"

The super stopped pushing and leaned back.

"I couldn't have that on my conscience." Alvin pulled a paper dust mask from his pocket, holding it over his face. "For your own safety and the future of all your little superintendents." Alvin pushed the door closed and bolted it.

The super inhaled deeply, held his breath, and leaned his ear against the door.

Inside, Alvin upended furniture, pulled down curtains, dragged out drawers and dropped them to the floor, all the while incanting, "I want to live forever!" and shouting, "Ah-ha! Got you! Take that! Thought you could hide from me!" And hissing, doing his best impersonation of a weaponized aerosol can of bug spray.

The super, listening at the door, flinched at each new crash, bang, and crunch.

"Look out, sir!" shouted Alvin, his voice muffled behind the locked door, "he's behind you."

Marisol parked Solomon in an isolation room. She laid a hospital gown on the examination table and put out a plastic tray.

"Gown ties in the back," she said. "Put any metal objects in the tray, so they don't interfere with the x-rays. I'll come back when you're done." Then she left, pulling the door shut behind her.

The room was rather spare, having a rolling chair, examination table, a cabinet of drawers and doors, all of which were locked, and a sink with a tall, narrow tube of a faucet. There was a framed print on the wall—flowers of some kind—and instructions to the room's occupants to mind their valuables.

Solomon tried the door. It wasn't locked.

He eased it open. Marisol stood talking to a police officer. She noticed Solomon in the doorway.

"Mr. Martin, you have to get changed so we can examine you. Do you need me to get you some help?"

A super-sized orderly in the same kind of light blue pajamas stepped into view. Wrestling him was out of the question, so Solomon closed the door.

He left his rags on the cabinet and slid into the gown, knotting the ties. It was a shameful travesty of a garment, which did nothing to cover his bare backside. But it might make him less conspicuous than the tatters he had been wearing. The cool breeze on his buttocks unnerved him.

"On you," said Griffin, "that actually looks good."

Solomon whirled around, trying to clutch the flaps closed over his backside.

"Get me out of here."

"And how do you propose I do that? There's a police officer on the other side."

"Whatever it was you did to me when you dragged me off to goldang Russia. Cloud their minds. Change into a polecat or skunk or something. You got all kinds of tricks you could use."

"I know, why not hang a neon sign over your head and say 'Here I am, last piece of Lucifer's armor, come get me! End of the world, right here, fresh for the taking!' "

"What's the big deal? You didn't think of that when you dragged me off before?"

"That was yesterday, before they got the scent of you. Before Shortwick had his proof. Before your media sensation of an accident with bread products flying everywhere. The hordes are gathering even as we speak. You can feel the great leathery wings beating up their hellacious tattoo—"

Solomon crossed his arms and cocked his head, squinting, one-eyed at Griffin.

"Is any of that the least bit true?"

"Which part was the most convincing?"

"None of it."

"None of it? Not even the part about the leathery wings beating up their hellacious tattoo?"

"No."

Griffin did a whip-dance of frustration, then flopped over at the waist. He rose up and breathed hard.

"Okay, some of it wasn't. But they do have your scent now. And it's nothing to do with personal hygiene. Pulling a mudfoot like you through the inter-dimensional realm leaves a terrible wake—like jet skis in a bird bath. Hard to miss. Now they have your scent. Any more supernatural interference will just draw attention to you."

"More malarky." Solomon wished he had a chaw of tobacco he could spit with, just to make his point.

"Hey! I'm the one who wants you to hang on to that doo-hickey as you call it. They find you, they find it, and we're both up Schlitz Creek without a beer stein. Or however you say it." Griffin looked around. "Speaking of which—where is it?"

"I got no idea. I was otherwise occupied with the front end of a moving bus!"

"You don't have it?"

"What did I just say?"

"We have to find it. The effective range of those pieces is greater inside the constraints of the time-space continuum. But—it's not limitless."

"How far's it reach?"

"I don't know. It's not like they've ever been tested."

"Now's a fine time to tell me."

"Aw, come on, Solly!"

There was a quick, brisk knock on the door, and a smallish young woman in those same light blue pajamas popped in.

"Hi, Mr. Martin." She consulted a sheet on a gray metal clipboard. "I'm Angie, the P.A., and I'm going to check your vitals before the doctor sees you. Let's start with your blood pressure."

Angie pulled the blood pressure cuff from its wall mount, wrapped it around Solomon's upper arm and squeezed the bulb to inflate the cuff, putting the chest piece of her stethoscope in the crook of Solomon's elbow.

"What's that supposed to do?"

Angie frowned, squeezing the bulb harder, moving the chest piece around over his veins.

"It's *supposed* to cut off circulation so we can measure how strong your pulse is." Angie squeezed the bulb until it just would not squeeze anymore. "Hunh."

"You seem a might perplexed."

She unwrapped the cuff. "I'll have to find another cuff. This one isn't working, so we'll get a bitsy bit of blood instead. Don't worry. It won't hurt. Just a little pinch. Hold out your finger."

Griffin and Solomon looked at each other.

Solomon stretched out his hand and Angie reached for it, holding the sharp stylus at the ready.

Then Solomon swooped his hand, a bird in flight, making whooshing sounds as he transcribed arcs with his hand.

"Mr. Martin," said Angie. "It won't hurt. I promise."

Solomon put all of his fingers in his mouth.

Angie went and opened the door, calling out, "Phil, could you give me a hand here?"

Phil, the mountainous orderly, stepped into the room.

"He's still delirious. Would you stabilize his hand for me?"

Phil, with amazing gentleness, took hold of Solomon's hands to pluck them from his jaws.

Solomon bit down on his fingers, determined to hold on, with Phil pulling on Solomon's hands, working back and forth. Solomon was a growling terrier unwilling to give up the frisbee.

"Mr. Martin, you're going to hurt yourself. Let go," said Angie.

Phil gave another shake of Solomon's head, tugging, unable to dislodge the digits.

"Forget it. We'll take him over to x-ray. Maybe he'll settle down by then," said Angie. "Come on, Mr. Martin. We'll do x-rays first instead, okay? Phil, you get the other arm."

Together they interlocked arms with Solomon and led him out of the examination room, past the cop and off down the corridor.

Despite her size, Angie managed to keep Solomon walking on his tippy-toes without any good traction to break free and run.

Griffin tagged along, whistling *Bogie's March*.

The super leaned back from the door of Solomon's apartment, took a quick sip of good air, and leaned in again. There was a final hard thump against the door which made the super flinch away.

Inside, Alvin slumped against the front door, his legs stretched out in front of him, spent.

"It's not here." Alvin surveyed the shambles he'd made of the place. "It's not here!" He slapped the floor. "It's got to be something on him."

Alvin struggled to his feet, unbolted the door, flinging it open. The super looked in on the destruction.

"What the hell?"

"It's all your fault, you know. If you'd called us sooner, they'd never have gotten to be so big. I'm sending my report to the Environmental Protection Agency and the Department of Agriculture. You know what you had in there? A mutant strain of super-cockroaches. They were huge! You'll be lucky if they only give you twenty years for negligence."

"Me?"

"I could've been killed."

"The guy never said anything to me."

"All right, all right," said Alvin, giving the agitated super his most patient and long-suffering sigh. "I'll let it go. Just this once. But when I come back, I better not find any more like that in there."

"Sure, man, sure. Thanks, man."

"Use this." Alvin slapped the empty can into the super's hand. "Just don't inhale. I'll be back."

Alvin dodged around the super and ran down the stairs, leaving him holding his breath and keeping the spray can at arm's length.

In the low light of the x-ray room, Solomon stood between the x-ray unit and the cold metal plate fastened to the wall, his hands on his hips, shoulders pressed forward.

The radiologist adjusted the projector against Solomon's back.

Griffin stood in the corner, his fingers in his ears.

"What're you doing?" Solomon asked Griffin.

"Just a precaution," said Griffin.

"I'm lining up so we can take a picture of your chest," said the radiologist.

"Just what do you expect's going to happen?" asked Solomon.

"Worse case, the beams get through, get trapped behind the armor field, bounce around inside you and cook your innards," said Griffin. "Which could be delicious. I'm just saying."

"I expect to take a picture of your skeletal structure and see if there's anything cracked or broken," said the radiologist.

"You don't think it'll cook my insides, really, do you?" asked Solomon.

"Beats the pants off of me," said Griffin.

"No, but you have to hold still."

The radiologist stepped behind a panel, to a control board, and peeked through the small square of glass set in the panel.

"Now hold reeeeal still." A soft hum started.

Solomon squeezed his eyes shut. Griffin kept his ears plugged and only closed one-eye, keeping watch with the other for what might happen to Solomon next.

"You can relax," said the radiologist, snapping off the machine.

Solomon exhaled, looking relieved. Griffin exhaled, looking disappointed.

"Now, let's do the front," said the radiologist.

Chapter Forty-Four

MARJORIE STEPPED UP to the emergency room's check-in desk.

"Is Skeeter Martin here?" she asked the guard on duty

The guard did a quick scan of her computer screen. "Yes. Are you family?"

"No. A friend. A close friend. A very close friend."

"Okay. They're still examining him. You can wait out here."

"I need to see him. To give him something."

"I can have someone take it back for you."

"I need to give it to him personally."

"Then have a seat until they can finish with him."

"She's with me," said a voice from behind. It was Lighter. "Mr. Martin's the one got hit by the bus." He nodded toward Marjorie. "She's part of the investigation."

"Isolation three, down and to the left." The guard pointed off to her left.

Lighter led Marjorie down the corridor past the open examination bays, weaving through the flow of medicos, patients, and orderlies.

"I guess you were right," said Lighter.

"About what?"

"It was bad luck to see the bride the day before the wedding." Lighter smiled, but Marjorie didn't.

"I don't know what Skeeter thought he was going to do."

"It's funny. They can't find a mark on him. Did the bus actually hit him?"

Marjorie stopped.

"Uh, I saw the whole thing, okay?"

"I'm just saying, a guy gets hit by a bus, there should be some kind of damage. Doesn't that seem odd to you?"

"Now the old lady needs her eyes examined?"

"You being an eye-witness sure is convenient. Pretty helpful if they are planning to sue the City."

"Maybe he should."

"I'm still checking, but there's no record of him anywhere. He's liv-ing off the grid. He pays the few bills he has either with cash or with money orders."

"Maybe he's in some kind of witness protection program. You stop to think about that?"

"I did. If he were, there'd be something somewhere saying who he was, even if it was fake."

"What do you have against Skeeter?"

"I don't want to see you get used by a couple of con men."

"I've known Skeeter since I was little."

"Which would make you the perfect choice to vouch for him."

"Stop being a cop all the time." Marjorie flung up her hands and headed on down the corridor, alone.

"I—uh—like what you did with your hair," Lighter called after her. "It's different?"

Back in the examination room for more waiting, Solomon tried the cabinets, looking for anything he could use to escape.

The knock on the door caused him to jack-knife erect and turn to face the door, holding the gaping garment closed behind him.

The door opened and Marisol let Marjorie in.

Solomon sighed. "I'm glad it's you."

"Skeeter—I wasn't going to meet him. I was trying to get a head start. You could've been killed."

"I'm a tough old bird."

Marjorie held out the artifact, dangling on its lanyard.

"Did you drop this?"

Something in the way Marjorie asked made Solomon hesitate reaching for it.

"That guy with the ponytail kept asking if you had it. Is what he said about the old lady true?"

Solomon realized he was playing for high stakes, with no idea of the game, the ante, or what was already on the table.

"You say anything special or feel anything peculiar when you picked it up?" asked Solomon.

"No. Why?"

"Nothing. No reason."

"Who is he? The guy with the ponytail? How does he know about me? What does he want with you?" She held up the artifact. "And what's with this thing?"

Solomon hoped his face showed more surprised ignorance than sheepish guilt.

"Is he someone from the old days? Is Skeeter Martin your real name? Are you—are you in some kind of witness protection program?"

Solomon still hadn't taken the artifact from her. She went over to drop it in the little plastic tray with his other personal effects.

"It would explain why no one knows anything about you," she started, then stopped. She spotted Solomon's locket and picked it up. She popped it open, seeing the tiny portrait of Solomon. She lifted her own locket from inside her blouse, and opened it, holding them side by side for a long moment.

She turned the two portraits to show Solomon.

"That's you, isn't it? Next to Abigail."

Solomon had been otherwise occupied, working on a plausible explanation for him having a locket just like hers, and he was sure it would be a mighty fine one, given the circumstances, but Marjorie's mention of Abigail tripped him up. It was Abigail's likeness there in Marjorie's locket that brought him to a dead stop.

"That's not Lavinia," said Solomon.

"Ohmygod, it's you! You're Abigail's lover. You're the one!"

"*Lavinia*," said Solomon. "I'm Lavinia's rightful suitor."

"You took poor Abigail, went to sea, and came back to haunt us for what you'd done." Marjorie turned and yanked open the door of the examination room, bolting down the corridor.

Lighter startled as the door banged open, then took out after Marjorie. Solomon started to chase after her, but Marisol blocked the way.

"Everything all right in here?" asked Marisol.

"I have to talk to that young lady who just left here."

"Once we finish examining you."

The other police officer stepped up behind Marisol.

"I promise you, we're being as quick as we can." Marisol pulled the door closed.

Marjorie dashed past the check-in desk, through the waiting area, and out the door into the street.

Lighter followed her as far as the street, but lost sight of her.

"Maybe I *should* find a new line of work." Lighter turned and went back into the hospital.

◆ ◆ ◆

Alvin popped up from behind the white van parked illegally just down from the entrance of the emergency room.

He'd just about made it to the front door when he saw Marjorie dashing at him, followed by the cop, forcing him to turn tail and hide behind his van.

Marjorie ran downtown, disappearing from view almost immediately. The cop gave up and went back inside.

Again, Alvin headed for the emergency room entrance.

He wore a painter's hooded overalls made of paper that he'd fashioned into a hazmat suit with a radiation symbol on the back done up with color markers. He wore black framed glasses with the lenses pushed out, a pair of clear safety goggles pushed up on his head, a paper dust mask over his nose and mouth, rubber dish washing gloves, and his utility belt buckled around his waist. He carried a clipboard and flashlight.

He'd pushed through the front door, but immediately pushed out again when he saw Lighter still standing at the check-in desk talking to the receiving nurse.

"How'd they get it so wrong? Why's Abigail got her picture in Marjorie's locket?" Solomon was shouting.

Solomon stalked around the tiny space, Griffin perched on the exam table, his legs drawn up out of Solomon's way.

"What was Abigail telling them all that time I was lost at sea? How'd it get so twisted up down through the years? I said it was a mistake me thinking Lavinia would let anything happen the night I snuck into her room. Didn't I say that?"

Marisol opened the door. "Keep it down Mr. Martin, I know it may feel like it, but you don't have the hospital all to yourself."

Solomon scowled at her, but kept his tongue, mad and embarrassed all at once.

Marisol closed the door.

Solomon turned his scowl on Griffin.

"There anything you been leaving out all these years?"

"The past is so overrated."

"There's something not right. I want to know what it is. If you don't spill it, I'm going to let them try to stick me. Then we'll see what a stink gets made."

"Who needs all that *agita*? There's nothing you can do about it now."

Solomon went to the door and grabbed the handle.

"Okayokayokay!"

Solomon let go of the door handle, still giving Griffin the eyeball.

"Have a seat. You may want to get comfortable for this."

Solomon sat in the chair, arms crossed, unwilling to relax on Griffin's say so.

Griffin hopped down and squatted next to Solomon, took his earlobe and leaned in. Solomon flinched away, elbow at the ready.

"You can tell me to my face."

"I'm going to refresh your recollection. I'll need to whisper it straight into your ear."

"Say it right out."

"It doesn't work that way. I have to get through to the basal ganglia to plant it deep enough so it becomes part of you, triggers every sense, every memory, every conjecture. I have to use my own language. A bit like a master key unlocking all the parts of your brain."

That gave Solomon a chill that ran all the way down the back of his legs.

"I don't cotton to having your teeth anywhere near my neck. I recall just fine your amigos back in St. Petersburg."

"Oh, come on, Solly. You never looked the least bit appetizing to me."

"All the same."

"You said you want to know. But I'm happy to leave you in your ignorance."

"Damn." But Solomon held still while Griffin leaned his mouth in close to Solomon's ear and whispered, a slushing, rhythmic, windless sound that did seem to swirl about as it flowed into his ear canal and pierce somewhere deep inside him.

Hudson River Valley – 1830s

Solomon stood outside at the back of Kantlingher House, watching.

Lavinia and Edwin were in the main parlor and Luther was up in his room, the lamps still burning.

Solomon planned to wait until Edwin left and Lavinia had retired for the night. He would scale the drainpipe, climb in at her window, and prove with so daring an act, risking discovery in her most sacred sanctum by her gun-toting father, the depth of his devotion to her.

But Edwin seemed like he'd pitched camp there in the parlor and would never leave.

Solomon had paced, kicked dirt clods, carved on the tree, played mumblety-peg, and tried whistling.

Finally, he decided not to wait for Edwin to leave. Instead, he slithered on up the drainpipe to wait for Lavinia in her room.

Once inside Lavinia's room, Solomon inhaled the fragrance and looked around, poking at this and handling that, then sat in the chair at her small mahogany secretary.

The squeak of the wooden seat seemed unnaturally loud in the quiet of a big house settling down for the night.

Lavinia's door flew open and Abigail stood there in her night dress and cap, holding an oil lamp high, shining on Solomon. Abigail inhaled as if to give out with a shout.

He bolted up out of the chair, grabbed Abigail around the waist, putting his hand to her mouth.

"Please, your daddy'll shoot me right between the eyes. You don't want to see that, do you?"

Abigail, eyes on Solomon, her mouth covered, nodded.

"Won't that give you terrible nightmares?"

Abigail, eyes on Solomon, her mouth covered, shook her head.

Solomon would've liked nothing better than flinging Abigail out the window and then go back to waiting for Lavinia. But there was something in Abigail's eyes as she fixed on Solomon. With her mouth covered up that way, Solomon somehow saw into Abigail's eyes differently. Missing was the twisty snarl she often gave him. Just for now, it was only her eyes with a deep longing that wouldn't have been as noticeable as it would have seemed had it been perched over a slight pinched corner of her lip.

"You are a cold-hearted daughter of Eve." Solomon eased his hand off her mouth. "If you aim to scream, get on with it. I guess I have it coming."

But she didn't.

"If daddy finds you here and shoots you, they'll make Lavinia sleep in my bed with me until they sponge your brains off her walls. We haven't slept under the same covers since we left the nursery. I'd like to keep it that way."

"I've always appreciated how practical you are, Abigail."

There was a flicker in Abigail's eye at the sound of her name on Solomon's lips.

"I wouldn't get a wink of sleep, all her visitors like you creeping in through the night."

"Who else is there?"

"Shhhh! Come on." Abigail took him by the hand. "You'll leave by the hall window in case anyone else is down there waiting, so they don't see your sorry carcass coming out of Lavinia's bedroom window." She gave a tug, but he held off. "You can't wait in here. Daddy always comes in to say good-night to each of us once we've gone to bed. He'll find you."

Solomon let her lead him out of Lavinia's bedroom, out to the back window at the end of the hallway.

Abigail stopped suddenly, then pushed back against Solomon.

"Oh, no! Another one."

"Who?" Solomon demanded.

"Another chucklehead like you." She pulled him back toward the door opposite Lavinia's room. "Quick! In my room. Daddy's already said his good-nights to me. He won't come in here."

She dragged him across to her bed and shoved him down onto the floor, out of view. He leaned his back against the frame, cushioned by the quilted comforter over the ticking.

It was a strange and comfortable smell of lavender and clean wool and sprigs of cinnamon of the potpourri wafting through the room, the fragrance blown by the breeze over a dish under the window.

"I'll be back and sneak you out of here."

"Why're you doing this?"

"I told you, I don't want—"

"—my brains all over Lavinia's walls. I appreciate your good heart."

Abigail left, taking the lamp with her.

Sitting in the dark, Solomon listened to the noises of the house, the voices from the parlor drifting up the stairs, the laughter. Lavinia's chirping goldfinch titter, Edwin's scraping goose honk.

The floorboards squeaked as the door opened again. Abigail flopped full-length onto the bed, her head close by Solomon's. She reached out an arm, holding a jug in her hand.

"Here. Entertain yourself with that."

"What's going on?"

"I have to save another sinner who's gotten himself lost in Lavinia's bedroom."

"Who?"

"You name them, they've been here. Might as well be a parade. Regular as clockwork." She pushed herself off the bed and slipped out the door.

Solomon, in spite of himself, began to doubt the firmness of Lavinia's affections for him.

He bit the cork out of the jug, spit it hard across the room and took a long swig, glad to drown his misgivings.

The floorboards continued their slow, rhythmic creaking, a sentinel walking his post.

It didn't take more than a half-dozen pulls on the jug before Solomon was singing a sad old ballad to himself.

Abigail flopped across the bed once more. When Solomon kept on singing, not looking around, Abigail just watched him. She reached out, a bit shaky, and touched his hair.

It stirred Solomon out of the reverie in which he'd lost himself.

"I must say, Miss Kantlingher, you are a mighty generous hostess." Solomon patted the jug.

"Shhhhh!"

"But, I would hate to overstay my welcome—oh, there's that song again. I wish I had my concertina."

Solomon got to his feet, unsteady, grabbing a bedpost to catch his balance.

"The weather's turned, mates. Rig lifelines and reef the main sail. We're in for a mighty blow."

Solomon leaned back, shading his eyes, and called out, "Mind the stays!" He looked at Abigail. "Can't even see the cross-trees in this gloom. Nothing for it but to shinny up." Solomon shucked his outer jacket, pushed up his sleeves, and then pitched headlong across Abigail's bed, completely out. Snoring, he lay with his head twisted to the side, his hind-end peaked upward by the incline of the bed ropes.

"Nooooo, no, no, you can't sleep here!" She hooked Solomon under his arm to wrestle him back onto his feet. "Come on." Unable to get leverage, she dropped his arm and then grabbed his ankles, thinking to drag him off her bed, but the mechanics of that was plain enough. He'd hit the floor chin first.

She pushed to roll Solomon over onto his back so he'd land butt first when she dragged him off the bed.

She got between his legs, hooked an arm under each knee, and pulled. He landed with a thump, sat erect for a moment, eyes opened, then they closed again, and he keeled over onto his side.

"Nonononononono!" Abigail squatted down across his lap, a foot on either side of him, getting her arms under his and lifting him back to a sitting position.

She didn't let go of him right away, his sleeping breath powerful on her neck.

It was enough to change her mind.

"I can't very well have you dying of exposure out in the cold."

Steadying him with one hand, she stood up and threw back the covers of her bed.

There was probably a twinge of good sense that called on her to stand back, have a good look at what she was doing, and consider the consequences. But she was long past thinking all that straight. She was in the grip of a powerful urge even she couldn't name. It dictated to her that it was nothing but common courtesy for her to undress Solomon and not leave him to sleep in his clothes like a common laborer.

Abigail squatted down and wrapped her arms around Solomon once more. She heaved up and got him onto the bed, again steadying him long enough to unbutton his shirt and slip it off him. Then she undid the buttons on the top of his longjohns and pushed them back off his shoulders, her hands stroking along the tight muscles of his chest.

She let go of him and he flopped backward.

Then flexing her fingers with the delicacy of a pickpocket, Abigail undid Solomon's belt and fly buttons and removed his trousers. Merely a precaution against him leaving any mud or silt from the harbor on her nice clean sheets.

She tugged off his trousers, then folded them up and set them on the chair by the bed, where he could find them in the morning.

Reaching under him, she rolled him onto his side so she could work his longjohns down over his hips and legs.

It was only after she got his longjohns off over his feet that she realized he wasn't wearing undershorts.

Solomon flopped onto his back and Abigail recoiled with a squeal, snake-bit, a mongoose dancing backward from a cobra's strike.

Abigail was certainly no stranger to the paintings of Michelangelo or the figures on Greek vases, but this was a revelation, a first in true flesh.

Abigail inched closer. She'd have bet money Solomon was a much smaller fella.

Keeping her fingers flexed back and stiff, using only the heels of her palms, she pushed on Solomon, shoving him to the middle of her bed, and then swept the covers over him. She exhaled deeply, relieved.

She came around the bed and took her robe from the hook by the bed and would have slipped into it and gone to the guest room, leaving him there, but Solomon gave out with a throaty whimper—the softest, sweetest, manliest sound Abigail ever heard. Solomon reached across the bed, his hand out, fingers stretched, feeling for something.

Abigail stretched to drop the robe on the chair behind her, never taking her eyes off Solomon. She missed the chair and the robe hit the floor. She didn't seem to notice.

She pulled off her nightcap shook her hair loose, and slipped out of her night dress. She would only stay long enough to warm the covers for him. He was dead to the world. He'd never notice. Then she'd leave.

She eased herself down onto the bed. She lifted the comforter, drew up her legs and slid under, alongside Solomon, the depression of the bed ropes rolling her up against him.

His eyelids flickered, the lashes seeming to brush Abigail's face, but he didn't open his eyes. His arm lifted and draped over her and she reached out to touch his hair. The warmth of their bodies on the cool of the bedclothes was a marvel to her.

There was still plenty of time before sunup. She would without fail pour him out the window in the morning.

New York City – Present Day

That fresh recollection melded with the one clear memory Solomon had started with—waking up on the roof over the back porch of Kantlingher House.

"That is a damn lie from start to finish." Solomon popped up out of the chair.

"You didn't sneak into Lavinia's bedroom?"

"Yes, but—"

"Abigail didn't hide you in her own room?"

"Yes, but—"

"She didn't give you a jug to keep you occupied?"

"Yes, but—"

"You didn't wake up on the porch roof, naked as a jaybird, outside Abigail's room, your clothes piled on top of you?"

"Yes, but—"

"You didn't have the dogs set on you at first light by Luther and the stable hands?"

"Yes, but the rest of it's a lie!"

"I'm just reminding you what happened."

"There's no way I could know what happened if I was dead drunk. There's no way I could know what her intentions were if I was dead drunk."

"Of course not. That's why I'm telling you. I knew what happened. I knew what she was thinking."

"No way in God's green earth."

"I was there."

"No, sir. I didn't meet up with you and get your damned doo-hickey until after that."

"That kind of mischief among you mudfoots is pretty hard to miss."

"You just happened to be there in the middle of the night when she accidentally got me drunk and took my clothes and left me naked on the roof?"

"No, I didn't just happen to be there in the middle of the night."

"Aha! I thought so."

"I made sure I was there. I gave her the idea. Why do you think I knew you'd likely die the night of Lavinia and Edwin's elopement? Luther was fed up with you. Everything was falling into place, until you decided you wanted to live forever."

Solomon inhaled deep and hard. "Damn your miserable hide to hell!" Solomon danced around, leaping and stomping, determined to penetrate the earth's crust so it could swallow them both.

"Hey! Solly!" Griffin gave himself both thumbs. "Been there, done that, and got the bacterial infection!"

Chapter Forty-Five

SOLOMON CONTINUED HIS TIRADE, storming around the tiny confines of the space.

"Bad enough I'm lied on by a wily female determined to stand in the way of true love, I got one of hell's very own filling her head with ideas!"

"Solly—"

"Don't you dare 'Solly' me." Solomon pointed at Griffin, arm stiff, finger shaking. "Abigail is a sneaking, conniving, underhanded, sneaking—"

"You already said she was sneaking," said Griffin, keeping count on his fingers.

"I know what I said." Solomon went back to pacing. "Abigail may be all of that, but there's no way she'd show herself naked to any man out of wedlock. No way."

"Yes way."

"That was all entirely made up by you."

"Okay. How do *you* remember it?"

"I—don't."

"You never wondered how it was you ended up naked on the roof? If not Abigail? Who else might it have been? Lavinia? Esther? Luther? You?"

"I never gave it much thought—I was being chased by dogs, if you recall."

"It never crossed your mind someone had to remove your clothes without you remembering? It just seemed a natural thing for you to wake up naked outside Abigail's window? The typical expression of the old Solomon Durnley charm?"

Solomon snapped his fingers. "You forgot the houseman. Maybe it was him, teaching me a lesson. Shaming me for breaking into the house."

"Well, it wasn't."

"Abigail may be devious, spiteful, and malicious, but she's no wanton."

"She may have had other reasons for such a thing, did you think of that?"

But Solomon wasn't listening to Griffin. "Now I've *got* to get back and straighten them all out."

"What do you care what they think? Have yourself a long, unnatural life. Be happy. Every single one of them have gone to dust a long time ago."

"That'd fit your pistol just fine, wouldn't it. One day they'll stand before the Almighty and tell that same cockamamie story. How do you think it'll go for me when it's my turn to speak and all I can say is I was too drunk to remember? Nossireebob! I'm getting back there one way or another. And I'm going to start by squaring things with little Marjorie."

Griffin didn't say anything. Solomon gave a quick bob of his head, satisfied he'd bested Griffin. Then he brightened.

"I can tell her the whole story. And once I'm back with Lavinia, I'll be out of their hair for good. I'll never bother them again."

"Marjorie's probably half-way to Texas by now."

"Then I'll go to Texas." Solomon yanked open the door. The police officer at the nurse's station straightened up, watching him. Solomon closed the door. "As soon as I get out of here."

"Solly, I just have to stop and say, apropos of nothing at all, mind you, the mudfoot's capacity for self-deception is truly breathtaking."

"Help me get shed of this place, or I haul myself out there and give them all a good gander at the amazing immortalman. We'll see how long it takes for your drooling amigos to get wind of me."

"Self-deception *and* self-destruction in one handy package." Griffin didn't move from where he sat. "I should let my amigos take turns gnawing on you just to teach you a lesson."

Solomon reached for the door handle.

"Okay okay okay. I'm working on it. Give me time to think, would you?" Griffin pulled the door open, already transforming into a hospital orderly wearing those same light blue pajamas.

The door stood ajar, no officer in sight. Solomon edged toward the door, just as the officer reached in and pulled the door shut.

Outside, Alvin plastered himself against the glass of the emergency room entrance watching for Lighter to leave.

When Lighter finally walked away, Alvin pushed through the entry doors, put his head down and did an arm-swinging quick-march right past the receiving nurse.

Straight into Marisol, bouncing off.

He tried a dance step to the right, then to the left, but there was no getting by her. She raised her arm and pointed back to the check-in desk.

Alvin walked backward, keeping an eye on her for any chance of daylight between her and the walls. Anything to let him slip by. But she seemed able to clog the corridor all by herself.

Alvin turned to the receiving nurse and lifted his clipboard.

"I'm from radiation repair. I have to do a tune-up on the x-ray machine."

"Your ID?"

"My, uh, name badge is on under my suit. I unzip and this place'll be flooded with all the radiation I've been walking around in today."

"I need to see some ID."

"Hey, I do that and this place becomes a nuclear hot spot."

"I'll call someone to help you." The nurse picked up the phone.

"Here. Let me." Alvin took the receiver from her, reached over and pushed about a dozen buttons then held the phone to his ear, listening and waiting.

He twisted the mouthpiece away from his mouth. "They need to know I'm not responsible if you don't let me in to get a look at it." Then he raised the mouthpiece. "Yes, it's me, uh, George. Could you put him on?" Alvin gave the nurse a dangerous widening of his eyes so she'd know how much trouble she'd caused herself.

He twisted the mouthpiece away again. "You'll be singing a different tune when it breaks down completely and cooks the liver of your next simple fracture case. Then you'll have a monster lawsuit on your hands, the kind they write about in the Times, and I'll just sit there reading about it, enjoying my morning coffee, saying, 'I told 'em so.'" Then he lifted the mouthpiece. "Yes. It's, uh, George. I'm here. And they're not letting me in." He listened for a minute, again with the wide, dangerous eyes at the nurse, then back to the phone. "I don't want to get her in trouble, but—"

The nurse reached up to take the handset away from Alvin. He jerked away. "You may have to send security," he said into the mouthpiece.

A hospital cop, all muscle and no neck, turned up at the desk.

"Whatcha got for me?"

"Patient's trying to use the intercom like it's an outside line. Talking to Mars, most likely." She grabbed the handset back from Alvin.

"There you are," said the hospital cop to Alvin. "We've been looking all over for you." The hospital cop gave the receiving nurse a wink.

"He slipped out before doc could finish his profile."

The nurse smiled at the hospital cop who had the kind of eyes, a deep silver-blue, that a married woman might risk getting lost in.

"Come on, buddy." The hospital cop hooked Alvin by the elbow and jacked his shoulder up to his ear.

"Are you out of your mind? I'm radioactive! Don't touch me!"

"Simmer down. See?" The hospital cop wiggled the fingers of his free hand at Alvin. "No sharp objects." He turned to the nurse. "Thinks he's a balloon."

"No, no. I'm here to fix the x-ray machine." Alvin squirmed in the vise-like grip.

"We'll put him in isolation next to Skeeter Martin our bus accident—" said the hospital cop, "then, do me a favor and page Doc Savage."

"Skeeter Martin?" Alvin stopped struggling.

"Is this character on the census?" The nurse scanned her computer screen. "I'm not seeing him."

"Boy," said Alvin, "it's lucky you found me. I almost floated away."

"We'll get you certified and then settle you in upstairs. Come on."

"Don't let go of me. I'm a balloon. I'll float right out the door and get caught in the trees." Alvin stuck a finger into his mouth and made a loud pop. He smiled at the nurse, filling his cheeks with air, an over-inflated balloon, bobbing along, lighter than air as the hospital cop walked him around the check-in desk and down the corridor.

In Isolation Three, Solomon stood with his ear up against the door, trying to hear anything that would tell him whether the way was clear or not.

Easing down the handle and pulling the door open ever so slightly, Solomon peeked through the slim crack. The cop was gone and the duty nurse had her back to him.

Solomon pushed the door closed, and dressed himself in his tattered clothes, then slipped the gown over top of the outfit. At least it covered up his chest. He reached into the tray for his personal effects. The artifact was no longer there.

Solomon looked around on the floor, behind the examination table, under the chair. Nothing.

He got down on his hands and knees, trying to see under the cabinet back against the wall.

• • •

Outside, in the corridor, the hospital cop gave a nod to the duty nurse as he moved Alvin along, coming to a stop at Isolation Room Four. He tried the handle.

"Locked. Wouldn't you know. I'll have to go get the key. Now you stay right here, understand? No funny stuff. Be a good screwball and don't go anywhere, we'll give you a sucker." The hospital cop disappeared around the corner.

Alvin stood frozen for half a heartbeat, unable to believe his luck. He looked right, then left, then did a discreet sidestep to put himself in front of Isolation Room Three. After another quick glance left and right, he opened the door and slipped in.

Solomon was still on the floor, so Alvin eased the door closed, but the loud click of the latch bolt snapping home made him flinch.

"You sure took your good sweet time about it." Solomon stood up and turned around.

"Where—?" Alvin started, but Solomon flew at him, putting him in a classic headlock before he got the second word out of his mouth.

Solomon hauled Alvin over to where the blood pressure cuff hung in its wall bracket.

With one arm locked around Alvin's head, Solomon used his free hand to wrap the cuff around Alvin's face and pumped it up tight. Alvin's forehead brightened to a cherry red, his eyes bugging out over the edge of the cuff.

"You remember that heart-to-heart I mentioned a while back?" said Solomon.

"Solly?" Griffin appeared over Solomon's shoulder.

"You listen and you listen good." Solomon had Alvin doubled over, locked to his waist.

"Uh, Solly?"

"You find yourself another hobby and leave Marjorie and Willa and all the rest of them gals alone. Or else, so help me, I will squeeze your brains right out the top of your head. You understand?"

Alvin shook his head.

"No, you don't understand, or no, you won't bother them ever again?"

"Solly, I think having that thing wrapped around his face is what's causing your breakdown in communication. If you want my opinion."

Solomon looked at Griffin and then down at Alvin.

Unable to breathe and not much of a puncher in the clinch, Alvin could barely slap at Solomon's back.

"I think he's pretty much used up all the air he had in him, Solly." Alvin sagged to his knees.

"I think that's it for this one. You want me to go fetch somebody else to help you get out of here?"

"You think this chucklehead can get me out of here?"

"Not now."

Against his better judgment, Solomon twisted the valve on the tube and released the pressure, ripping the cuff off Alvin's head.

Alvin's eyes deflated and he sucked in the biggest gulp of air that he might possibly ever had to gasp in his entire life.

Alvin wheezed as he tried to talk. "It's him—isn't it? Here—in the room—somewhere? That angel. He's in here with us, isn't he? That proves you've got it."

"I don't have anything."

Now with the color back in his face, and the object of his desire within reach, Alvin's courage bloomed once more.

"Oh, yes, you do. Look at this." Alvin pushed up the sleeves of his paper overalls, holding out his arms for Solomon to see.

"Nothing. Nothing, you see? Un-hunh, un-hunh. Don't try telling me you don't have it. This is all the proof I need. Not a scratch. I jumped into a dumpster full of nails and glass and bricks. And now, nothing. Not one single scratch." Alvin pulled up his pant leg to give Solomon a look at his thigh. "Stabbed myself with your pen, right? Now? Nothing. Must've happened the first time I was there."

Solomon flicked a glance at Griffin, who shrugged.

"News to me," said Griffin.

"I tore your place apart, but it's not there. So—you must have it on you."

"How'm I supposed to know what it is you want, if you can't even describe it?"

"I don't need to describe it. I'll know it when I see it." Alvin went for the tray of Solomon's personal effects, pawing through them, coming up empty.

"Not here," Alvin turned to face Solomon. "You're wearing it."

"All I got left is rags and no pockets to hide anything, thanks to you. But—you get me out of here and I'll take you where it is."

"I get you out of here and you're gone. No way. But I've got a good idea where to look next. That chick's place. That Kantlingher chick? I knew I should've torn her place apart while I was at it." Alvin turned for the door.

"There's no way you'll find it if you don't get me out of here."

"I can't make you tell me. But that Kantlingher chick—she can't live forever like you." Alvin pulled a pair of pliers out of his tool belt. "So, you tell me, or I make her tell me."

"She makes me no nevermind now."

"Oh, come on!" Alvin flung himself in a whipsnap of irritation. "Every record of you I find, there's a Kantlingher somewhere nearby. She's got to mean something."

"This knucklehead is useless," said Solomon to Griffin. "I'm finding my own way out."

Alvin slapped himself against the door, arms out.

Solomon stepped back. "Okay, fine. We'll wait for the doctor."

"Let's just do that. You know what'll happen, smart guy?"

"They'll bend a few needles on my hide, then lock me away to find out what makes me tick?"

"That's right, mister smarty-pants. Then your secret will be out, then—" The realization hit him. "No! They can't do that!"

Alvin grabbed Solomon by the wrist and dragged him to the door.

"We've got to get you out of here."

Chapter Forty-Six

ALVIN YANKED OPEN THE DOOR, surprising the doctor standing on the other side, studying an open file folder.

"Ah, Mr. Martin," said the doctor.

Alvin, out of view behind the open door, hunkered down and pulled the dust mask up over his face.

"I'm Dr. Campbell." He stepped into the room, followed by Angie. Phil, the humongous orderly, stood just outside the door.

"I have to say, you really are a spry guy, for someone who was hit by a bus."

"It's my high fiber diet, doctor. That it for the questions? Can I go?"

"This is a hit-and-run, Mr. Martin. I have to do a bunch of tests, check for spinal damage, broken bones, stuff like that. After I give the all-clear, the police need to talk to you. Then you can go."

Sensing a presence, Dr. Campbell looked behind the door.

"Hello. What are you doing in here? What's with the mask? Are you contagious?"

"Umm, ummm, ummmmmmm." Alvin couldn't seem to find words to answer this simple question.

"Phil," said Dr. Campbell. The man-mountain ducked his head and made to squeeze himself into the room.

"He's my nephew. He's a little tetched." Solomon tapped his temple and winked at the doctor. "He thinks I got beri-beri when I was in the Pacific. That's why he's done up the way he is. Wears it whenever he visits me."

"So. You're a veteran?" asked Dr. Campbell.

"After a fashion."

Dr. Campbell turned to Angie. "Give the V.A. a call. See if they have anything on file for him." Dr. Campbell flipped open the file folder he'd been holding. "Let's do another series of x-rays. The first set was fogged. And let's take some blood."

Angie unlocked the cabinet and pulled out the syringe tube, vacu-tainers, a packet of fresh needles, rubber tubing, and iodine swabs.

"I hope you're using extra-sharp needles." Solomon kept his eye on Alvin whose lip began to quiver.

"Don't worry." Angie gave Solomon a wink. "I only use the big, square needles on bad boys."

"I don't know. I been told I got a mighty tough hide."

"Okay, hold out your arm." Angie gave the tubing a stretch.

Solomon pushed up his sleeve and lifted his arm.

"Wait!"

Everyone looked at Alvin who bolted across the room, grabbing a handful of specimen cups from the medical cabinet.

"How about we do the hard part first?" said Alvin. "Here." He held out two cups to Solomon.

"What am I supposed to do with these?"

"Pee in them."

"The hell you say."

"We can get that afterwards," said Dr. Campbell.

"The sight of needles makes you dry up. Remember?"

"I ain't got it in me."

"Come on, you're ninety-eight percent water." Alvin pushed the cups at Solomon.

"This won't take but a minute." Angie started to wrap the tubing around Solomon's arm.

Alvin tugged on Solomon's other arm. "Wouldn't you rather go to the bathroom? Out there? Alone?" Alvin gave a jerk of his head in the general direction of freedom. "No doctor? No nurse? No—cops?"

"Oh. Oohhhh. Why didn't you say so? I thought you expected me to do my business here in front of everybody. Lead the way."

Alvin, nodding and smiling, backed out of the door, holding out the cups, like doggie treats, for Solomon to follow.

Solomon did one last glance around the room, still trying to spot the lost artifact.

"Let me know when he's back." Dr. Campbell handed the file to Angie. "And see what the V.A. has to say about him."

Outside, parked curbside, Wood sat in the driver's seat while Lighter leaned against the front fender, folding and re-folding his arms.

"They're not going to find anything," said Lighter. "It's a scam. Ponytail and the old guy are both in on it. Ponytail wrecked the bus and the old guy was hiding under the car."

"The bus hit something that flew through the bread truck and the livery cab."

"A dummy?"

"Something really heavy."

"I don't know? A mailbox? Something."

"Rudy's handling it. He'll make his report and if there's anything funny, the detectives will look into it."

"Ponytail looks squishy. But the old guy, he's one tough character."

"You want to help Rudy play a little good cop, bad cop? That make you feel better?"

"I'd like to play a little bad cop, bad cop."

"You're getting all worked up, and it's because of the girl, right?"

"Why pick on her? What's she got they could possibly want?"

"Maybe she's a European princess. Or a secret heiress, pretending to be a single mom in a run-down apartment."

"With a two-year old?"

"Maybe the kid's rented."

Lighter leaned down to look in on Wood, who smiled from behind her shades.

In the corridor, Alvin dragged Solomon by the wrist toward the exit, but stopped and turned back, flat into Solomon.

"What'n hell're you doing?"

"Cops," whined Alvin. "What's with all the cops!"

Two police officers had a man in handcuffs between them.

Alvin dragged Solomon in the opposite direction, dancing around a janitor's cart parked in the corridor. Around the corner, Marisol and a phalanx of nurses came straight at them.

"What's with all the nurses!" Alvin did a two-step of indecision, pinched between the cops and the nurses.

"In here." Solomon grabbed the janitor's cart and herded Alvin into the restroom.

Inside, Alvin looked around. Three stalls, three sinks, no windows leading outside, and no air vents large enough to climb through. The trash bins were too small to hide in.

"What're we doing in here?"

"You got any bright ideas?"

"Um. No."

"Good thing I got me one." Solomon pushed the cart at Alvin.

"Empty the bag."

"What for?"

"You're gonna ride me out of here in it."

"That's disgusting. You empty the bag."

"If you expect me to do the thinking, you'll do the lifting. Don't stand there eyeballing me. Get to it, before they come looking for us."

Alvin unhooked the bag and held it out. "Where should I empty it?"

"On the floor! We're about to become fugitives. Now is not the time to go all dainty."

Alvin upended the bag and dumped out the contents, scattering paper, wadded napkins, food waste, and sloshing half-filled coffee cups onto the floor.

"Oh, jeez!" Alvin winced as trash splashed over his sandals and between his toes. He kicked out, trying to dislodge the nasty particulates that clung to his skin.

"Gimme that." Solomon took the bag.

"Okay. Now what?"

"Point your head thataway and bend over."

"Okay." Alvin bent over. Just as the thought struck him this might not be a good idea, Solomon scooped the vinyl bag over Alvin's head, encapsulating him in a single swoop, then tugged the bag all the way down to his waist.

Outside by the cruiser, Lighter pushed himself away from the fender. "This is taking forever." Lighter strode toward the entrance.

"No rough stuff, or you'll end up the one on the carpet."

Back in the corridor, Solomon poked his head out of the restroom. Now dressed in Alvin's radiation get-up, with the mask over his mouth and nose, and the goggles down over his eyes, he strolled along the corridor toward the exit.

Lighter came through the waiting area, heading for the check-in desk, spotting Marisol.

"Hey, Marisol. What's taking so long with Mr. Martin? Let me have a minute with him. It'll just be one minute, I promise."

"His nephew's got him in doing a urine sample. He'll be done soon."

"Nephew? I don't think he has a nephew."

"Big guy? Balding? Gray ponytail?"

Lighter dodged around Marisol and ran for the restroom.

Solomon walked over to the waiting area, keeping his head down. He picked up a magazine, stood behind a pillar, and pretended to read.

Once they were both out of sight, Solomon dropped the magazine and left the hospital.

Lighter found Alvin on the restroom floor in his underwear, trapped in the yellow bag cinched down over his head and arms. Alvin whimpered as he kicked, spinning himself around, going nowhere in a great big hurry.

"I know who the bad guy is." Lighter ran back into the corridor, heading for the front.

Solomon walked until he reached Riverside Drive, then headed downtown.

A bus pulled up beside him in the middle of the block. The door squeaked open.

"Need a lift?" Griffin sat at the wheel, wearing mirrored sunglasses, a bus driver's uniform with the sleeves rolled up, and black leather driving gloves.

Solomon climbed aboard. There were no other passengers. Griffin closed the door and pulled back into traffic.

"Where'd you get this thing?"

"They're everywhere. They're a cinch to start, easy to drive, and best of all," Griffin swerved to scatter a pack of bicyclists, "you rule the road. Shortwick had the right idea." Griffin gave a regal wave at the cursing and swearing cyclists.

"I rescued your things from the hospital." Griffin held out a bundle tied up in Solomon's big red handkerchief.

Solomon took the hankie and opened it.

"What about the doo-hickey?"

Griffin handed him a styrofoam clamshell container. Inside was the artifact.

"Sorry about the mayonnaise and pickle parts. It was all I could find to pick it up with. There's no way I'm touching that thing with my bare hands."

"Where was it?"

"I was standing on it. You should have seen me trying to flick it onto the floor with a tongue depressor before Shortwick got there and saw it."

Solomon sat with the open container on his lap, studying the artifact.

"What'd happen to Marjorie and Willa if I did decide to let go and snap backwards?"

Griffin shrugged.

"You don't know or you won't say."

"Like I told you maybe a hundred years ago, it's all about probabilities becoming eventualities."

"They oughta get some kind of second chance."

"Maybe they do and maybe they don't."

"Will they just disappear?"

"You think your soul comes in a soda bottle? All you have to do is pour it back, put a cork in it and wait till next time?"

"I never gave much thought to things like that."

"The Hereafter's going to be a real eye-opener for you, Solly. If you make it that far."

"If I do start over, will all that's happened the first time around count against me?"

"Careful, Solly m'lad, regret leads to repentance, and repentance is as bad as altruism. That thing'll go off in your lap."

"If I was to give up this doo-hickey—what'd happen?"

"I told you. Armageddon. The Crack o' Doom. The End of All Things. The Big Finito. The Fat Lady Finally Sings. You want the gory details?"

"But it wouldn't happen right away, would it, the minute I got back? We all made it this far, didn't we? There might be time, wouldn't there?"

"What are you asking, Solly?" Griffin glanced up at the mirror, looking back at him.

"I'm just wondering if there'd be time for me to—to fix things."

"Ah, got it. You're asking at what point along the space-time continuum it falls apart. Back in the eighteen-thirties or here in the Right Now."

"That's it, that's it."

"Won't matter. To you. You'll be dead. No way you survive getting shot in the heart at point blank range."

"But you keep saying—"

Griffin leaned around to look over his sunglasses at Solomon. "You're kidding, right?"

"I forgot. You're a lying, conniving son-of-a-bitch."

"And if it's one thing you know all about, Solly me boyo, it's lying conniving sons-of-bitches." Griffin steered the bus up over the curb onto the sidewalk, sending a clutch of joggers diving over park benches.

"So there'd be nothing left of me. Nothing to remember."

Griffin sighed hard, steering back onto the street.

"Let me show you." Griffin came back to sit beside Solomon.

"Who'n hell's driving the bus?"

"Don't worry. The thing practically drives itself."

Speeding along, the bus careened from side to side, weaving into oncoming traffic, glancing off parked cars, running up behind the vehicles ahead of it, forcing them onto the sidewalk, sending pedestrians dodging and scampering.

"This is you." Griffin wiggled his fingertip. "And this is you in time." He thrust his finger into an unrolled condom, pushing and stretching the prophylactic open.

Solomon looked at the slick, latex cylinder, then at Griffin.

"I'm using tools you'll understand. Shall I continue? Okay. You're walking along in a corridor that shouldn't exist. People on the outside see and hear you, have a notion of you. But—" Griffin pinched the tip, withdrew his finger, keeping tension on the elastic sleeve, "when you give it up—" He let go, the condom snapping back.

"You'll be an empty spot in everyone's memory, a gap, an odd recollection, a face that can't quite be pictured. A memory that will not be pinned down. And—with so much else going on in the human brain—forgotten. But that's good. For them. Otherwise, the halfway-knowing would drive them crazy. Or crazi-*er*."

"Everything happens just like it did? But I'm not there for any of it?"

"Some yes, some no. Probabilities remain. Some will turn out as before, some will be different, some may never happen." Griffin climb back into the driver's seat. "Look on the bright side. Once you snap back, you'll forget everything that came after. Because it won't be there anymore. That should be a load off your mind. It would be for me."

"I don't like the idea of not knowing." Solomon remained fixed on the artifact in his lap.

"If you hadn't escaped with that thing, you wouldn't know."

"But I do know. I know now." Solomon closed the lid on the artifact. "You sure made a mess of things for me, didn't you?"

"Me? You've had nearly two hundred years you weren't entitled to. I should get some thanks for that." Griffin struck a hot dog cart and sent it spinning, spraying weiners, buns, and soda cans everywhere.

"Fat lot of good it's done."

"Not for you, maybe. But it did a hell of a lot of good for me. And that suits me right down to my tippy-toes. You know, Solly-boy, not having to pretend with you anymore is kind of liberating." Griffin smiled behind his shades as he gave a twist to the wheel and nudged a couple on a tandem bike into a bank of leaves.

It was clear that Griffin was making the most of his time behind the wheel.

Chapter Forty-Seven

GRIFFIN BROUGHT THE BUS TO A STOP with a skillful combination of brakes, steering, and a crunching impact into the rear end of a large, parked SUV.

Griffin opened the curbside door.

"We're here," said Griffin, pulling off his gloves and throwing them in the driver's seat. "Let's grab your stuff and put some serious asphalt between us and all our troubles."

"About time," said the old lady standing at the door, jabbing her Metrocard at him.

"There's a half-a-tank of gas left in it." Griffin stepped down from the bus, hanging the keys on the old lady's pinky.

Solomon and Griffin hot-footed it across Riverside Drive and up to the sidewalk fronting the buildings along the Drive, then headed downtown toward Solomon's block.

As Solomon got closer to his street, he spotted Marjorie hopping out of Gayle's car parked at the corner. It looked like she was heading for their building.

Solomon rounded on Griffin. "You lying stack a flapjacks. You said she was half-way to Texas by now."

"I keep telling you I'm not omniscient."

Solomon ran to catch her, but pivoted hard, flat into Griffin following close behind him.

"Get out the way!" Solomon jigged, ducking down between two of the parked cars.

A police cruiser rolled toward them, made the turn, then parked in front of Solomon's building.

"Dang. Wouldn't you know."

"Oh, well, tough luck. Let's get out here. We can be in New Jersey by lunch. I'm hungry. Are you hungry?"

"You have anything to do with those cops showing up? Never mind.

What's the good asking you anything anymore."

Moving along the line of parked cars, Solomon scuttled toward Gayle, keeping low until he reached the driver's side window. He tapped on the glass and Gayle lowered the window. Willa sat in the back seat.

"Marjorie said you got hit by a bus."

"I did. Sort of."

"Well, it sort of convinced her you're the hex she's been running from all her life. I'm not supposed to talk to you or that police officer." Gayle nodded toward the police cruiser.

"I can explain everything, if she'll just give me the chance."

"Solly, I thought we'd been all through this." Griffin stood on the other side of the car. "Whatever you're planning right now? There's no way it turns out well for anyone."

Solomon leaned across the roof of the car, hissing in a harsh whisper. "And I told you, I won't be snookered the way you all did Adam and Eve."

"You're going to throw it all away on the off-chance I'm lying about something as important as this?"

"I won't have a lie that big hanging over my immortal soul. Not when there's something I can do about it." Solomon leaned back down to Gayle. "Did she go upstairs?"

"To your place. She wants her angel back."

"I got to find a way to talk to her." Solomon checked on the police cruiser again. "Can't go in the front."

"If she sees you or that cop, she's gone. She made me promise to keep the motor running."

"I'll try to catch her upstairs. If she comes down before I get to speak with her, keep her here, please. I have a way to fix everything, but she's got to hear me out."

But Gayle wasn't listening. She batted at her ear, fighting off some irritant. Then she looked up at Solomon. "Sorry. What'd you say?"

"I said—" Solomon started, but Gayle went back to batting at some unseen, flying insect.

Solomon leaned down to look through to the other side of the car.

Griffin had a straw, working on Gayle's ear, making mosquito noises.

"You cut that out! Right now, you hear me? Leave her be!"

"This damn mosquito needs something more than a good talking-to," said Gayle, still slapping the air around her. Griffin lowered the straw, but kept buzzing, watching Solomon.

"I need Marjorie to hear me out. Then she can do whatever she sees fit once I've had my say."

Solomon ran for the next block down, turned and went about twenty paces. He stopped at a tall iron gate closing off the little alleyway between the buildings. Beyond he could see the back of his building.

Solomon pulled at the gate. The ironwork was solid, secured with a large, stainless steel padlock. No way he could force it open. He'd have to climb.

"You want to transmogrify me inside the building?"

"I told you, it'll just bring a lot of unwanted company down on you."

"You could melt a couple of these bars so I can slip through."

Griffin crossed his arms.

"Let's see. I could help you give up immortality and get back your precious reputation and, oh, by the way, help myself into the lake of fire? Or I could leave you to struggle on by yourself for a few more centuries and let the world go spinning along in one piece." Griffin stroked his chin. "Gosh, Solly, that's a tough one."

"I could just say the words and it'd all be over."

"You could, but you won't."

"Why won't I?"

"Marjorie and Willa."

"You're a jackass, you know that? You're as bad as Shortwick, raising them up against me." Solomon took hold of the bars like a rope and walked up the face of the building, levering himself over the pointed finials. Easing himself down the other side, he trotted toward the dividing walls of the interconnected rear courtyards. The brick wall behind his building was too high, and bare of any hand holds. The wall behind the building next door was lower and topped with a chain link fence.

On the street, Alvin's white van slammed to a stop in front of the gate. He jumped out, leaving the door wide open and the engine running. He flung himself at the gate, bouncing off, knocking himself to the ground. Struggling to his feet, Alvin grabbed at the lock, yanking on it, his eyes still on Solomon in the courtyard beyond.

Alvin leaped for the top of the gate, missed, and landed hard, wrenching his ankle. Alvin could only watch as Solomon used a garden hose for a lasso to snare a stanchion of the chain link fence and scale the wall. Alvin slammed at the gate again as Solomon hooked the fire escape ladder with a push broom, pulled it down, then scampered up toward the roof.

Alvin turned and ran, circling the block to come around on the other side, his wrenched ankle causing him to run in a syncopated gallop.

Making the corner, Alvin saw Lighter cop coming out of Solomon's building, shaking his head at Wood who stood by the cruiser.

Alvin skidded to a stop, his arms flailing to keep his balance. He ducked behind the street-side mound of trash bags and recyclables.

Alvin grabbed a bag of paper recycling, hefted it up on his shoulder, and walked past the two officers, keeping his face behind the bag until he got beyond them and into the building next door.

Above, Solomon stood gauging the distance between the buildings. Too far to jump, he'd have to find something to bridge the gap. There wasn't much lying around. A couple of broken-down lawn chairs, a plastic wading pool filled with rainwater, several wooden sawhorses, five-gallon cans of roofing tar, and a stash of decaying construction supplies under a tarp held down by an aluminum extension ladder.

Inside the building, Alvin and the building's handyman rode the elevator, both of them watching the numbers as they headed up.

"I told her and told her," said Alvin, "clip his wings, or come mating season, he's gone, looking for Mrs. Macaw. But, we don't have children, and he's an only parrot."

Still up on the roof, Solomon extended the ladder to its full length, then rested it on the parapet to pivot across the gap between the buildings. Using the cans as a step, he stood on the end of the ladder. Then, with his arms out for balance, Solomon walked, rung-to-rung, across the ladder to the other side.

Inside, Alvin and the handyman reached the access door to the roof. As the handyman got the door open, Alvin dodged around him, out onto the roof. Slamming the door behind him, Alvin blocked it with the heavy tar buckets.

Alvin reached the parapet edge as Solomon hopped down onto the roof the building opposite. Alvin ran back to the rooftop door, but the handyman was still cursing and trying to break through the obstructions.

Alvin skittered over to the street-side fire escape. Officer Wood leaned against the cruiser, watching the buildings.

Alvin dashed back to the parapet edge.

Solomon watched Alvin from behind the elevator machinery shed.

"You think it wise to leave that ladder?" asked Griffin.

"Fella his size? He'd be a fool to try getting across on that flimsy thing."

"Seems to me he's wearing the spurs of desire."

Alvin edged up onto the ladder, on his hands and knees, reaching out to grip the nearest rung.

"I don't know, Solly."

Alvin took a deep breath and held it. Then, squinting to see only the end of the ladder and not the chasm below him, he crawled rung-to-rung over the breezeway. Just as he reached the far parapet, the ladder buckled and fell out from under him.

"Told you." Solomon turned for the fire escape at the front of the building.

Griffin eased up to the parapet edge and looked over. Alvin hung by his fingertips.

"Hunh," said Griffin. "Solly was right." Griffin followed Solomon.

At the front of the building, looking down on the street, Solomon could see Wood and Lighter still leaning on the police cruiser. He eased himself down the fire escape steps, soft and easy, keeping his eye on the cops.

Reaching the window of his apartment, Solomon slid open the sash and climbed through, then pulled the sash down behind him.

He took up the kerosene lamp and lit it. He picked up the lamp's chimney, slightly cracked, and slid it over the flame.

Alvin had done a real job on his place. No way to tell if Marjorie had already been here and then gone.

"Marjorie?" Solomon called to her, soft and low. "I got something you need to hear."

Solomon continued to look around. Everything was pulled open, dumped out, left ajar.

Except the closet, which was closed.

Solomon moved as silently as the debris underfoot would allow. He put his hand on the knob of the little closet door. Then gave it a quick twist and yanked it open.

"Stay back!" Marjorie pointed his pistol at him, both hands gripping the butt. "You might as well go back wherever you came from. I know who you are now."

Solomon held his hand up. "Take it easy. I'm glad you're still here. I need to talk to you."

"There's nothing for us to talk about."

"It's something you'll want to hear. I promise."

"I don't want to hear anything you have to say. I just want my angel back."

"Seems a fool thing to come back for. But I'm glad you did." Then he stopped and looked over at Griffin. "What're you up to?"

"*Me?* What am *I* up to?" Marjorie demanded.

"Did you put that idea in her head?"

"You said you wanted a chance to speak with her," said Griffin,

"So. Speak."

"Yeah, but what's in it for you, is what's got me wondering."

"I never trusted anyone in my whole life the way I trusted you," said Marjorie. "Even Skip."

Solomon finally realized Marjorie was talking to him.

"Now it turns out you're the one hounding us for what you did to Abigail."

"I never did anything to Abigail. Whatever was done, was done to me. It sure beats all, what I ever did to her, but pay court to Lavinia, like every other fella in that valley. Why she took up against me never made a lick of sense."

"What's Lavinia got to do with anything?" Marjorie lowered the pistol.

"She was my intended, until that skunk Edwin Greene spirited her away."

"So. You were just stringing Abigail along."

Solomon was about to launch into his spiel about being Lavinia Kantlingher's long-lost sweetheart, but stopped. "Stringing Abigail along? Abigail? I never did no such thing."

"Are you saying you never had sex with her?" Marjorie's cynical scowl burned through the air at him.

Solomon flinched as if struck, something so private flung at him. He'd lived a long time seeing how people's ways had changed, but little, dancing Marjorie, being so free with loose talk stung him.

"No!"

"Then where'd we all come from? The good fairy leave us under mushrooms in the moonlight?"

None of this was making any sense to Solomon. He took a breath and started again. "I'm Lavinia Kantlingher's long-lost sweetheart, charged by her to be a blessing to her children wherever I might encounter them on the road of life—"

Marjorie jumped in. "So Abigail never meant anything to you?"

"Why would she?"

"How'd she get your locket, then?"

"I gave Lavinia that locket the night she ran off to marry Edwin. I put her picture and mine in it. I got no idea how Abigail come by it."

"That's her picture in it. Isn't it?"

"It's a tolerable likeness, yes. But she must've done that herself."

"Well, Abigail had it and gave it to Salomé so she'd know you by sight if you ever did come back."

"That'd be just like her. For all they knew I was dead, lost at sea, and Abigail's still trying to get the last word in against me."

"Abigail loved you."

"I don't know how everything got so mixed up in the telling from that time to this, but she never had a solitary civil word to say to me or about me. It was Lavinia that loved me. Abigail was doing her level best to keep us apart."

"Then why'd Abigail ask her mother—what was her name?"

"Esther."

"She told Esther to give the locket to Salomé when she was old enough to understand who you were."

"I'm dead for all they knew and that vindictive harpy's bad-mouthing me to Lavinia's young'uns."

"*Abigail* was Salomé's mother."

"No, Lavinia was. She's the one married Edwin."

"You're confusing them completely. Lavinia was her sister."

"I know that. I was there."

"Abigail told Lavinia how she looked forward to joining you in heaven—"

Griffin barked out a laugh at that.

"—so she'd finally have the chance to tell you how much she loved you. She regretted never telling you. But Lavinia, being Lavinia, said you were probably toasting in hell that very minute. Can you imagine? Telling her sister, dying in childbirth right there in front of her, that the man she loved, the father of her baby, is burning in hell? Lavinia must've seen it as a comfort, putting all the blame on you for what Abigail did."

"Childbirth?"

"I told you. Abigail was Salomé's mother."

Solomon started to speak, but stopped, his head tilted as he tried to make sense of what she was saying.

"Salomé was your daughter."

Solomon's face was still crossed up, and unmoving.

Marjorie chuffed, slapping her arms against her side. "You've been haunting us all these years, and this is news to you? Abigail is the one who kept the locket. Abigail's the one who had your baby. Salomé. She named your daughter for you."

The air seemed to leave the room, because, try as he might, Solomon's lungs weren't pulling anything in.

"And now the fog clears," said Griffin, sitting on the back of the

379

sofa, rocking, his elbows on his knees, his chin resting on his laced fingers. "Solly, I have got to tell you, that stupefied look on your face almost makes me wish I still had my day job, tormenting you mudfoot short-timers.

Chapter Forty-Eight

SOLOMON STRETCHED HIS HAND OUT for some solid surface. Finding none, he flopped down hard onto the sofa.

Solomon shook his head, then shook it harder, as if he could prevent what he'd heard from getting any kind of foothold in reality. He couldn't and everything came crashing in on him. Willa, Marjorie, Francie—and all the rest of them, his blood kin. The whole history of his accidental torment of every single one, straight on back to Salomé, all came rising up before him, a cresting wall of water that swamped him. They'd never really been anything more to him than a means to an end, and all the while—

That one thing—if true—made everything Abigail had done look different.

Abigail's hard words covering up a warm desire. Having him under her roof for the musicale that night, against her daddy's wishes. Hiding him the night he snuck in to be with Lavinia. Slipping between the covers with him. Holding—having—

"I don't remember any of that last part," said Solomon.

"Oh, it's all there."

Solomon closed his eyes, trying to recall, trying to picture it, if only to prove Griffin wrong.

Sure enough, there it was, the tiniest of memories, overlooked in his anger at what he'd thought was Abigail's betrayal with her scheming ways.

Now he could see her sitting on the bedside next to him, lifting the covers, tucking her legs under, rolling against him, then him taking her in his arms. For a woman that out-sized him, how small she seemed, tucked in his embrace, the smell of her hair, the springy curls on his face.

Them—being together like that. It had been Griffin's idea to start with, having bragged as much. But she'd gone along because she loved Solomon and wanted to believe it was from inside her ownself.

Then naming her—their—daughter after him. Salomé. He was already lost at sea by then.

Salomé. So everyone would know she belonged to him, in spite of what people would think of her. And of him.

The aged, crystalline desire he'd felt for Lavinia cracked, then shattered under the percussive strokes of Abigail's soft heartbeat as he remembered it. Or perhaps fantasized, feeling her heartbeat against his back, carrying her when she'd twisted her ankle. Showing off for Lavinia with a clumsy effort to win Livy's affection and easy access, even as the one true heart was pressed firm against his spine.

Lavinia had been the dancing doll in the distance of his hillside memories, and there on the road, close at hand was Abigail, standing in the dust of his ignorant longing.

He was a fool, stretched, grasping for Lavinia so far beyond his touch, while Abigail was there, within easy reach, her own hand hanging at her side for the taking. A bend of the elbow, a simple interlacing of their fingers, and he would have been loved back like he'd never been loved before. No longer alone and solitary.

He wished he could blame Griffin. But he couldn't. He'd like to, great God A'mighty, the words would come easy enough. But he couldn't. Griffin was a dang jackass, but none of what Solomon felt and what Abigail felt and what Lavinia felt was Griffin's fault. It was just something handy for him to use against them.

"You strung me along, making me think I could change my history, just by getting one of these gals to choose a good man over a scoundrel."

"Who're you talking to now?" asked Marjorie.

"For your own good," said Griffin. "Seemed a safe choice. I could have kept you occupied with petty crime and self-destructive habits, but there's always the risk of regret. I've never had to worry about moralizing and meddling do-gooders bothering with regret."

In the stairwell of the other building, Lighter put his shoulder to the rooftop door, firmly blocked by the tar buckets on the other side.

"I think maybe he's planning to jump," said the handyman. "He had a really crazy look in his eyes."

Lighter took hold of the handrails on either side, and slammed both feet against the door, bursting it outward and scattering the tar buckets. He stepped through, followed by the handyman and Officer Wood.

◆ ◆ ◆

"There's no need to keep clear of that lawman," said Solomon. "Ain't fair to him. He's probably a good enough fella. Better than some, no worse than others."

"Oh, right. Of course. I should drop everything and go pick out my trousseau right now. I mean, I have it on the solemn word of an angel—and the world's oldest deadbeat dad."

"Marjorie, I been a horse's ass—"

"Care—ful," said Griffin, then flashed an exploding bomb burst with his air-filled cheeks and splaying hands, waggling his fingers for raining debris.

Solomon cut himself off.

"No sense me playing cupid to you girls anymore. Find your own fellas. Good, bad, or indifferent, makes no nevermind to me." Solomon looked back at Griffin for his approval.

Griffin nodded, smiling, and pulled his hands back to his chest.

"This'll be the last you see of me."

"All right," said Griffin, hopping up. "Let's scat while the scattin's good."

"Forever? No popping back in on the night before Willa's wedding?"

"Never again," said Solomon.

"And that ponytail guy? Is he immortal like you are?"

"No. That's why he's been hounding me."

Marjorie pointed the pistol toward the fire escape window and fired, splintering glass and wood, the shot echoing around the breezeway as the shards fell, tinkling onto the steel grating on down to the ground.

"That was next door," said Wood.

Both cops bolted back down the stairs, the handyman right behind them.

Marjorie stared at the smokey gun barrel. "That's loud. And loaded."

"Not much use if it ain't." Solomon took the gun from her. "The cops are sure to have heard that."

"You think I scared him off?" Marjorie nodded toward the shattered window.

Solomon went and looked out onto the fire escape.

Cringing just underneath the window, covered in tiny, glittering fragments of glass, Alvin had his head as far between his knees as he could manage.

383

Marjorie approached with some caution. "So. Was he? Immortal?"

Griffin and Solomon watched Alvin as he searched himself over for any new holes.

"With her aim, he might as well be," said Griffin.

"What good is it, me disappearing if this rascal's hounding her the rest of her days, trying to get to me? I can't just up and leave her."

"Who? Me?" asked Marjorie.

"Sure you can. She's doing her small part to keep Armageddon at bay. A little personal sacrifice to keep the cosmos all tickety-boo. Think of it that way. Doesn't look so bad in that light, right?"

"If I never had this thing in the first place, he'd a never connected her to me."

"Who? Me?" Marjorie asked again.

"Water under the bridge, over the dam, down the toilet—pick one and let's get out of here."

"Looks like the only for-sure way to fix it all now is give up the doo-hickey and be carried back. If I never have it, he never finds her."

"Am I part of this conversation? Because I'm not keeping up."

"Solly! C'mon! You just learned that you've been a father all these years. You're still going to throw it all away? Doesn't this news just make you want to take to your heels and fly? Lead Shortwick here on a merry chase? Spin this out for decades? C'mon, it could be fun. What'dya say?"

"The only way to fix it with Abigail is for me to go back and face Luther."

Griffin leaned against the window frame and crossed his arms. "Oh, good. That takes care of your eensy-teensie little self-image problem. And the rest of us? We just watch as the apocalypse unfolds across creation! Dammit all, Solly. You are one selfish mudfoot, you know that!"

Down on the street, the super held the door open for Wood and Lighter who dashed through the lobby and up the stairs, with Lighter leading the way. Wood, on her walkie as she ran, reported shots fired at their location.

Solomon looked from Marjorie, to Griffin, to Alvin who winced every time the gun barrel came anywhere near him.

Solomon snapped his fingers. "I just had me a humdinger of an idea."

"You did, did you?" asked Griffin.

"I get rid of the doo-hickey. Hide it somewhere safe."

"There's nowhere on this planet you could hide that thing now that everyone's got your scent."

"What if I hide it with someone they ain't smelt yet? I think I know someone who'd move heaven and earth to keep this thing secret, if he had hold of it."

Griffin's eyes shifted to the liver-spotted scalp right beneath them. "Him?"

"Him." Solomon pointed the gun barrel at Alvin, for emphasis.

"Him what?" Alvin kept his hands clamped onto his head. "Uh—could you not point that thing at me?"

"You'd give it to a sociopath like him?"

"That's the humdinger part."

"If where you come from, 'humdinger' means 'terrible,' then, yes, it's a humdinger. You can't trust him to keep it secret. He's just itching to use it for fame and fortune. And once he does, it'll bring every hellhound hunting for it down on him."

"I think he'd be quite happy to keep it secret—once he got an up-close look at your amigos."

Griffin's mouth sprung open, ready with new objections, obviously. But he stopped, considered, then his eyes went wide. He smiled.

Solomon gave Griffin a poke in the chest. "*That's* the humdinger part."

"That could be arranged," said Griffin. "What do I do with him after that?"

"Find a place where his kind of crazy don't stand out?"

"Are you really that desperate to see Abigail one last time? Because Luther will shoot you. I can't prevent that, and there's nothing to protect you."

Solomon nodded.

The front door rattled under a pounding fist.

"Police," Lighter called out through the door. "Mr. Martin. Open up. It's the police."

"Then I guess I'm desperate enough to let you give it a try. I may have to pervert the local justice system." Griffin shrugged. "Not like anyone would notice."

Steadying the pistol at Alvin's forehead, Solomon raised the sash, more wood bits and glass pieces falling.

"Why don't you come inside," said Solomon. "I got a proposition for you."

Alvin climbed over the sill, hauling himself through the window, pouring himself onto the floor.

Lighter pounded on the door again.

"Mr. Martin? We know you're in there. Open up."

"They think you two are a couple of con men working rich old ladies." Marjorie pointed at Alvin. "They say he's wanted in Minnesota for the disappearance of someone named Philippa Waverly, and you're his accomplice."

Solomon scowled at Alvin as he dusted glass and pigeon feathers off himself.

"That's even better." Solomon, his eye and pistol still on Alvin, said to Marjorie, "Go keep that lawman busy. We'll all be out of your hair directly."

"No! She stays in here," said Alvin.

"They'll bust down the door before our business is done. You want that?"

Clearly, he didn't. All Alvin could manage was some twisty-faced anger and a lot of heavy breathing.

"Get to it." Solomon waved the pistol toward the door.

"Forever?" asked Marjorie.

"Forever."

Marjorie nodded and went to the front door, paused a moment, then slipped out and into the hall, pulling the door closed behind herself. Solomon, right behind her, locked the door.

"Okay, pops. Where is it?"

"I need to leave a note. Explain my untimely disappearance. You don't want the police asking a lot of questions."

"Okay, okay. But hurry it up. I don't have all day."

In the hallway, Marjorie stood against the door, facing the two officers "Oh, hi! Thanks, I don't need to get married anymore. Nice of you to stop by."

"It sounded like a gunshot," said Wood. "Something heavy caliber."

"We'd like to take a look," said Lighter.

"Uh. Extra-strength popcorn! I'd invite you in, but I know you're busy fighting crime and all."

"This is Mr. Martin's apartment, isn't it?" asked Wood. "What were you doing in there?"

"I'm minding the dog?"

"I don't remember him having a dog."

"Cat! Minding the cat. You probably never saw her. She's shy. Because she looks like a dog."

From the other side, Solomon listened at the door for a moment, putting the pistol on the bureau. He turned the coffee table back onto its legs, and picked up his writing kit off the floor. He took out a sheet of paper and sat down to write.

Griffin leaned over his shoulder, reading as Solomon wrote.

"Solly. I know a confession when I see one. You could level this entire block."

Solomon continued to write, then signed it, blew the ink dry, and folded it into an envelope.

"Don't get your knickers in a knot. Ain't a bit of truth in it, so we're safe."

"That angel's here, isn't he." Alvin swept his hands in a wide arc around himself.

"You're okay leaving her to think that what you wrote is true?" Griffin nodded at the envelope in Solomon's hand.

"Once I spring back. I won't ever have the chance to write this note in the first place, now will I? She won't have it to read."

"Solly, you are almost as good as me."

"I'll take that as a criticism."

"We could arrest you for obstruction," said Wood.

"He gave me a key." Marjorie dug the key out of her pocket and held it up. "I'm minding his place for him."

Wood reached for the key. "We could take a quick look."

"You have a warrant?" Marjorie tucked it back into her pocket. "I'll wait while you go get one." She whistled, examining her fingernails.

Inside the apartment, Solomon dropped his locket into the envelope.

"That's it, isn't it!" Alvin lunged for the locket, landing on the coffee table, collapsing it with a crunching crash.

In the hall, hearing the noise, Wood and Lighter looked at each other.

"Now we've got something better," said Lighter. "Probable cause." Then he said to Wood, "You get this door. I got the one on the roof."

Marjorie spread out her arms, blocking their way.

Wood sighed, gave a tilt of her head toward Marjorie and said to Lighter, "Would you mind? She's your fiancé."

"Right. Pardon me, ma'am," said Lighter as he hefted Marjorie over his shoulder, then stepped back from the door.

Wood kept her body to one side and leaned toward the jamb, her hand on her sidearm.

"Mr. Martin. Step away from the door. We're coming in."

Inside, Alvin still sat on the collapsed coffee table, rocking, holding his arm. Solomon licked the flap and sealed the envelope, then rested it against the pistol on the bureau by the door. From his pocket he took the ceramic angel and set it down next to the note.

Outside, Marjorie stiffened, arching backward, like a four-year-old. "Put me down!"

"Think of this as practice for when I carry you over the threshold."

Wood planted herself and mule-kicked the door, the lockset cracking, separating slightly from the wood.

"Stop it! Stop it!" Marjorie shouted. "You'll ruin everything!"

Solomon lifted the lanyard from around his neck and stood over Alvin, lowering it over Alvin's head, the artifact resting against his chest. Alvin took hold of it, lifting it up, staring at the dark, shimmery mass in his palm.

Another banging crack shimmied the front door in its frame, the lockset sagging more as the wood tore further away but still held.

Outside the door, Lighter put Marjorie down and drew his sidearm.

Chapter Forty-Nine

INSIDE, ALVIN STILL SAT ON THE FLOOR, fixed on the artifact in his hand.

Solomon gave a nod to Griffin, ready for whatever might happen next. "Make your wish, Shortwick."

Griffin, clearly at war with himself, his face twisted up in indecision, raised a hand. "Solly, what is it about you that brings out the worst in me?"

Solomon wasn't listening, still focused on Alvin. "I give it to you free and clear."

"I want to live forever," whispered Alvin, his eyes squeezed shut.

Griffin grabbed hold of Solomon's collar as the unnatural departure took hold of Solomon, folding him up into himself, yanked away, amid swirling debris, kicked up by the sucking blast of wind that carried him off.

Griffin, still holding onto Solomon as they both disappeared, whirled, sucked through the small, glowing vortex.

Alvin, hair whipped by the violence in the air, ignored the debris thrashing around him as the artifact warmed and glowed in his hands, his skin streaking with light where the artifact rested on his chest.

With Wood's third booming kick, the door sprang open, vibrating against its hinges.

Lighter came through, followed by Wood, both of them parsing the room with their sidearms, high and low.

Alvin sat on the floor, rocking and cackling, the artifact clutched in his fist.

Lighter was on him in an instant.

"Where's Martin!" Lighter shouted. "Where's your partner?"

Alvin scowled, keeping his eyes averted, wrapping himself over the artifact.

"Where is he? What did you do with him?"

"He tried to kill me," said Alvin. "Up on the roof."

"Is that where he is? Up on the roof?" asked Wood.

"He's gone. Melted away." Alvin rocked and cackled, covering the artifact.

"Is that a confession?" asked Wood.

"What've you got there?"

"Nothing." Alvin tightened himself over the artifact, smiling. "Nothing at all."

Wood turned to search further through the rooms.

Marjorie followed them into the apartment, picking up Solomon's note. She opened it, lifting out the locket and unfolding the note.

"Leave it," said Wood, seeing the note in her hands. "Might be needed as evidence."

Marjorie was already reading.

"What's he say?" asked Lighter.

"He admits he and this guy Shortwick are responsible for what happened to that old woman back in Minnesota."

"Waverly?" Lighter got Alvin to his feet and Wood handcuffed him.

"Hey!" Alvin's day-dreaming cut short, he started to twist. "You can't arrest me!"

"He say what they did with the body?" Wood nodded at the note in Marjorie's hand.

Marjorie, eyes already filled with tears, shook her head.

"She didn't leave a body," shouted Alvin. "No body, no crime! I know my habeas corpus. Lemme go!"

"Looks like that note's your ticket back to Minnesota. Think what you'll save on air fare," said Wood.

Alvin bucked and whipped in Lighter's grip.

"You can't do this to me now. I'm immortal. I can finally live forever. Lemme go!"

Lighter and Wood escorted Alvin down the stairs onto the street, now blocked off with more police vehicles.

Wood put him in the back of their cruiser.

Marjorie followed down after them.

"I wonder where he did go," said Marjorie.

Shutting the door on Alvin, Lighter turned back to Marjorie. "He'll turn up again. Bad pennies, and all that." He opened the door to get into the cruiser. "Maybe I'll see you at the arraignment? Have another coffee with me? If I promise to stick around and finish it?"

Marjorie opened her purse and took out a pair of handcuffs.

"I guess you could have used these."

Lighter took the handcuffs. "Thanks for not dropping them off at the station."

"I was hoping it'd be a good reason to call me."

"Look. What say we don't wait until the arraignment. How about right now? Your building's a crime scene." He nodded back at the officers entering the building. "These guys'll be crawling all over it for the next few hours. It's the end of my shift and if we're still engaged, we should probably get serious about planning the honeymoon. Before the offer expires."

"Hey, partner," Wood called out to him, "Let's get this guy processed, and then you can live happily ever after, okay?"

Lighter winked at Marjorie and slid into the cruiser, closing the door, still looking up at her. He held up a finger phone to his ear and then pointed between himself and Marjorie.

Gayle came up, holding Willa, who reached out for Marjorie.

"What happened up there?"

"I think I may be getting married in the morning." Marjorie took Willa from Gayle, and watched as the cruiser disappeared up the block under the large, citified moon just now visible over the building tops.

Hudson River Valley – 1830s

That same large moon shone through the window, onto Solomon holding Lavinia's hand.

For a fair instant, the room melded with the night, the stars breaking in, then subtracted, leaving the walls intact as they'd been, and a blowing wind that disturbed nothing around him.

Solomon's guts were electrified for the barest clock tick, nearly knocking him off his feet, his insides contracting then expanding, a ball bounced hard against a barn-side wall, springing back to the hand that threw him.

Solomon got control of himself and managed to say, "I want to live forever," which tasted funny in his mouth, like a practiced speech he'd written out beforehand. He brought her knuckles to his lips and kissed them hard, sending Abigail into further paroxysms of shock.

Solomon again felt a churning, a chasm seeming to open under his feet, his insides dropping, a high-fall and the hard landing yet to come. It was a vast emptiness and a breath-taking disconnect from the solid ground and walls and ceiling, under, around, and over him.

Lavinia pulled back, as if Solomon might be sick all over her.

Luther burst through the hallway door, into the room, both pistols leveled.

Behind him, Edwin followed, holding onto Luther's night shirt, keeping the old man between him and Solomon.

"Dimsley! It'll ease my sense of guilt having to shoot you, seeing as I've caught you in the very act of trespassing my daughter's bedchamber."

Solomon's life flashed in front of his eyes. Including things he didn't recall ever doing. Impossible things. Hellacious things. Which he didn't think was fair at a moment like this.

Then he remembered. Everything.

"We're properly chaperoned," said Solomon, backing up, circling to keep the women between himself and Luther. He seemed to be speaking against his will. What he wanted to say was that he was an astonishing fact of nature and had something wild to share with them.

"Step into the hallway, woman!" Luther bobbed to get a clear shot at Solomon.

"Don't leave, Missus Kantlingher. You'll be washing innocent blood out of the bedsheets for weeks." His mouth moved in spite of himself, his memories crystal clear.

"Oh, no, dear. I have help."

Luther moved Esther to one side with his forearm keeping the pistol aimed in Solomon's general direction.

"I'll remember you fondly," said Lavinia, helping steer Esther and Abigail out of the bedroom.

He watched Abigail go, seeing no sign from her of being in a family way. Given how little time since that night in her bed, she might not even know yet.

A terrible thought crossed his mind. This was divine punishment and Griffin was the avenging angel. He'd said it often enough. Maybe it was all a scheme cooked up by Griffin for Solomon to be the instrument of his own destruction, all the while thinking it a noble gesture. Poetic and pathetic in a single body.

"Momma, does Daddy have to shoot him?" asked Abigail. "We'll have to repaint the room."

"Mister Durnley is awfully stubborn. May not be any other way, hon."

Solomon clinched his face, unable to avoid the point-blank impact he knew to be coming.

Luther fired the left-hand pistol.

Even as he shut his eyes against the sparks and smoke filling the room, Solomon saw for the barest moment what looked like a ghostly glowing hand reaching for the onrushing bullet.

He would have opened his eyes again to see if what he'd seen was real, but the bullet struck him, knocking him backward through the open window, carrying the curtains, frame, and glass crashing after him onto the roof.

Lavinia and Abigail both shrieked.

Abigail rushed to the window in time to see Solomon roll to the edge of the roof and fall off.

Out of view, falling, face up to the stars, Solomon felt cushioned and suspended, lowered on cloudy hands, instead of rushing toward the collision with the ground.

Griffin leaned in close over him, his glowing face obscuring the darkened sky overhead.

Solomon tried to understand the peculiar sensations, then he realized he was in that watery-curtained place again, betwixt time and eternity.

"I am such an old softy," said Griffin. "Although I'm not sure I did you any good." He looked at the rude red bloom in the meat to the left of Solomon's heart. "Medical care being what it is in this century, and how far away you are even from that, out here in the middle of nowhere."

Solomon tucked his chin trying to look down at the painful hole in him.

"Sorry that I had to let Luther shoot you. Otherwise, those plug uglies on the roof will think you still have it."

Solomon turned his head so he could see where Griffin had jerked his thumb.

Settling along the roof ridge of Kantlingher House, a leathered flock of handsome creatures crouched on the peaks, watching like pestilential ravens.

"Solly, as always, it's been an education and a pleasure. Good luck with the rest of your life—however much is left of it." Griffin took up Solomon's hand to shake it. "I'll miss that winsome stubbornness of yours."

Griffin then reached over and folded Marjorie's ceramic angel into Solomon's other hand. Solomon looked at it, causing himself pain as he twisted his wrist to see it.

"Just a little something I picked up in all the commotion. Sort of like a parting gift."

"I'm starting to forget it all," Solomon croaked out, barely enough air to form the words.

"That's natural. Your little corridor of time no longer exists."

"I'll forget—?"

"Everything."

"I don't want to forget. Not now."

"Sorry, Solly. That's got to be."

"Leave me something." Solomon sipped at the air, trying to hold back enough for whatever else needed to be said.

"Isn't forgetting better? Out of all that was and now can't possibly be, what do you really want to remember in what little time is left?"

Solomon tried to speak again, but the air was nearly gone from his lungs, too little for his larynx to make enough sound to form the words.

Griffin leaned his ear close to Solomon's moving lips and listened, then jerked his head back.

"Really? Out of everything? Solly, m'lad, you never cease to amaze me. You're sure?"

Solomon nodded, the pain now engulfing his shoulder, back and buttocks, his legs splayed, arms windmilling slowly as he neared the ground.

Griffin put his mouth to Solomon's ear and whispered.

Solomon smiled, no more than a crook in the corner of his lip, his eyes closed, then time rushed back to normal and he hit the ground, hard.

Solomon lay still for the longest time, blood soaking his shirt.

Above, Luther had stepped onto the roof and edged out to see where Solomon fell.

Behind Luther, Abigail clambered out after him.

Solomon jerked and arched as he took air back into his lungs, then rolled over to his right and levered himself up on one arm. His faced opened up in a silent howl at the pain.

"How in hell did I miss plugging you square in the middle?"

Solomon shook his head, trying to recover his thoughts. There'd been something all-fired important he wanted to tell them. Something to reassure them he was a man of purpose. That some extraordinary thing was taking place. Would take place. Perhaps even greatness that would wash away any vile thought they might hold of him.

It was flickering away, a dream that binds until fluttered away in wakefulness, there being no mortal means to hold onto it.

He strained to remember. But it was all nearly gone, gossamer lace curtains scorched away to nothing in a house fire of forgetting, then furnishings, floorboards, walls, until nothing but a single memory stood, the fire-blackened stones of the chimney stack, resisting and remaining after everything else was consumed.

It was the memory of Abigail in his arms and the overwhelming rush of love that he'd breathed in remembering how he'd held her, lying there, his face to her hair. Everything else was gone.

"Abby!" Solomon cried out.

He struggled to take in more air.

"I love you, Abigail!"

Lavinia, leaning out of the window behind them, her own face wide open with astonishment.

"He must've hit his head when he fell, knocking the sense clean out of him," said Lavinia.

"Abigail Kantlingher, I'm saying it out where everyone can hear me. I love you!" Then he flopped backward, arms out, breathing hard, the exertion too much for him.

Sane or not, Abigail was going to him. She tottered to the roof's edge, bellied over the side and down to the ground, tearing loose the copper rain gutter as she went.

Abigail knelt down next to Solomon. She hefted him up by the shoulders, laying his head in her lap.

"Abby." The effort wore on him. He took her hand and pressed it to his cheek, wanting to hold something of her.

Abigail cocked an eyebrow at him. "Did you mean what you said to Livy up there?" Her voice cool, covering her hot, boiling heart.

His breathing was harder, but he shook his head, firm and strong.

"Why'd you say it, then, and me standing right there, hearing every word?"

Solomon's brains were in a whirl, great vacancies opened up in his memory, water shrinking in the heat of a hot skillet, evaporated and misted away.

"Was it to make me jealous and declare myself right there in front of God and everybody?"

He nodded and smiled. That would do. That seemed right.

"That's a mean trick, Solomon Durnley. Letting daddy shoot you. What would you've done if I hadn't let myself be taken in by such a thing?"

"Let him shoot me again?" Solomon rasped out.

"I'd be more'n obliged," shouted Luther.

"So would I," said Lavinia.

"Livy!" said Edwin, who'd wedged himself between Esther and Lavinia. "You don't mean to say you covet that scalawag's attentions?"

Lavinia whirled on Edwin, but relaxed and said, "Of course not—*dear*."

"He'll do no such a thing." Abigail held tight to Solomon.

Solomon nodded, his eyes half-closing.

"I've finally got you, and now I'm going to lose you." She rocked and squeezed him, Solomon's eyes crossing with the pain, but having no strength to resist her.

Above them, like hounds seeking a lost scent, the demons nosed the air, gave a last look back at the fallen man. Satisfied he wasn't the one they were seeking, they each straightened up in turn, and stretched to the four corners of the wind, leaving to the beat of leathery wings, to rove and roam in their search.

Griffin, sitting on the eaves, his legs dangling over the edge, shook his head.

"I am such an old softy," he said again.

Chapter Fifty

Hudson River Valley – 1830s

FROM OUT OF THE DARKNESS, a one-horse buggy crunched on the hard-dirt drive, its lanterns pooling light dimly along the path as it pulled into the clear patch of ground just to the other side of the picket fence.

A tall, gaunt man in a long, dark coat, unbuttoned collar, with an untucked shirt peeking out from under the points of his half-buttoned vest, stepped down from the rig, carrying a black bag.

"Dr. Hackenbush?" Luther cried out. "What'n hell brings you out this time a night. We didn't send for you."

"Just riding by," said the doctor. "I was seeing to Miz Klein down the way. Saw the lights on and thought I'd stop in."

Abigail was up and had the doctor by the wrist, hauling him over to where Solomon lay, blood running down his side, puddling on the ground under him.

The doctor stood over Solomon, still talking up at Luther.

"Miz Klein had a terrible fright, and the baby came early. She'd worked herself up into quite a state. Said she'd come down to the parlor and found a big old jackass there in her best room, eating the antimacassars like they were cabbage leaves, right off her good sofa."

"Doctor, he's bleeding!" Abigail shook him by the wrist.

"She yelled at the critter, but he just kept on munching. Dangedest silver-blue eyes, staring right at her, daring her to stop him, she said."

"Doctor!"

The doctor squatted down on his haunches, still looking up at everyone perched out on the roof and clustered back at the window.

"Didn't sound like any animal from around here." He set down his bag, opening it up.

"Please!" cried Abigail.

Dr. Hackenbush adjusted his spectacles to look at the wound in Solomon's chest, then rested his forearms on his thighs.

"Yep. Your aim isn't what it used to be, is it, Luther? Missed his heart by more than an inch." He looked up at Luther. "So, like I was saying, Miz Klein commenced to having herself a regular conniption fit right there in the parlor."

The doctor reached under Solomon's shoulder, feeling for an exit wound, but found none. He put a large square of cotton over the bloody hole. "Put your finger on that," he said to Abigail, then looked up at everyone. "She set to chasing it round and round with a broom, and the baby came early. A boy. Mother and child are doing fine." The Doctor leaned his head in close to Abigail. "I was heading home when I heard the shooting. Thought I ought to check in just in case someone needed to be looked to." Then he winked at Abigail.

The cotton quickly soaked red. Abigail looked up at the doctor.

"Edwin! Luther! Come down here and give a hand. We'll get him inside. Let's see if I can get the bullet out. He's likely to die. Let's not make him do it out here in your door yard."

Abigail held onto the hand of Solomon's good arm.

"Of course," said the doctor, nodding at the white-knuckle hold Abigail had on Solomon's hand, "with the grip she's got on you, son, it's unlikely she's going to let you go anywhere anytime soon."

Luther and Edwin stood over them. Dr. Hackenbush directed Luther to heft Solomon up by the shoulders, easy, and directed Edwin to grab his feet. Edwin pulled back, not wanting to touch a dead body, or a near-dead body.

"Oh, for crying out loud, Edwin. You aren't thinking to make the ladies do it, are you? I'm busy carrying the bag. That leaves you. Get to it."

Luther had him up, sitting.

"I can walk." Solomon got to his feet, favoring his left side. He leaned on Abigail as he got his balance, still cocked slightly, his left arm clinched across his chest.

Edwin was enormously relieved he didn't have to carry his nemesis by his muddy shoes.

"You just might live out the night," said the doctor as they helped Solomon up onto the porch.

Griffin was sitting in the porch swing.

"Goodbye, Solly," said Griffin as they moved Solomon to the door. Solomon stopped, sensing something, then turned toward the swing. But Griffin was gone, the swing still in motion, a glow fading away.

Solomon opened his hand and saw the ceramic angel he'd been holding onto. He couldn't remember why he had it. But he knew it was precious. He closed his fingers around it and let Abigail lead him into the house.

State Correctional Facility – 21st Century

The no-contact room was small, pale green, and over-lit with fluorescent lights. The half-glass partition along one wall separated a bank of eight cubicles on one side, with an equal number on the other side. Each cubicle had a telephone handset and a list of instructions to visitor and prisoner alike. Mostly a list of 'will nots' and 'must nots.'

All eight chairs on both sides were occupied. Alvin, wearing an orange jumpsuit, cheap sneakers, and his hair untied, was in the middle, talking to his attorney, a short, wirey, unkempt little man in a three-piece suit and bow-tie, poorly tied.

Alvin, at that moment was trying to squeeze the handset in half, since he was not able to put his fingers around his attorney's throat.

His attorney was trying to be reasonable.

"Solomon Durnley—the only one we can find—died in 1887. I've seen the grave. I've photocopied the death certificate. He didn't live into the twentieth century, much less the twenty-first." The attorney tried to keep his voice down.

"He went by a lot of different names," said Alvin.

"We tried every one you gave us. Lucky Smoke, Shotwad, Axel, Old Squirt, Gummy. A few anecdotes here and there. Nothing we can pin down."

"What about Skeeter Martin?"

"Nothing."

"Nothing! They arrested me in his apartment!"

The corrections officer looked over, a tilt of his head was usually enough to quiet the unruly ones.

Alvin exhaled, gathering control.

"Other than the note implicating you in Philippa Waverly's disappearance, there is no record of a Skeeter Martin. Anywhere."

"Then why am I still in prison? If the only witness against me is a f—" Alvin looked over at the corrections officer. "—figment of my imagination? Hunh? Tell me that?"

"The prison psychologist has tried explaining it to you. But you resist."

"I did not write that note!" Alvin wanted to smash something, aiming the handset at the attorney, wishing it had a trigger, a barrel, and about five rounds of high caliber ammunition. "I did not confess!"

The corrections officer cleared his throat.

Alvin settled himself, smiled, giving a glance up at the corrections officer, petting the handset, showing how in control of himself he was. Then he whirled back around to his attorney. "I did nothing to Philippa Waverly. She vanished. Of her own free will. She was over four-hundred years old."

"You'd help your case enormously if you would tell them what you did with the body. It would prove you're serious about your rehabilitation. You'll get out of here sooner."

"She was immortal. She had this little piece of—"

"Ah-ah-ah," said Griffin, suddenly at his elbow, miming a winged creature with his hands, flying it under Alvin's nose.

Alvin clamped down, his teeth gnashed together, his eyes scanning for invaders.

"Why doesn't anyone remember him, but me?" Alvin asked, tilting his head toward Griffin, his eyes still on his attorney.

"Have I ever showed you this one?" Griffin held up his index finger and a rolled-up condom. "This is you," he said, wiggling his finger, "and this is—"

"Not me! Durnley!" Alvin slapped at the condom. "I watched him write that note!"

"Mr. Shortwick, we've gone over this time and time again," said the attorney.

"When he gave you that—" Griffin and Alvin both did a quick scan overhead, "—that doo-hickey, you and Solomon shared the same improbable time corridor. That's why you remember him and no one else does."

"But they have his note. Why didn't that disappear with him when he vanished back into the past?"

"Mr. Shortwick, if you keep talking like that—"

"Everyone remembers Philippa. And she got sucked back through some kind of time hole, just like Durnley did."

"Funny, the little things people remember, isn't it?" said Griffin.

"—they are never going to let you out of here," said the attorney, trying to talk over Alvin's ranting.

"Oh, shut up! I'm not talking to you. I'm talking to him," said Alvin.

The inmate sitting in the next cubicle leaned back and looked around the partition at Alvin. He was hard, bald, heavily tattooed, and had a fresh slash over his right eye.

"Nasty gash there," said Alvin, giving him an open-mouthed, lip-curled smile, then ducking back behind his own partition.

Griffin, sitting on the floor behind them with his back against the wall, fixed on cutting out paper dolls as he whistled a sea shanty he'd often heard Solomon play.

"Must you?" Alvin closed his eyes, then looked back at Griffin. "I'm sick of that tune."

"Sorry. You ever get a piece of music stuck in your head and you just can't get it out?" Griffin went back to whistling, giving Alvin a wide-eyed, shoulder-shrug of an apology. But he kept on whistling and cutting.

"Shut up!"

The inmate leaned back again to look at Alvin.

Alvin gave Griffin a quick sneer. "You think you've got me, don't you. I can't do anything with this—thing of mine. I'll show you how I can make some money with it. Good money."

Griffin kept whistling and cutting.

"Hey!" Alvin hissed at the inmate. "I got something'll fix that gash right up." Alvin patted his chest. "Want to hold my doo-hickey? Cures what ails you. Fifty bucks."

Alvin reached down inside his jumpsuit, but before he could get the artifact pulled free, the inmate sprang at him, knocking the chair backward across the room, knocking Alvin out of his chair, fists flailing, pounding Alvin around the head and shoulders.

The corrections officer and his partners were on them both instantly, pulling at the tussling, tangling mass. The other inmates sprung out of their chairs and lined up against the walls, cheering on the battlers.

"Griffin! Griffin!" shouted Alvin over the mayhem, his head bouncing off the floor. "What kind of guardian angel are you!"

"I'm more the avenging angel type," said Griffin, opening up a string of paper angels, and went back to whistling over his handiwork.

"GRIIIIIIIIFFIN!"

Hudson River Valley – 21st Century

Paper banners of the Junior High Talent Show Spectacular hung across the stage of the Saugerties Central Schools auditorium.

Griffin, hunched down and made his way along the aisle, sidling in toward an empty seat, two rows behind where Marjorie and Ray Lighter sat. Ray squinted, peering through the viewfinder of his camera aimed at the stage.

The lights dimmed over the audience who applauded for the start of the performances and then quieted.

On stage, Willa, now twelve, wearing an angel costume of white taffeta and a halo of silver tinsel wrapped around a wire frame, came out with a short stool in one hand and her concertina tucked under her arm. She placed the stool in the middle of the pond of bluish light aimed at the center of the stage.

She sat, slipped her hands under the straps of the concertina, and looked down to check the placement of her fingers. Satisfied, she looked up, cleared her throat, and started to play—a sea shanty she'd never been able to get out of her head.

Now she was playing it, body weaving, tapping heel-and-toe to keep time, her silver-slippered foot dancing, her halo shaking.

Up in the audience, Marjorie smiled and nodded along with the music. She looked over at Lighter who smiled as well, his eye fixed on the viewfinder, catching it all.

Griffin behind them, bobbed his head with the music. "I am *such* an old softy."

The music filled the auditorium as Willa played for all she was worth, her foot bouncing harder and harder, at one with the music, dancing in the dust as if it were only yesterday.

SCOTT PARSON writes fiction that embraces the comic, the surreal, and the romantic. He moved to New York City to be an actor where he added juggling, fire-eating, and swordplay to his resumé. After working as an actor he shifted his focus to writing. He lives in New York with his wife. Find out more at www.scottparson.com.